Everyman, I will go with thee,
and be thy guide

THE EVERYMAN
LIBRARY

*The Everyman Library was founded by J. M. Dent
in 1906. He chose the name Everyman because he wanted
to make available the best books ever written in every
field to the greatest number of people at the cheapest possible
price. He began with Boswell's 'Life of Johnson';
his one-thousandth title was Aristotle's 'Metaphysics',
by which time sales exceeded forty million.*

*Today Everyman paperbacks remain true to
J. M. Dent's aims and high standards, with a wide range
of titles at affordable prices in editions which address
the needs of today's readers. Each new text is reset to give
a clear, elegant page and to incorporate the latest thinking
and scholarship. Each book carries the pilgrim logo,
the character in 'Everyman', a medieval morality play,
a proud link between Everyman
past and present.*

Mary Shelley

FRANKENSTEIN

Introduced by
PADDY LYONS
University of Glasgow

Other Critical Apparatus by
PHILIP GOODEN

EVERYMAN
J. M. DENT · LONDON
CHARLES E. TUTTLE
VERMONT

Introduction copyright © J.M.Dent 1992

Chronology, notes and other critical apparatus
copyright © J. M. Dent, 1994

First published in Everyman's Library in 1992
This edition first published in Everyman in 1994

Reprinted 1995, 1996, 1998

J.M.Dent
Orion Publishing Group
Orion House, 5 Upper St Martin's Lane,
London WC2H 9EA
and
Charles E. Tuttle Co. Inc
28 South Main Street,
Rutland, Vermont
05701, USA

Typeset in Sabon by CentraCet Limited, Cambridge
Printed in Great Britain by
The Guernsey Press Co. Ltd, Guernsey, C.I.

British Library Cataloguing-in-Publication Data
is available on request.

ISBN 0 460 87528 0

CONTENTS

NOTE ON THE AUTHOR AND EDITORS

MARY WOLLSTONECRAFT SHELLEY was born in London on 30 August 1797, the only daughter of William Godwin and of Mary Wollstonecraft, who died some days after her birth. In 1814 she ran away and set up house with Percy Bysshe Shelley. She married him on 30 December 1816, three weeks after the suicide of his estranged wife, in the hope this might secure them custody of the children of his first marriage – a hope that was to be disappointed. Of the four children Mary bore by Shelley, three died in infancy. From mid-1818, the couple lived in Italy, where Shelley drowned in a boating accident in 1822. After his death, Mary returned to London, where she lived by her writing, reared her surviving child and edited Shelley's essays, letters, and poems. Though best remembered as the author of *Frankenstein* (1818), Mary Shelley wrote other novels – notably, *The Last Man* (1826) – as well as biographies, journals, and many short stories. She died on 1st February 1851.

PADDY LYONS lectures in English at Glasgow University. He is a translator of Althusser and has written extensively on literary theory. In 1991 he co-edited *Female Playwrights of the Restoration: Five Comedies* for Everyman.

PHILIP GOODEN teaches in the English Department of Kingswood School, Bath. He contributed an article on Mary Shelley to *Makers of Nineteenth-Century Culture* (RKP 1982).

CHRONOLOGY OF MARY SHELLEY'S LIFE

Year	Age	Life
1797		Mary Goodwin born 30 August in London. Her mother, Mary Wollstonecraft Godwin, dies 10 September
1801	4	Mary Godwin's father, William Godwin, marries Mary Clairemont
1803	6	Mary Godwin's stepbrother, William Godwin jnr, born
1805	8	Godwins start children's publishing company
1807	10	Godwins move to central London, live on business premises
1808	11	Mary Godwin's version of comic song, 'Mounseer Nongtonpaw', published by father's firm
1811	14	Mary Godwin first sees Lord Byron at public lecture; spends six months at Ramsgate for salt-water treatment for skin condition
1812	15	Stays in Scotland with family of William Baxter, Godwin sympathiser. Meets Percy Bysshe Shelley, who dines with then wife at Godwins
1813	13	Mary Godwin returns to Baxters in Scotland
1814	17	Leaves Scotland; meets Percy Shelley again and intimate friendship begins; couple elope to France with Mary's stepsister, Jane, in July. Return to England in September. Godwin disowns daughter
1815	18	Mary Godwin gives birth to Clara; baby dies within eleven days. She and Shelley rent cottage near Windsor

CHRONOLOGY OF HER TIMES

Year	Literary Context	Historical Events
1797	Mrs Radcliffe, *The Italian*	
1798	Wordsworth and Coleridge, *Lyrical Ballads*	Irish rebellion
1801		William Pitt resigns as Prime Minister; succeeded by Henry Addington
1804		Pitt returns as PM; Napoleon crowned Emperor of France
1805		Battle of Trafalgar
1807	Charles and Mary Lamb, *Tales from Shakespeare* (Published by M. Godwin & Co.)	Peninsular War begins
1808	Leigh Hunt editor of *The Examiner*	
1811	Jane Austen, *Sense and Sensibility* Shelley sent down from Oxford for producing atheist pamphlet	
1812	Birth of Dickens	Napoleon invades Russia War between Britain and U.S. over trade
1813	Scott, *Waverley*	
1814	Jane Austen, *Mansfield Park*	Napoleon exiled to Elba; accession of Louis XVIII
1815		Battle of Waterloo

Year	Age	Life
1816	19	Mary Godwin gives birth to William. Claire (Jane) Clairmont becomes Byron's lover. May, Mary, Shelley and Claire stay with Byron on Lake Geneva. 22 June, Mary has dream which inspires *Frankenstein* and starts story. Fanny Godwin (Mary Wollstonecraft's child by Gilbert Imlay) commits suicide. In December Mary and Shelley marry
1817	20	*Frankenstein* finished, offered anonymously to publishers. Shelleys take lease on house in Marlow. *Frankenstein* accepted by Shelley's publishers. In September Mary gives birth to Clara Everina. Appearance of *Six Weeks' Tour*, edition of her and Shelley's travel letters
1818	21	In March Shelleys go to Italy to take Alba (Claire Clairmont's daughter by Byron) to Lord Byron; in September Mary's child Clara dies while they are en route to Venice
1819	22	Mary Shelley's son William dies in Rome aged three. In November she gives birth to Percy
1820	23	Shelleys move to Pisa. Mary begins research for *Valperga*, writes most of *Matilda* (unpublished in her life)
1822	25	Shelleys move to Casa Magni near La Spezia; Mary Shelley suffers miscarriage. Shelley drowned attempting to sail from Leghorn to Lerici with Edward Williams in July. In September Mary moves to Genoa
1823	26	Mary returns to England. *Valperga* published. First stage version of *Frankenstein* (titled *Presumption*) acclaimed
1824	27	Mary oversees publication of *Posthumous Poems* by Shelley until Shelley's father objects. Mary moves to Kentish Town; close friendship with Jane Williams
1826	29	Godwin declared bankrupt; children's publishers dissolved. Publication of *The Last Man*. Mary begins to write stories for Christmas Annuals
1827	30	Breakdown of friendship with Jane Williams
1828	31	Visits Paris and catches smallpox; meets Prosper Mérimée (author of *Carmen*) and starts correspondence with him
1829	32	Leases flat near Portman Square; assists her father financially. Continued tension and negotiation with Shelley's father over allowances for Percy, Mary's surviving child

Year	Literary Context	Historical Events
1816	Peacock, *Headlong Hall* (novel part inspired by friendship with Mary and Shelley)	Public disorder over prices and unemployment
1817	Keats publishes early poems Coleridge, *Biographia Literaria*	
1818	Byron begins *Don Juan* Jane Austen, *Northanger Abbey* (Austen's response to Gothic novel fad)	
1819		Peterloo Massacre
1820	Charles Maturin, *Melmoth the Wanderer* (influential Gothic novel)	Death of George III; accession of George IV
1821	Death of Keats; Shelley produces *Adonais* elegy	Start of Greek War of Independence
1822	de Quincey, *Confessions of an English Opium Eater*	
1824	Death of Byron at Missolonghi in Greece	
1825		Stockton and Darlington railway opened
1826	John Martin, admirer of Godwin, produces first of *Last Man* sequence of pictures	
1827	Death of William Blake	
1828		Duke of Wellington is Prime Minister

Year	Age	Life
1830	33	Publication of historical novel, *Perkin Warbeck*
1831	34	Publication of revised edition of *Frankenstein*
1832	35	Percy Shelley goes to Harrow
1833	36	Mary forms close friendship with Aubrey Beauclerk, radical MP
1834	37	Finishes first volume of *Literary and Scientific Lives* for encyclopedia series
1835	38	Publication of *Lodore*
1836	39	William Godwin dies. Mary suffers minor breakdown at end of year
1837	40	Percy goes to Trinity College, Cambridge
1839	42	Mary Shelley oversees publication of Shelley's *Poetical Works* in four volumes, followed by edition of his essays
1840	43	Mary returns to Italy (Lake Como) for first time since death of Shelley, also Geneva and Paris
1841	44	Death of Mrs Godwin, Mary's stepmother
1842	45	Mary Shelley travels to Germany and Italy with her son
1844	47	Shelley's father dies; as a result Mary's financial position is less precarious. *Rambles in Germany and Italy* is published
1845	48	Mary Shelley and son Percy buy house in Pimlico (first she has owned). Early signs of illness
1847	50	Mary operated on for back trouble
1848	51	Percy Shelley marries Jane St. John
1850	53	Travels to Lake Como with son and daughter-in-law
1851		Mary dies of a brain tumour on February 1. Buried with her parents in St Peter's, Bournemouth, at the insistence of Jane Shelley. She and Percy dedicate themselves to Mary's memory

Year	Literary Context	Historical Events
1830	Stendhal, *Le Rouge et le Noir*	Death of George IV; accession of William IV
1832	Death of Sir Walter Scott	Reform Bill extending voting rights
1833		Factory Act limits employment of children
1834		Tolpuddle Martyrs sent to Australia
1836	Dickens, *Pickwick Papers*, published monthly	
1837		Death of William IV; accession of Victoria
1839	Poe, *Tales of Grotesque and Arabesque*	
1840	Birth of Thomas Hardy	Victoria marries Prince Albert. Opium War with China
1844	Death of William Beckford, author of *Vathek*	
1845		Potato famine in Ireland
1847	Charlotte Bronte, *Jane Eyre*	
1848	Emily Bronte, *Wuthering Heights* Thackeray, *Vanity Fair*, published monthly	Outbreak of revolutionary activity across Europe Marx and Engels issue *Communist Manifesto*
1850	Death of Wordsworth Tennyson is Poet Laureate	
1851	Ruskin publishes first volume of *Stones of Venice* Melville, *Moby Dick*	Great Exhibition at Crystal Palace

INTRODUCTION

TEXT AND TEXTS

The text of *Frankenstein* given in this volume is that of the three-volume first edition of 1818.[1] It was completed before Mary Shelley was twenty, published anonymously a year later, and for a century and a half it has been unavailable to the all but the specialist reader.[2] The versions of *Frankenstein* circulating since the 1840s either reprint or derive from a revised text which Mary Shelley prepared in 1831; included here as an appendix is the retrospective preface which Mary Shelley added to that publication.

Modern scholarship prefers – and prefers strongly – the first edition text of *Frankenstein* over later versions. In a study of Mary Shelley first published in 1951, the novelist Muriel Spark found her to be a writer whose talent peaked early, commenting that from her late twenties onward 'her creative faculty dwindled' (Spark 1987, p. 151).[3] From a comparison of the 1831

[1] Five hundred copies were printed. This edition is based on the copy now held in the rare books collection of Glasgow University Library. I am grateful to the staff there for helpful assistance and untailing kindness – most especially, to Irene Kennedy, who located this copy-text for me, and to Elizabeth Watson, who prepared an archive copy on my behalf.

[2] The many editions of the novel have been collated by W. H. Lylys, *Mary Shelley: An Annotated Bibliography* (New York: Garland, 1975). James Rieger's scholarly edition, *Frankenstein, or The Modern Prometheus (The 1818 Text)* (New York: Bobbs-Merrill, 1974) is in fact more than its title indicates: it incorporates variant revisions which Mary Shelley made in 1823 in the copy she gave to her friend Mrs Talbot – despite of Rieger's view that few of these additions 'can be said to improve the style, and several detract from the imaginative integrity' (p. xxii). Based on a copy of the 1818 *Frankenstein* held in Smith College Library, a limited edition deluxe printing (with added woodcuts) was produced in 1983 by the Pennyroyal Press, and subsequently reproduced in 1984 by the University of California Press as an expensive coffee-table book. The 1818 text is also included in the compendious *Mary Shelley Reader* ed. Bennett and Robinson (New York: Oxford University Press, 1990) which also includes *Mathilda*, an autobiographical novel not published in Mary Shelley's lifetime, together with a generous selection from the writings of her later years.

[3] Full details of works cited in this short form are given in the list of works for further reading, which follows this Introduction.

revision with the 1818 first edition, a more recent critic concludes that 'in her depiction of the monster and the 1831 Frankenstein, Mary Shelley essentially raises feminine powerlessness to the status of myth.' (Poovey 1984, p. 142). Mary Shelley's most recent biographer has been no less forthright: 'The 1831 *Frankenstein* is as different from the 1818 *Frankenstein* as Wordsworth's 1850 *Prelude* is different from his 1805 version, and in somewhat the same ways.' (Mellor 1988, p. 170.) As if in shy deference to these views, an odd practice has emerged in recent paperback editions, which continue to reprint the later 1831 text – but prefix to it a facsimile of the 1818 title page!

The inordinate survival in print of the later versions of *Frankenstein* was possible so long as differences between the first and later editions could be sidelined and elided. While critics have vexed over the relative merits of alternative texts of *Hamlet*, there has been little similar concern about *Frankenstein*. Moreover, *any* version of the novel stands in significant contrast to a parallel series of stage and screen Frankensteins, which have sustained a quite independent existence. These have not been direct adaptations of Mary Shelley's novel but have instead have cloned each upon the other, following in tracks set out by *Presumption or the Fate of Frankenstein*, the play which Richard Brinsley Peake fashioned from her tale in 1823.[4] Like much early nineteenth-century melodrama, his play addressed a middle-class in need of reassurance and – once it had established servants as laughable buffoons – achieved its aim by rendering the Monster mute. The eloquent protests against misery and injustice were removed, and what remained was a figure without language, who could be viewed as but marginally human. Though this unbalanced Mary Shelley's work, it projected a scapegoat that caught the public imagination. By the mid-nineteenth century, the name Frankenstein had become a focus for dreads that beset the Victorian bourgeoisie:

The actions of the uneducated seem to me typified in those of Frankenstein, that monster of many human qualities, ungifted with a soul, a knowledge of the difference between good and evil. The people

---

[4] For details of the evolution of these plays, see Forry (1990) and Nitchie (1953). Printed copies of Peake's play vary considerably: the text given in Appendix B was compiled with a view to fullness. I am grateful to Chris Baldick for advice in locating some of the material on which it draws.

rise up to life; they irritate us, they terrify us, and we become their enemies. Then, in the sorrowful moment of our triumphant power, their eyes gaze on us with mute reproach. Why have we made them what they are: a powerful monster, yet without the inner means for peace and happiness?[5]

Occurring casually in a well-known novel of 1848, this passage makes apparent how quickly – thanks to the popularity of Peake's play and those that followed it – Mary Shelley's story had been absorbed without being read: the name 'Frankenstein' has shifted over from maker to monster. And when Hollywood brought *Frankenstein* to the screen in 1931, the script was based not on the novel but on a successful dramatisation (by Peggy Webling) which descended from Peake. The Creature was again speechless, wearing a large bolt through his throat, and could represent new dreads, those of Depression America:

What Universal's *Frankenstein* seeks to say specifically to the mass audience at whom it is aimed concerns above all mass activity in times of crisis: where that activity might be assertive and democratic and beneficial (the Walton story), it is removed and concealed; where it is violent and insurrectionary (the monster's story), it is systematically denigrated . . . (O'Flinn 1986, pp. 213–14.)

The co-existence of these *Frankensteins*[6] alongside – though apart from and in striking contrast to the book – has until recently deflected attention from differences between versions of the novel.

Two developments in particular have led to a reconsideration of Mary Shelley and her work. One is a general tendency of contemporary fiction towards fantasy and the Gothic; this has had the effect of promoting the Gothic from subgenre status into the literary mainstream, and it is now no longer necessary to present Frankenstein as an angst-torn Victorian scientist, halfway between Captain Nemo and Madame Curie. Secondly, the rise of Women's Studies marks a shift from the times when Mary Shelley could be summed up and dismissed as no more than an appendage to her poetical husband – 'an excellent widow, whatever kind of wife she made' is how she was described by John Masefield, then Poet Laureate, when inter-

[5] Elizabeth Gaskell, *Mary Barton* (Harmondsworth: Penguin, 1970), pp. 219–20.
[6] Extensively detailed and discussed by Baldick (1987).

viewed by Muriel Spark in 1950.[7] For the visions of emancipation into calm and serenity which attracted Victorian and Edwardian feminists, Gothic fiction could hold small importance. But to critics schooled in the Women's Movement of the later twentieth century, Gothic strangeness can be an enlargement to the map of female achievement: that *Frankenstein* was written in the midst of (and bears the traces of) child-bearing, grief, and domestic upheaval can be recognised without apology. Yet as much as the biographical approach may illuminate, it can also dazzle, and Mary Shelley's life was, especially while she worked on *Frankenstein*, unnervingly eventful. The unorthodoxy of her approach to authorship in her presentation of *Frankenstein* is, therefore, particularly worthy of further attention.

AUTHORSHIP, ROMANTICISM, AND FEMINISM

No author's name appears on the 1818 title-page of *Frankenstein*, and this is not merely a triumph of shyness over pride, or of delicacy lest attention be drawn to sensitive areas of her domestic life. Printed immediately beneath the title are lines from Milton's *Paradise Lost* which put in question the relations between an author and what he has created:

> Did I request thee, Maker, from my clay
> To mould me man? Did I solicit thee
> From darkness to promote me?

The outcry is that of Milton's Adam, against the Divine Author, against the God who created him and who has rejected his creation. The issue raised is that of authorial responsibility, and it echoes through the novel:

I am thy creature. I ought to be thy Adam; but I am rather the fallen angel, whom thou drivest from joy for no misdeed. (p. 81)

The plea impresses Frankenstein, who understands and concurs – '. . . I felt what the duties of a creator towards his creature were, and that I ought to render him happy before I complained of his wickedness.' (p. 83) – giving his attention as his creature tells his story. But setting these sentiments on the title-page where an author's name might be expected, is discordant: the effect is

[7] Noted in her introduction to the revised edition of her study: Muriel Spark, *John Masefield* (London: Hutchinson, 1992), p. ix.

that authorial responsibility is asserted while, simultaneously and by the same means, authorial identity is held back in concealment. The tension here is not limited to the typographical details of one page, but becomes a recurrent motif in the novel that follows, as Frankenstein first shys off from the Creature he has brought into being, then reaches out towards the Creature, only to hold off again. It is apparent too as the Creature admits to crimes, then shifts blame onto his maker, only to take back responsibility on himself, first with pride, and later with shame. And this process results from a contradiction which was implicit in the Romantic involvement with authorship, a contradiction which Mary Shelley opened up and utilised to propel her fiction.

Authorship was enshrined in Romantic poetic manifestos: Wordsworth described the Poet as 'a man speaking to men'. His famous phrase is suggestive of directness and intimacy, of egalitarianism and the democratic principle which had enabled the French Revolution. But alongside this is a different, more hierarchical stance, which emerges as the description is amplified to that of:

a man endowed with more lively sensibility, more enthusiasm and tenderness, who has a greater knowledge of human nature, and a more comprehensive soul, than are supposed to be common among mankind; a man pleased with his own passions and volitions . . .[8]

This dualism of stance was to be a shaping principle in much Romantic poetry, most immediately evident in the treatment of the authorial persona within a poem, and often sufficiently crucial to constitute a poetic device in itself. It can be illustrated in as brief a piece as Wordsworth's elegiac lyric 'She dwelt among the untrodden ways' (1800), which concludes:

> She lived unknown, and few could know
>   When Lucy ceased to be;
> But she is in her grave, and, oh,
>   The difference to me.[9]

The tone is hushed and intimate, as is the inclusive democratic concern, the sentiment that everyone matters, that no life is to be dismissed; but counter to this there is an insistence on specialness, most of all on the important singularity of the Poet's

[8] Preface to the 1800 edition of *Lyrical Ballads: The Poetical Works of Wordsworth*, ed. Hutchinson and revised De Selincourt (London: Oxford University Press, 1950), p. 737.
[9] Wordsworth, *op. cit.*, p. 86

feelings, which set him apart from a less sensitive multitude ('few could know . . . the difference to me'). As the poem encodes it, the figure of the author is at once on a level footing with all humankind and is also somehow aloof and superior. Supporting this double effect is a teasing deployment of the biographical: grief is manifested in a single exclamation ('and, oh,') and then is not expanded; the personal is at once asserted as if for sharing and yet is withheld and veiled. A similar use of biographical half-hints recurs in the glancing mentions of private friendships that run through the poetry of Wordsworth, Coleridge and Shelley and underpins Byron's insinuations that his Don Juan or Childe Harold may at once be, and yet not be, Byron himself. Thus a haughty aristocratic distance and a levelling egalitarianism – unresolved and together in suspension – constituted the poetic figure of the Romantic author.

Much the same forces can be seen as shaping many novels of this era, most obviously in the relations between narration and dialogue. For example, in the Scottish novels of Sir Walter Scott, the dialogue frequently presents the difficulty of dialect and 'untrodden ways', whereas the narration is conducted in self-effacing and metropolitan 'standard' English. The effect is on the one hand to produce understanding and intelligibility (levelling), while at the same time setting up what Catherine Belsey has usefully described[10] as a 'hierarchy of discourses', in which 'a privileged discourse . . . places as subordinate all the discourses that are literally or figuratively between inverted commas'. And in his analysis of how a reader may feel a sense of 'shared' irony at the conclusion of a novel by Jane Austen, Wayne Booth indicates how this also involves a tacit acceptance of hierarchy:

'Jane Austen' has learned nothing at the end of the novel that she did not know at the beginning. She needed to learn nothing. She knew everything of importance already. We have been privileged to watch with her as she observes her favorite character climb from a considerably lower platform to join the exalted company of Knightly, 'Jane Austen', and those of us readers who are wise enough, good enough, and perceptive enough to belong up there too.[11]

[10] Catherine Belsey, *Critical Practice* (London and New York: Routledge, 1980), p. 70.
[11] Wayne Booth, *The Rhetoric of Fiction* (Chicago: Chicago University Press, 1961), p. 265.

Once a narrating voice can be readily designated as if it is that
of the Author ('"Jane Austen"'), a hierarchy of discourses
emerges, and authority is conferred under the author's name.
But Mary Shelley authorised no such knowingness. *Frankenstein*
is narrated by a male trio – Walton, Frankenstein, and the
Creature – and, between the rival narratives of Frankenstein
and the Creature, neither Walton nor the implied reader can
infer a hierarchy or adjudication: '. . . Margaret, what comment
can I make . . . ?' (p. 187)

In an intricate comparative discussion of *Frankenstein* and
Charlotte Brontë's *Jane Eyre*, Gayatri Spivak links this absence
of a dominant authorative voice to a relative absence from
Frankenstein of the racism with which she finds *Jane Eyre*
collusive. *Jane Eyre* allows Adèle (who is part French) and the
first Mrs Rochester (who is part Creole) to seem subhuman,
whereas Safie (the Turkish girl) is idealised and on a par with
Frankenstein's Elizabeth (Spivak, 1985). Spivak relates this
absence of a directing imperial authority to a unusual association between the author and the imaginary female addressee of
Frankenstein, an association that is not one between the author
and any narrating discourse: Walton's sister, to whom are
addressed the letters that enfold the stories of Frankenstein and
the Creature, and whose voice is never audible in the novel, has
the name Margaret Walton Saville; her initials – MWS – are
those of Mary Wollstonecraft Shelley. In other words, if the
personal is to be found encoded in the novel, it is outside the
frame, and not as a slyly assertive support to authority. None-
theless, to some critics of the novel, this absence of a directly
personal voice constitutes a failing and not an asset. According
to Anne K. Mellor:

Mary Shelley systematically censored her own speech in *Frankenstein*.
The structure of the novel builds a series of screens around her authentic
voice. The monster's autobiographical account of a benevolent disposition perverted by social neglect drew most directly on Mary Shelley's
own experience of childhood abandonment and emotional deprivation
in the Godwin household after her father's remarriage to the unsympa-
thetic Mrs Clairmont. Mary Shelley's decision to enclose that narrative
within not one but two other narratives (Frankenstein's account of his
own history as recorded in Walton's journal or his voyage towards the
North Pole) has the effect of twice distancing her private voice from
public speech. (Mellor 1988, p. 57.)

At issue in the difference between Spivak and Mellor is a larger debate within late twentieth-century feminist criticism – the (separatist) question of whether or not to argue in favour of a distinctively 'feminine prose'. On this matter Mary Wollstonecraft was in no doubt, and in 1792 had put forward her position with vigour :

A wild wish has just flown from my heart to my head, and I will not stifle it, . . . I do earnestly wish to see the distinction of sex confounded in society, unless where love animates the behaviour. For this distinction is, I believe, the foundation of the weakness of character ascribed to woman.[12]

As Mary Wollstonecraft's daughter, it is very likely that Mary Shelley endorsed these views. She would also have been familiar with her mother's dismissal of a gendered literature designed to direct young women towards 'femininity' – a literature such as Rousseau had advocated and provided for her generation :

If fear in girls, instead of being cherished, perhaps created, were treated in the same manner as cowardice in boys, we should quickly see women with more dignified aspects. It is true they could not then with equal propriety be termed the sweet flowers that smile in the walk of man ; but they would be more respectable members of society. 'Educate women like men,' says Rousseau, 'and the more they ressemble our sex the less power will they have over us.' This is the very point I aim at. I do not wish them to have power over men ; but over themselves.[13]

In the letters from Walton to his sister, Margaret Walton is not addressed so as to set her apart for being female. Against the view that Mary Shelley was 'self-censoring', it is arguable that, in the construction of the voices which compose *Frankenstein*, she was engaged in an aesthetic based strategically on principles absorbed from the feminist writings of her mother.

BIOGRAPHY AND COMPOSITION

In her 1831 *Preface*, Mary Shelley distances her past self from autobiographical impulses :

I did not make myself the heroine of my tales. Life appeared to me too commonplace an affair as regarded myself. I could not figure to myself

---

[12] Mary Wollstonecraft, *A Vindication of the Rights of Woman* (London : J M Dent, Everyman, 1992), p. 63.
[13] Mary Wolllstonecraft, *op. cit.*, p. 69.

that romantic woes or wonderful events would ever be my lot; but I was not confined to my own identity, and I could people the hours with creations far more interesting to me at that age, than my own sensations. (p. 196)

She concludes by allowing no more personal dimension to *Frankenstein* beyond that 'Its several pages speak of many a walk, many a drive, and many a conversation, when I was not alone;' (p. 199) and associates her novel with 'days when death and grief were but words which found no true echo in my heart.'

Shelley's death by drowning in 1822 had left Mary Shelley with a sense of inconsolable loss, but it was not her first acquaintance with grief. But it is arguable too that by 1831 she had come to focus all pain around that bereavement, as if it might be unbearable to admit there had been pain mixed in with the happiness she had once enjoyed. The very brilliance with which she describes the beginnings of *Frankenstein*, as given in a dream like a surrealist poem, is then, arguably, a deflection, a refusal not to acknowledge suffering as scarring those times too. It is difficult to dissociate completely her tale of guilt and responsibility, painful begettings and violent deaths from events that surrounded her while the novel was in progress.

When she began work on *Frankenstein*, her name was Mary Wollstonecraft Godwin. She was not yet nineteen, and for nearly two years she and Percy Bysshe Shelley, had been living together, mostly in contentment and delight. The novel was begun in mid-June 1816, while she, Shelley and their baby son William were holidaying in Switzerland; they were accompanied by Mary's step-sister Claire, who was by now also in the throes of a love affair with a well-known poet, Byron, by whom she had successfully become pregnant. In October 1816, within weeks of their return to England, Fanny Imlay, daughter of Mary Wollstonecraft and half-sister to Mary, had committed suicide, swallowing poison in a hotel room in Swansea. Shelley went to the scene, and, it is said, there was such disfigurement to the corpse that he could only identify the body by embroidery on her stays. During the time Mary and Shelley had been abroad, Fanny had written several letters despairing of her life in London, and proposed to move to Ireland, where an aunt kept a school. But when the aunt refused her application on the grounds that her associating with a couple who lived as Mary and Shelley made her unfit to work in a school, Fanny had set off for Ireland regardless, and given way to despair in the course of her journey. In December there was further suicide: Shelley's estranged wife Harriet drowned herself in the Serpentine. She was advanced in pregnancy, perhaps as the result of a liaison with an army officer. Three weeks after her body was discovered, Mary and Shelley were married, in the hope this would obtain for them custody of Shelley's two children by Harriet. Their plea was refused by the Courts on the grounds that they were unfit as parents, and the children were sent to a foster home.

Bleak in themselves, these events held terrible resonances for Mary Shelley, not least in bringing together childbearing and violent death. Mary knew that when Mary Wollstonecraft was giving birth to her, the placenta had failed to descend, and owing to the efforts of a surgeon to dislodge it, an infection had set in which was to prove fatal: her mother died ten days afterwards. In February 1815, aged 17 and pregnant by Shelley, Mary had given premature birth to a daughter, who died some days later, and who then haunted her waking thoughts and dreams. Her journal entries from the time are chilling:

March 13: . . . whenever I am left alone to my own thoughts, and do not read to divert them, they always come back to the same point – that I was a mother and am no longer.

March 19: Dream that my little baby came to life again; that it had been only cold, and that we rubbed it before the fire, and it lived. Awake and find no baby. I think about the little thing all day. Not in good spirits. (*Journals*, 198, Vol. 1, pp. 69–70)

To say the least, these sad statements evidence too much sorrow to allow that 'death and grief were but words' to her in the years before Shelley's death; it is hard to suppose that these feelings were not reawakened in Mary by the distressing events surrounding her in the winter of 1816/17 as she worked on *Frankenstein*.

The fortitude which kept her going in these trying times is quite remarkable. In January 1816 Mary had given birth to her son William – a sickly boy, who was to die in mid–1819. She nursed him with care throughout the time she was writing. And by early 1817 she was pregnant again; her daughter Clara (named after the child who died) was born in September 1817, though she was to live only a year. That her child's illness would have given rise to worries for the well-being of the baby she was carrying is likely. And the similarity of name between Mary Shelley's infant son and the boy William Frankenstein, who is murdered because of the name he carries, goes beyond casual coincidence. Though it is hard to quarrel with the view that '*Frankenstein* is a book about what happens when a man tries to have a baby without a woman' (Mellor 1988, p. 40), it is difficult to gauge how far events and anxieties may have actually shaped *Frankenstein*.[14] It is feasible, however, to posit a distance of feeling between the time when the book was written and the secure tones of fond maternal sarcasm that emerge in the 1831 *Preface*:

I bid my hideous progeny go forth and prosper. I have an affection for it, for it was the offspring of happy days . . .' (p. 199)

'We will each write a ghost story,' said Lord Byron. (p. 197)

GENRE AND NARRATIVE

By 1818 the supernaturalism of eighteenth-century Gothic fiction was looking increasingly dated and bookish. In her response to Byron's challenge, Mary Shelley did not rely on haunted castles and antique vaults, and *Frankenstein* is without the mysterious monks and eerie spectres which had peopled the Gothic. To the genre she brought an acute ear for shifts in stylistic register, and the unrealism her story engages with is that of male hysteria. For example, for the scene where Frankenstein first encounters the Creature he has brought into being and attempted to evade, the setting is outdoors, the Mer de Glace at Chamoix – which Mary Shelley had visited – and the confrontation develops through a counterpoint of voices:

'Devil,' I exclaimed, 'do you dare approach me? And do you not fear the fierce vengeance of my arm wreaked on your miserable head? Begone, vile insect! Or rather stay, that I may trample you to dust! And oh, that I could, with the extinction of your miserable existence, restore those victims whom you have so diabolically murdered!'
'I expected this reception,' said the demon. 'All men hate the wretched'. (p. 80)

Facing each other are the windiness of melodramatic posturing and the lucidity of plain speaking. Admirably clear when the

---

[14] This issue has been much scrutinised in recent criticism; see Johnson 1985, Kahane 1985, Moers 1976, Rubenstein 1976, and Sedgwick 1986.

goal is practical – describing a landscape or calming the muti-nous sailors – Frankenstein's language moves into emptiness once it is driven by evasiveness and by his efforts to escape the consequences of having usurped the process of giving life. His nightmares, too, are triggered by denial and avoidance; at the moment when his creation begins to move, he turns away, and his daydream of Elizabeth slides into surreal disturbance :

> ... as I imprinted the first kiss on her lips, they became livid with the hue of death, her features appeared to change, and I though that I held the corpse of my dead mother in my arms; a shroud enveloped her form, and I saw grave-worms crawling in the folds of the flannel ...
> (p.41)

In contrast to his creator, the Creature has the appeal of directness and freshness : 'I distinguished the insect from the herb, and, by degrees, one herb from another. I found that the sparrow uttered none but harsh notes, whilst those of the blackbird and thrush were sweet and enticing.' (p. 85) But though the effect of the Creature's account of himself is one of original innocence, it too has a background of bookish encounters :

> ... the most decisive experience ... is the Monster's discovery of Frankenstein's detailed journal of the four months preceding its cre-ation. What the discovery and perusal of this journal allows the Monster is a reading of its own coming into existence ... What the journal reveals is that the Monster had not been born but made, that its originality was essentially derivative ... in this very moment the Monster discovers its negative relations with all that constitute it ...
> (Musselwhite 1987, p. 70.)

And as decisive, though not mentioned when the Creature lists the books that advanced him, is the work of William Godwin, novelist, philosopher, father of Mary Shelley and the dedicatee of *Frankenstein*. Underwriting the powerful insistence on the relations between exclusion and violence is Godwin's political philosophy. Opposed to the penitentiary system that advocated the solitary confinement and exclusion from community as a method to reform the criminal, Godwin argued that Law was itself social and communal, not natural, and that offence against communal bonds could only be augmented under a regime of isolation and exclusion from human fellowship :

Will his heart become much either softened or expanded, who breathes the atmosphere of a dungeon ? Surely it would be better in this respect to imitate the system of the universe, and, if we would teach justice and humanity, transplant those we would teach into a simple and reasonable state of society ? Solitude, absolutely considered, may instigate us to serve ourselves, but not to serve our neighbours. Solitude, imposed under too few limitations, may be a nursery for madmen and idiots, but not for useful members of society.[15]

Frankenstein's refusals to take responsibility for the being he has created make his Creature an outcast; the Creature's analysis of his own violence and murderousness makes vivid Godwin's arguments :

Everywhere I see bliss, from which I alone am irrevocably excluded. I was benevolent and good: misery made me a fiend. Make me happy, and I shall again be virtuous. (p. 81)

The plot pattern of pursuit-encounter-pursuit derives too from Godwin, from his novel *Caleb William, or Things as They are* (1794). There are no heroes, only anti-heroes who are interchangeably hunter and quarry, and – as with Caleb and Falkland – the movement is that of a reversible chase : Frankenstein is in flight from the Creature, who haunts his dreams ; the Creature pursues Frankenstein, in search of either companionship or vengeance; and in the final pursuit of each other they head towards mutual destruction. Against the stark vividness of this pattern, family and community become subsidiary, shadowy, ultimately to be left behind in what Eve Sedgwick has characterised as the paranoid dynamic of Gothic fiction. She elaborates :

The fate of the family in *Frankenstein* and throughout the paranoid Gothic presents the pared-down nuclear Oedipal family, first, as compulsory, but second, as a somewhat ephemeral stage on the way to ... the tableau of two men chasing one another across a landscape. It is importantly undecidable in this tableau ... whether the two men represent two consciousnesses or only one; and it is importantly undecidable whether their bond ... is murderous or amorous.

(Sedgwick 1986, p. ix)[16]

---

[15] William Godwin, *Enquiry Concerning Political Justice*, ed. Isaac Kramnick (Harmondsworth : Pelican Classics, 1976) p. 678.

[16] She analyses how 'the absolute omnipresence of this homophobic, paranoid tableau' in nineteenth-century writing relates to '*The absence of* a widely-available sense of a possible homosexual role' *op.cit.*p. x. For a further literary-historical account, see Eve Kosofski–Sedgwick *Between Men : English Literature and Male Homosocial Desire* (New York : Colombia University Press, 1985), especially pp. 82–117.

By the end of the novel, capture or defeat matters less than pursuit itself:

You will feel the misery of cold and frost, to which I am impassive ... Come on my enemy, we have yet to wrestle ... wrap yourself in furs ... (p. 191)

The taunts sound almost affectionate; and when death brings the chase to its end, the prospect of his own extinction becomes ecstatic to the survivor:

He is dead who called me into being; and when I shall be no more, the very remembrance of us both will speedily vanish ... I shall ascend my funeral pile triumphantly, and exult in the agony of the torturing flames. (p. 191)

There are casualties. In this vicious scenario of man-to-man bonding, women are not merely left behind, but suffer unjustly. Justine is executed for a crime she did not commit, Elizabeth is slain in revenge for Frankenstein's destruction of his Creature's future companion. Though neither of these women comes to an understanding of how she has been jeopardised, there is an advance beyond the conventions of Gothic fiction whereby female speech was destined to issue as wordless screams: Elizabeth is at once generous and eloquent in pleading on behalf of Justine; Justine is in no doubt about her own innocence, and is clear that a false confession of guilt was bullied from her simply to satisfy the Church. What Mary Shelley's novel exposes is the mechanism whereby these women have been excluded and destroyed.

PADDY LYONS

FRANKENSTEIN;

OR,

THE MODERN PROMETHEUS.*

———◆———

IN THREE VOLUMES.

———◆———

Did I request thee, Maker, from my clay
To mould me man? Did I solicit thee
From darkness to promote me?——
                            PARADISE LOST.

———

VOL. I.

═══════════

LonDon :

PRINTED FOR

LACKINGTON, HUGHES, HARDING, MAVOR, & JONES,
FINSBURY SQUARE.

———

1818.

TO

WILLIAM GODWIN,*

AUTHOR OF POLITICAL JUSTICE, CALEB WILLIAMS, &C.

THESE VOLUMES

Are respectfully inscribed

BY

THE AUTHOR.

PREFACE

[*Written entirely by Mary Shelley's husband, the poet
Percy Bysshe Shelley — see p. 199.*]

The event on which this fiction is founded has been supposed,
by Dr Darwin,* and some of the physiological writers of
Germany, as not of impossible occurrence. I shall not be
supposed as according the remotest degree of serious faith to
such an imagination; yet, in assuming it as the basis of a work
of fancy, I have not considered myself as merely weaving a series
of supernatural terrors. The event on which the interest of the
story depends is exempt from the disadvantages of a mere tale
of spectres or enchantment. It was recommended by the novelty
of the situations which it develops; and, however impossible as
a physical fact, affords a point of view to the imagination for
the delineating of human passions more comprehensive and
commanding than any which the ordinary relations of existing
events can yield.

I have thus endeavoured to preserve the truth of the elementary principles of human nature, while I have not scrupled to
innovate upon their combinations. The *Iliad*, the tragic poetry
of Greece — Shakespeare, in the *Tempest* and *Midsummer
Night's Dream* — and most especially Milton, in *Paradise Lost*,
conform to this rule; and the most humble novelist, who seeks
to confer or receive amusement from his labours, may, without
presumption, apply to prose fiction a licence, or rather a rule,
from the adoption of which so many exquisite combinations of
human feeling have resulted in the highest specimens of poetry.

The circumstance on which my story rests was suggested in
casual conversation. It was commenced, partly as a source of
amusement, and partly as an expedient for exercising any
untried resources of mind. Other motives were mingled with
these, as the work proceeded. I am by no means indifferent to
the manner in which whatever moral tendencies exist in the
sentiments or characters it contains shall affect the reader; yet

my chief concern in this respect has been limited to the avoiding
the enervating effects of the novels of the present day and to the
exhibition of the amiableness of domestic affection, and the
excellence of universal virtue. The opinions which naturally
spring from the character and situation of the hero are by no
means to be conceived as existing always in my own conviction;
nor is any inference justly to be drawn from the following pages
as prejudicing any philosophical doctrine of whatever kind.

It is a subject also of additional interest to the author that this
story was begun in the majestic region where the scene is
principally laid, and in society which cannot cease to be regretted. I passed the summer of 1816 in the environs of Geneva.
The season was cold and rainy, and in the evenings we crowded
around a blazing wood fire, and occasionally amused ourselves
with some German stories of ghosts, which happened to fall
into our hands. These tales excited in us a playful desire of
imitation. Two other friends (a tale from the pen of one of
whom would be far more acceptable to the public than anything
I can ever hope to produce) and myself agreed to write each a
story founded on some supernatural occurrence.

The weather, however, suddenly became serene ; and my two
friends left me on a journey among the Alps, and lost, in the
magnificent scenes which they present, all memory of their
ghostly visions. The following tale is the only one which has
been completed.

Marlow, September 1817

FRANKENSTEIN

Volume I

LETTER I

To Mrs Saville, England.
St Petersburgh, Dec. 11, 17—.

You will rejoice to hear that no disaster has accompanied the commencement of an enterprise which you have regarded with such evil forebodings. I arrived here yesterday; and my first task is to assure my dear sister of my welfare, and increasing confidence in the success of my undertaking.

I am already far north of London; and as I walk in the streets of Petersburgh, I feel a cold northern breeze play upon my cheeks, which braces my nerves, and fills me with delight. Do you understand this feeling? This breeze, which has travelled from the regions towards which I am advancing, gives me a foretaste of those icy climes. Inspirited by this wind of promise, my day dreams become more fervent and vivid. I try in vain to be persuaded that the pole is the seat of frost and desolation; it ever presents itself to my imagination as the region of beauty and delight.* There, Margaret, the sun is forever visible; its broad disk just skirting the horizon, and diffusing a perpetual splendour. There – for with your leave, my sister, I will put some trust in preceding navigators – there snow and frost are banished; and, sailing over a calm sea, we may be wafted to a land surpassing in wonders and in beauty every region hitherto discovered on the habitable globe. Its productions and features may be without example, as the phenomena of the heavenly bodies undoubtedly are in those undiscovered solitudes. What may not be expected in a country of eternal light? I may there discover the wondrous power which attracts the needle; and may regulate a thousand celestial observations, that require only this voyage to render their seeming eccentricities consistent forever. I shall satiate my ardent curiosity with the sight of a part of the world never before visited, and may tread a land never before imprinted by the foot of man. These are my enticements, and they are sufficient to conquer all fear of danger or death, and to induce me to commence this laborious voyage with the joy a child feels when he embarks in a little boat, with his holiday mates, on an expedition of discovery up his native river. But, supposing all these conjectures to be false, you cannot contest the inestimable benefit which I shall confer on all mankind to the last generation, by discovering a passage near the pole* to those countries, to reach which at present so many months are requisite; or by ascertaining the secret of the magnet, which, if at all possible, can only be effected by an undertaking such as mine.

These reflections have dispelled the agitation with which I began my letter, and I feel my heart glow with an enthusiasm which elevates me to heaven; for nothing contributes so much to tranquillize the mind as a steady purpose, – a point on which the soul may fix its intellectual eye. This expedition has been the favourite dream of my early years. I have read with ardour the accounts of the various voyages which have been made in the prospect of arriving at the North Pacific Ocean through the seas which surround the pole. You may remember, that a history of all the voyages made for purposes of discovery composed the whole of our good uncle Thomas's library. My education was neglected, yet I was passionately fond of reading. These volumes were my study day and night, and my familiarity with them increased that regret which I had felt, as a child, on learning that my father's dying injunction had forbidden my uncle to allow me to embark in a sea-faring life.

These visions faded when I perused, for the first time, those poets whose effusions entranced my soul, and lifted it to heaven. I also became a poet, and for one year lived in a Paradise of my own creation; I imagined that I also might obtain a niche in the temple where the names of Homer and Shakespeare are consecrated. You are well acquainted with my failure, and how heavily I bore the disappointment. But just at that time I inherited the fortune of my cousin, and my thoughts were turned into the channel of their earlier bent.

Six years have passed since I resolved on my present undertaking. I can, even now, remember the hour from which I dedicated myself to this great enterprise. I commenced by inuring my body to hardship. I accompanied the whale-fishers on several expeditions to the North Sea; I voluntarily endured cold, famine, thirst, and want of sleep ; I often worked harder than the common sailors during the day, and devoted my nights to the study of mathematics, the theory of medicine, and those branches of physical science from which a naval adventurer might derive the greatest practical advantage. Twice I actually hired myself as an undermate in a Greenland whaler, and acquitted myself to admiration. I must own I felt a little proud, when my captain offered me the second dignity in the vessel, and entreated me to remain with the greatest earnestness ; so valuable did he consider my services.

And now, dear Margaret, do I not deserve to accomplish some great purpose. My life might have been passed in ease and luxury ; but I preferred glory to every enticement that wealth placed in my path. Oh, that some encouraging voice would answer in the affirmative ! My courage and my resolution is firm ; but my hopes fluctuate, and my spirits are often depressed. I am about to proceed on a long and difficult voyage ; the emergencies of which will demand all my fortitude : I am required not only to raise the spirits of others, but sometimes to sustain my own, when their's are failing.

This is the most favourable period for travelling in Russia. They fly quickly over the snow in their sledges ; the motion is pleasant, and, in my opinion, far more agreeable than that of an English stage-coach. The cold is not excessive, if you are wrapt in furs, a dress which I have already adopted ; for there is a great difference between walking the deck and remaining seated motionless for hours, when no exercise prevents the blood from actually freezing in your veins. I have no ambition to lose my life on the post-road between St Petersburgh and Archangel.

I shall depart from the latter town in a fortnight or three weeks ; and my intention is to hire a ship there, which can easily be done by paying the insurance for the owner, and to engage as many sailors as I think necessary among those who are accustomed to the whale-fishing. I do not intend to sail until the month of June : and when shall I return ? Ah, dear sister, how can I answer this question ? If I succeed, many, many months, perhaps years, will pass before you and I may meet. If I fail, you will see me again soon, or never.

Farewell, my dear, excellent, Margaret. Heaven shower down blessings on you, and save me, that I may again and again testify my gratitude for all your love and kindness.

Your affectionate brother,
R. *Walton.*

LETTER II

To Mrs Saville, England.
Archangel, 28 March, 17—.

How slowly the time passes here, encompassed as I am by frost and snow; yet a second step is taken towards my enterprise. I have hired a vessel, and am occupied in collecting my sailors; those whom I have already engaged appear to be men on whom I can depend, and are certainly possessed of dauntless courage.

But I have one want which I have never yet been able to satisfy; and the absence of the object of which I now feel as a most severe evil. I have no friend, Margaret: when I am glowing with the enthusiasm of success, there will be none to participate my joy; if I am assailed by disappointment, no one will endeavour to sustain me in dejection. I shall commit my thoughts to paper, it is true; but that is a poor medium for the communication of feeling. I desire the company of a man who could sympathize with me; whose eyes would reply to mine. You may deem me romantic, my dear sister, but I bitterly feel the want of a friend. I have no-one near me, gentle yet courageous, possessed of a cultivated as well as of a capacious mind, whose tastes are like my own, to approve or amend my plans. How would such a friend repair the faults of your poor brother! I am too ardent in execution, and too impatient of difficulties. But it is a still greater evil to me that I am self-educated: for the first fourteen years of my life I ran wild on a common, and read nothing but our uncle Thomas's books of voyages. At that age I became acquainted with the celebrated poets of our own country; but it was only when it had ceased to be in my power to derive its most important benefits from such a conviction, that I perceived the necessity of becoming acquainted with more languages than that of my native country.

Now I am twenty-eight, and am in reality more illiterate than many school-boys of fifteen. It is true that I have thought more, and that my day dreams are more extended and magnificent; but they want (as the painters call it) *keeping*;* and I greatly need a friend who would have sense enough not to despise me as romantic, and affection enough for me to endeavour to regulate my mind.

Well, these are useless complaints; I shall certainly find no friend on the wide ocean, nor even here in Archangel, among merchants and seamen. Yet some feelings, unallied to the dross of human nature, beat even in these rugged bosoms. My lieutenant, for instance, is a man of wonderful courage and enterprise; he is madly desirous of glory. He is an Englishman, and in the midst of national and professional prejudices, unsoftened by cultivation, retains some of the noblest endowments of humanity. I first became acquainted with him on board a whale vessel: finding that he was unemployed in this city, I easily engaged him to assist in my enterprise.

The master is a person of an excellent disposition, and is remarkable in the ship for his gentleness, and the mildness of his discipline. He is, indeed, of so amiable a nature, that he will not hunt (a favourite, and almost the only amusement here), because he cannot endure to spill blood. He is, moreover, heroically generous. Some years ago he loved a young Russian lady, of moderate fortune; and having amassed a considerable sum in prize-money, the father of the girl consented to the match. He saw his mistress once before the destined ceremony; but she was bathed in tears, and, throwing herself at his feet, entreated him to spare her, confessing at the same time that she loved another, but that he was poor, and that her father would never consent to the union. My generous friend reassured the suppliant, and on being informed of the name of her lover instantly abandoned his pursuit. He had already bought a farm with his money, on which he had designed to pass the remainder of his life; but he bestowed the whole on his rival, together with the remains of his prize-money* to purchase stock, and then himself solicited the young woman's father to consent to her marriage with her lover. But the old man decidedly refused, thinking himself bound in honour to my friend; who, when he found the father inexorable, quitted his country, nor returned until he heard that his former mistress was married according to her inclinations. 'What a noble fellow !' you will exclaim. He is so;

but then he has passed all his life on board a vessel, and has scarcely an idea beyond the rope and the shroud.

But do not suppose that, because I complain a little, or because I can conceive a consolation for my toils which I may never know, that I am wavering in my resolutions. Those are as fixed as fate; and my voyage is only now delayed until the weather shall permit my embarkation. The winter has been dreadfully severe; but the spring promises well, and it is considered as a remarkably early season; so that, perhaps, I may sail sooner than I expected. I shall do nothing rashly; you know me sufficiently to confide in my prudence and considerateness whenever the safety of others is committed to my care.

I cannot describe to you my sensations on the near prospect of my undertaking. It is impossible to communicate to you a conception of the trembling sensation, half pleasurable and half fearful, with which I am preparing to depart. I am going to unexplored regions, to 'the land of mist and snow;' but I shall kill no albatross,* therefore do not be alarmed for my safety.

Shall I meet you again, after having traversed immense seas, and returned by the most southern cape of Africa or America? I dare not expect such success, yet I cannot bear to look on the reverse of the picture. Continue to write to me by every opportunity: I may receive your letters (though the chance is very doubtful) on some occasions when I need them most to support my spirits. I love you very tenderly. Remember me with affection, should you never hear from me again.

Your affectionate brother,
Robert Walton.

LETTER III

To Mrs Saville, England.
July 7, 17—.

MY DEAR SISTER,
I write a few lines in haste, to say that I am safe, and well advanced on my voyage. This letter will reach England by a merchant-man now on its homeward voyage from Archangel; more fortunate than I, who may not see my native land, perhaps, for many years. I am, however, in good spirits: my men are bold, and apparently firm of purpose; nor do the floating sheets of ice that continually pass us, indicating the dangers of the region towards which we are advancing, appear to dismay them. We have already reached a very high latitude; but it is the height of summer, and although not so warm as in England, the southern gales, which blow us speedily towards those shores which I so ardently desire to attain, breathe a degree of renovating warmth which I had not expected.

No incidents have hitherto befallen us, that would make a figure in a letter. One or two stiff gales, and the breaking of a mast, are accidents which experienced navigators scarcely remember to record; and I shall be well content, if nothing worse happen to us during our voyage.

Adieu, my dear Margaret. Be assured, that for my own sake, as well as your's, I will not rashly encounter danger. I will be cool, persevering, and prudent.

Remember me to all my English friends.

Most affectionately yours,
R. W.

LETTER IV

To Mrs Saville, England.
August 5, 17—.

So strange an accident has happened to us, that I cannot forbear recording it, although it is very probable that you will see me before these papers can come into your possession.

Last Monday (July 31), we were nearly surrounded by ice, which closed in the ship on all sides, scarcely leaving her the sea room in which she floated. Our situation was somewhat dangerous, especially as we were compassed round by a very thick fog. We accordingly lay to, hoping that some change would take place in the atmosphere and weather.

About two o'clock the mist cleared away, and we beheld, stretched out in every direction, vast and irregular plains of ice, which seemed to have no end. Some of my comrades groaned, and my own mind began to grow watchful with anxious thoughts, when a strange sight suddenly attracted our attention, and diverted our solicitude from our own situation. We perceived a low carriage, fixed on a sledge and drawn by dogs, pass on towards the north, at the distance of half a mile: a being which had the shape of a man, but apparently of gigantic stature, sat in the sledge, and guided the dogs. We watched the rapid progress of the traveller with our telescopes, until he was lost among the distant inequalities of the ice.

This appearance excited our unqualified wonder. We were, as we believed, many hundred miles from any land; but this apparition seemed to denote that it was not, in reality, so distant as we had supposed. Shut in, however, by ice, it was impossible to follow his track, which we had observed with the greatest attention.

About two hours after this occurrence, we heard the ground

sea ;* and before night the ice broke, and freed our ship. We, however, lay to until the morning, fearing to encounter in the dark those large loose masses which float about after the breaking up of the ice. I profited of this time to rest for a few hours.

In the morning, however, as soon as it was light, I went upon deck, and found all the sailors busy on one side of the vessel, apparently talking to someone in the sea. It was, in fact, a sledge, like that we had seen before, which had drifted towards us in the night, on a large fragment of ice. Only one dog remained alive ; but there was a human being within it, whom the sailors were persuading to enter the vessel. He was not, as the other traveller seemed to be, a savage inhabitant of some undiscovered island, but an European. When I appeared on deck, the master said, 'Here is our captain, and he will not allow you to perish on the open sea.'

On perceiving me, the stranger addressed me in English, although with a foreign accent. 'Before I come on board your vessel,' said he, 'will you have the kindness to inform me whither you are bound ?'

You may conceive my astonishment on hearing such a question addressed to me from a man on the brink of destruction, and to whom I should have supposed that my vessel would have been a resource which he would not have exchanged for the most precious wealth the earth can afford. I replied, however, that we were on a voyage of discovery towards the northern pole.

Upon hearing this he appeared satisfied, and consented to come on board. Good God ! Margaret, if you had seen the man who thus capitulated* for his safety, your surprise would have been boundless. His limbs were nearly frozen, and his body dreadfully emaciated by fatigue and suffering. I never saw a man in so wretched a condition. We attempted to carry him into the cabin ; but as soon as he had quitted the fresh air, he fainted. We accordingly brought him back to the deck, and restored him to animation by rubbing him with brandy, and forcing him to swallow a small quantity. As soon as he showed signs of life, we wrapped him up in blankets, and placed him near the chimney of the kitchen-stove. By slow degrees he recovered, and ate a little soup, which restored him wonderfully.

Two days passed in this manner before he was able to speak ; and I often feared that his sufferings had deprived him of understanding. When he had in some measure recovered, I removed him to my own cabin, and attended on him as much as my duty would permit. I never saw a more interesting creature: his eyes have generally an expression of wildness, and even madness; but there are moments when, if anyone performs an act of kindness towards him, or does him any the most trifling service, his whole countenance is lighted up, as it were, with a beam of benevolence and sweetness that I never saw equalled. But he is generally melancholy and despairing; and sometimes he gnashes his teeth, as if impatient of the weight of woes that oppresses him.

When my guest was a little recovered, I had great trouble to keep off the men, who wished to ask him a thousand questions; but I would not allow him to be tormented by their idle curiosity, in a state of body and mind whose restoration evidently depended upon entire repose. Once, however, the lieutenant asked, Why he had come so far upon the ice in so strange a vehicle?

His countenance instantly assumed an aspect of the deepest gloom; and he replied, 'To seek one who fled from me.'

'And did the man whom you pursued travel in the same fashion?'

'Yes.'

'Then I fancy we have seen him; for, the day before we picked you up, we saw some dogs drawing a sledge, with a man in it, across the ice.'

This aroused the stranger's attention; and he asked a multitude of questions concerning the route which the dæmon,* as he called him, had pursued. Soon after, when he was alone with me, he said, 'I have, doubtless, excited your curiosity, as well as that of these good people; but you are too considerate to make inquiries.'

'Certainly; it would indeed be very impertinent and inhuman in me to trouble you with any inquisitiveness of mine.'

'And yet you rescued me from a strange and perilous situation; you have benevolently restored me to life.'

Soon after this he inquired, if I thought that the breaking up of the ice had destroyed the other sledge? I replied, that I could not answer with any degree of certainty; for the ice had not broken until near midnight, and the traveller might have arrived at a place of safety before that time; but of this I could not judge.

From this time the stranger seemed very eager to be upon deck, to watch for the sledge which had before appeared; but I have persuaded him to remain in the cabin, for he is far too week to sustain the rawness of the atmosphere. But I have promised that some one should watch for him, and give him instant notice if any new object should appear in sight.

Such is my journal of what relates to this strange occurrence up to the present day. The stranger has gradually improved in health, but is very silent, and appears uneasy when any one except myself enters his cabin. Yet his manners are so conciliating and gentle, that the sailors are all interested in him, although they have had very little communication with him. For my own part, I begin to love him as a brother; and his constant and deep grief fills me with sympathy and compassion. He must have been a noble creature in his better days, being even now in wreck so attractive and amiable.

I said in one of my letters, my dear Margaret, that I should find no friend on the wide ocean; yet I have found a man who, before his spirit had been broken by misery, I should have been happy to have possessed as the brother of my heart.

I shall continue my journal concerning the stranger at intervals, should I have any fresh incidents to record.

August 13, 17—.

My affection for my guest increases every day. He excites at once my admiration and my pity to an astonishing degree. How can I see so noble a creature destroyed by misery without feeling the most poignant grief? He is so gentle, yet so wise; his mind is so cultivated; and when he speaks, although his words are culled with the choicest art, yet they flow with rapidity and unparalleled eloquence.

He is now much recovered from his illness, and is continually on the deck, apparently watching for the sledge that preceded his own. Yet, although unhappy, he is not so utterly occupied by his own misery, but that he interests himself deeply in the employments of others. He has asked me many questions concerning my design; and I have related my little history frankly to him. He appeared pleased with the confidence, and suggested several alterations in my plan, which I shall find exceedingly useful. There is no pedantry in his manner; but all he does appears to spring solely from the interest he instinctively takes in the welfare of those who surround him. He is often overcome by gloom, and then he sits by himself, and tries to overcome all that is sullen or unsocial in his humour. These paroxysms pass from him like a cloud from before the sun, though his dejection never leaves him. I have endeavoured to win his confidence; and I trust that I have succeeded. One day I mentioned to him the desire I had always felt of finding a friend who might sympathize with me, and direct me by his counsel. I said, I did not belong to that class of men who are offended by advice. 'I am self-educated, and perhaps I hardly rely sufficiently upon my own powers. I wish therefore that my companion should be wiser and more experienced than myself, to confirm and support me; nor have I believed it impossible to find a true friend.'

'I agree with you,' replied the stranger, 'in believing that friendship is not only a desirable, but a possible acquisition. I once had a friend, the most noble of human creatures, and am entitled, therefore, to judge respecting friendship. You have hope, and the world before you, and have no cause for despair. But I—I have lost every thing, and cannot begin life anew.'

As he said this, his countenance became expressive of a calm settled grief, that touched me to the heart. But he was silent, and presently retired to his cabin.

Even broken in spirit as he is, noone can feel more deeply than he does the beauties of nature. The starry sky, the sea, and every sight afforded by these wonderful regions, seems still to have the power of elevating his soul from earth. Such a man has a double existence: he may suffer misery, and be overwhelmed by disappointments; yet when he has retired into himself, he will be like a celestial spirit, that has a halo around him, within whose circle no grief or folly ventures.

Will you laugh at the enthusiasm I express concerning this divine wanderer? If you do, you must have certainly lost the simplicity which was once your characteristic charm. Yet, if you will, smile at the warmth of my expressions, while I find every day new causes for repeating them.

August 19, 17—.

Yesterday the stranger said to me, 'You may easily perceive, Captain Walton, that I have suffered great and unparalleled misfortunes. I had determined, once, that the memory of these evils should die with me; but you have won me to alter my determination. You seek for knowledge and wisdom, as I once did; and I ardently hope that the gratification of your wishes may not be a serpent to sting you, as mine has been. I do not know that the relation of my misfortunes will be useful to you, yet, if you are inclined, listen to my tale. I believe that the strange incidents connected with it will afford a view of nature, which may enlarge your faculties and understanding. You will hear of powers and occurrences such as you have been accustomed to believe impossible: but I do not doubt that my tale conveys in its series* internal evidence of the truth of the events of which it is composed.'

You may easily conceive that I was much gratified by the offered communication; yet I could not endure that he should renew his grief by a recital of his misfortunes. I felt the greatest eagerness to hear the promised narrative, partly from curiosity, and partly from a strong desire to ameliorate his fate, if it were in my power. I expressed these feelings in my answer.

'I thank you,' he replied, 'for your sympathy, but it is useless; my fate is nearly fulfilled. I wait but for one event, and then I shall repose in peace. I understand your feeling,' continued he, perceiving that I wished to interrupt him; 'but you are mistaken, my friend, if thus you will allow me to name you; nothing can alter my destiny: listen to my history, and you will perceive how irrevocably it is determined.

He then told me, that he would commence his narrative the next day when I should be at leisure. This promise drew from me the warmest thanks. I have resolved every night, when I am not engaged, to record, as nearly as possible in his own words, what he has related during the day. If I should be engaged, I will at least make notes. This manuscript will doubtless afford you the greatest pleasure: but to me, who know him, and who hear it from his own lips, with what interest and sympathy shall I read it in some future day!

CHAPTER I

I am by birth a Genevese; and my family is one of the most distinguished of that republic. My ancestors had been for many years counsellors and syndics;* and my father had filled several public situations with honour and reputation. He was respected by all who knew him for his integrity and indefatigable attention to public business. He passed his younger days perpetually occupied by the affairs of his country; and it was not until the decline of life that he thought of marrying, and bestowing on the state sons who might carry his virtues and his name down to posterity.

As the circumstances of his marriage illustrate his character, I cannot refrain from relating them. One of his most intimate friends was a merchant, who, from a flourishing state, fell, through numerous mischances, into poverty. This man, whose name was Beaufort, was of a proud and unbending disposition, and could not bear to live in poverty and oblivion in the same country where he had formerly been distinguished for his rank and magnificence. Having paid his debts, therefore, in the most honourable manner, he retreated with his daughter to the town of Lucerne, where he lived unknown and in wretchedness. My father loved Beaufort with the truest friendship, and was deeply grieved by his retreat in these unfortunate circumstances. He grieved also for the loss of his society, and resolved to seek him out and endeavour to persuade him to begin the world again through his credit and assistance.

Beaufort had taken effectual measures to conceal himself; and it was ten months before my father discovered his abode. Overjoyed at this discovery, he hastened to the house, which was situated in a mean street, near the Reuss. But when he entered, misery and despair alone welcomed him. Beaufort had saved but a very small sum of money from the wreck of his fortunes; but it was sufficient to provide him with sustenance for some months, and in the mean time he hoped to procure some respectable employment in a merchant's house. The interval was consequently spent in inaction; his grief only became more deep and rankling, when he had leisure for reflection; and at length it took so fast hold of his mind, that at the end of three months he lay on a bed of sickness, incapable of any exertion.

His daughter attended him with the greatest tenderness; but she saw with despair that their little fund was rapidly decreasing, and that there was no other prospect of support. But Caroline Beaufort possessed a mind of an uncommon mould; and her courage rose to support her in her adversity. She procured plain work;* she plaited straw; and by various means contrived to earn a pittance scarcely sufficient to support life.

Several months passed in this manner. Her father grew worse; her time was more entirely occupied in attending him; her means of subsistence decreased; and in the tenth month her father died in her arms, leaving her an orphan and a beggar. This last blow overcame her; and she knelt by Beaufort's coffin, weeping bitterly, when my father entered the chamber. He came like a protecting spirit to the poor girl, who committed herself to his care, and after the interment of his friend he conducted her to Geneva, and placed her under the protection of a relation. Two years after this event Caroline became his wife.

When my father became a husband and a parent, he found his time so occupied by the duties of his new situation, that he relinquished many of his public employments, and devoted himself to the education of his children. Of these I was the eldest, and the destined successor to all his labours and utility. No creature could have more tender parents than mine. My improvement and health were their constant care, especially as I remained for several years their only child. But before I continue my narrative, I must record an incident which took place when I was four years of age.

My father had a sister, whom he tenderly loved, and who had married early in life an Italian gentleman. Soon after her marriage, she had accompanied her husband into his native country, and for some years my father had very little communication with her. About the time I mentioned she died; and a few months afterwards he received a letter from her husband, acquainting him with his intention of marrying an Italian lady, and requesting my father to take charge of the infant Elizabeth, the only child of his deceased sister. 'It is my wish,' he said, 'that you should consider her as your own daughter, and educate her thus. Her mother's fortune is secured to her, the documents of which I will commit to your keeping. Reflect upon this proposition; and decide whether you would prefer educating your niece yourself to her being brought up by a stepmother.'

My father did not hesitate, and immediately went to Italy, that he might accompany the little Elizabeth to her future home. I have often heard my mother say, that she was at that time the most beautiful child she had ever seen, and showed signs even then of a gentle and affectionate disposition. These indications, and a desire to bind as closely as possible the ties of domestic love, determined my mother to consider Elizabeth as my future wife; a design which she never found reason to repent.

From this time Elizabeth Lavenza became my playfellow, and, as we grew older, my friend. She was docile and good tempered, yet gay and playful as a summer insect. Although she was lively and animated, her feelings were strong and deep, and her disposition uncommonly affectionate. No one could better enjoy liberty, yet no one could submit with more grace than she did to constraint and caprice. Her imagination was luxuriant, yet her capability of application was great. Her person was the image of her mind; her hazel eyes, although as lively as a bird's, possessed an attractive softness. Her figure was light and airy; and, though capable of enduring great fatigue, she appeared the most fragile creature in the world. While I admired her understanding and fancy, I loved to tend on her, as I should on a favourite animal; and I never saw so much grace both of person and mind united to so little pretension.

Every one adored Elizabeth. If the servants had any request to make, it was always through her intercession. We were strangers to any species of disunion and dispute; for although there was a great dissimilitude in our characters, there was an harmony in that very dissimilitude. I was more calm and philosophical than my companion; yet my temper was not so yielding. My application was of longer endurance; but it was not so severe whilst it endured. I delighted in investigating the facts relative to the actual world; she busied herself in following the aërial creations of the poets. The world was to me a secret, which I desired to discover; to her it was a vacancy, which she sought to people with imaginations of her own.

My brothers were considerably younger than myself; but I

had a friend in one of my schoolfellows, who compensated for this deficiency. Henry Clerval was the son of a merchant of Geneva, an intimate friend of my father. He was a boy of singular talent and fancy. I remember, when he was nine years old, he wrote a fairy tale, which was the delight and amazement of all his companions. His favourite study consisted in books of chivalry and romance; and when very young, I can remember, that we used to act plays composed by him out of these favourite books, the principal characters of which were Orlando, Robin Hood, Amadis, and St George.*

No youth could have passed more happily than mine. My parents were indulgent, and my companions amiable. Our studies were never forced; and by some means we always had an end placed in view, which excited us to ardour in the prosecution of them. It was by this method, and not by emulation, that we were urged to application. Elizabeth was not incited to apply herself to drawing, that her companions might not outstrip her; but through the desire of pleasing her aunt, by the representation of some favourite scene done by her own hand. We learned Latin and English, that we might read the writings in those languages; and so far from study being made odious to us through punishment, we loved application, and our amusements would have been the labours of other children. Perhaps we did not read so many books, or learn languages so quickly, as those who are disciplined according to the ordinary methods; but what we learned was impressed the more deeply on our memories.

In this description of our domestic circle I include Henry Clerval; for he was constantly with us. He went to school with me, and generally passed the afternoon at our house; for being an only child, and destitute of companions at home, his father was well pleased that he should find associates at our house; and we were never completely happy when Clerval was absent.

I feel pleasure in dwelling on the recollections of childhood, before misfortune had tainted my mind, and changed its bright visions of extensive usefulness into gloomy and narrow reflections upon self. But, in drawing the picture of my early days, I must not omit to record those events which led, by insensible steps to my after tale of misery: for when I would account to myself for the birth of that passion, which afterwards ruled my destiny, I find it arise, like a mountain river, from ignoble and almost forgotten sources; but, swelling as it proceeded, it became the torent which, in its course, has swept away all my hopes and joys.

Natural philosophy* is the genius that has regulated my fate; I desire therefore, in this narration, to state those facts which led to my predilection for that science. When I was thirteen years of age, we all went on a party of pleasure to the baths near Thonon: the inclemency of the weather obliged us to remain a day confined to the inn. In this house I chanced to find a volume of the works of Cornelius Agrippa.* I opened it with apathy; the theory which he attempts to demonstrate, and the wonderful facts which he relates, soon changed this feeling into enthusiasm. A new light seemed to dawn upon my mind; and, bounding with joy, I communicated my discovery to my father. I cannot help remarking here the many opportunities instructors possess of directing the attention of their pupils to useful knowledge, which they utterly neglect. My father looked carelessly at the title-page of my book, and said, 'Ah! Cornelius Agrippa! My dear Victor, do not waste your time upon this; it is sad trash.'

If, instead of this remark, my father had taken the pains to explain to me, that the principles of Agrippa had been entirely exploded, and that a modern system of science had been introduced, which possessed much greater powers than the ancient, because the powers of the latter were chimerical,* while those of the former were real and practical; under such circumstances, I should certainly have thrown Agrippa aside, and, with my imagination warmed as it was, should probably have applied myself to the more rational theory of chemistry which has resulted from modern discoveries. It is even possible, that the train of my ideas would never have received the fatal impulse that led to my ruin. But the cursory glance my father had taken of my volume by no means assured me that he was acquainted with its contents; and I continued to read with the greatest avidity.

When I returned home, my first care was to procure the whole works of this author, and afterwards of Paracelsus and Albertus Magnus.* I read and studied the wild fancies of these writers with delight; they appeared to me treasures known to few beside myself; and although I often wished to communicate these secret stores of knowledge to my father, yet his indefinite censure of my favourite Agrippa always withheld me. I disclosed my discoveries to Elizabeth, therefore, under a promise of strict secrecy; but she did not interest herself in the subject, and I was left by her to pursue my studies alone.

It may appear very strange, that a disciple of Albertus Magnus should arise in the eighteenth century; but our family was not scientifical, and I had not attended any of the lectures given at the schools of Geneva. My dreams were therefore undisturbed by reality; and I entered with the greatest diligence into the search of the philosopher's stone and the elixir of life.* But the latter obtained my most undivided attention: wealth was an inferior object; but what glory would attend the discovery, if I could banish disease from the human frame, and render man invulnerable to any but a violent death!

Nor were these my only visions. The raising of ghosts or devils was a promise liberally accorded by my favourite authors, the fulfilment of which I most eagerly sought; and if my incantations were always unsuccessful, I attributed the failure rather to my own inexperience and mistake, than to a want of skill or fidelity in my instructors.

The natural phenomena that take place every day before our eyes did not escape my examinations. Distillation, and the wonderful effects of steam, processes of which my favourite authors were utterly ignorant, excited my astonishment; but my utmost wonder was engaged by some experiments on an air-pump, which I saw employed by a gentleman whom we were in the habit of visiting.

The ignorance of the early philosophers on these and several other points served to decrease their credit with me: but I could not entirely throw them aside, before some other system should occupy their place in my mind.

When I was about fifteen years old, we had retired to our house near Belrive, when we witnessed a most violent and terrible thunder-storm. It advanced from behind the mountains of Jura; and the thunder burst at once with frightful loudness from various quarters of the heavens. I remained, while the storm lasted, watching its progress with curiosity and delight. As I stood at the door, on a sudden I beheld a stream of fire issue from an old and beautiful oak, which stood about twenty yards from our house; and so soon as the dazzling light vanished, the oak had disappeared, and nothing remained but a blasted stump. When we visited it the next morning, we found the tree shattered in a singular manner. It was not splintered by the shock, but entirely reduced to thin ribbands of wood. I never beheld any thing so utterly destroyed.

The catastrophe of this tree excited my extreme astonishment; and I eagerly inquired of my father the nature and origin of thunder and lightning. He replied, 'Electricity;' describing at the same time the various effects of that power. He constructed a small electrical machine, and exhibited a few experiments; he made also a kite, with a wire and string, which drew down that fluid from the clouds.

This last stroke completed the overthrow of Cornelius Agrippa, Albertus Magnus, and Paracelsus, who had so long reigned the lords of my imagination. But by some fatality I did not feel inclined to commence the study of any modern system; and this disinclination was influenced by the following circumstance.

My father expressed a wish that I should attend a course of lectures upon natural philosophy, to which I cheerfully consented. Some accident prevented my attending these lectures until the course was nearly finished. The lecture, being therefore one of the last, was entirely incomprehensible to me. The professor discoursed with the greatest fluency of potassium and boron, of sulphates and oxids, terms to which I could affix no idea; and I became disgusted with the science of natural philosophy, although I still read Pliny and Buffon* with delight, authors, in my estimation, of nearly equal interest and utility.

My occupations at this age were principally the mathematics, and most of the branches of study appertaining to that science. I was busily employed in learning languages; Latin was already familiar to me, and I began to read some of the easiest Greek authors without the help of a lexicon. I also perfectly understood English and German. This is the list of my accomplishments at the age of seventeen; and you may conceive that my hours were fully employed in acquiring and maintaining a knowledge of this various literature.

Another task also devolved upon me, when I became the instructor of my brothers. Ernest was six years younger than myself, and was my principal pupil. He had been afflicted with ill health from his infancy, through which Elizabeth and I had been his constant nurses: his disposition was gentle, but he was incapable of any severe application. William, the youngest of our family, was yet an infant, and the most beautiful little fellow in the world ; his lively blue eyes, dimpled cheeks, and endearing manners, inspired the tenderest affection.

Such was our domestic circle, from which care and pain seemed for ever banished. My father directed our studies, and my mother partook of our enjoyments. Neither of us possessed the slightest pre-eminence over the other ; the voice of command was never heard amongst us ; but mutual affection engaged us all to comply with and obey the slightest desire of each other.

CHAPTER II

When I had attained the age of seventeen, my parents resolved that I should become a student at the university of Ingolstadt.* I had hitherto attended the schools of Geneva; but my father thought it necessary, for the completion of my education, that I should be made acquainted with other customs than those of my native country. My departure was therefore fixed at an early date; but, before the day resolved upon could arrive, the first misfortune of my life occurred – an omen, as it were, of my future misery.

Elizabeth had caught the scarlet fever; but her illness was not severe, and she quickly recovered. During her confinement, many arguments had been urged to persuade my mother to refrain from attending upon her. She had, at first, yielded to our entreaties; but when she heard that her favourite was recovering, she could no longer debar herself from her society, and entered her chamber long before the danger of infection was past. The consequences of this imprudence were fatal. On the third day my mother sickened; her fever was very malignant, and the looks of her attendants prognosticated the worst event. On her death-bed the fortitude and benignity of this admirable woman did not desert her. She joined the hands of Elizabeth and myself: 'My children,' she said, 'my firmest hopes of future happiness were placed on the prospect of your union. This expectation will now be the consolation of your father. Elizabeth, my love, you must supply my place to your younger cousins. Alas! I regret that I am taken from you; and, happy and beloved as I have been, is it not hard to quit you all? But these are not thoughts befitting me; I will endeavour to resign myself cheerfully to death, and will indulge a hope of meeting you in another world.'

She died calmly; and her countenance expressed affection

even in death. I need not describe the feelings of those whose dearest ties are rent by that most irreparable evil, the void that presents itself to the soul, and the despair that is exhibited on the countenance. It is so long before the mind can persuade itself that she, whom we saw every day, and whose very existence appeared a part of our own, can have departed for ever – that the brightness of a beloved eye can have been extinguished, and the sound of a voice so familiar, and dear to the ear, can be hushed, never more to be heard. These are the reflections of the first days; but when the lapse of time proves the reality of the evil, then the actual bitterness of grief commences. Yet from whom has not that rude hand rent away some dear connexion; and why should I describe a sorrow which all have felt, and must feel? The time at length arrives, when grief is rather an indulgence than a necessity; and the smile that plays upon the lips, although it may be deemed a sacrilege, is not banished. My mother was dead, but we had still duties which we ought to perform; we must continue our course with the rest, and learn to think ourselves fortunate, whilst one remains whom the spoiler has not seized.

My journey to Ingolstadt, which had been deferred by these events, was now again determined upon. I obtained from my father a respite of some weeks. This period was spent sadly; my mother's death, and my speedy departure, depressed our spirits; but Elizabeth endeavoured to renew the spirit of cheerfulness in our little society. Since the death of her aunt, her mind had acquired new firmness and vigour. She determined to fulfil her duties with the greatest exactness; and she felt that that most imperious duty, of rendering her uncle and cousins happy, had devolved upon her. She consoled me, amused her uncle, instructed my brothers; and I never beheld her so enchanting as at this time, when she was continually endeavouring to contribute to the happiness of others, entirely forgetful of herself.

The day of my departure at length arrived. I had taken leave of all my friends, excepting Clerval, who spent the last evening with us. He bitterly lamented that he was unable to accompany me: but his father could not be persuaded to part with him, intending that he should become a partner with him in business, in compliance with his favourite theory, that learning was superfluous in the commerce of ordinary life. Henry had a refined mind; he had no desire to be idle, and was well pleased to become his father's partner, but he believed that a man might be a very good trader, and yet possess a cultivated understanding.

We sat late, listening to his complaints, and making many little arrangements for the future. The next morning early I departed. Tears guished from the eyes of Elizabeth; they proceeded partly from sorrow at my departure, and partly because she reflected that the same journey was to have taken place three months before, when a mother's blessing would have accompanied me.

I threw myself into the chaise that was to convey me away, and indulged in the most melancholy reflections. I, who had ever been surrounded by amiable companions, continually engaged in endeavouring to bestow mutual pleasure, I was now alone. In the university, whither I was going, I must form my own friends, and be my own protector. My life had hitherto been remarkably secluded and domestic; and this had given me invincible repugnance to new countenances. I loved my brothers, Elizabeth, and Clerval; these were 'old familiar faces;' but I believed myself totally unfitted for the company of strangers. Such were my reflections as I commenced my journey; but as I proceeded, my spirits and hopes rose. I ardently desired the acquisition of knowledge. I had often, when at home, thought it hard to remain during my youth cooped up in one place, and had longed to enter the world, and take my station among other human beings. Now my desires were complied with, and it would, indeed, have been folly to repent.

I had sufficient leisure for these and many other reflections during my journey to Ingolstadt, which was long and fatiguing. At length the high white steeple of the town met my eyes. I alighted, and was conducted to my solitary apartment, to spend the evening as I pleased.

The next morning I delivered my letters of introduction, and paid a visit to some of the principal professors, and among others to M. Krempe, professor of natural philosophy. He received me with politeness, and asked me several questions concerning my progress in the different branches of science appertaining to natural philosophy. I mentioned, it is true, with fear and trembling, the only authors I had ever read upon those subjects. The professor stared: 'Have you,' he said, 'really spent your time in studying such nonsense?'

I replied in the affirmative. 'Every minute,' continued M. Krempe with warmth, 'every instant that you have wasted on those books is utterly and entirely lost. You have burdened your memory with exploded systems, and useless names. Good God! in what desert land have you lived, where no one was kind enough to inform you that these fancies, which you have so greedily imbibed, are a thousand years old, and as musty as they are ancient? I little expected in this enlightened and scientific age to find a disciple of Albertus Magnus and Paracelsus. My dear Sir, you must begin your studies entirely anew.'

So saying, he stept aside, and wrote down a list of several books treating of natural philosophy, which he desired me to procure, and dismissed me, after mentioning that in the beginning of the following week he intended to commence a course of lectures upon natural philosophy in its general relations, and that M. Waldman, a fellow-professor, would lecture upon chemistry the alternate days that he missed.

I returned home, not disappointed, for I had long considered those authors useless whom the professor had so strongly reprobated;* but I did not feel much inclined to study the books which I procured at his recommendation. M. Krempe was a little squat man, with a gruff voice and repulsive countenance; the teacher, therefore, did not prepossess me in favour of his doctrine. Besides, I had a contempt for the uses of modern natural philosophy. It was very different, when the masters of the science sought immortality and power; such views, although futile, were grand: but now the scene was changed. The ambition of the inquirer seemed to limit itself to the annihilation of those visions on which my interest in science was chiefly founded. I was required to exchange chimeras of boundless grandeur for realities of little worth.

Such were my reflections during the first two or three days spent almost in solitude. But as the ensuing week commenced, I thought of the information which M. Krempe had given me concerning the lectures. And although I could not consent to go and hear that little conceited fellow deliver sentences out of a pulpit, I recollected what he had said of M. Waldman, whom I had never seen, as he had hitherto been out of town.

Partly from curiosity, and partly from idleness, I went into the lecturing room, which M. Waldman entered shortly after. This professor was very unlike his colleague. He appeared about fifty years of age, but with an aspect expressive of the greatest benevolence; a few gray hairs covered his temples, but those at the back of his head were nearly black. His person was short, but remarkably erect; and his voice the sweetest I had ever heard. He began his lecture by a recapitulation of the history of chemistry and the various improvements made by different men of learning, pronouncing with fervour the names of the most distinguished discoverers. He then took a cursory view of the present state of the science, and explained many of its elementary terms. After having made a few preparatory experiments, he concluded with a panegyric upon modern chemistry, the terms of which I shall never forget : —

'The ancient teachers of this science,' said he, 'promised impossibilities, and performed nothing. The modern masters promise very little; they know that metals cannot be transmuted, and that the elixir of life is a chimera. But these philosophers, whose hands seem only made to dabble in dirt, and their eyes to pour over the microscope or crucible, have indeed performed miracles. They penetrate into the recesses of nature, and shew how she works in her hiding places. They ascend into the heavens; they have discovered how the blood circulates, and the nature of the air we breathe. They have acquired new and almost unlimited powers; they can command the thunders of heaven, mimic the earthquake, and even mock the invisible world with its own shadows.'

I departed highly pleased with the professor and his lecture, and paid him a visit the same evening. His manners in private were even more mild and attractive than in public; for there was a certain dignity in his mien during his lecture, which in his own house was replaced by the greatest affability and kindness. He heard with attention my little narration concerning my studies, and smiled at the names of Cornelius Agrippa, and Paracelsus, but without the contempt that M. Krempe had exhibited. He said, that 'these were men to whose indefatigable zeal modern philosophers were indebted for most of the foundations of their knowledge. They had left to us, as an easier task, to give new names, and arrange in connected classifications, the facts which they in a great degree had been the instruments of bringing to light. The labours of men of genius, however erroneously directed, scarcely ever fail in ultimately turning to the solid advantage of mankind.' I listened to his statement, which was delivered without any presumption or affectation; and then added, that his lecture had removed my prejudices against modern chemists; and I, at the same time, requested his advice concerning the books I ought to procure.

'I am happy,' said M. Waldman, 'to have gained a disciple; and if your application equals your ability, I have no doubt of your success. Chemistry is that branch of natural philosophy in which the greatest improvements have been and may be made; it is on that account that I have made it my peculiar study; but at the same time I have not neglected the other branches of science. A man would make but a very sorry chemist, if he attended to that department of human knowledge alone. If your wish is to become really a man of science, and not merely a petty experimentalist, I should advise you to apply to every branch of natural philosophy, including mathematics.'

He then took me into his laboratory, and explained to me the uses of his various machines; instructing me as to what I ought to procure, and promising me the use of his own, when I should have advanced far enough in the science not to derange their mechanism. He also gave me the list of books which I had requested; and I took my leave.

Thus ended a day memorable to me; it decided my future destiny.

CHAPTER III

From this day natural philosophy, and particularly chemistry, in the most comprehensive sense of the term, became nearly my sole occupation. I read with ardour those works, so full of genius and discrimination, which modern inquirers have written on these subjects. I attended the lectures, and cultivated the acquaintance, of the men of science of the university; and I found even in M. Krempe a great deal of sound sense and real information, combined, it is true, with a repulsive physiognomy and manners, but not on that account the less valuable. In M. Waldman I found a true friend. His gentleness was never tinged by dogmatism; and his instructions were given with an air of frankness and good nature, that banished every idea of pedantry. It was, perhaps, the amiable character of this man that inclined me more to that branch of natural philosophy which he professed, than an intrinsic love for the science itself. But this state of mind had place only in the first steps towards knowledge: the more fully I entered into the science, the more exclusively I pursued it for its own sake. That application, which at first had been a matter of duty and resolution, now became so ardent and eager, that the stars often disappeared in the light of morning whilst I was yet engaged in my laboratory.

As I applied so closely, it may be easily conceived that I improved rapidly. My ardour was indeed the astonishment of the students; and my proficiency, that of the masters. Professor Krempe often asked me, with a sly smile, how Cornelius Agrippa went on? whilst M. Waldman expressed the most heartfelt exultation in my progress. Two years passed in this manner, during which I paid no visit to Geneva, but was engaged, heart and soul, in the pursuit of some discoveries, which I hoped to make. None but those who have experienced them can conceive of the enticements of science. In other studies you go as far as others have gone before you, and there is nothing more to know; but in a scientific pursuit there is continual food for discovery and wonder. A mind of moderate capacity, which closely pursues one study, must infallibly arrive at great proficiency in that study; and I, who continually sought the attainment of one object of pursuit, and was solely wrapt up in this, improved so rapidly, that, at the end of two years, I made some discoveries in the improvement of some chemical instruments, which procured me great esteem and admiration at the university. When I had arrived at this point, and had become as well acquainted with the theory and practice of natural philosophy as depended on the lessons of any of the professors at Ingolstadt, my residence there being no longer conducive to my improvements, I thought of returning to my friends and my native town, when an incident happened that protracted my stay.

One of the phenonema which had peculiarly attracted my attention was the structure of the human frame, and, indeed, any animal endued with life. Whence, I often asked myself, did the principle of life proceed? It was a bold question, and one which has ever been considered as a mystery; yet with how many things are we upon the brink of becoming acquainted, if cowardice or carelessness did not restrain our inquiries. I revolved these circumstances in my mind, and determined thenceforth to apply myself more particularly to those branches of natural philosophy which relate to physiology. Unless I had been animated by an almost supernatural enthusiasm, my application to this study would have been irksome, and almost intolerable. To examine the causes of life, we must first have recourse to death. I became acquainted with the science of anatomy: but this was not sufficient; I must also observe the natural decay and corruption of the human body. In my education my father had taken the greatest precautions that my mind should be impressed with no supernatural horrors. I do not ever remember to have trembled at a tale of superstition, or to have feared the apparition of a spirit. Darkness had no effect upon my fancy; and a church-yard was to me merely the receptacle of bodies deprived of life, which, from being the seat of beauty and strength had become food for the worm. Now I was led to examine the cause and progress of this decay, and forced to spend days and nights in vaults and charnel houses.*
My attention was fixed upon every object the most insupportable to the delicacy of the human feelings. I saw how the fine

form of man was degraded and wasted; I beheld the corruption
of death succeed to the blooming cheek of life; I saw how the
worm inherited the wonders of the eye and brain. I paused,
examining and analysing all the minutiæ of causation, as
exemplified in the change from life to death, and death to life,
until from the midst of this darkness a sudden light broke in
upon me – a light so brilliant and wondrous, yet so simple, that
while I became dizzy with the immensity of the prospect which
it illustrated, I was surprised that among so many men of genius,
who had directed their inquiries towards the same science, that
I alone should be reserved to discover so astonishing a secret.

Remember, I am not recording the vision of a madman. The
sun does not more certainly shine in the heavens, than that
which I now affirm is true. Some miracle might have produced
it, yet the stages of the discovery were distinct and probable.
After days and nights of incredible labour and fatigue, I succeeded in discovering the cause of generation and life; nay,
more, I became myself capable of bestowing animation upon
lifeless matter.

The astonishment which I had at first experienced on this
discovery soon gave place to delight and rapture. After so much
time spent in painful labour, to arrive at once at the summit of
my desires, was the most gratifying consummation of my toils.
But this discovery was so great and overwhelming, that all the
steps by which I had been progressively led to it were obliterated,
and I beheld only the result. What had been the study and desire
of the wisest men since the creation of the world, was now
within my grasp. Not that, like a magic scene, it all opened upon
me at once: the information I had obtained was of a nature
rather to direct my endeavours so soon as I should point them
towards the object of my search, than to exhibit that object
already accomplished. I was like the Arabian* who had been
buried with the dead, and found a passage to life aided only by
one glimmering, and seemingly ineffectual, light.

I see by your eagerness, and the wonder and hope which your
eyes express, my friend, that you expect to be informed of the
secret with which I am acquainted; that cannot be: listen
patiently until the end of my story, and you will easily perceive
why I am reserved upon that subject. I will not lead you on,
unguarded and ardent as I then was, to your destruction and
infallible misery. Learn from me, if not by my precepts, at least
by my example, how dangerous is the acquirement of knowl-

edge, and how much happier that man is who believes his native town to be the world, than he who aspires to become greater than his nature will allow.

When I found so astonishing a power placed within my hands, I hesitated a long time concerning the manner in which I should employ it. Although I possessed the capacity of bestowing animation, yet to prepare a frame for the reception of it, with all its intricacies of fibres, muscles, and veins, still remained a work of inconceivable difficulty and labour. I doubted at first whether I should attempt the creation of a being like myself or one of simpler organization; but my imagination was too much exalted by my first success to permit me to doubt of my ability to give life to an animal as complex and wonderful as man. The materials at present within my command hardly appeared adequate to so arduous an undertaking; but I doubted not that I should ultimately succeed. I prepared myself for a multitude of reverses; my operations might be incessantly baffled, and at last my work be imperfect: yet, when I considered the improvement which every day takes place in science and mechanics, I was encouraged to hope my present attempts would at least lay the foundations of future success. Nor could I consider the magnitude and complexity of my plan as any argument of its impracticability. It was with these feelings that I began the creation of a human being. As the minuteness of the parts formed a great hindrance to my speed, I resolved, contrary to my first intention, to make the being of a gigantic stature; that is to say, about eight feet in height, and proportionably large. After having formed this determination, and having spent some months in successfully collecting and arranging my materials, I began.

No one can conceive the variety of feelings which bore me onwards, like a hurricane, in the first enthusiasm of success. Life and death appeared to me ideal bounds, which I should first break through, and pour a torrent of light into our dark world. A new species would bless me as its creator and source; many happy and excellent natures would owe their being to me. No father could claim the gratitude of his child so completely as I should deserve their's. Pursuing these reflections, I thought, that if I could bestow animation upon lifeless matter, I might in process of time (although I now found it impossible) renew life where death had apparently devoted the body to corruption.

These thoughts supported my spirits, while I pursued my undertaking with unremitting ardour. My cheek had grown pale

with study, and my person had become emaciated with confinement. Sometimes, on the very brink of certainty, I failed; yet
still I clung to the hope which the next day or the next hour
might realize. One secret which I alone possessed was the hope
to which I had dedicated myself; and the moon gazed on my
midnight labours, while, with unrelaxed and breathless eagerness, I pursued nature to her hiding places. Who shall conceive
the horrors of my secret toil, as I dabbled among the unhallowed
damps of the grave, or tortured the living animal to animate the
lifeless clay? My limbs now tremble, and my eyes swim with the
remembrance; but then a resistless, and almost frantic impulse,
urged me forward; I seemed to have lost all soul or sensation
but for this one pursuit. It was indeed but a passing trance, that
only made me feel with renewed acuteness so soon as, the
unnatural stimulus ceasing to operate, I had returned to my old
habits. I collected bones from charnel houses; and disturbed,
with profane fingers, the tremendous secrets of the human
frame. In a solitary chamber, or rather cell, at the top of the
house, and separated from all the other apartments by a gallery
and staircase, I kept my workshop of filthy creation; my eyeballs
were starting from their sockets in attending to the details of my
employment. The dissecting room and the slaughter-house furnished many of my materials; and often did my human nature
turn with loathing from my occupation, whilst, still urged on by
an eagerness which perpetually increased, I brought my work
near to a conclusion.

The summer months passed while I was thus engaged, heart
and soul, in one pursuit. It was a most beautiful season; never
did the fields bestow a more plentiful harvest, or the vines yield
a more luxuriant vintage: but my eyes were insensible to the
charms of nature. And the same feelings which made me neglect
the scenes around me caused me also to forget those friends who
were so many miles absent, and whom I had not seen for so
long a time. I knew my silence disquieted them; and I well
remembered the words of my father: 'I know that while you are
pleased with yourself, you will think of us with affection, and
we shall hear regularly from you. You must pardon me, if I
regard any interruption in your correspondence as a proof that
your other duties are equally neglected.'

I knew well therefore what would be my father's feelings; but
I could not tear my thoughts from my employment, loathsome
in itself, but which had taken an irresistible hold of my imagin-

ation. I wished, as it were, to procrastinate all that related to my feelings of affection until the great object, which swallowed up every habit of my nature, should be completed.

I then thought that my father would be unjust if he ascribed my neglect to vice, or faultiness on my part; but I am now convinced that he was justified in conceiving that I should not be altogether free from blame. A human being in perfection ought always to preserve a calm and peaceful mind, and never to allow passion or a transitory desire to disturb his tranquillity. I do not think that the pursuit of knowledge is an exception to this rule. If the study to which you apply yourself has a tendency to weaken your affections, and to destroy your taste for those simple pleasures in which no alloy can possibly mix, then that study is certainly unlawful, that is to say, not befitting the human mind. If this rule were always observed; if no man allowed any pursuit whatsoever to interfere with the tranquillity of his domestic affections, Greece had not been enslaved; Cæsar would have spared his country; America would have been discovered more gradually; and the empires of Mexico and Peru had not been destroyed.

But I forget that I am moralizing in the most interesting part of my tale; and your looks remind me to proceed.

My father made no reproach in his letters; and only took notice of my silence by inquiring into my occupations more particularly than before. Winter, spring, and summer, passed away during my labours; but I did not watch the blossom or the expanding leaves – sights which before always yielded me supreme delight, so deeply was I engrossed in my occupation. The leaves of that year had withered before my work drew near to a close; and now every day showed me more plainly how well I had succeeded. But my enthusiasm was checked by my anxiety, and I appeared rather like one doomed by slavery to toil in the mines, or any other unwholesome trade, than an artist occupied by his favourite employment. Every night I was oppressed by a slow fever, and I became nervous to a most painful degree; a disease that I regretted the more because I had hitherto enjoyed most excellent health, and had always boasted of the firmness of my nerves. But I believed that exercise and amusement would soon drive away such symptoms; and I promised myself both of these, when my creation should be complete.

CHAPTER IV

It was on a dreary night of November, that I beheld the accomplishment of my toils. With an anxiety that almost amounted to agony, I collected the instruments of life around me, that I might infuse a spark of being into the lifeless thing that lay at my feet. It was already one in the morning; the rain pattered dismally against the panes, and my candle was nearly burnt out, when by the glimmer of the half-extinguished light, I saw the dull yellow eye of the creature open; it breathed hard, and a convulsive motion agitated its limbs.

How can I describe my emotions at this catastrophe, or how delineate the wretch whom with such infinite pains and care I had endeavoured to form? His limbs were in proportion, and I had selected his features as beautiful. Beautiful! – Great God! His yellow skin scarcely covered the work of muscles and arteries beneath; his hair was of a lustrous black, and flowing; his teeth of a pearly whiteness; but these luxuriances only formed a more horrid contrast with his watery eyes, that seemed almost of the same colour as the dun white sockets in which they were set, his shrivelled complexion, and straight black lips.

The different accidents* of life are not so changeable as the feelings of human nature. I had worked hard for nearly two years, for the sole purpose of infusing life into an inanimate body. For this I had deprived myself of rest and health. I had desired it with an ardour that far exceeded moderation; but now that I had finished, the beauty of the dream vanished, and breathless horror and disgust filled my heart. Unable to endure the aspect of the being I had created, I rushed out of the room, and continued a long time traversing my bed-chamber, unable to compose my mind to sleep. At length lassitude succeeded to the tumult I had before endured; and I threw myself on the bed in my clothes, endeavouring to seek a few moments of forgetfulness. But it was in vain: I slept indeed, but I was disturbed by the wildest dreams. I thought I saw Elizabeth, in the bloom of health, walking in the streets of Ingolstadt. Delighted and surprised, I embraced her; but as I imprinted the first kiss on her lips, they became livid with the hue of death; her features appeared to change, and I thought that I held the corpse of my dead mother in my arms; a shroud enveloped her form, and I saw the grave-worms crawling in the folds of the flannel. I started from my sleep with horror; a cold dew covered my forehead, my teeth chattered, and every limb became convulsed; when, by the dim and yellow light of the moon, as it forced its way through the window-shutters, I beheld the wretch — the miserable monster whom I had created. He held up the curtain of the bed; and his eyes, if eyes they may be called, were fixed on me. His jaws opened, and he muttered some inarticulate sounds, while a grin wrinkled his cheeks. He might have spoken, but I did not hear; one hand was stretched out, seemingly to detain me, but I escaped, and rushed down stairs. I took refuge in the court-yard belonging to the house which I inhabited; where I remained during the rest of the night, walking up and down in the greatest agitation, listening attentively, catching and fearing each sound as if it were to announce the approach of the demoniacal corpse to which I had so miserably given life.

Oh! no mortal could support the horror of that countenance. A mummy again endued with animation could not be so hideous as that wretch. I had gazed on him while unfinished; he was ugly then; but when those muscles and joints were rendered capable of motion, it became a thing such as even Dante* could not have conceived.

I passed the night wretchedly. Sometimes my pulse beat so quickly and hardly, that I felt the palpitation of every artery; at others, I nearly sank to the ground through languor and extreme weakness. Mingled with this horror, I felt the bitterness of disappointment: dreams that had been my food and pleasant rest for so long a space, were now become a hell to me; and the change was so rapid, the overthrow so complete!

Morning, dismal and wet, at length dawned, and discovered to my sleepless and aching eyes the church of Ingolstadt, its white steeple and clock, which indicated the sixth hour. The porter opened the gates of the court, which had that night been my asylum, and I issued into the streets, pacing them with quick steps, as if I sought to avoid the wretch whom I feared every

turning of the street would present to my view. I did not dare
return to the apartment which I inhabited, but felt impelled to
hurry on, although wetted by the rain, which poured from a
black and comfortless sky.

I continued walking in this manner for some time, endeavouring, by bodily exercise, to ease the load that weighed upon my
mind. I traversed the streets, without any clear conception of
where I was, or what I was doing. My heart palpitated in the
sickness of fear; and I hurried on with irregular steps, not daring
to look about me:

> Like one who, on a lonely road,
>   Doth walk in fear and dread,
> And, having once turn'd round, walks on,
>   And turns no more his head;
> Because he knows a frightful fiend
>   Doth close behind him tread.*

Continuing thus, I came at length opposite to the inn at which
the various diligences* and carriages usually stopped. Here I
paused, I knew not why; but I remained some minutes with my
eyes fixed on a coach that was coming towards me from the
other end of the street. As it drew nearer, I observed that it was
the Swiss diligence: it stopped just where I was standing; and,
on the door being opened, I perceived Henry Clerval, who, on
seeing me, instantly sprung out. 'My dear Frankenstein,'
exclaimed he, 'how glad I am to see you! how fortunate that
you should be here at the very moment of my alighting!

Nothing could equal my delight on seeing Clerval; his presence brought back to my thoughts my father, Elizabeth, and all
those scenes of home so dear to my recollection. I grasped his
hand, and in a moment forgot my horror and misfortune; I felt
suddenly, and for the first time during many months, calm and
serene joy. I welcomed my friend, therefore, in the most cordial
manner, and we walked towards my college. Clerval continued
talking for some time about our mutual friends, and his own
good fortune in being permitted to come to Ingolstadt. 'You
may easily believe,' said he, 'how great was the difficulty to
persuade my father that it was not absolutely necessary for a
merchant not to understand any thing except book-keeping;
and, indeed, I believe I left him incredulous to the last, for his

---

* Coleridge's 'Ancient Mariner.'

constant answer to my unwearied entreaties was the same as that of the Dutch school-master in the Vicar of Wakefield:* "I have ten thousand florins a year without Greek, I eat heartily without Greek." But his affection for me at length overcame his dislike of learning, and he has permitted me to undertake a voyage of discovery to the land of knowledge.'

'It gives me the greatest delight to see you; but tell me how you left my father, brothers, and Elizabeth.'

'Very well, and very happy, only a little uneasy that they hear from you so seldom. By the bye, I mean to lecture you a little upon their account myself. — But, my dear Frankenstein,' continued he, stopping short, and gazing full in my face, 'I did not before remark how very ill you appear; so thin and pale; you look as if you had been watching for several nights.'

'You have guessed right; I have lately been so deeply engaged in one occupation, that I have not allowed myself sufficient rest, as you see: but I hope, I sincerely hope, that all these employments are now at an end, and that I am at length free.'

I trembled excessively; I could not endure to think of, and far less to allude to the occurrences of the preceding night. I walked with a quick pace, and we soon arrived at my college. I then reflected, and the thought made me shiver, that the creature whom I had left in my apartment might still be there, alive, and walking about. I dreaded to behold this monster; but I feared still more that Henry should see him. Entreating him therefore to remain a few minutes at the bottom of the stairs, I darted up towards my own room. My hand was already on the lock of the door before I recollected myself. I then paused; and a cold shivering came over me. I threw the door forcibly open, as children are accustomed to do when they expect a spectre to stand in waiting for them on the other side; but nothing appeared. I stepped fearfully in: the apartment was empty; and my bedroom was also freed from its hideous guest. I could hardly believe that so great a good-fortune could have befallen me; but when I became assured that my enemy had indeed fled, I clapped my hands for joy, and ran down to Clerval.

We ascended into my room, and the servant presently brought breakfast; but I was unable to contain myself. It was not joy only that possessed me; I felt my flesh tingle with excess of sensitiveness, and my pulse beat rapidly. I was unable to remain for a single instant in the same place; I jumped over the chairs, clapped my hands, and laughed aloud. Clerval at first attributed my unusual spirits to joy on his arrival; but when he observed me more attentively, he saw a wildness in my eyes for which he could not account; and my loud, unrestrained, heartless laughter, frightened and astonished him.

'My dear Victor,' cried he, 'what for God's sake, is the matter? Do not laugh in that manner. How ill you are! What is the cause of all this?

'Do not ask me,' cried I, putting my hands before my eyes, for I thought I saw the dreaded spectre glide into the room; '*he* can tell. — Oh, save me! save me!' I imagined that the monster seized me; I struggled furiously, and fell down in a fit.

Poor Clerval! what must have been his feelings? A meeting, which he anticipated with such joy, so strangely turned to bitterness. But I was not the witness of his grief; for I was lifeless, and did not recover my senses for a long, long time.

This was the commencement of a nervous fever, which confined me for several months. During all that time Henry was my only nurse. I afterwards learned that, knowing my father's advanced age, and unfitness for so long a journey, and how wretched my sickness would make Elizabeth, he spared them this grief by concealing the extent of my disorder. He knew that I could not have a more kind and attentive nurse than himself; and, firm in the hope he felt of my recovery, he did not doubt that, instead of doing harm, he performed the kindest action that he could towards them.

But I was in reality very ill; and surely nothing but the unbounded and unremitting attentions of my friend could have restored me to life. The form of the monster on whom I had bestowed existence was for ever before my eyes, and I raved incessantly concerning him. Doubtless my words surprised Henry: he at first believed them to be the wanderings of my disturbed imagination; but the pertinacity with which I continually recurred to the same subject persuaded him that my disorder indeed owed its origin to some uncommon and terrible event.

By very slow degrees, and with frequent relapses, that alarmed and grieved my friend, I recovered. I remember the first time I became capable of observing outward objects with any kind of pleasure, I perceived that the fallen leaves had disappeared, and that the young buds were shooting forth from the trees that shaded my window. It was a divine spring; and the season contributed greatly to my convalescence. I felt also sentiments of joy and affection revive in my bosom; my gloom disappeared, and in a short time I became as cheerful as before I was attacked by the fatal passion.

'Dearest Clerval,' exclaimed I, 'how kind, how very good you are to me. This whole winter, instead of being spent in study, as you promised yourself, has been consumed in my sick room. How shall I ever repay you? I feel the greatest remorse for the disappointment of which I have been the occasion; but you will forgive me.'

'You will repay me entirely, if you do not discompose yourself, but get well as fast as you can; and since you appear in such good spirits, I may speak to you on one subject, may I not?'

I trembled. One subject! what could it be? Could he allude to an object on whom I dared not even think?

'Compose yourself,' said Clerval, who observed my change of colour, 'I will not mention it, if it agitates you; but your father and cousin would be very happy if they received a letter from you in your own hand-writing. They hardly know how ill you have been, and are uneasy at your long silence.'

'Is that all? my dear Henry. How could you suppose that my first thought would not fly towards those dear, dear friends whom I love, and who are so deserving of my love.'

'If this is your present temper, my friend, you will perhaps be glad to see a letter that has been lying here some days for you: it is from your cousin, I believe.'

CHAPTER V

Clerval then put the following letter into my hands.

'To V. *Frankenstein*.

'MY DEAR COUSIN,
    'I cannot describe to you the uneasiness we have all felt concerning your health. We cannot help imagining that your friend Clerval conceals the extent of your disorder: for it is now several months since we have seen your hand-writing; and all this time you have been obliged to dictate your letters to Henry. Surely, Victor, you must have been exceedingly ill; and this makes us all very wretched, as much so nearly as after the death of your dear mother. My uncle was almost persuaded that you were indeed dangerously ill, and could hardly be restrained from undertaking a journey to Ingolstadt. Clerval always writes that you are getting better; I eagerly hope that you will confirm this intelligence soon in your own hand-writing; for indeed, indeed, Victor, we are all very miserable on this account. Relieve us from this fear, and we shall be the happiest creatures in the world. Your father's health is now so vigorous, that he appears ten years younger since last winter. Ernest also is so much improved, that you would hardly know him: he is now nearly sixteen, and has lost that sickly appearance which he had some years ago; he is grown quite robust and active.
    'My uncle and I conversed a long time last night about what profession Ernest should follow. His constant illness when young has deprived him of the habits of application; and now that he enjoys good health, he is continually in the open air, climbing the hills, or rowing on the lake. I therefore proposed that he should be a farmer; which you know, Cousin, is a favourite scheme of mine. A farmer's is a very healthy happy

life; and the least hurtful, or rather the most beneficial profession of any. My uncle had an idea of his being educated as an advocate, that through his interest he might become a judge. But, besides that he is not at all fitted for such an occupation, it is certainly more creditable to cultivate the earth for the sustenance of man, than to be the confidant, and sometimes the accomplice, of his vices; which is the profession of a lawyer. I said, that the employments of a prosperous farmer, if they were not a more honourable, they were at least a happier species of occupation than that of a judge, whose misfortune it was always to meddle with the dark side of human nature. My uncle smiled, and said, that I ought to be an advocate myself, which put an end to the conversation on that subject.

'And now I must tell you a little story that will please, and perhaps amuse you. Do you not remember Justine Moritz? Probably you do not; I will relate her history, therefore, in a few words. Madame Moritz, her mother, was a widow with four children, of whom Justine was the third. This girl had always been the favourite of her father; but, through a strange perversity, her mother could not endure her, and, after the death of M. Moritz, treated her very ill. My aunt observed this; and, when Justine was twelve years of age, prevailed on her mother to allow her to live at her house. The republican institutions of our country have produced simpler and happier manners than those which prevail in the great monarchies that surround it. Hence there is less distinction between the several classes of its inhabitants; and the lower orders being neither so poor nor so despised, their manners are more refined and moral. A servant in Geneva does not mean the same thing as a servant in France and England. Justine, thus received in our family, learned the duties of a servant; a condition which, in our fortunate country, does not include the idea of ignorance, and a sacrifice of the dignity of a human being.

'After what I have said, I dare say you well remember the heroine of my little tale: for Justine was a great favourite of your's; and I recollect you once remarked, that if you were in an ill humour, one glance from Justine could dissipate it, for the same reason that Ariosto gives concerning the beauty of Angelica* — she looked so frank-hearted and happy. My aunt conceived a great attachment for her, by which she was induced to give her an education superior to that which she had at first intended. This benefit was fully repaid; Justine was the most grateful little creature in the world: I do not mean that she made any professions, I never heard one pass her lips; but you could see by her eyes that she almost adored her protectress. Although her disposition was gay, and in many respects inconsiderate, yet she paid the greatest attention to every gesture of my aunt. She thought her the model of all excellence, and endeavoured to imitate her phraseology and manners, so that even now she often reminds me of her.

'When my dearest aunt died, every one was too much occupied in their own grief to notice poor Justine, who had attended her during her illness with the most anxious affection. Poor Justine was very ill; but other trials were reserved for her.

'One by one, her brothers and sister died; and her mother, with the exception of her neglected daughter, was left childless. The conscience of the woman was troubled; she began to think that the deaths of her favourites was a judgment from heaven to chastise her partiality. She was a Roman Catholic; and I believe her confessor confirmed the idea which she had conceived. Accordingly, a few months after your departure for Ingolstadt, Justine was called home by her reptentant mother. Poor girl! she wept when she quitted our house: she was much altered since the death of my aunt; grief had given softness and a winning mildness to her manners, which had before been remarkable for vivacity. Nor was her residence at her mother's house of a nature to restore her gaiety. The poor woman was very vacillating in her repentance. She sometimes begged Justine to forgive her unkindness, but much oftener accused her of having caused the deaths of her brothers and sister. Perpetual fretting at length threw Madame Moritz into a decline, which at first increased her irritability, but she is now at peace for ever. She died on the first approach of cold weather, at the beginning of this last winter. Justine has returned to us; and I assure you I love her tenderly. She is very clever and gentle, and extremely pretty; as I mentioned before, her mien and her expressions continually remind me of my dear aunt.

'I must say also a few words to you, my dear cousin, of little darling William. I wish you could see him; he is very tall of his age, with sweet laughing blue eyes, dark eye-lashes, and curling hair. When he smiles, two little dimples appear on each cheek, which are rosy with health. He has already had one or two little *wives*, but Louisa Biron is his favourite, a pretty little girl of five years of age.

'Now, dear Victor, I dare say you wish to be indulged in a little gossip concerning the good people of Geneva. The pretty Miss Mansfield has already received the congratulatory visits on her approaching marriage with a young Englishman, John Melbourne, Esq. Her ugly sister, Manon, married M. Duvillard, the rich banker, last autumn. Your favourite schoolfellow, Louis Manoir, has suffered several misfortunes since the departure of Clerval from Geneva. But he has already recovered his spirits, and is reported to be on the point of marrying a very lively pretty Frenchwoman, Madame Tavernier. She is a widow, and much older than Manoir; but she is very much admired, and a favourite with every body.

'I have written myself into good spirits, dear cousin; yet I cannot conclude without again anxiously inquiring concerning your health. Dear Victor, if you are not very ill, write yourself, and make your father and all of us happy; or – I cannot bear to think of the other side of the question; my tears already flow. Adieu, my dearest cousin.

Elizabeth Lavenza.

Geneva, March 18th, 17—.'

'Dear, dear Elizabeth!' I exclaimed when I had read her letter, 'I will write instantly, and relieve them from the anxiety they must feel.' I wrote, and this exertion greatly fatigued me; but my convalescence had commenced, and proceeded regularly. In another fortnight I was able to leave my chamber.

One of my first duties on my recovery was to introduce Clerval to the several professors of the university. In doing this, I underwent a kind of rough usage, ill befitting the wounds that my mind had sustained. Ever since the fatal night, the end of my labours, and the beginning of my misfortunes, I had conceived a violent antipathy even to the name of natural philosophy. When I was otherwise quite restored to health, the sight of a chemical instrument would renew all the agony of my nervous symptoms. Henry saw this, and had removed all my apparatus from my view. He had also changed my apartment; for he perceived that I had acquired a dislike for the room which had previously been my laboratory. But these cares of Clerval were made of no avail when I visited the profesors. M. Waldman inflicted torture when he praised, with kindness and warmth, the astonishing progress I had made in the sciences. He soon perceived that I disliked the subject; but, not guessing the real cause, he attributed my feelings to modesty, and changed the subject from my improvement to the science itself, with a desire, as I evidently saw, of drawing me out. What could I do ? He meant to please, and he tormented me. I felt as if he had placed carefully, one by one, in my view those instruments which were to be afterwards used in putting me to a slow and cruel death. I writhed under his words, yet dared not exhibit the pain I felt. Clerval, whose eyes and feelings were always quick in discerning the sensations of others, declined the subject, alleging, in excuse, his total ignorance ; and the conversation took a more general turn. I thanked my friend from my heart, but I did not speak. I saw plainly that he was surprised, but he never attempted to draw my secret from me ; and although I loved him with a mixture of affection and reverence that knew no bounds, yet I could never persuade myself to confide to him that event which was so often present to my recollection, but which I feared the detail to another would only impress more deeply.

M. Krempe was not equally docile; and in my condition at that time, of almost insupportable sensitiveness, his harsh blunt encomiums gave me even more pain than the benevolent approbation of M. Waldman. 'D—n the fellow !' cried he ; 'why, M. Clerval, I assure you he has outstripped us all. Aye, stare if you please ; but it is nevertheless true. A youngster who, but a few years ago, believed Cornelius Agrippa as firmly as the gospel, has now set himself at the head of the university ; and if he is not soon pulled down, we shall all be out of countenance. – Aye, aye,' continued he, observing my face expressive of suffering, 'M. Frankenstein is modest ; an excellent quality in a young man. Young men should be diffident of themselves, you know, M. Clerval ; I was myself when young : but that wears out in a very short time.'

M. Krempe had now commenced an eulogy on himself, which happily turned the conversation from a subject that was so annoying to me.

Clerval was no natural philosopher. His imagination was too vivid for the minutiæ of science. Languages were his principal study ; and he sought, by acquiring their elements, to open a field for self-instruction on his return to Geneva. Persian, Arabic, and Hebrew, gained his attention, after he had made himself perfectly master of Greek and Latin. For my own part, idleness had ever been irksome to me ; and now that I wished to fly from reflection, and hated my former studies, I felt great relief in being the fellow-pupil with my friend, and found not only instruction but consolation in the works of the orientalists. Their melancholy is soothing, and their joy elevating to a degree I never experienced in studying the authors of any other country. When you read their writings, life appears to consist in a warm sun and garden of roses – in the smiles and frowns of a fair enemy, and the fire that consumes your own heart. How different from the manly and heroical poetry of Greece and Rome.

Summer passed away in these occupations, and my return to Geneva was fixed for the latter end of autumn; but being delayed by several accidents, winter and snow arrived, the roads were deemed impassable, and my journey was retarded until the ensuing spring. I felt this delay very bitterly; for I longed to see my native town, and my beloved friends. My return had only been delayed so long from an unwillingness to leave Clerval in a strange place, before he had become acquainted with any of its inhabitants. The winter, however, was spent cheerfully; and although the spring was uncommonly late, when it came, its beauty compensated for its dilatoriness.

The month of May had already commenced, and I expected the letter daily which was to fix the date of my departure, when Henry proposed a pedestrian tour in the environs of Ingoldstadt that I might bid a personal farewell to the country I had so long inhabited. I acceded with pleasure to this proposition: I was fond of exercise, and Clerval had always been my favourite companion in the rambles of this nature that I had taken among the scenes of my native country.

We passed a fortnight in these perambulations: my health and spirits had long been restored, and they gained additional strength from the salubrious air I breathed, the natural incidents of our progress, and the conversation of my friend. Study had before secluded me from the intercourse of my fellow-creatures, and rendered me unsocial; but Clerval called forth the better feelings of my heart; he again taught me to love the aspect of nature, and the cheerful faces of children. Excellent friend! how sincerely did you love me, and endeavour to elevate my mind, until it was on a level with your own. A selfish pursuit had cramped and narrowed me, until your gentleness and affection warmed and opened my senses; I became the same happy creature who, a few years ago, loving and beloved by all, had no sorrow or care. When happy, inanimate nature had the power of bestowing on me the most delightful sensations. A serene sky and verdant fields filled me with ecstacy. The present season was indeed divine; the flowers of spring bloomed in the hedges, while those of summer were already in bud: I was undisturbed by thoughts which during the preceding year had pressed upon me, notwithstanding my endeavours to throw them off, with an invincible burden.

Henry rejoiced in my gaiety, and sincerely sympathized in my feelings: he exerted himself to amuse me, while he expressed the sensations that filled his soul. The resources of his mind on this occasion were truly astonishing: his conversation was full of imagination; and very often, in imitation of the Persian and Arabic writers, he invented tales of wonderful fancy and passion. At other times he repeated my favourite poems, or drew me out into arguments, which he supported with great ingenuity.

We returned to our college on a Sunday afternoon: the peasants were dancing, and every one we met appeared gay and happy. My own spirits were high, and I bounded along with feelings of unbridled joy and hilarity.

CHAPTER VI

On my return, I found the following letter from my father:

'To V. Frankenstein.

'MY DEAR VICTOR,

'You have probably waited impatiently for a letter to fix the date of your return to us; and I was at first tempted to write only a few lines, merely mentioning the day on which I should expect you. But that would be a cruel kindness, and I dare not do it. What would be your surprise, my son, when you expected a happy and gay welcome, to behold, on the contrary, tears and wretchedness? And how, Victor, can I relate our misfortune? Absence cannot have rendered you callous to our joys and griefs; and how shall I inflict pain on an absent child? I wish to prepare you for the woeful news, but I know it is impossible; even now your eye skims over the page, to seek the words which are to convey to you the horrible tidings.

'William is dead! – that sweet child, whose smiles delighted and warmed my heart, who was so gentle, yet so gay! Victor, he is murdered!

'I will not attempt to console you; but will simply relate the circumstances of the transaction.

'Last Thursday (May 7th) I, my niece, and your two brothers, went to walk in Plainpalais. The evening was warm and serene, and we prolonged our walk farther than usual. It was already dusk before we thought of returning; and then we discovered that William and Ernest, who had gone on before, were not to be found. We accordingly rested on a seat until they should return. Presently Ernest came, and inquired if we had seen his brother: he said, that they had been playing together, that William had run away to hide himself, and that he vainly sought for him, and afterwards waited for him a long time, but that he did not return.

'This account rather alarmed us, and we continued to search for him until night fell, when Elizabeth conjectured that he might have returned to the house. He was not there. We returned again, with torches; for I could not rest, when I thought that my sweet boy had lost himself, and was exposed to all the damps and dews of night: Elizabeth also suffered extreme anguish. About five in the morning I discovered my lovely boy, whom the night before I had seen blooming and active in health, stretched on the grass livid and motionless: the print of the murderer's finger was on his neck.

'He was conveyed home, and the anguish that was visible in my countenance betrayed the secret to Elizabeth. She was very earnest to see the corpse. At first I attempted to prevent her; but she persisted, and entering the room where it lay, hastily examined the neck of the victim, and clasping her hands exclaimed, "O God! I have murdered my darling infant!"

'She fainted, and was restored with extreme difficulty. When she again lived, it was only to weep and sigh. She told me, that that same evening William had teased her to let him wear a very valuable miniature that she possessed of your mother. This picture is gone, and was doubtless the temptation which urged the murderer to the deed. We have no trace of him at present, although our exertions to discover him are unremitted; but they will not restore my beloved William.

'Come, dearest Victor; you alone can console Elizabeth. She weeps continually, and accuses herself unjustly as the cause of his death; her words pierce my heart. We are all unhappy; but will not that be an additional motive for you, my son, to return and be our comforter? Your dear mother! Alas, Victor! I now say, Thank God she did not live to witness the cruel, miserable death of her youngest darling!

'Come, Victor; not brooding thoughts of vengeance against the assassin, but with feelings of peace and gentleness, that will heal, instead of festering the wounds of our minds. Enter the house of mourning, my friend, but with kindness and affection for those who love you, and not with hatred for your enemies.

'Your affectionate and afflicted father,

Alphonse Frankenstein.
Geneva, May 12th, 17—.'

Clerval, who had watched my countenance as I read this letter, was surprised to observe the despair that succeeded to the joy I at first expressed on receiving news from my friends. I threw the letter on the table, and covered my face with my hands.

'My dear Frankenstein,' exclaimed Henry, when he perceived me weep with bitterness, 'are you always to be unhappy? My dear friend, what has happened?'

I motioned to him to take up the letter, while I walked up and down the room in the extremest agitation. Tears also gushed from the eyes of Clerval, as he read the account of my misfortune.

'I can offer you no consolation, my friend,' said he; 'your disaster is irreparable. What do you intend to do?'

'To go instantly to Geneva: come with me, Henry, to order the horses.'

During our walk, Clerval endeavoured to raise my spirits. He did not do this by common topics of consolation, but by exhibiting the truest sympathy. 'Poor William!' said he, 'that dear child; he now sleeps with his angel mother. His friends mourn and weep, but he is at rest: he does not now feel the murderer's grasp; a sod covers his gentle form, and he knows no pain. He can no longer be a fit subject for pity; the survivors are the greatest sufferers, and for them time is the only consolation. Those maxims of the Stoics,* that death was no evil, and that the mind of man ought to be superior to despair on the eternal absence of a beloved object, ought not to be urged. Even Cato wept over the dead body of his brother.'

Clerval spoke thus as we hurried through the streets; the words impressed themselves on my mind, and I remembered them afterwards in solitude. But now, as soon as the horses arrived, I hurried into a cabriole,* and bade farewell to my friend.

My journey was very melancholy. At first I wished to hurry on, for I longed to console and sympathize with my loved and sorrowing friends; but when I drew near my native town, I slackened my progress. I could hardly sustain the multitude of feelings that crowded into my mind. I passed through scenes familiar to my youth, but which I had not seen for nearly six years. How altered every thing might be during that time? One sudden and desolating change had taken place; but a thousand little circumstances might have by degrees worked other alterations, which, although they were done more tranquilly, might not be the less decisive. Fear overcame me; I dared not advance, dreading a thousand nameless evils that made me tremble, although I was unable to define them.

I remained two days at Lausanne, in this painful state of mind. I contemplated the lake: the waters were placid; all around was calm, and the snowy mountains, 'the palaces of nature,'* were not changed. By degress the calm and heavenly scene restored me, and I continued my journey towards Geneva.

The road ran by the side of the lake, which became narrower as I approached my native town. I discovered more distinctly the black sides of Jura, and the bright summit of Mont Blanc; I wept like a child: 'Dear mountains! my own beautiful lake! how do you welcome your wanderer? Your summits are clear; the sky and lake are blue and placid. Is this to prognosticate peace, or to mock at my unhappiness?'

I fear, my friend, that I shall render myself tedious by dwelling on these preliminary circumstances; but they were days of comparative happiness, and I think of them with pleasure. My country, my beloved country! who but a native can tell the delight I took in again beholding thy streams, thy mountains, and, more than all, thy lovely lake.

Yet, as I drew nearer home, grief and fear again overcame me. Night also closed around; and when I could hardly see the dark mountains, I felt still more gloomily. The picture appeared a vast and dim scene of evil, and I foresaw obscurely that I was destined to become the most wretched of human beings. Alas! I prophesied truly, and failed only in one single circumstance, that in all the misery I imagined and dreaded, I did not conceive the hundredth part of the anguish I was destined to endure.

It was completely dark when I arrived in the environs of Geneva; the gates of the town were already shut; and I was obliged to pass the night at Secheron, a village half a league to the east of the city. The sky was serene; and, as I was unable to rest, I resolved to visit the spot where my poor William had been murdered. As I could not pass through the town, I was obliged to cross the lake in a boat to arrive at Plainpalais. During this short voyage I saw the lightnings playing on the summit of Mont Blanc in the most beautiful figures. The storm appeared to approach rapidly; and, on landing, I ascended a low hill, that I might observe its progress. It advanced; the heavens were clouded, and I soon felt the rain coming slowly in large drops, but its violence quickly increased.

I quitted my seat, and walked on, although the darkness and

storm increased every minute, and the thunder burst with a terrific crash over my head. It was echoed from Salêve, the Juras, and the Alps of Savoy; vivid flashes of lightning dazzled my eyes, illuminating the lake, making it appear like a vast sheet of fire; then for an instant every thing seemed of a pitchy darkness, until the eye recovered itself from the preceding flash. The storm, as is often the case in Switzerland, appeared at once in various parts of the heavens. The most violent storm hung exactly north of the town, over that part of the lake which lies between the promontory of Belrive and the village of Copêt. Another storm enlightened Jura with faint flashes; and another darkened and sometimes disclosed the Môle, a peaked mountain to the east of the lake.

While I watched the storm, so beautiful yet terrific, I wandered on with a hasty step. This noble war in the sky elevated my spirits; I clasped my hands, and exclaimed aloud, 'William, dear angel! this is thy funeral, this thy dirge!' As I said these words, I perceived in the gloom a figure which stole from behind a clump of trees near me; I stood fixed, gazing intently: I could not be mistaken. A flash of lightning illuminated the object, and discovered* its shape plainly to me; its gigantic stature, and the deformity of its aspect, more hideous than belongs to humanity, instantly informed me that it was the wretch, the filthy dæmon to whom I had given life. What did he there? Could he be (I shuddered at the conception) the murderer of my brother? No sooner did that idea cross my imagination, than I became convinced of its truth; my teeth chattered, and I was forced to lean against a tree for support. The figure passed me quickly, and I lost it in the gloom. Nothing in human shape could have destroyed that fair child. *He* was the murderer! I could not doubt it. The mere presence of the idea was an irresistible proof of the fact. I thought of pursuing the devil; but it would have been in vain, for another flash discovered him to me hanging among the rocks of the nearly perpendicular ascent of Mont Salêve, a hill that bounds Plainpalais on the south. He soon reached the summit, and disappeared.

I remained motionless. The thunder ceased; but the rain still continued, and the scene was enveloped in an impenetrable darkness. I revolved in my mind the events which I had until now sought to forget: the whole train of my progress towards the creation; the appearance of the work of my own hands alive at my bed side; its departure. Two years had now nearly elapsed since the night on which he first received life ; and was this his first crime ? Alas ! I had turned loose into the world a depraved wretch, whose delight was in carnage and misery ; had he not murdered my brother ?

No one can conceive the anguish I suffered during the remainder of the night, which I spent, cold and wet, in the open air. But I did not feel the inconvenience of the weather ; my imagination was busy in scenes of evil and despair. I considered the being whom I had cast among mankind, and endowed with the will and power to effect purposes of horror, such as the deed which he had now done, nearly in the light of my own vampire, my own spirit let loose from the grave, and forced to destroy all that was dear to me.

Day dawned ; and I directed my steps towards the town. The gates were open ; and I hastened to my father's house. My first thought was to discover what I knew of the murderer, and cause instant pursuit to be made. But I paused when I reflected on the story that I had to tell. A being whom I myself had formed, and endued with life, had met me at midnight among the precipices of an inaccessible mountain. I remembered also the nervous fever with which I had been seized just at the time that I dated my creation, and which would give an air of delirium to a tale otherwise so utterly improbable. I well knew that if any other had communicated such a relation to me, I should have looked upon it as the ravings of insanity. Besides, the strange nature of the animal would elude all pursuit, even if I were so far credited as to persuade my relatives to commence it. Besides, of what use would be pursuit ? Who could arrest a creature capable of scaling the overhanging sides of Mont Salêve. These reflections determined me, and I resolved to remain silent.

It was about five in the morning when I entered my father's house. I told the servants not to disturb the family, and went into the library to attend their usual hour of rising.

Six years had elapsed, passed as a dream but for one indelible trace, and I stood in the same place where I had last embraced my father before my departure for Ingoldstadt. Beloved and respectable parent ! He still remained to me. I gazed on the picture of my mother, which stood over the mantelpiece. It was an historical subject, painted at my father's desire, and represented Caroline Beaufort in an agony of despair, kneeling by the coffin of her dead father. Her garb was rustic, and her cheek pale ; but there was an air of dignity and beauty, that hardly permitted the sentiment of pity. Below this picture was a miniature of William; and my tears flowed when I looked upon it. While I was thus engaged, Ernest entered: he had heard me arrive, and hastened to welcome me. He expressed a sorrowful delight to see me: 'Welcome, my dearest Victor,' said he. 'Ah! I wish you had come three months ago, and then you would have found us all joyous and delighted. But we are now unhappy; and, I am afraid, tears instead of smiles will be your welcome. Our father looks so sorrowful: this dreadful event seems to have revived in his mind his grief on the death of Mamma. Poor Elizabeth also is quite inconsolable.' Ernest began to weep as he said these words.

'Do not,' said I, 'welcome me thus; try to be more calm, that I may not be absolutely miserable the moment I enter my father's house after so long an absence. But, tell me, how does my father support his misfortunes? and how is my poor Elizabeth?'

'She indeed requires consolation; she accused herself of having caused the death of my brother, and that made her very wretched. But since the murderer has been discovered—'

'The murderer discovered! Good God! how can that be? who could attempt to pursue him? It is impossible; one might as well try to overtake the winds, or confine a mountain-stream with a straw.'

'I do not know what you mean; but we were all very unhappy when she was discovered. No one would believe it at first; and even now Elizabeth will not be convinced, notwithstanding all the evidence. Indeed, who would credit that Justine Moritz, who was so amiable, and fond of all the family, could all at once become so extremely wicked?'

'Justine Moritz! Poor, poor girl, is she the accused? But it is wrongfully; every one knows that; no one believes it, surely, Ernest?'

'No one did at first; but several circumstances came out, that have almost forced conviction upon us: and her own behaviour has been so confused, as to add to the evidence of facts a weight that, I fear, leaves no hope for doubt. But she will be tried to-day, and you will then hear all.'

He related that, the morning on which the murder of poor William had been discovered, Justine had been taken ill, and confined to her bed; and, after several days, one of the servants, happening to examine the apparel she had worn on the night of

the murder, had discovered in her pocket the picture of my
mother, which had been judged to be the temptation of the
murderer. The servant instantly showed it to one of the others,
who, without saying a word to any of the family, went to a
magistrate; and, upon their deposition, Justine was appre-
hended. On being charged with the fact, the poor girl confirmed
the suspicion in a great measure by her extreme confusion of
manner.

This was a strange tale, but it did not shake my faith; and I
replied earnestly, 'You are all mistaken; I know the murderer.
Justine, poor, good Justine, is innocent.'

At that instant my father entered. I saw unhappiness deeply
impressed on his countenance, but he endeavoured to welcome
me cheerfully; and, after we had exchanged our mournful
greeting, would have introduced some other topic than that of
our disaster, had not Ernest exclaimed, 'Good God, Papa!
Victor says that he knows who was the murderer of poor
William.'

'We do also, unfortunately,' replied my father; 'for indeed I
had rather have been for ever ignorant than have discovered so
much depravity and ingratitude in one I valued so highly.'

'My dear father, you are mistaken; Justine is innocent.'

'If she is, God forbid that she should suffer as guilty. She is to
be tried to-day, and I hope, I sincerely hope, that she will be
acquitted.'

This speech calmed me. I was firmly convinced in my own
mind that Justine, and indeed every human being, was guiltless
of this murder. I had no fear, therefore, that any circumstantial
evidence could be brought forward strong enough to convict
her; and, in this assurance, I calmed myself, expecting the trial
with eagerness, but without prognosticating an evil result.

We were soon joined by Elizabeth. Time had made great
alterations in her form since I had last beheld her. Six years
before she had been a pretty, good-humoured girl, whom every
one loved and caressed. She was now a woman in stature and
expression of countenance, which was uncommonly lovely. An
open and capacious forehead gave indications of a good understanding, joined to great frankness of disposition. Her eyes were
hazel, and expressive of mildness, now through recent affliction
allied to sadness. Her hair was of a rich dark auburn, her
complexion fair, and her figure slight and graceful. She welcomed me with the greatest affection. 'Your arrival, my dear

cousin,' said she, 'fills me with hope. You perhaps will find some means to justify my poor guiltless Justine. Alas! who is safe, if she be convicted of crime? I rely on her innocence as certainly as I do upon my own. Our misfortune is doubly hard to us; we have not only lost that lovely darling boy, but this poor girl, whom I sincerely love, is to be torn away by even a worse fate. If she is condemned, I never shall know joy more. But she will not, I am sure she will not; and then I shall be happy again, even after the sad death of my little William.'

'She is innocent, my Elizabeth,' said I, 'and that shall be proved; fear nothing, but let your spirits be cheered by the assurance of her acquittal.'

'How kind you are! everyone else believes in her guilt, and that made me wretched; for I knew that it was impossible: and to see every one else prejudiced in so deadly a manner, rendered me hopeless and despairing.' She wept.

'Sweet niece,' said my father, 'dry your tears. If she is, as you believe, innocent, rely on the justice of our judges, and the activity with which I shall prevent the slightest shadow of partiality.'

CHAPTER VII

We passed a few sad hours, until eleven o'clock, when the trial was to commence. My father and the rest of the family being obliged to attend as witnesses, I accompanied them to the court. During the whole of this wretched mockery of justice, I suffered living torture. It was to be decided, whether the result of my curiosity and lawless devices would cause the death of two of my fellow-beings : one a smiling babe, full of innocence and joy ; the other far more dreadfully murdered, with every aggravation of infamy that could make the murder memorable in horror. Justine also was a girl of merit, and possessed qualities which promised to render her life happy : now all was to be obliterated in an ignominious grave ; and I the cause ! A thousand times rather would I have confessed myself guilty of the crime ascribed to Justine ; but I was absent when it was committed, and such a declaration would have been considered as the ravings of a madman, and would not have exculpated her who suffered through me.

The appearance of Justine was calm. She was dressed in mourning ; and her countenance, always engaging, was rendered, by the solemnity of her feelings, exquisitely beautiful. Yet she appeared confident in innocence, and did not tremble, although gazed on and execrated by thousands ; for all the kindness which her beauty might otherwise have excited, was obliterated in the minds of the spectators by the imagination of the enormity she was supposed to have committed. She was tranquil, yet her tranquillity was evidently constrained ; and as her confusion had before been adduced as a proof of her guilt, she worked up her mind to an appearance of courage. When she entered the court, she threw her eyes round it, and quickly discovered where we were seated. A tear seemed to dim her eye when she saw us ; but she quickly recovered herself, and a look of sorrowful affection seemed to attest her utter guiltlessness.

The trial began ; and after the advocate against her had stated the charge, several witnesses were called. Several strange facts combined against her, which might have staggered any one who had not such proof of her innocence as I had. She had been out the whole of the night on which the murder had been committed, and towards morning had been perceived by a market-woman not far from the spot where the body of the murdered child had been afterwards found. The woman asked her what she did there ; but she looked very strangely, and only returned a confused and unintelligible answer. She returned to the house about eight o'clock ; and when one inquired where she had passed the night, she replied, that she had been looking for the child, and demanded earnestly, if any thing had been heard concerning him. When shown the body, she fell into violent hysterics, and kept her bed for several days. The picture was then produced, which the servant had found in her pocket ; and when Elizabeth, in a faltering voice, proved that it was the same which, an hour before the child had been missed, she had placed round his neck, a murmur of horror and indignation filled the court.

Justine was called on for her defence. As the trial had proceeded, her countenance had altered. Surprise, horror, and misery, were strongly expressed. Sometimes she struggled with her tears ; but when she was desired to plead, she collected her powers, and spoke in an audible although variable voice : —

'God knows,' she said, 'how entirely I am innocent. But I do not pretend that my protestations should acquit me : I rest my innocence on a plain and simple explanation of the facts which have been adduced against me ; and I hope the character I have always borne will incline my judges to a favourable interpretation, where any circumstance appears doubtful or suspicious.'

She then related that, by the permission of Elizabeth, she had passed the evening of the night on which the murder had been committed, at the house of an aunt at Chêne, a village situated at about a league from Geneva. On her return, at about nine o'clock, she met a man, who asked her if she had seen any thing of the child who was lost. She was alarmed by this account, and passed several hours in looking for him, when the gates of Geneva were shut, and she was forced to remain several hours of the night in a barn belonging to a cottage, being unwilling to call up the inhabitants, to whom she was well known. Unable to rest or sleep, she quitted her asylum early, that she might again endeavour to find my brother. If she had gone near the spot where his body lay, it was without her knowledge. That she had been bewildered when questioned by the market-woman, was not surprising, since she had passed a sleepless night, and the fate of poor William was yet uncertain. Concerning the picture she could give no account.

'I know,' continued the unhappy victim, 'how heavily and fatally this one circumstance weighs against me, but I have no power of explaining it; and when I have expressed my utter ignorance, I am only left to conjecture concerning the probabilities by which it might have been placed in my pocket. But here also I am checked. I believe that I have no enemy on earth, and none surely would have been so wicked as to destroy me wantonly. Did the murderer place it there? I know of no opportunity afforded him for so doing; or if I had, why should he have stolen the jewel, to part with it again so soon?

'I commit my cause to the justice of my judges, yet I see no room for hope. I beg permission to have a few witnesses examined concerning my character; and if their testimony shall not overweigh my supposed guilt, I must be condemned, although I would pledge my salvation on my innocence.'

Several witnesses were called, who had known her for many years, and they spoke well of her; but fear, and hatred of the crime of which they supposed her guilty, rendered them timorous, and unwilling to come forward. Elizabeth saw even this last resource, her excellent dispositions and irreproachable conduct, about to fail the accused, when, although violently agitated, she desired permission to address the court.

'I am,' said she, 'the cousin of the unhappy child who was murdered, or rather his sister, for I was educated by and have lived with his parents ever since and even long before his birth. It may therefore be judged indecent in me to come forward on this occasion; but when I see a fellow-creature about to perish through the cowardice of her pretended friends, I wish to be allowed to speak, that I may say what I know of her character. I am well acquainted with the accused. I have lived in the same house with her, at one time for five, and at another for nearly two years. During all that period she appeared to me the most amiable and benevolent of human creatures. She nursed Madame Frakenstein, my aunt, in her last illness with the greatest affection and care; and afterwards attended her own mother during a tedious illness, in a manner that excited the admiration of all who knew her. After which she again lived in my uncle's house, where she was beloved by all the family. She was warmly attached to the child who is now dead, and acted towards him like a most affectionate mother. For my own part, I do not hesitate to say, that, notwithstanding all the evidence produced against her, I believe and rely on her perfect innocence. She had no temptation for such an action: as to the bauble on which the chief proof rests, if she had earnestly desired it, I should have willingly given it to her; so much do I esteem and value her.'

Excellent Elizabeth! A murmur of approbation was heard; but it was excited by her generous interference, and not in favour of poor Justine, on whom the public indignation was turned with renewed violence, charging her with the blackest ingratitude. She herself wept as Elizabeth spoke, but she did not answer. My own agitation and anguish was extreme during the whole trial. I believed in her innocence; I knew it. Could the demon, who had (I did not for a minute doubt) murdered my brother, also in his hellish sport have betrayed the innocent to death and ignominy. I could not sustain the horror of my situation; and when I perceived that the popular voice, and the countenances of the judges, had already condemned my unhappy victim, I rushed out of the court in agony. The tortures of the accused did not equal mine; she was sustained by innocence, but the fangs of remorse tore my bosom, and would not forego their hold.

I passed a night of unmingled wretchedness. In the morning I went to the court; my lips and throat were parched. I dared not ask the fatal question; but I was known, and the officer guessed the cause of my visit. The ballots had been thrown; they were all black, and Justine was condemned.

I cannot pretend to describe what I then felt. I had before experienced sensations of horror; and I have endeavoured to bestow upon them adequate expressions, but words cannot convey an idea of the heart-sickening despair that I then endured. The person to whom I addressed myself added, that Justine had already confessed her guilt. 'That evidence,' he observed, 'was hardly required in so glaring a case, but I am glad of it; and, indeed, none of our judges like to condemn a criminal upon circumstantial evidence, be it ever so decisive.'

When I returned home, Elizabeth eagerly demanded the result.

'My cousin,' replied I, 'it is decided as you may have expected; all judges had rather that ten innocent should suffer, than that one guilty should escape. But she has confessed.'

This was a dire blow to poor Elizabeth, who had relied with firmness upon Justine's innocence. 'Alas!' said she, 'how shall I ever again believe in human benevolence? Justine, whom I loved and esteemed as my sister, how could she put on those smiles of innocence only to betray; her mild eyes seemed incapable of any severity or ill-humour, and yet she has committed a murder.'

Soon after we heard that the poor victim had expressed a wish to see my cousin. My father wished her not to go; but said, that he left it to her own judgment and feelings to decide. 'Yes,' said Elizabeth, 'I will go, although she is guilty; and you, Victor, shall accompany me : I cannot go alone.' The idea of this visit was torture to me, yet I could not refuse.

We entered the gloomy prison-chamber, and beheld Justine sitting on some straw at the further end; her hands were manacled, and her head rested on her knees. She rose on seeing us enter; and when we were left alone with her, she threw herself at the feet of Elizabeth, weeping bitterly. My cousin wept also.

'Oh, Justine!' said she, 'why did you rob me of my last consolation. I relied on your innocence; and although I was then very wretched, I was not so miserable as I am now.'

'And do you also believe that I am so very, very wicked? Do you also join with my enemies to crush me?' Her voice was suffocated with sobs.

'Rise, my poor girl,' said Elizabeth, 'why do you kneel, if you are innocent? I am not one of your enemies; I believed you guiltless, notwithstanding every evidence, until I heard that you had yourself declared your guilt. That report, you say, is false; and be assured, dear Justine, that nothing can shake my confidence in you for a moment, but your own confession.'

'I did confess; but I confessed a lie. I confessed, that I might obtain absolution; but now that falsehood lies heavier at my heart than all my other sins. The God of heaven forgive me! Ever since I was condemned, my confessor has besieged me; he threatened and menaced, until I almost began to think that I was the monster that he said I was. He threatened excommunication and hell fire in my last moments, if I continued obdurate. Dear lady, I had none to support me; all looked on me as a wretch doomed to ignominy and perdition. What could I do? In an evil hour I subscribed to a lie; and now only am I truly miserable.'

She paused, weeping, and then continued – 'I thought with horror, my sweet lady, that you should believe your Justine, whom your blessed aunt had so highly honoured, and whom you loved, was a creature capable of a crime which none but the devil himself could have perpetrated. Dear William! dearest blessed child! I soon shall see you again in heaven, where we shall all be happy; and that consoles me, going as I am to suffer ignominy and death.'

'Oh, Justine! forgive me for having for one moment distrusted you. Why did you confess? But do not mourn, my dear girl; I will every where proclaim your innocence, and force belief. Yet you must die; you, my playfellow, my companion, my more than sister. I never can survive so horrible a misfortune.'

'Dear, sweet Elizabeth, do not weep. You ought to raise me with thoughts of a better life, and elevate me from the petty cares of this world of injustice and strife. Do not you, excellent friend, drive me to despair.'

'I will try to confort you; but this, I fear, is an evil too deep and poignant to admit of consolation, for there is no hope. Yet heaven bless thee, my dearest Justine, with resignation, and a confidence elevated beyond this world. Oh! how I hate its shows and mockeries! when one creature is murdered, another is immediately deprived of life in a slow torturing manner; then the executioners, their hands yet reeking with the blood of innocence, believe that they have done a great deed. They call this *retribution*. Hateful name! When that word is pronounced, I know greater and more horrid punishments are going to be inflicted than the gloomiest tyrant has ever invented to satiate his utmost revenge. Yet this is not consolation for you, my Justine, unless indeed that you may glory in escaping from so miserable a den. Alas! I would I were in peace with my aunt and my lovely William, escaped from a world which is hateful to me, and the visages of men which I abhor.'

Justine smiled languidly. 'This dear lady, is despair, and not resignation. I must not learn the lesson that you would teach me. Talk of something else, something that will bring peace, and not increase of misery.'

During this conversation I had retired to a corner of the prison-room, where I could conceal the horrid anguish that possessed me. Despair! Who dared talk of that? The poor victim, who on the morrow was to pass the dreary boundary between life and death, felt not as I did, such deep and bitter agony. I gnashed my teeth, and ground them together, uttering a groan that came from my inmost soul. Justine started. When she saw who it was, she approached me, and said, 'Dear Sir, you are very kind to visit me; you, I hope, do not believe that I am guilty.'

I could not answer. 'No, Justine,' said Elizabeth; 'he is more convinced of your innocence than I was; for even when he heard that you had confessed, he did not credit it.'

'I truly thank him. In these last moments I feel the sincerest gratitude towards those who think of me with kindness. How sweet is the affection of others to such a wretch as I am! It removes more than half my misfortune; and I feel as if I could die in peace, now that my innocence is acknowledged by you, dear lady, and your cousin.'

Thus the poor sufferer tried to comfort others and herself. She indeed gained the resignation she desired. But I, the true murderer, felt the never-dying worm alive in my bosom, which allowed of no hope or consolation. Elizabeth also wept, and was unhappy; but hers also was the misery of innocence, which, like a cloud that passes over the fair moon, for a while hides, but cannot tarnish its brightness. Anguish and despair had penetrated into the core of my heart; I bore a hell within me, which nothing could extinguish. We stayed several hours with Justine; and it was with great difficulty that Elizabeth could tear herself away. 'I wish,' cried she, 'that I were to die with you; I cannot live in this world of misery.'

Justine assumed an air of cheerfulness, while she with difficulty repressed her bitter tears. She embraced Elizabeth, and said, in a voice of half-suppressed emotion, 'Farewell, sweet lady, dearest Elizabeth, my beloved and only friend; may heaven in its bounty bless and preserve you; may this be the last misfortune that you will ever suffer. Live, and be happy, and make others so.'

As we returned, Elizabeth said, 'You know not, my dear Victor, how much I am relieved, now that I trust in the innocence of this unfortunate girl. I never could again have known peace, if I had been deceived in my reliance on her. For the moment that I did believe her guilty, I felt an anguish that I could not have long sustained. Now my heart is lightened. The innocent suffers ; but she whom I thought amiable and good has not betrayed the trust I reposed in her, and I am consoled.

Amiable cousin ! such were your thoughts, mild and gentle as your own dear eyes and voice. But I – I was a wretch, and none ever conceived of the misery that I then endured.

END OF VOL. I

FRANKENSTEIN
Volume II

CHAPTER I

Nothing is more painful to the human mind, than, after the feelings have been worked up by a quick succession of events, the dead calmness of inaction and certainty which follows, and deprives the soul both of hope and fear. Justine died; she rested; and I was alive. The blood flowed freely in my veins, but a weight of despair and remorse pressed on my heart, which nothing could remove. Sleep fled from my eyes; I wandered like an evil spirit, for I had committed deeds of mischief beyond description horrible, and more, much more, (I persuaded myself) was yet behind. Yet my heart overflowed with kindness, and the love of virtue. I had begun life with benevolent intentions, and thirsted for the moment when I should put them in practice, and make myself useful to my fellow-beings. Now all was blasted: instead of that serenity of conscience, which allowed me to look back upon the past with self-satisfaction, and from thence to gather promise of new hopes, I was seized by remorse and the sense of guilt, which hurried me away to a hell of intense tortures, such as no language can describe.

This state of mind preyed upon my health, which had entirely recovered from the first shock it had sustained. I shunned the face of man; all sound of joy or complacency was torture to me; solitude was my only consolation – deep, dark, death-like solitude.

My father observed with pain the alteration perceptible in my disposition and habits, and endeavoured to reason with me on the folly of giving way to immoderate grief. 'Do you think, Victor,' said he, 'that I do not suffer also? No one could love a child more than I loved your brother;' (tears came into his eyes as he spoke); 'but is it not a duty to the survivors, that we should refrain from augmenting their unhappiness by an appearance of immoderate grief? It is also a duty owed to yourself;

for excessive sorrow prevents improvement or enjoyment, or even the discharge of daily usefulness, without which no man is fit for society.'

This advice, although good, was totally inapplicable to my case; I should have been the first to hide my grief, and console my friends, if remorse had not mingled its bitterness with my other sensations. Now I could only answer my father with a look of despair, and endeavour to hide myself from his view.

About this time we retired to our house at Belrive. This change was particularly agreeable to me. The shutting of the gates regularly at ten o'clock, and the impossibility of remaining on the lake after that hour, had rendered our residence within the walls of Geneva very irksome to me. I was now free. Often, after the rest of the family had retired for the night, I took the boat, and passed many hours upon the water. Sometimes, with my sails set, I was carried by the wind; and sometimes, after rowing into the middle of the lake, I left the boat to pursue its own course, and gave way to my own miserable reflections. I was often tempted, when all was at peace around me, and I the only unquiet thing that wandered restless in a scene so beautiful and heavenly, if I except some bat, or the frogs, whose harsh and interrupted croaking was heard only when I approached the shore – often, I say, I was tempted to plunge into the silent lake, that the waters might close over me and my calamities for ever. But I was restrained, when I thought of the heroic and suffering Elizabeth, whom I tenderly loved, and whose existence was bound up in mine. I thought also of my father, and surviving brother: should I by my base desertion leave them exposed and unprotected to the malice of the fiend whom I had let loose among them?

At these moments I wept bitterly, and wished that peace would revisit my mind only that I might afford them consolation and happiness. But that could not be. Remorse extinguished every hope. I had been the author of unalterable evils; and I lived in daily fear, lest the monster whom I had created should perpetrate some new wickedness. I had an obscure feeling that all was not over, and that he would still commit some signal crime, which by its enormity should almost efface the recollection of the past. There was always scope for fear, so long as any thing I loved remained behind. My abhorrence of this fiend cannot be conceived. When I thought of him, I gnashed my teeth, my eyes became inflamed, and I ardently wished to extinguish that life which I had so thoughtlessly bestowed. When I reflected on his crimes and malice, my hatred and revenge burst all bounds of moderation. I would have made a pilgrimage to the highest peak of the Andes, could I, when there, have precipitated him to their base. I wished to see him again, that I might wreak the utmost extent of anger on his head, and avenge the deaths of William and Justine.

Our house was the house of mourning. My father's health was deeply shaken by the horror of the recent events. Elizabeth was sad and desponding; she no longer took delight in her ordinary occupations; all pleasure seemed to her sacrilege toward the dead; eternal woe and tears she then thought was the just tribute she should pay to innocence so blasted and destroyed. She was no longer that happy creature, who in earlier youth wandered with me on the banks of the lake, and talked with ecstacy of our future prospects. She had become grave, and often conversed of the inconstancy of fortune, and the instability of human life.

'When I reflect, my dear cousin,' said she, 'on the miserable death of Justine Moritz, I no longer see the world and its works as they before appeared to me. Before, I looked upon the accounts of vice and injustice, that I read in books or heard from others, as tales of ancient days, or imaginary evils; at least they were remote, and more familiar to reason than to the imagination; but now misery has come home, and men appear to me as monsters thirsting for each other's blood. Yet I am certainly unjust. Everybody believed that poor girl to be guilty; and if she could have committed the crime for which she suffered, assuredly she would have been the most depraved of human creatures. For the sake of a few jewels, to have murdered the son of her benefactor and friend, a child whom she had nursed from its birth, and appeared to love as if it had been her own! I could not consent to the death of any human being; but certainly I should have thought such a creature unfit to remain in the society of men. Yet she was innocent. I know, I feel she was innocent; you are of the same opinion, and that confirms me. Alas! Victor, when falsehood can look so like the truth, who can assure themselves of certain happiness? I feel as if I were walking on the edge of a precipice, towards which thousands are crowding, and endeavouring to plunge me into the abyss. William and Justine were assassinated, and the murderer escapes; he walks about the world free, and perhaps respected.

But even if I were condemned to suffer on the scaffold for the same crimes, I would not change places with such a wretch.'

I listened to this discourse with the extremest agony. I, not in deed, but in effect, was the true murderer. Elizabeth read my anguish in my countenance, and kindly taking my hand said, 'My dearest cousin, you must calm yourself. These events have affected me, God knows how deeply; but I am not so wretched as you are. There is an expression of despair, and sometimes of revenge, in your countenance, that makes me tremble. Be calm, my dear Victor; I would sacrifice my life to your peace. We surely shall be happy: quiet in our native country, and not mingling in the world, what can disturb our tranquillity?'

She shed tears as she said this, distrusting the very solace that she gave; but at the same time she smiled, that she might chase away the fiend that lurked in my heart. My father, who saw in the unhappiness that was painted in my face only an exaggeration of that sorrow which I might naturally feel, thought that an amusement suited to my taste would be the best means of restoring to me my wonted serenity. It was from this cause that he had removed to the country; and, induced by the same motive, he now proposed that we should all make an excursion to the valley of Chamounix. I had been there before, but Elizabeth and Ernest never had; and both had often expressed an earnest desire to see the scenery of this place, which had been described to them as so wonderful and sublime. Accordingly we departed from Geneva on this tour about the middle of the month of August, nearly two months after the death of Justine.

The weather was uncommonly fine; and if mine had been a sorrow to be chased away by any fleeting circumstance, this excursion would certainly have had the effect intended by my father. As it was, I was somewhat interested in the scene; it sometimes lulled, although it could not extinguish my grief. During the first day we travelled in a carriage. In the morning we had seen the mountains at a distance, towards which we gradually advanced. We perceived that the valley through which we wound, and which was formed by the river Arve, whose course we followed, closed in upon us by degrees; and when the sun had set, we beheld immense mountains and precipices overhanging us on every side, and heard the sound of the river raging among rocks, and the dashing of waterfalls around.

The next day we pursued our journey upon mules; and as we ascended still higher, the valley assumed a more magnificent and astonishing character. Ruined castles hanging on the precipices of piny mountains; the impetuous Arve, and cottages every here and there peeping forth from among the trees, formed a scene of singular beauty. But it was augmented and rendered sublime by the mighty Alps, whose white and shining pyramids and domes towered above all, as belonging to another earth, the habitations of another race of beings.

We passed the bridge of Pelissier, where the ravine, which the river forms, opened before us, and we began to ascend the mountain that overhangs it. Soon after we entered the valley of Chamounix. This valley is more wonderful and sublime, but not so beautiful and picturesque as that of Servox, through which we had just passed. The high and snowy mountains were its immediate boundaries; but we saw no more ruined castles and fertile fields. Immense glaciers approached the road; we heard the rumbling thunder of the falling avalanche, and marked the smoke of its passage. Mont Blanc, the supreme and magnificent Mont Blanc, raised itself from the surrounding *aiguilles*,* and its tremendous *dome** overlooked the valley.

During this journey, I sometimes joined Elizabeth, and exerted myself to point out to her the various beauties of the scene. I often suffered my mule to lag behind, and indulged in the misery of reflection. At other times I spurred on the animal before my companions, that I might forget them, the world, and, more than all, myself. When at a distance, I alighted, and threw myself on the grass, weighed down by horror and despair. At eight in the evening I arrived at Chamounix. My father and Elizabeth were very much fatigued; Ernest, who accompanied us, was delighted, and in high spirits: the only circumstance that detracted from his pleasure was the south wind, and the rain it seemed to promise for the next day.

We retired early to our apartments, but not to sleep; at least I did not. I remained many hours at the window, watching the pallid lightning that played above Mont Blanc, and listening to the rushing of the Arve, which ran below my window.

CHAPTER II

The next day, contrary to the prognostications of our guides, was fine, although clouded. We visited the source of the Arveiron, and rode about the valley until evening. These sublime and magnificent scenes afforded me the greatest consolation that I was capable of receiving. They elevated me from all littleness of feeling; and although they did not remove my grief, they subdued and tranquillized it. In some degree, also, they diverted my mind from the thoughts over which it had brooded for the last month. I returned in the evening, fatigued, but less unhappy, and conversed with my family with more cheerfulness than had been my custom for some time. My father was pleased, and Elizabeth overjoyed. 'My dear cousin,' said she, 'you see what happiness you diffuse when you are happy; do not relapse again!'

The following morning the rain poured down in torrents, and thick mists hid the summits of the mountains. I rose early, but felt unusually melancholy. The rain depressed me; my old feelings recurred, and I was miserable. I knew how disappointed my father would be at this sudden change, and I wished to avoid him until I had recovered myself so far as to be enabled to conceal those feelings that overpowered me. I knew that they would remain that day at the inn; and as I had ever inured myself to rain, moisture, and cold, I resolved to go alone to the summit of Montanvert. I remembered the effect that the view of the tremendous and ever-moving glacier had produced upon my mind when I first saw it. It had then filled me with a sublime ecstacy that gave wings to the soul, and allowed it to soar from the obscure world to light and joy. The sight of the awful and majestic in nature had indeed always the effect of solemnizing my mind, and causing me to forget the passing cares of life. I determined to go alone, for I was well acquainted with the path, and the presence of another would destroy the solitary grandeur of the scene.

The ascent is precipitous, but the path is cut into continual and short windings, which enable you to surmount the perpendicularity of the mountain. It is a scene terrifically desolate. In a thousand spots the traces of the winter avalanche may be perceived, where trees lie broken and strewed on the ground; some entirely destroyed, others bent, leaning upon the jutting rocks of the mountain, or transversely upon other trees. The path, as you ascend higher, is intersected by ravines of snow, down which stones continually roll from above; one of them is particularly dangerous, as the slightest sound, such as even speaking in a loud voice, produces a concussion of air sufficient to draw destruction upon the head of the speaker. The pines are not tall or luxuriant, but they are sombre, and add an air of severity to the scene. I looked on the valley beneath; vast mists were rising from the rivers which ran through it, and curling in thick wreaths around the opposite mountains, whose summits were hid in the uniform clouds, while rain poured from the dark sky, and added to the melancholy impression I received from the objects around me. Alas! why does man boast of sensibilities superior to those apparent in the brute; it only renders them more necessary beings.* If our impulses were confined to hunger, thirst, and desire, we might be nearly free; but now we are moved by every wind that blows, and a chance word or scene that that word may convey to us.

> We rest; a dream has power to poison sleep.
> We rise; one wand'ring thought pollutes the day.
> We feel, conceive, or reason; laugh, or weep.
> Embrace fond woe, or cast our cares away;
> It is the same: for, be it joy or sorrow,
> The path of its departure still is free.
> Man's yesterday may ne'er be like his morrow;
> Nought may endure but mutability!*

It was nearly noon when I arrived at the top of the ascent. For some time I sat upon the rock that overlooks the sea of ice. A mist covered both that and the surrounding mountains. Presently a breeze dissipated the cloud, and I descended upon the glacier. The surface is very uneven, rising like the waves of a troubled sea, descending low, and interspersed by rifts that sink deep. The field of ice is almost a league in width, but I spent nearly two hours in crossing it. The opposite mountain is a bare perpendicular rock. From the side where I now stood Montanvert was exactly opposite, at the distance of a league; and above it rose Mont Blanc, in awful majesty. I remained in a recess of the rock, gazing on this wonderful and stupendous scene. The sea, or rather the vast river of ice, wound among its dependent mountains, whose aerial summits hung over its recesses. Their icy and glittering peaks shone in the sunlight over the clouds. My heart, which was before sorrowful, now swelled with something like joy; I exclaimed – 'Wandering spirits, if indeed ye wander, and do not rest in your narrow beds, allow me this faint happiness, or take me, as your companion, away from the joys of life.'

As I said this, I suddenly beheld the figure of a man, at some distance, advancing towards me with superhuman speed. He bounded over the crevices in the ice, among which I had walked with caution; his stature also, as he approached, seemed to exceed that of man. I was troubled: a mist came over my eyes, and I felt a faintness seize me; but I was quickly restored by the cold gale of the mountains. I perceived, as the shape came nearer, (sight tremendous and abhorred!) that it was the wretch whom I had created. I trembled with rage and horror, resolving to wait his approach, and then close with him in mortal combat. He approached; his countenance bespoke bitter anguish, combined with disdain and malignity, while its unearthly ugliness rendered it almost too horrible for human eyes. But I scarcely observed this; anger and hatred had at first deprived me of utterance, and I recovered only to overwhelm him with words expressive of furious detestation and contempt.

'Devil!' I exclaimed, 'do you dare approach me? and do not you fear the fierce vengeance of my arm wreaked on your miserable head? Begone, vile insect! or rather stay, that I may trample you to dust! and, oh, that I could, with the extinction of your miserable existence, restore those victims whom you have so diabolically murdered!'

'I expected this reception,' said the demon. 'All men hate the wretched; how then must I be hated, who am miserable beyond all living things! Yet you, my creator, detest and spurn me, thy creature, to whom thou art bound by ties only dissoluble by the annihilation of one of us. You purpose to kill me. How dare you sport thus with life? Do your duty towards me, and I will do mine towards you and the rest of mankind. If you will comply with my conditions, I will leave them and you at peace; but if you refuse, I will glut the maw of death, until it be satiated with the blood of your remaining friends.'

'Abhorred monster! fiend that thou art! the tortures of hell are too mild a vengeance for thy crimes. Wretched devil! you reproach me with your creation; come on then, that I may extinguish the spark which I so negligently bestowed.'

My rage was without bounds; I sprang on him, impelled by all the feelings which can arm one being against the existence of another.

He easily eluded me, and said,

'Be calm! I entreat you to hear me, before you give vent to your hatred on my devoted head. Have I not suffered enough, that you seek to increase my misery? Life, although it may only be an accumulation of anguish, is dear to me, and I will defend it. Remember, thou hast made me more powerful than thyself; my height is superior to thine; my joints more supple. But I will not be tempted to set myself in opposition to thee. I am thy creature, and I will be ever mild and docile to my natural lord and king, if thou wilt also perform thy part, the which thou owest me. Oh, Frankenstein, be not equitable to every other, and trample upon me alone, to whom thy justice, and even thy clemency and affection, is most due. Remember, that I am thy creature: I ought to be thy Adam; but I am rather the fallen angel,* whom thou drivest from joy for no misdeed. Everywhere I see bliss, from which I alone am irrevocably excluded. I was benevolent and good; misery made me a fiend. Make me happy, and I shall again be virtuous.'

'Begone! I will not hear you. There can be no community between you and me; we are enemies. Begone, or let us try our strength in a fight, in which one must fall.'

'How can I move thee? Will no entreaties cause thee to turn a favourable eye upon thy creature, who implores thy goodness and compassion. Believe me, Frankenstein: I was benevolent; my soul glowed with love and humanity: but am I not alone, miserably alone? You, my creator, abhor me; what hope can I gather from your fellow-creatures, who owe me nothing? they spurn and hate me. The desert mountains and dreary glaciers are my refuge. I have wandered here many days; the caves of ice, which I only do not fear, are a dwelling to me, and the only one which man does not grudge. These bleak skies I hail, for they are kinder to me than your fellow-beings. If the multitude of mankind knew of my existence, they would do as you do, and arm themselves for my destruction. Shall I not then hate them who abhor me? I will keep no terms with my enemies. I am miserable, and they shall share my wretchedness. Yet it is in your power to recompense me, and deliver them from an evil which it only remains for you to make so great, that not only you and your family, but thousands of others, shall be swallowed up in the whirlwinds of its rage. Let your compassion be moved, and do not disdain me. Listen to my tale: when you have heard that, abandon or commiserate me, as you shall judge that I deserve. But hear me. The guilty are allowed, by human laws, bloody as they may be, to speak in their own defence before they are condemned. Listen to me, Frankenstein. You accuse me of murder; and yet you would, with a satisfied conscience, destroy your own creature. Oh, praise the eternal justice of man! Yet I ask you not to spare me: listen to me; and then, if you can, and if you will, destroy the work of your hands.'

'Why do you call to my remembrance circumstances of which I shudder to reflect, that I have been the miserable origin and author? Cursed be the day, abhorred devil, in which you first saw light! Cursed (although I curse myself) be the hands that formed you! You have made me wretched beyond expression. You have left me no power to consider whether I am just to you, or not. Begone! relieve me from the sight of your detested form.'

'Thus I relieve thee, my creator,' he said, and placed his hated hands before my eyes, which I flung from me with violence; 'thus I take from thee a sight which you abhor. Still thou canst listen to me, and grant me thy compassion. By the virtues that I once possessed, I demand this from you. Hear my tale; it is long and strange, and the temperature of this place is not fitting to your fine sensations; come to the hut upon the mountain. The sun is yet high in the heavens; before it descends to hide itself behind yon snowy precipices, and illuminate another world, you will have heard my story, and can decide. On you it rests, whether I quit for ever the neighbourhood of man, and lead a harmless life, or become the scourge of your fellow-creatures, and the author of your own speedy ruin.'

As he said this, he led the way across the ice: I followed. My heart was full, and I did not answer him; but, as I proceeded, I weighed the various arguments that he had used, and determined at least to listen to his tale. I was partly urged by curiosity, and compassion confirmed my resolution. I had hitherto supposed him to be the murderer of my brother, and I eagerly sought a confirmation or denial of this opinion. For the first time, also, I felt what the duties of a creator towards his creature were, and that I ought to render him happy before I complained of his wickedness. These motives urged me to comply with his demand. We crossed the ice, therefore, and ascended the opposite rock. The air was cold, and the rain again began to descend: we entered the hut, the fiend with an air of exultation, I with a heavy heart, and depressed spirits. But I consented to listen; and, seating myself by the fire which my odious companion had lighted, he thus began his tale.

CHAPTER III

'It is with considerable difficulty that I remember the original era of my being: all the events of that period appear confused and indistinct. A strange multiplicity of sensations seized me, and I saw, felt, heard, and smelt, at the same time; and it was, indeed, a long time before I learned to distinguish between the operations of my various senses. By degrees, I remember, a stronger light pressed upon my nerves, so that I was obliged to shut my eyes. Darkness then came over me, and troubled me; but hardly had I felt this, when, by opening my eyes, as I now suppose, the light poured in upon me again. I walked, and, I believe, descended; but I presently found a great alteration in my sensations. Before, dark and opaque bodies had surrounded me, impervious to my touch or sight; but I now found that I could wander on at liberty, with no obstacles which I could not either surmount or avoid. The light became more and more oppressive to me; and, the heat wearying me as I walked, I sought a place where I could receive shade. This was the forest near Ingoldstadt; and here I lay by the side of a brook resting from my fatigue, until I felt tormented by hunger and thirst. This roused me from my nearly dormant state, and I ate some berries which I found hanging on the trees, or lying on the ground. I slaked my thirst at the brook; and then lying down, was overcome by sleep.

'It was dark when I awoke; I felt cold also, and half-frightened as it were instinctively, finding myself so desolate. Before I had quitted your apartment, on a sensation of cold, I had covered myself with some clothes; but these were insufficient to secure me from the dews of night. I was a poor, helpless, miserable wretch; I knew, and could distinguish, nothing; but, feeling pain invade me on all sides, I sat down and wept.

'Soon a gentle light stole over the heavens, and gave me a sensation of pleasure. I started up, and beheld a radiant form rise from among the trees. I gazed with a kind of wonder. It moved slowly, but it enlightened my path; and I again went out in search of berries. I was still cold, when under one of the trees I found a huge cloak, with which I covered myself, and sat down upon the ground. No distinct ideas occupied my mind; all was confused. I felt light, and hunger, and thirst, and darkness; innumerable sounds rung in my ears, and on all sides various scents saluted me: the only object that I could distinguish was the bright moon, and I fixed my eyes on that with pleasure.

'Several changes of day and night passed, and the orb of night had greatly lessened when I began to distinguish my sensations from each other. I gradually saw plainly the clear stream that supplied me with drink, and the trees that shaded me with their foliage. I was delighted when I first discovered that a pleasant sound, which often saluted my ears, proceeded from the throats of the little winged animals who had often intercepted the light from my eyes. I began also to observe, with greater accuracy, the forms that surrounded me, and to perceive the boundaries of the radiant roof of light which canopied me. Sometimes I tried to imitate the pleasant songs of the birds, but was unable. Sometimes I wished to express my sensations in my own mode, but the uncouth and inarticulate sounds which broke from me frightened me into silence again.

'The moon had disappeared from the night, and again, with a lessened form, shewed itself, while I still remained in the forest. My sensations had, by this time, become distinct, and my mind received every day additional ideas. My eyes became accustomed to the light, and to perceive objects in their right forms; I distinguished the insect from the herb, and, by degrees, one herb from another. I found that the sparrow uttered none but harsh notes, whilst those of the blackbird and thrush were sweet and enticing.

'One day, when I was oppressed by cold, I found a fire which had been left by some wandering beggars, and was overcome with delight at the warmth I experienced from it. In my joy I thrust my hand into the live embers, but quickly drew it out again with a cry of pain. How strange, I thought, that the same cause should produce such opposite effects! I examined the materials of the fire, and to my joy found it to be composed of wood. I quickly collected some branches; but they were wet, and would not burn. I was pained at this, and sat still watching the operation of the fire. The wet wood which I had placed near the heat dried, and itself became inflamed. I reflected on this; and, by touching the various branches, I discovered the cause, and busied myself in collecting a great quantity of wood, that I might dry it, and have a plentiful supply of fire. When night came on, and brought sleep with it, I was in the greatest fear lest my fire should be extinguished. I covered it carefully with dry wood and leaves, and placed wet branches upon it; and then, spreading my cloak, I lay on the ground, and sunk into sleep.

'It was morning when I awoke, and my first care was to visit the fire. I uncovered it, and a gentle breeze quickly fanned it into a flame. I observed this also, and contrived a fan of branches, which roused the embers when they were nearly extinguished. When night came again, I found, with pleasure, that the fire gave light as well as heat; and that the discovery of this element was useful to me in my food; for I found some of the offals that the travellers had left had been roasted, and tasted much more savoury than the berries I gathered from the trees. I tried, therefore, to dress my food in the same manner, placing it on the live embers. I found that the berries were spoiled by this operation, and the nuts and roots much improved.

'Food, however, became scarce; and I often spent the whole day searching in vain for a few acorns to assuage the pangs of hunger. When I found this, I resolved to quit the place that I had hitherto inhabited, to seek for one where the few wants I experienced would be more easily satisfied. In this emigration, I exceedingly lamented the loss of the fire which I had obtained through accident, and knew not how to reproduce it. I gave several hours to the serious consideration of this difficulty; but I was obliged to relinquish all attempt to supply it; and, wrapping myself up in my cloak, I struck across the wood towards the setting sun. I passed three days in these rambles, and at length discovered the open country. A great fall of snow had taken place the night before, and the fields were of one uniform white; the appearance was disconsolate, and I found my feet chilled by the cold damp substance that covered the ground.

'It was about seven in the morning, and I longed to obtain food and shelter; at length I perceived a small hut, on a rising ground, which had doubtless been built for the convenience of some shepherd. This was a new sight to me; and I examined the structure with great curiosity. Finding the door open, I entered. An old man sat in it, near a fire, over which he was preparing his breakfast. He turned on hearing a noise; and, perceiving me, shrieked loudly, and, quitting the hut, ran across the fields with a speed of which his debilitated form hardly appeared capable. His appearance, different from any I had ever before seen, and his flight, somewhat surprised me. But I was enchanted by the appearance of the hut: here the snow and rain could not penetrate; the ground was dry; and it presented to me then as exquisite and divine a retreat as Pandæmonium* appeared to the dæmons of hell after their sufferings in the lake of fire. I greedily devoured the remnants of the shepherd's breakfast, which consisted of bread, cheese, milk, and wine; the latter, however, I did not like. Then, overcome by fatigue, I lay down among some straw, and fell asleep.

'It was noon when I awoke; and, allured by the warmth of the sun, which shone brightly on the white ground, I determined to recommence my travels; and, depositing the remains of the peasant's breakfast in a wallet I found, I proceeded across the fields for several hours, until at sunset I arrived at a village. How miraculous did this appear! the huts, the neater cottages, and stately houses, engaged my admiration by turns. The vegetables in the gardens, the milk and cheese that I saw placed at the windows of some of the cottages, allured my appetite. One of the best of these I entered; but I had hardly placed my foot within the door, before the children shrieked, and one of the women fainted. The whole village was roused; some fled, some attacked me, until, grievously bruised by stones and many other kinds of missile weapons, I escaped to the open country, and fearfully took refuge in a low hovel, quite bare, and making a wretched appearance after the palaces I had beheld in the village. This hovel, however, joined a cottage of a neat and pleasant appearance; but, after my late dearly-bought experience, I dared not enter it. My place of refuge was constructed of wood, but so low, that I could with difficulty sit upright in it. No wood, however, was placed on the earth, which formed the floor, but it was dry; and although the wind entered it by innumerable chinks, I found it an agreeable asylum from the snow and rain.

'Here then I retreated, and lay down, happy to have found a shelter, however miserable, from the inclemency of the season, and still more from the barbarity of man.

'As soon as morning dawned, I crept from my kennel, that I might view the adjacent cottage, and discover if I could remain in the habitation I had found. It was situated against the back of the cottage, and surrounded on the sides which were exposed by a pig-stye and a clear pool of water. One part was open, and by that I had crept in; but now I covered every crevice by which I might be perceived with stones and wood, yet in such a manner that I might move them on occasion to pass out: all the light I enjoyed came through the stye, and that was sufficient for me.

'Having thus arranged my dwelling, and carpeted it with clean straw, I retired; for I saw the figure of a man at a distance, and I remembered too well my treatment the night before, to trust myself in his power. I had first, however, provided for my sustenance for that day, by a loaf of coarse bread, which I purloined, and a cup with which I could drink, more conveniently than from my hand, of the pure water which flowed by my retreat. The floor was a little raised, so that it was kept perfectly dry, and by its vicinity to the chimney of the cottage it was tolerably warm.

'Being thus provided, I resolved to reside in this hovel, until something should occur which might alter my determination. It was indeed a paradise, compared to the bleak forest, my former residence, the rain-dropping branches, and dank earth. I ate my breakfast with pleasure, and was about to remove a plank to procure myself a little water, when I heard a step, and, looking through a small chink, I beheld a young creature, with a pail on her head, passing before my hovel. The girl was young and of gentle demeanour, unlike what I have since found cottagers and farm-house servants to be. Yet she was meanly dressed, a coarse blue petticoat and a linen jacket being her only garb; her fair hair was plaited, but not adorned; she looked patient, yet sad. I lost sight of her; and in about a quarter of an hour she returned, bearing the pail, which was now partly filled with milk. As she walked along, seemingly incommoded by the burden, a young man met her, whose countenance expressed a deeper despondence. Uttering a few sounds with an air of melancholy, he took the pail from her head, and bore it to the cottage himself. She followed, and they disappeared. Presently I saw the young man again, with some tools in his hand, cross the field behind the cottage; and the girl was also busied, sometimes in the house, and sometimes in the yard.

'On examining my dwelling, I found that one of the windows

of the cottage had formerly occupied a part of it, but the panes
had been filled up with wood. In one of these was a small and
almost imperceptible chink, through which the eye could just
penetrate. Through this crevice, a small room was visible, white-
washed and clean, but very bare of furniture. In one corner,
near a small fire, sat an old man, leaning his head on his hands
in a disconsolate attitude. The young girl was occupied in
arranging the cottage; but presently she took something out of
a drawer, which employed her hands, and she sat down beside
the old man, who, taking up an instruments began to play, and
to produce sounds, sweeter than the voice of the thrush or the
nightingale. It was a lovely sight, even to me, poor wretch! who
had never beheld aught beautiful before. The silver hair and
benevolent countenance of the aged cottager, won my reverence; while the gentle manners of the girl enticed my love. He
played a sweet mournful air, which I perceived drew tears from
the eyes of his amiable companion, of which the old man took
no notice, until she sobbed audibly; he then pronounced a few
sounds, and the fair creature, leaving her work, knelt at his feet.
He raised her, and smiled with such kindness and affection, that
I felt sensations of a peculiar and over-powering nature: they
were a mixture of pain and pleasure, such as I had never before
experienced, either from hunger or cold, warmth or food; and I
withdrew from the window, unable to bear these emotions.

'Soon after this the young man returned, bearing on his
shoulders a load of wood. The girl met him at the door, helped
to relieve him of his burden, and, taking some of the fuel into
the cottage, placed it on the fire; then she and the youth went
apart into a nook of the cottage, and he shewed her a large loaf
and a piece of cheese. She seemed pleased; and went into the
garden for some roots and plants, which she placed in water,
and then upon the fire. She afterwards continued her work,
whilst the young man went into the garden, and appeared busily
employed in digging and pulling up roots. After he had been
employed thus about an hour, the young woman joined him,
and they entered the cottage together.

'The old man had, in the mean time, been pensive; but, on
the appearance of his companions, he assumed a more cheerful
air, and they sat down to eat. The meal was quickly dispatched.
The young woman was again occupied in arranging the cottage;
the old man walked before the cottage in the sun for a few
minutes, leaning on the arm of the youth. Nothing could exceed

in beauty the contrast between these two excellent creatures. One was old, with silver hairs and a countenance beaming with benevolence and love : the younger was slight and graceful in his figure, and his features were moulded with the finest symmetry ; yet his eyes and attitude expressed the utmost sadness and despondency. The old man returned to the cottage ; and the youth, with tools different from those he had used in the morning, directed his steps across the fields.

'Night quickly shut in ; but, to my extreme wonder, I found that the cottagers had a means of prolonging light, by the use of tapers, and was delighted to find, that the setting of the sun did not put an end to the pleasure I experienced in watching my human neighbours. In the evening, the young girl and her companion were employed in various occupations which I did not understand ; and the old man again took up the instrument, which produced the divine sounds that had enchanted me in the morning. So soon as he had finished, the youth began, not to play, but to utter sounds that were monotonous, and neither resembling the harmony of the old man's instrument or the songs of the birds ; I since found that he read aloud, but at that time I knew nothing of the science of words or letters.

'The family, after having been thus occupied for a short time, extinguished their lights, and retired, as I conjectured, to rest.

CHAPTER IV

'I lay on my straw, but I could not sleep. I thought of the occurrences of the day. What chiefly struck me was the gentle manners of these people; and I longed to join them, but dared not. I remembered too well the treatment I had suffered the night before from the barbarous villagers, and resolved, whatever course of conduct I might hereafter think it right to pursue, that for the present I would remain quietly in my hovel, watching, and endeavouring to discover the motives which influenced their actions.

'The cottagers arose the next morning before the sun. The young woman arranged the cottage, and prepared the food; and the youth departed after the first meal.

'This day was passed in the same routine as that which preceded it. The young man was constantly employed out of doors, and the girl in various laborious occupations within. The old man, whom I soon perceived to be blind, employed his leisure hours on his instrument, or in contemplation. Nothing could exceed the love and respect which the younger cottagers exhibited towards their venerable companion. They performed towards him every little office of affection and duty with gentleness; and he rewarded them by his benevolent smiles.

'They were not entirely happy. The young man and his companion often went apart, and appeared to weep. I saw no cause for their unhappiness; but I was deeply affected by it. If such lovely creatures were miserable, it was less strange that I, an imperfect and solitary being, should be wretched. Yet why were these gentle beings unhappy? They possessed a delightful house (for such it was in my eyes), and every luxury; they had a fire to warm them when chill, and delicious viands* when hungry; they were dressed in excellent clothes; and, still more, they enjoyed one another's company and speech, interchanging each day looks of affection and kindness. What did their tears imply ? Did they really express pain ? I was at first unable to solve these questions ; but perpetual attention, and time, explained to me many appearances which were at first enigmatic.

'A considerable period elapsed before I discovered one of the causes of the uneasiness of this amiable family ; it was poverty : and they suffered that evil in a very distressing degree. Their nourishment consisted entirely of the vegetables of their garden, and the milk of one cow, who gave very little during the winter, when its masters could scarcely procure food to support it. They often, I believe, suffered the pangs of hunger very poignantly, especially the two younger cottagers ; for several times they placed food before the old man, when they reserved none for themselves.

'This trait of kindness moved me sensibly. I had been accustomed, during the night, to steal a part of their store for my own consumption ; but when I found that in doing this I inflicted pain on the cottagers, I abstained, and satisfied myself with berries, nuts, and roots, which I gathered from a neighbouring wood.

'I discovered also another means through which I was enabled to assist their labours. I found that the youth spent a great part of each day in collecting wood for the family fire ; and, during the night, I often took his tools, the use of which I quickly discovered, and brought home firing sufficient for the consumption of several days.

'I remember, the first time that I did this, the young woman, when she opened the door in the morning, appeared greatly astonished on seeing a great pile of wood on the outside. She uttered some words in a loud voice, and the youth joined her, who also expressed surprise. I observed, with pleasure, that he did not go to the forest that day, but spent it in repairing the cottage, and cultivating the garden.

'By degrees I made a discovery of still greater moment. I found that these people possessed a method of communicating their experience and feelings to one another by articulate sounds. I perceived that the words they spoke sometimes produced pleasure or pain, smiles or sadness, in the minds and countenances of the hearers. This was indeed a godlike science, and I ardently desired to become acquainted with it. But I was baffled in every attempt I made for this purpose. Their pronunciation was quick ; and the words they uttered, not having any apparent connexion with visible objects, I was unable to discover any clue by which I could unravel the mystery of their reference. By great

application, however, and after having remained during the
space of several revolutions of the moon in my hovel, I discovered the names that were given to some of the most familiar
objects of discourse: I learned and applied the words *fire, milk,
bread,* and *wood.* I learned also the names of the cottagers
themselves. The youth and his companion had each of them
several names, but the old man had only one, which was *father.*
The girl was called *sister,* or *Agatha*; and the youth *Felix,
brother,* or *son.* I cannot describe the delight I felt when I
learned the ideas appropriated to each of these sounds, and was
able to pronounce them. I distinguished several other words,
without being able as yet to understand or apply them; such as
good, dearest, unhappy.

'I spent the winter in this manner. The gentle manners and
beauty of the cottagers greatly endeared them to me: when they
were unhappy, I felt depressed; when they rejoiced, I sympathized in their joys. I saw few human beings beside them; and if
any other happened to enter the cottage, their harsh manners
and rude gait only enhanced to me the superior accomplishments
of my friends. The old man, I could perceive, often endeavoured
to encourage his children, as sometimes I found that he called
them, to cast off their melancholy. He would talk in a cheerful
accent, with an expression of goodness that bestowed pleasure
even upon me. Agatha listened with respect, her eyes sometimes
filled with tears, which she endeavoured to wipe away unperceived; but I generally found that her countenance and tone
were more cheerful after having listened to the exhortations of
her father. It was not thus with Felix. He was always the saddest
of the group; and, even to my unpractised senses, he appeared
to have suffered more deeply than his friends. But if his
countenance was more sorrowful, his voice was more cheerful
than that of his sister, especially when he addressed the old man.

'I could mention innumerable instances, which, although
slight, marked the dispositions of these amiable cottagers. In the
midst of poverty and want, Felix carried with pleasure to his
sister the first little white flower that peeped out from beneath
the snowy ground. Early in the morning before she had risen, he
cleared away the snow that obstructed her path to the milk-
house, drew water from the well, and brought the wood from
the out-house, where, to his perpetual astonishment, he found
his store always replenished by an invisible hand. In the day, I
believe, he worked sometimes for a neighbouring farmer,

because he often went forth, and did not return until dinner, yet brought no wood with him. At other times he worked in the garden; but, as there was little to do in the frosty season, he read to the old man and Agatha.

'This reading had puzzled me extremely at first; but, by degrees, I discovered that he uttered many of the same sounds when he read as when he talked. I conjectured, therefore, that he found on the paper signs for speech which he understood, and I ardently longed to comprehend these also; but how was that possible, when I did not even understand the sounds for which they stood as signs? I improved, however, sensibly in this science, but not sufficiently to follow up any kind of conversation, although I applied my whole mind to the endeavour: for I easily perceived that, although I eagerly longed to discover myself to the cottagers, I ought not to make the attempt until I had first become master of their language; which knowledge might enable me to make them overlook the deformity of my figure; for with this also the contrast perpetually presented to my eyes had made me acquainted.

'I had admired the perfect forms of my cottagers – their grace, beauty, and delicate complexions: but how was I terrified, when I viewed myself in a transparent pool! At first I started back, unable to believe that it was indeed I who was reflected in the mirror; and when I became fully convinced that I was in reality the monster that I am, I was filled with the bitterest sensations of despondence and mortification. Alas! I did not yet entirely know the fatal effects of this miserable deformity.

'As the sun became warmer, and the light of day longer, the snow vanished, and I beheld the bare trees and the black earth. From this time Felix was more employed; and the heart-moving indications of impending famine disappeared. Their food, as I afterwards found, was coarse, but it was wholesome; and they procured a sufficiency of it. Several new kinds of plants sprung up in the garden, which they dressed; and these signs of comfort increased daily as the season advanced.

'The old man, leaning on his son, walked each day at noon, when it did not rain, as I found it was called when the heavens poured forth its waters. This frequently took place; but a high wind quickly dried the earth, and the season became far more pleasant than it had been.

'My mode of life in my hovel was uniform. During the morning I attended the motions of the cottagers; and when they were dispersed in various occupations, I slept : the remainder of the day was spent in observing my friends. When they had retired to rest, if there was any moon, or the night was star-light, I went into the woods, and collected my own food and fuel for the cottage. When I returned, as often as it was necessary, I cleared their path from the snow, and performed those offices that I had seen done by Felix. I afterwards found that these labours, performed by an invisible hand, greatly astonished them ; and once or twice I heard them, on these occasions, utter the words *good spirit, wonderful* ; but I did not then understand the signification of these terms.

'My thoughts now became more active, and I longed to discover the motives and feelings of these lovely creatures ; I was inquisitive to know why Felix appeared so miserable, and Agatha so sad. I thought (foolish wretch !) that it might be in my power to restore happiness to these deserving people. When I slept, or was absent, the forms of the venerable blind father, the gentle Agatha, and the excellent Felix, flitted before me. I looked upon them as superior beings, who would be the arbiters of my future destiny. I formed in my imagination a thousand pictures of presenting myself to them, and their reception of me. I imagined that they would be disgusted, until, by my gentle demeanour and conciliating words, I should first win their favour, and afterwards their love.

'These thoughts exhilarated me, and led me to apply with fresh ardour to the acquiring the art of language. My organs were indeed harsh, but supple ; and although my voice was very unlike the soft music of their tones, yet I pronounced such words as I understood with tolerable ease. It was as the ass and the lap-dog ;* yet surely the gentle ass, whose intentions were affectionate, although his manners were rude, deserved better treatment than blows and execration.

'The pleasant showers and genial warmth of spring greatly altered the aspect of the earth. Men, who before this change seemed to have been hid in caves, dispersed themselves, and were employed in various arts of cultivation. The birds sang in more cheerful notes, and the leaves began to bud forth on the trees. Happy, happy earth ! fit habitation for gods, which, so short a time before, was bleak, damp, and unwholesome. My spirits were elevated by the enchanting appearance of nature ; the past was blotted from my memory, the present was tranquil, and the future gilded by bright rays of hope, and anticipations of joy.

CHAPTER V

'I now hasten to the more moving part of my story. I shall relate events that impressed me with feelings which, from what I was, have made me what I am.

'Spring advanced rapidly; the weather became fine, and the skies cloudless. It surprised me, that what before was desert and gloomy should now bloom with the most beautiful flowers and verdure. My senses were gratified and refreshed by a thousand scents of delight, and a thousand sights of beauty.

'It was on one of these days, when my cottagers periodically rested from labour – the old man played on his guitar, and the children listened to him – I observed that the countenance of Felix was melancholy beyond expression: he sighed frequently; and once his father paused in his music, and I conjectured by his manner that he inquired the cause of his son's sorrow. Felix replied in a cheerful accent, and the old man was recommencing his music, when some one tapped at the door.

'It was a lady on horseback, accompanied by a countryman as a guide. The lady was dressed in a dark suit, and covered with a thick black veil. Agatha asked a question; to which the stranger only replied by pronouncing, in a sweet accent, the name of Felix. Her voice was musical, but unlike that of either of my friends. On hearing this word, Felix came up hastily to the lady; who, when she saw him, threw up her veil, and I beheld a countenance of angelic beauty and expression. Her hair of a shining raven black, and curiosly braided; her eyes were dark, but gentle, although animated; her features of a regular proportion, and her complexion wondrously fair, each cheek tinged with a lovely pink.

'Felix seemed ravished with delight when he saw her, every trait of sorrow vanished from his face, and it instantly expressed a degree of ecstatic joy, of which I could hardly have believed it capable; his eyes sparkled, as his cheek flushed with pleasure; and at that moment I thought him as beautiful as the stranger. She appeared affected by different feelings; wiping a few tears from her lovely eyes, she held out her hand to Felix, who kissed it rapturously, and called her, as well as I could distinguish, his sweet Arabian. She did not appear to understand him, but smiled. He assisted her to dismount, and, dismissing her guide, conducted her into the cottage. Some conversation took place between him and his father; and the young stranger knelt at the old man's feet, and would have kissed his hand, but he raised her, and embraced her affectionately.

'I soon perceived, that although the stranger uttered articulate sounds, and appeared to have a language of her own, she was neither understood by, or herself understood, the cottagers. They made many signs which I did not comprehend; but I saw that her presence diffused gladness through the cottage, dispelling their sorrow as the sun dissipates the morning mists. Felix seemed peculiarly happy, and with smiles of delight welcomed his Arabian. Agatha, the ever-gentle Agatha, kissed the hands of the lovely stranger; and, pointing to her brother, made signs which appeared to me to mean that he had been sorrowful until she came. Some hours passed thus, while they, by their countenances, expressed joy, the cause of which I did not comprehend. Presently I found, by the frequent recurrence of one sound which the stranger repeated after them, that she was endeavouring to learn their language; and the idea instantly occurred to me, that I should make use of the same instructions to the same end. The stranger learned about twenty words at the first lesson, most of them indeed were those which I had before understood, but I profited by the others.

'As night came on, Agatha and the Arabian retired early. When they separated, Felix kissed the hand of the stranger, and said, "Good night, sweet Safie." He sat up much longer, conversing with his father; and, by the frequent repetition of her name, I conjectured that their lovely guest was the subject of their conversation. I ardently desired to understand them, and bent every faculty towards that purpose, but found it utterly impossible.

'The next morning Felix went out to his work; and, after the usual occupations of Agatha were finished, the Arabian sat at the feet of the old man, and, taking his guitar, played some airs so entrancingly beautiful, that they at once drew tears of sorrow and delight from my eyes. She sang, and her voice flowed in a rich cadence, swelling or dying away, like a nightingale of the woods.

'When she had finished, she gave the guitar to Agatha, who at first declined it. She played a simple air, and her voice accompanied it in sweet accents, but unlike the wondrous strain of the stranger. The old man appeared enraptured, and said some words, which Agatha endeavoured to explain to Safie, and by which he appeared to wish to express that she bestowed on him the greatest delight by her music.

'The days now passed as peaceably as before, with the sole alteration, that joy had taken place of sadness in the countenances of my friends. Safie was always gay and happy; she and I improved rapidly in the knowledge of language, so that in two months I began to comprehend most of the words uttered by my protectors.

'In the meanwhile also the black ground was covered with herbage, and the green banks interspersed with innumerable flowers, sweet to the scent and the eyes, stars of pale radiance among the moonlit woods; the sun became warmer, the nights clear and balmy; and my nocturnal rambles were an extreme pleasure to me, although they were considerably shortneed by the late setting and early rising of the sun; for I never ventured abroad during daylight, fearful of meeting with the same treatment as I had formerly endured in the first village which I entered.

'My days were spent in close attention, that I might more speedily master the language; and I may boast that I improved more rapidly than the Arabian, who understood very little, and conversed in broken accents, whilst I comprehended and could imitate almost every word that was spoken.

'While I improved in speech, I also learned the science of letters, as it was taught to the stranger; and this opened before me a wide field for wonder and delight.

'The book from which Felix instructed Safie was Volney's *Ruins of Empires.** I should not have understood the purport of this book, had not Felix, in reading it, given very minute explanations. He had chosen this work, he said, because the declamatory style was framed in imitation of the eastern authors. Through this work I obtained a cursory knowledge of history, and a view of the several empires at present existing in the world; it gave me an insight into the manners, governments, and religions of the different nations of the earth. I heard of the slothful Asiatics; of the stupendous genius and mental activity of the Grecians; of the wars and wonderful virtue of the early Romans – of their subsequent degeneration – of the decline of that mighty empire; of chivalry, christianity, and kings. I heard of the discovery of the American hemisphere, and wept with Safie over the hapless fate of its original inhabitants.

'These wonderful narrations inspired me with strange feelings. Was man, indeed, at once so powerful, so virtuous, and magnificent, yet so vicious and base? He appeared at one time a mere scion of the evil principle, and at another as all that can be conceived of noble and godlike. To be a great and virtuous man appeared the highest honour that can befall a sensitive being; to be base and vicious, as many on record have been, appeared the lowest degradation, a condition more abject than that of the blind mole or harmless worm. For a long time I could not conceive how one man could go forth to murder his fellow, or even why there were laws and governments; but when I heard details of vice and bloodshed, my wonder ceased, and I turned away with disgust and loathing.

'Every conversation of the cottagers now opened new wonders to me. While I listened to the instructions which Felix bestowed upon the Arabian, the strange system of human society was explained to me. I heard of the division of property, of immense wealth and squalid poverty; of rank, descent, and noble blood.

'The words induced me to turn towards myself. I learned that the possession most esteemed by your fellow-creatures were, high and unsullied descent united with riches. A man might be respected with only one of these acquisitions; but without either he was considered, except in very rare instances, as a vagabond and a slave, doomed to waste his powers for the profit of the chosen few. And what was I? Of my creation and creator I was absolutely ignorant; but I knew that I possessed no money, no friends, no kind of property. I was, besides, endowed with a figure hideously deformed and loathsome; I was not even of the same nature as man. I was more agile than they, and could subsist upon coarser diet; I bore the extremes of heat and cold with less injury to my frame; my stature far exceeded their's. When I looked around, I saw and heard of none like me. Was I then a monster, a blot upon the earth, from which all men fled, and whom all men disowned?

'I cannot describe to you the agony that these reflections

inflicted upon me; I tried to dispel them, but sorrow only increased with knowledge. Oh, that I had for ever remained in my native wood, nor known or felt beyond the sensations of hunger, thirst, and heat!

'Of what a strange nature is knowledge! It clings to the mind, when it has once seized on it, like a lichen on the rock. I wished sometimes to shake off all thought and feeling; but I learned that there was but one means to overcome the sensation of pain, and that was death – a state which I feared yet did not understand. I admired virtue and good feelings, and loved the gentle manners and amiable qualities of my cottagers; but I was shut out from intercourse with them, except through means which I obtained by stealth, when I was unseen and unknown, and which rather increased than satisfied the desire I had of becoming one among my fellows. The gentle words of Agatha, and the animated smiles of the charming Arabian, were not for me. The mild exhortations of the old man, and the lively conversation of the loved Felix, were not for me. Miserable, unhappy wretch!

'Other lessons were impressed upon me even more deeply. I heard of the difference of sexes; of the birth and growth of children; how the father doated on the smiles of the infant, and the lively sallies of the older child; how all the life and cares of the mother were wrapt up in the precious charge; how the mind of youth expanded and gained knowlege; of brother, sister, and all the various relationships which bind one human being to another·in mutual bonds.

'But where were my friends and relations? No father had watched my infant days, no mother had blessed me with smiles and caresses; or if they had, all my past life was now a blot, a blind vacancy in which I distinguished nothing. From my earliest remembrance I had been as I then was in height and proportion. I had never yet seen a being resembling me, or who claimed any intercourse with me. What was I? The question again recurred, to be answered only with groans.

'I will soon explain to what these feelings tended; but allow me now to return to the cottagers, whose story excited in me such various feelings of indignation, delight, and wonder, but which all terminated in additional love and reverence for my protectors (for so I loved, in an innocent, half painful self-deceit, to call them).

CHAPTER VI

'Some time elapsed before I learned the history of my friends. It was one which could not fail to impress itself deeply on my mind, unfolding as it did a number of circumstances each interesting and wonderful to one so utterly inexperienced as I was.

'The name of the old man was De Lacey. He was descended from a good family in France, where he had lived for many years in affluence, respected by his superiors, and beloved by his equals. His son was bred in the service of his country; and Agatha had ranked with ladies of the highest distinction. A few months before my arrival, they had lived in a large and luxurious city, called Paris, surrounded by friends, and possessed of every enjoyment which virtue, refinement of intellect, or taste, accompanied by a moderate fortune, could afford.

'The father of Safie had been the cause of their ruin. He was a Turkish merchant, and had inhabited Paris for many years, when some reason which I could not learn, he became obnoxious to the government. He was seized and cast into prison the very day that Safie arrived from Constantinople to join him. He was tried, and condemned to death. The injustice of his sentence was very flagrant; all Paris was indignant; and it was judged that his religion and wealth, rather than the crime alleged against him, had been the cause of his condemnation.

'Felix had been present at the trial; his horror and indignation were uncontrollable, when he heard the decision of the court. He made, at that moment, a solemn vow to deliver him, and then looked around for the means. After many fruitless attempts to gain admittance to the prison, he found a strongly grated window in an unguarded part of the building, which lighted the dungeon of the unfortunate Mahometan;* who, loaded with chains, waited in despair the execution of the barbarous sentence. Felix visited the grate at night, and made known to the prisoner his intentions in his favour. The Turk, amazed and delighted, endeavoured to kindle the zeal of his deliverer by promises of reward and wealth. Felix rejected his offers with contempt; yet when he saw the lovely Safie, who was allowed to visit her father, and who, by her gestures, expressed her lively gratitude, the youth could not help owning to his own mind, that the captive possessed a treasure which would fully reward his toil and hazard.

'The Turk quickly perceived the impression that his daughter had made on the heart of Felix, and endeavoured to secure him more entirely in his interests by the promise of her hand in marriage, so soon as he should be conveyed to a place of safety. Felix was too delicate to accept this offer; yet he looked forward to the probability of that event as to the consummation of his happiness.

'During the ensuing days, while the preparations were going forward for the escape of the merchant, the zeal of Felix was warmed by several letters that he received from this lovely girl, who found means to express her thoughts in the language of her lover by the aid of an old man, a servant of her father's, who understood French. She thanked him in the most ardent terms of his intended services towards her father; and at the same time she gently deplored her own fate.

'I have copies of these letters; for I found means, during my residence in the hovel, to procure the implements of writing; and the letters were often in the hands of Felix or Agatha. Before I depart, I will give them to you, they will prove the truth of my tale; but at present, as the sun is already far declined, I shall only have time to repeat the substance of them to you.

'Safie related, that her mother was a Christian Arab, seized and made a slave by the Turks; recommended by her beauty, she had won the heart of the father of Safie, who married her. The young girl spoke in high and enthusiastic terms of her mother, who, born in freedom spurned the bondage to which she was now reduced. She instructed her daughter in the tenets of her religion, and taught her to aspire to higher powers of intellect, and an independence of spirit, forbidden to the female followers of Mahomet. This lady died; but her lessons were indelibly impressed on the mind of Safie, who sickened at the prospect of again returning to Asia, and the being immured within the walls of a haram, allowed only to occupy herself with puerile amusements, ill suited to the temper of her soul, now accustomed to grand ideas and a noble emulation for virtue. The prospect of marrying a Christian, and remaining in a country where women were allowed to take a rank in society, was enchanting to her.

'The day for the execution of the Turk was fixed; but, on the night previous to it, he had quitted prison, and before morning was distant many leagues from Paris. Felix had procured passports in the name of his father, sister, and himself. He had previously communicated his plan to the former, who aided the deceit by quitting his house, under the pretence of a journey, and concealed himself, with his daughter, in an obscure part of Paris.

'Felix conducted the fugitives through France to Lyons, and across Mont Cenis to Leghorn, where the merchant had decided to wait a favourable opportunity of passing into some part of the Turkish dominions.

'Safie resolved to remain with her father until the moment of his departure, before which time the Turk renewed his promise that she should be united to his deliverer; and Felix remained with them in expectation of that event; and in the mean time he enjoyed the society of the Arabian, who exhibited towards him the simplest and tenderest affection. They conversed with one another through the means of an interpreter, and sometimes with the interpretation of looks; and Safie sang to him the divine airs of her native country.

'The Turk allowed this intimacy to take place, and encouraged the hopes of the youthful lovers, while in his heart he had formed far other plans. He loathed the idea that his daughter should be united to a Christian; but he feared the resentment of Felix if he should appear lukewarm; for he knew that he was still in the power of his deliverer, if he should choose to betray him to the Italian state which they inhabited. He revolved a thousand plans by which he should be enabled to prolong the deceit until it might be no longer necessary, and secretly to take his daughter with him when he departed. His plans were greatly facilitated by the news which arrived from Paris.

'The government of France were greatly enraged at the escape of their victim, and spared no pains to detect and punish his deliverer. The plot of Felix was quickly discovered, and De Lacey and Agatha were thrown into prison. The news reached Felix, and roused him from his dream of pleasure. His blind and aged father, and his gentle sister, lay in a noisome dungeon, while he enjoyed the free air, and the society of her whom he loved. This idea was torture to him. He quickly arranged with the Turk, that if the latter should find a favourable opportunity for escape before Felix could return to Italy, Safie should remain as a boarder at a convent at Leghorn; and then, quitting the lovely Arabian, he hastened to Paris, and delivered himself up to the vengeance of the law, hoping to free De Lacey and Agatha by this proceeding.

'He did not succeed. They remained confined for five months before the trial took place; the result of which deprived them of their fortune, and condemned them to a perpetual exile from their native country.

'They found a miserable asylum in the cottage in Germany, where I discovered them. Felix soon learned that the treacherous Turk, for whom he and his family endured such unheard-of oppression, on discovering that his deliverer was thus reduced to poverty and impotence, became a traitor to good feeling and honour, and had quitted Italy with his daughter, insultingly sending Felix a pittance of money to aid him, as he said, in some plan of future maintenance.

'Such were the events that preyed on the heart of Felix, and rendered him, when I first saw him, the most miserable of his family. He could have endured poverty, and when this distress had been the meed of his virtue, he would have gloried in it: but the ingratitude of the Turk, and the loss of his beloved Safie, were misfortunes more bitter and irreparable. The arrival of the Arabian now infused new life into his soul.

'When the news reached Leghorn, that Felix was deprived of his wealth and rank, the merchant commanded his daughter to think no more of her lover, but to prepare to return with him to her native country. The generous nature of Safie was outraged by this command; she attempted to expostulate with her father, but he left her angrily, reiterating his tyrannical mandate.

'A few days after, the Turk entered his daughter's apartment, and told her hastily, that he had reason to believe that his residence at Leghorn had been divulged, and that he should speedily be delivered up to the French government; he had, consequently, hired a vessel to convey him to Constantinople, for which city he should sail in a few hours. He intended to leave his daughter under the care of a confidential servant, to follow at her leisure with the greater part of his property, which had not yet arrived at Leghorn.

'When alone, Safie resolved in her own mind the plan of conduct that it would become her to pursue in this emergency. A residence in Turkey was abhorrent to her; her religion and feelings were alike adverse to it. By some papers of her father's, which fell into her hands, she heard of the exile of her lover, and learnt the name of the spot where he then resided. She hesitated some time, but at length she formed her determination. Taking with her some jewels that belonged to her, and a small sum of money, she quitted Italy, with an attendant, a native of Leghorn, but who understood the common language of Turkey, and departed for Germany.

'She arrived in safety at a town about twenty leagues from the cottage of De Lacey, when her attendant fell dangerously ill. Safie nursed her with the most devoted affection; but the poor girl died, and the Arabian was left alone, unacquainted with the language of the country, and utterly ignorant of the customs of the world. She fell, however, into good hands. The Italian had mentioned the name of the spot for which they were bound; and, after her death, the woman of the house in which they had lived took care that Safie should arrive in safety at the cottage of her lover.

CHAPTER VII

'Such was the history of my beloved cottagers. It impressed me deeply. I learned, from the views of social life which it developed, to admire their virtues, and to deprecate the vices of mankind.

As yet I looked upon crime as a distant evil; benevolence and generosity were ever present before me, inciting within me a desire to become an actor in the busy scene where so many admirable qualities were called forth and displayed. But, in giving an account of the progress of my intellect, I must not omit a circumstance which occurred in the beginning of the month of August of the same year.

'One night, during my accustomed visit to the neighbouring wood, where I collected my own food, and brought home firing for my protectors, I found on the ground a leathern portmanteau, containing several articles of dress and some books. I eagerly seized the prize, and returned with it to my hovel. Fortunately the books were written in the language the elements of which I had acquired at the cottage; they consisted of *Paradise Lost*,* a volume of *Plutarch's Lives*,* and the *Sorrows of Werter*.* The possession of these treasures gave me extreme delight; I now continually studied and exercised my mind upon these histories, whilst my friends were employed in their ordinary occupations.

'I can hardly describe to you the effect of these books. They produced in me an infinity of new images and feelings, that sometimes raised me to ecstasy, but more frequently sunk me into the lowest dejection. In the *Sorrows of Werter*, besides the interest of its simple and affecting story, so many opinions are canvassed; and so many lights thrown upon what had hitherto been to me obscure subjects, that I found in it a never-ending source of speculation and astonishment. The gentle and domestic manners it described, combined with lofty sentiments and feelings, which had for their object something out of self, accorded well with my experience among my protectors, and with the wants which were for ever alive in my own bosom. But I thought Werter himself a more divine being than I had ever beheld or imagined; his character contained no pretension, but it sunk deep. The disquisitions upon death and suicide were calculated to fill me with wonder. I did not pretend to enter into the merits of the case, yet I inclined towards the opinions of the hero, whose extinction I wept, without precisely understanding it.

'As I read, however, I applied much personally to my own feelings and condition. I found myself similar, yet at the same time strangely unlike the beings concerning whom I read, and to whose conversation I was a listener. I sympathized with, and partly understood them, but I was unformed in mind; I was dependent on none, and related to none. "The path of my departure was free;"* and there was none to lament my annihilation. My person was hideous, and my stature gigantic: what did this mean? Who was I? What was I? Whence did I come? What was my destination? These questions continually recurred, but I was unable to solve them.

'The volume of *Plutarch's Lives* which I possessed, contained the histories of the first founders of the ancient republics. This book had a far different effect upon me from the *Sorrows of Werter*. I learned from Werter's imaginations despondency and gloom: but Plutarch taught me high thoughts; he elevated me above the wretched sphere of my own reflections, to admire and love the heroes of past ages. Many things I read surpassed my understanding and experience. I had a very confused knowledge of kingdoms, wide extents of country, mighty rivers, and boundless seas. But I was perfectly unacquainted with towns, and large assemblages of men. The cottage of my protectors had been the only school in which I had studied human nature; but this book developed new and mightier scenes of action. I read of men concerned in public affairs governing or massacring their species. I felt the greatest ardour for virtue rise within me, and abhorrence for vice, as far as I understood the signification of those terms, relative as they were, as I applied them, to pleasure and pain alone. Induced by these feelings, I was of course led to admire peaceable law-givers, Numa, Solon, and Lycurgus,* to preference to Romulus and Theseus.* The patriarchal lives of my protectors caused these impressions to take a firm hold on my mind; perhaps, if my first introduction to humanity had been made by a young soldier, burning for glory and slaughter, I should have been imbued with different sensations.

'But *Paradise Lost* excited different and far deeper emotions. I read it, as I had read the other volumes which had fallen into my hands, as a true history. It moved every feeling of wonder and awe, that the picture of an omnipotent God warring with his creatures was capable of exciting. I often referred the several situations, as their similarity struck me, to my own. Like Adam, I was created apparently united by no link to any other being in existence; but his state was far different from mine in every other respect. He had come forth from the hands of God a perfect creature, happy and prosperous, guarded by the especial care of his Creator; he was allowed to converse with, and acquire knowledge from beings of a superior nature: but I was wretched, helpless, and alone. Many times I considered Satan as the fitter emblem of my condition; for often, like him, when I viewed the bliss of my protectors, the bitter gall of envy rose within me.

'Another circumstance strengthened and confirmed these feelings. Soon after my arrival in the hovel, I discovered some papers in the pocket of the dress which I had taken from your laboratory. At first I had neglected them; but now that I was able to decypher the characters in which they were written, I began to study them with diligence. It was your journal of the four months that preceded my creation. You minutely described in these papers every step you took in the progress of your work; this history was mingled with accounts of domestic occurrences. You, doubtless, recollect these papers. Here they are. Every thing is related in them which bears reference to my accursed origin; the whole detail of that series of disgusting circumstances which produced it is set in view; the minutest description of my odious and loathsome person is given, in language which painted your own horrors, and rendered mine ineffaceable. I sickened as I read. "Hateful day when I received life!" I exclaimed in agony. "Cursed creator! Why did you form a monster so hideous that even you turned from me in disgust? God in pity made man beautiful and alluring, after his own image; but my form is a filthy type of yours, more horrid from its very resemblance. Satan had his companions, fellow-devils, to admire and encourage him; but I am solitary and detested."

'These were the reflections of my hours of despondency and solitude; but when I contemplated the virtues of the cottagers, their amiable and benevolent dispositions, I persuaded myself that when they should become acquainted with my admiration of their virtues, they would compassionate me, and overlook my personal deformity. Could they turn from their door one, however monstrous, who solicited their compassion and friendship? I resolved, at least, not to despair, but in every way to fit myself for an interview with them which would decide my fate. I postponed this attempt for some months longer; for the importance attached to its success inspired me with a dread lest I should fail. Besides, I found that my understanding improved so much with every day's experience, that I was unwilling to commence this undertaking until a few more months should have added to my wisdom.

'Several changes, in the mean time, took place in the cottage. The presence of Safie diffused happiness among its inhabitants; and I also found that a greater degree of plenty reigned there. Felix and Agatha spent more time in amusement and conversation, and were assisted in their labours by servants. They did not appear rich, but they were contented and happy; their feelings were serene and peaceful, while mine became every day more tumultuous. Increase of knowledge only discovered to me more clearly what a wretched outcast I was. I cherished hope, it is true; but it vanished, when I beheld my person reflected in water, or my shadow in the moon-shine, even as that frail image and that inconstant shade.

'I endeavoured to crush these fears and to fortify myself for the trial which in a few months I resolved to undergo; and sometimes I allowed my thoughts, unchecked by reason, to ramble in the fields of Paradise, and dared to fancy amiable and lovely creatures sympathizing with my feelings and cheering my gloom; their angelic countenances breathed smiles of consolation. But it was all a dream: no Eve soothed my sorrows, or shared my thoughts; I was alone. I remembered Adam's supplication to his Creator; but where was mine? he had abandoned me, and, in the bitterness of my heart, I cursed him.

'Autumn passed thus. I saw, with surprise and grief, the leaves decay and fall, and nature again assume the barren and bleak appearance it had worn when I first beheld the woods and the lovely moon. Yet I did not heed the bleakness of the weather; I was better fitted by my conformation for the endurance of cold than heat. But my chief delights were the sight of the flowers, the birds, and all the gay apparel of summer; when those deserted me, I turned with more attention towards the cottagers. Their happiness was not decreased by the absence of summer. They loved, and sympathized with one another; and their joys, depending on each other, were not interrupted by the casualties that took place around them. The more I saw of them, the greater became my desire to claim their protection and kindness; my heart yearned to be known and loved by these amiable creatures: to see their sweet looks turned towards me with affection, was the utmost limit of my ambition. I dared not think that they would turn them from me with disdain and horror. The poor that stopped at their door were never driven away. I asked, it is true, for greater treasures than a little food or rest; I required kindness and sympathy; but I did not believe myself utterly unworthy of it.

'The winter advanced, and an entire revolution of the seasons had taken place since I awoke into life. My attention, at this time, was solely directed towards my plan of introducing myself into the cottage of my protectors. I revolved* many projects; but that on which I finally fixed was, to enter the dwelling when the blind old man should be alone. I had sagacity enough to discover, that the unnatural hideousness of my person was the chief object of horror with those who had formerly beheld me. My voice, although harsh, had nothing terrible in it; I thought, therefore, that if, in the absence of his children, I could gain the good-will and mediation of the old De Lacy, I might, by his means, be tolerated by my younger protectors.

'One day, when the sun shone on the red leaves that strewed the ground, and diffused cheerfulness, although it denied warmth, Safie, Agatha, and Felix, departed on a long country walk, and the old man, at his own desire, was left alone in the cottage. When his children had departed, he took up his guitar, and played several mournful, but sweet airs, more sweet and mournful than I had ever heard him play before. At first his countenance was illuminated with pleasure, but, as he continued, thoughtfulness and sadness succeeded; at length, laying aside the instrument, he sat absorbed in reflection.

'My heart beat quick; this was the hour and moment of trial which would decide my hopes, or realize my fears. The servants were gone to a neighbouring fair. All was silent in and around the cottage: it was an excellent opportunity; yet, when I proceeded to execute my plan, my limbs failed me, and I sunk to the ground. Again I rose; and, exerting all the firmness of which I was master, removed the planks which I had placed before my hovel to conceal my retreat. The fresh air revived me, and, with renewed determination, I approached the door of their cottage.

'I knocked. "Who is there?" said the old man – "Come in."

'I entered; "Pardon this intrusion," said I, "I am a traveller in want of a little rest; you would greatly oblige me, if you would allow me to remain a few minutes before the fire."

' "Enter," said De Lacy; "and I will try in what manner I can relieve your wants; but, unfortunately, my children are from home, and, as I am blind, I am afraid I shall find it difficult to procure food for you."

' "Do not trouble yourself, my kind host, I have food; it is warmth and rest only that I need."

'I sat down, and silence ensued. I knew that every minute was precious to me, yet I remained irresolute in what manner to commence the interview; when the old man addressed me –

' "By your language, stranger, I suppose you are my countryman; – are you French?"

' "No; but I was educated by a French family, and understand that language only. I am now going to claim the protection of some friends, whom I sincerely love, and of whose favour I have some hopes."

' "Are these Germans?"

' "No, they are French. But let us change the subject. I am an unfortunate and deserted creature; I look around, and I have no relation or friend upon earth. These amiable people to whom I go have never seen me, and know little of me. I am full of fears; for if I fail there, I am an outcast in the world for ever."

' "Do not despair. To be friendless is indeed to be unfortunate; but the hearts of men, when unprejudiced by any obvious self-interest, are full of brotherly love and charity. Rely, therefore, on your hopes; and if these friends are good and amiable, do not despair."

' "They are kind – they are the most excellent creatures in the world; but, unfortunately, they are prejudiced against me. I have good dispositions; my life has been hitherto harmless, and, in some degree, beneficial; but a fatal prejudice clouds their eyes, and where they ought to see a feeling and kind friend, they behold only a detestable monster."

' "That is indeed unfortunate; but if you are really blameless, cannot you undeceive them?"

' "I am about to undertake that task; and it is on that account that I feel so many overwhelming terrors. I tenderly love these friends; I have, unknown to them, been for many months in the habits of daily kindness towards them; but they believe that I wish to injure them, and it is that prejudice which I wish to overcome."

' "Where do these friends reside?"

' "Near this spot."

'The old man paused, and then continued, "If you will unreservedly confide to me the particulars of your tale, I perhaps may be of use in undeceiving them. I am blind, and cannot judge of your countenance, but there is something in your words which persuades me that you are sincere. I am poor, and an exile; but it will afford me true pleasure to be in any way serviceable to a human creature."

' "Excellent man! I thank you, and accept your generous offer. You raise me from the dust by this kindness; and I trust that, by your aid, I shall not be driven from the society and sympathy of your fellow-creatures.

' "Heaven forbid! even if you were really criminal; for that can only drive you to desperation, and not instigate you to virtue. I also am unfortunate; I and my family have been condemned, although innocent: judge, therefore, if I do not feel for your misfortunes."

' "How can I thank you, my best and only benefactor? from your lips first have I heard the voice of kindness directed towards me; I shall be for ever grateful; and your present humanity assures me of success with those friends whom I am on the point of meeting."

' "May I know the names and residence of those friends?"

'I paused. This, I thought, was the moment of decision, which was to rob me of, or bestow happiness on me for ever. I struggled vainly for firmness sufficient to answer him, but the effort destroyed all my remaining strength; I sank on the chair, and sobbed aloud. At that moment I heard the steps of my younger protectors. I had not a moment to lose; but, seizing the hand of the old man, I cried, "Now is the time! — save and protect me! You and your family are the friends whom I seek. Do not you desert me in the hour of trial!"

' "Great God!" exclaimed the old man, "who are you?"

'At that instant the cottage door was opened, and Felix, Safie and Agatha entered. Who can describe their horror and consternation on beholding me ? Agatha fainted; and Safie, unable to attend to her friend, rushed out of the cottage. Felix darted forward, and with supernatural force tore me from his father, to whose knees I clung: in a transport of fury, he dashed me to the ground, and struck me violently with a stick. I could have torn him limb from limb, as the lion rends the antelope. But my heart sunk within me as with bitter sickness, and I refrained. I saw him on the point of repeating his blow, when, overcome by pain and anguish, I quitted the cottage, and in the general tumult escaped unperceived to my hovel.

CHAPTER VIII

'Cursed, cursed creator! Why did I live? Why, in that instant, did I not extinguish the spark of existence which you had so wantonly bestowed? I know not; despair had not yet taken possession of me; my feelings were those of rage and revenge. I could with pleasure have destroyed the cottage and its inhabitants, and have glutted myself with their shrieks and misery.

'When night came, I quitted my retreat, and wandered in the wood; and now, no longer restrained by the fear of discovery, I gave vent to my anguish in fearful howlings. I was like a wild beast that had broken the toils;* destroying the objects that obstructed me, and ranging through the wood with a stag-like swiftness. Oh! what a miserable night I passed! the cold stars shone in mockery, and the bare trees waved their branches above me: now and then the sweet voice of a bird burst forth amidst the universal stillness. All, save I, were at rest or in enjoyment: I, like the arch fiend, bore a hell within me;* and, finding myself unsympathized with, wished to tear up the trees, spread havoc and destruction around me, and then to have sat down and enjoyed the ruin.

'But this was a luxury of sensation that could not endure; I became fatigued with excess of bodily exertion, and sank on the damp grass in the sick impotence of despair. There was none among the myriads of men that existed who would pity or assist me; and should I feel kindness towards my enemies? No: from that moment I declared everlasting war against the species, and, more than all, against him who had formed me, and sent me forth to this unsupportable misery.

'The sun rose; I heard the voices of men, and knew that it was impossible to return to my retreat during that day. Accordingly I hid myself in some thick underwood, determining to devote the ensuing hours to reflection on my situation.

'The pleasant sunshine, and the pure air of day, restored me to some degree of tranquillity; and when I considered what had passed at the cottage, I could not help believing that I had been too hasty in my conclusions. I had certainly acted imprudently. It was apparent that my conversation had interested the father in my behalf, and I was a fool in having exposed my person to the horror of his children. I ought to have familiarized the old De Lacey to me, and by degrees have discovered myself to the rest of his family, when they should have been prepared for my approach. But I did not believe my errors to be irretrievable; and, after much consideration, I resolved to return to the cottage, seek the old man, and by my representations win him to my party.

'These thoughts calmed me, and in the afternoon I sank into a profound sleep; but the fever of my blood did not allow me to be visited by peaceful dreams. The horrible scene of the preceding day was for ever acting before my eyes; the females were flying, and the enraged Felix tearing me from his father's feet. I awoke exhausted; and, finding that it was already night, I crept forth from my hiding-place, and went in search of food.

'When my hunger was appeased, I directed my steps towards the well-known path that conducted to the cottage. All there was at peace. I crept into my hovel, and remained in silent expectation of the accustomed hour when the family arose. That hour past, the sun mounted high in the heavens, but the cottagers did not appear. I trembled violently, apprehending some dreadful misfortune. The inside of the cottage was dark, and I heard no motion; I cannot describe the agony of this suspence.

'Presently two countrymen passed by; but, pausing near the cottage, they entered into conversation, using violent gesticulations; but I did not understand what they said, as they spoke the language of the country, which differed from that of my protectors. Soon after, however, Felix approached with another man: I was surprised, as I knew that he had not quitted the cottage that morning, and waited anxiously to discover, from his discourse, the meaning of these unusual appearances.

' "Do you consider," said his companion to him, "that you will be obliged to pay three months' rent, and to lose the produce of your garden? I do not wish to take any unfair advantage, and I beg therefore that you will take some days to consider of your determination."

'"It is utterly useless," replied Felix, "we can never again inhabit your cottage. The life of my father is in the greatest danger, owing to the dreadful circumstance that I have related. My wife and my sister will never recover their horror. I entreat you not to reason with me any more. Take possession of your tenement, and let me fly from this place."

'Felix trembled violently as he said this. He and his companion entered the cottage, in which they remained for a few minutes, and then departed. I never saw any of the family of De Lacey more.

'I continued for the remainder of the day in my hovel in a state of utter and stupid despair. My protectors had departed, and had broken the only link that held me to the world. For the first time the feelings of revenge and hatred filled my bosom, and I did not strive to controul them ; but, allowing myself to be borne away by the stream, I bent my mind towards injury and death. When I thought of my friends, of the mild voice of De Lacey, the gentle eyes of Agatha, and the exquisite beauty of the Arabian, these thoughts vanished, and a gush of tears somewhat soothed me. But again, when I reflected that they had spurned and deserted me, anger returned, a rage of anger ; and, unable to injure anything human, I turned my fury towards inanimate objects. As night advanced, I placed a variety of combustibles around the cottage ; and, after having destroyed every vestige of cultivation in the garden, I waited with forced impatience until the moon had sunk to commence my operations.

'As the night advanced, a fierce wind arose from the woods, and quickly dispersed the clouds that had loitered in the heavens : the blast tore along like a mighty avalanche, and produced a kind of insanity in my spirits, that burst all bounds of reason and reflection. I lighted the dry branch of a tree, and danced with fury around the devoted cottage, my eyes still fixed on the western horizon, the edge of which the moon nearly touched. A part of its orb was at length hid, and I waved my brand ; it sunk, and, with a loud scream, I fired the straw, and heath, and bushes, which I had collected. The wind fanned the fire, and the cottage was quickly enveloped by the flames, which clung to it, and licked it with their forked and destroying tongues.

'As soon as I was convinced that no assistance could save any part of the habitation, I quitted the scene, and sought for refuge in the woods.

'And now, with the world before me, whither should I bend my steps? I resolved to fly far from the scene of my misfortunes; but to me, hated and depised, every country must be equally horrible. At length the thought of you crossed my mind. I learned from your papers that you were my father, my creator; and to whom could I apply with more fitness than to him who had given me life? Among the lessons that Felix had bestowed upon Safie geography had not been omitted: I had learned from these the relative situations of the different countries of the earth. You had mentioned Geneva as the name of your native town; and towards this place I resolved to proceed.

'But how was I to direct myself? I knew that I must travel in a south-westerly direction to reach my destination; but the sun was my only guide. I did not know the names of the towns that I was to pass through, nor could I ask information from a single human being; but I did not despair. From you only could I hope for succour, although towards you I felt no sentiment but that of hatred. Unfeeling, heartless creator! you had endowed me with perceptions and passions, and then cast me abroad an object for the scorn and horror of mankind. But on you only had I any claim for pity and redress, and from you I determined to seek that justice which I vainly attempted to gain from any other being that wore the human form.

'My travels were long, and the sufferings endured intense. It was late in autumn when I quitted the district where I had so long resided. I travelled only at night, fearful of encountering the visage of a human being. Nature decayed around me, and the sun became heatless; rain and snow poured around me; mighty rivers were frozen; the surface of the earth was hard, and chill, and bare, and I found no shelter. Oh, earth! how often did I imprecate curses on the cause of my being! The mildness of my nature had fled, and all within me was turned to gall and bitterness. The nearer I approached to your habitation, the more deeply did I feel the spirit of revenge enkindled in my heart. Snow fell, and the waters were hardened, but I rested not. A few incidents now and then directed me, and I possessed a map of the country; but I often wandered wide from my path. The agony of my feelings allowed me no respite: no incident occurred from which my rage and misery could not extract its food; but a circumstance that happened when I arrived on the confines of Switzerland, when the sun had recovered it warmth, and the earth again began to look green, confirmed in an especial manner the bitterness and horror of my feelings.

'I generally rested during the day, and travelled only when I was secured by night from the view of man. One morning, however, finding that my path lay through a deep wood, I ventured to continue my journey after the sun had risen; the day, which was one of the first of spring, cheered even me by the loveliness of its sunshine and the balminess of the air. I felt emotions of gentleness and pleasure, that had long appeared dead, revive within me. Half surprised by the novelty of these sensations, I allowed myself to be borne away by them; and, forgetting my solitude and deformity, dared to be happy. Soft tears again bedewed my cheeks, and I even raised my humid eyes with thankfulness towards the blessed sun which bestowed such joy upon me.

'I continued to wind among the paths of the wood, until I came to its boundary, which was skirted by a deep and rapid river, into which many of the trees bent their branches, now budding with the fresh spring. Here I paused, not exactly knowing what path to pursue, when I heard the sound of voices, that induced me to conceal myself under the shade of a cypress. I was scarcely hid, when a young girl came running towards the spot where I was concealed, laughing as if she ran from some one in sport. She continued her course along the precipitous sides of the river, when suddenly her foot slipt; and she fell into the rapid stream. I rushed from my hiding place, and, with extreme labour from the force of the current, saved her, and dragged her to shore. She was senseless; and I endeavoured, by every means in my power, to restore animation, when I was suddenly interrupted by the approach of a rustic, who was probably the person from whom she had playfully fled. On seeing me, he darted towards me, and, tearing the girl from my arms, hastened towards the deeper parts of the wood. I followed speedily, I hardly knew why; but when the man saw me draw near, he aimed a gun, which he carried, at my body, and fired. I sunk to the ground, and my injurer, with increased swiftness, escaped into the woods.

'This was then the reward of my benevolence! I had saved a human being from destruction, and, as a recompense, I now writhed under the miserable pain of a wound, which shattered the flesh and bone. The feelings of kindness and gentleness, which I had entertained but a few moments before, gave place to hellish rage and gnashing of teeth. Inflamed by pain, I vowed eternal hatred and vengeance to all mankind. But the agony of my wound overcame me ; my pulses paused, and I fainted.

'For some weeks I led a miserable life in the woods, endeavouring to cure the wound which I had received. The ball had entered my shoulder, and I knew not whether it had remained there or passed through ; at any rate I had no means of extracting it. My sufferings were augmented also by the oppressive sense of the injustice and ingratitude of their infliction. My daily vows rose for revenge – a deep and deadly revenge, such as would alone compensate for the outrages and anguish I had endured.

'After some weeks my wound healed, and I continued my journey. The labours I endured were no longer to be alleviated by the bright sun or gentle breezes of spring ; all joy was but a mockery, which insulted my desolate state, and made me feel more painfully that I was not made for the enjoyment of pleasure.

'But my toils now drew near a close ; and, two months from this time, I reached the environs of Geneva.

'It was evening when I arrived, and I retired to a hiding-place among the fields that surround it, to meditate in what manner I should apply to you. I was oppressed by fatigue and hunger, and far too unhappy to enjoy the gentle breezes of evening, or the prospect of the sun setting behind the stupendous mountains of Jura.

'At this time a slight sleep relieved me from the pain of reflection, which was disturbed by the approach of a beautiful child, who came running into the recess I had chosen with all the sportiveness of infancy. Suddenly, as I gazed on him, an idea seized me, that this little creature was unprejudiced, and had lived too short a time to have imbibed a horror of deformity. If, therefore, I could seize him, and educate him as my companion and friend, I should not be so desolate in this peopled earth.

'Urged by this impulse, I seized on the boy as he passed, and drew him towards me. As soon as he beheld my form, he placed his hands before his eyes, and uttered a shrill scream : I drew his hand forcibly from his face, and said, "Child, what is the meaning of this ? I do not intend to hurt you ; listen to me."

'He struggled violently ; "Let me go," he cried ; "monster ! ugly wretch ! you wish to eat me, and tear me to pieces – You are an ogre – Let me go, or I will tell my papa."

' "Boy, you will never see your father again; you must come with me."

' "Hideous monster! let me go; My papa is a Syndic – he is M. Frankenstein – he would punish you. You dare not keep me."

' "Frankenstein! you belong then to my enemy – to him towards whom I have sworn eternal revenge; you shall be my first victim."

'The child still struggled, and loaded me with epithets which carried despair to my heart: I grasped his throat to silence him, and in a moment he lay dead at my feet.

'I gazed on my victim, and my heart swelled with exultation and hellish triumph: clapping my hands, I exclaimed, "I, too, can create desolation; my enemy is not impregnable; this death will carry despair to him, and a thousand other miseries shall torment and destroy him."

'As I fixed my eyes on the child, I saw something glittering on his breast. I took it; it was a portrait of a most lovely woman. In spite of my malignity, it softened and attracted me. For a few moments I gazed with delight on her dark eyes, fringed by deep lashes, and her lovely lips; but presently my rage returned: I remembered that I was for ever deprived of the delights that such beautiful creatures could bestow; and that she whose resemblance I contemplated would, in regarding me, have changed that air of divine benignity to one expressive of disgust and affright.

'Can you wonder that such thoughts transported me with rage? I only wonder that at that moment, instead of venting my sensations in exclamations and agony, I did not rush among mankind, and perish in the attempt to destroy them.

'While I was overcome by these feelings, I left the spot where I had committed the murder, and was seeking a more secluded hiding-place, when I perceived a woman passing near me. She was young, not indeed so beautiful as her whose portrait I held, but of an agreeable aspect, and blooming in the loveliness of youth and health. Here, I thought, is one of those whose smiles are bestowed on all but me; she shall not escape: thanks to the lessons of Felix, and the sanguinary* laws of man, I have learned how to work mischief. I approached her unperceived, and placed the portrait securely in one of the folds of her dress.

'For some days I haunted the spot where these scenes had taken place; sometimes wishing to see you, sometimes resolved to quit the world and its miseries for ever. At length I wandered towards these mountains, and have ranged through their immense recesses, consumed by a burning passion which you alone can gratify. We may not part until you have promised to comply with my requisition. I am alone, and miserable; man will not associate with me; but one as deformed and horrible as myself would not deny herself to me. My companion must be of the same species, and have the same defects. This being you must create.'

CHAPTER IX

The being finished speaking, and fixed his looks upon me in expectation of a reply. But I was bewildered, perplexed, and unable to arrange my ideas sufficiently to understand the full extent of his proposition. He continued –

'You must create a female for me, with whom I can live in the interchange of those sympathies necessary for my being. This you alone can do; and I demand it of you as a right which you must not refuse.'

The latter part of his tale had kindled anew in me the anger that had died away while he narrated his peaceful life among the cottagers, and as he said this, I could no longer suppress the rage that burned within me.

'I do refuse it,' I replied; 'and no torture shall ever extort a consent from me. You may render me the most miserable of men, but you shall never make me base in my own eyes. Shall I create another like yourself, whose joint wickedness might desolate the world. Begone! I have answered you; you may torture me, but I will never consent.'

'You are in the wrong,' replied the fiend; 'and, instead of threatening, I am content to reason with you. I am malicious because I am miserable; am I not shunned and hated by all mankind? You, my creator, would tear me to pieces, and triumph; remember that, and tell me why I should pity man more than he pities me? You would not call it murder, if you could precipitate me into one of those ice-rifts, and destroy my frame, the work of your own hands. Shall I respect man, when he contemns* me? Let him live with me in the interchange of kindness, and, instead of injury, I would bestow every benefit upon him with tears of gratitude at his acceptance. But that cannot be; the human senses are insurmountable barriers to our union. Yet mine shall not be the submission of abject slavery. I will revenge my injuries: if I cannot inspire love, I will cause fear; and chiefly towards you my arch-enemy, because my creator, do I swear inextinguishable hatred. Have a care: I will work at your destruction, nor finish until I desolate your heart, so that you curse the hour of your birth.'

A fiendish rage animated him as he said this; his face was wrinkled into contortions too horrible for human eyes to behold; but presently he calmed himself, and proceeded –

'I intended to reason. This passion is detrimental to me; for you do not reflect that you are the cause of its excess. If any being felt emotions of benevolence towards me, I should return them an hundred and an hundred-fold; for that one creature's sake, I would make peace with the whole kind! But I now indulge in dreams of bliss that cannot be realized. What I ask of you is reasonable and moderate; I demand a creature of another sex, but as hideous as myself: the gratification is small, but it is all that I can receive, and it shall content me. It it true, we shall be monsters, cut off from all the world; but on that account we shall be more attached to one another. Our lives will not be happy, but they will be harmless, and free from the misery I now feel. Oh! my creator, make me happy; let me feel gratitude towards you for one benefit! Let me see that I excite the sympathy of some existing thing; do not deny me my request!'

I was moved. I shuddered when I thought of the possible consequences of my consent; but I felt that there was some justice in his argument. His tale, and the feelings he now expressed, proved him to be a creature of fine sensations; and did I not, as his maker, owe him all the portion of happiness that it was in my power to bestow? He saw my change of feeling, and continued –

'If you consent, neither you nor any other human being shall ever see us again: I will go to the vast wilds of South America. My food is not that of man; I do not destroy the lamb and the kid, to glut my appetite; acorns and berries afford me sufficient nourishment. My companion will be of the same nature as myself, and will be content with the same fare. We shall make our bed of dried leaves; the sun will shine on us as on man, and will ripen our food. The picture I present to you is peaceful and human, and you must feel that you could deny it only in the wantonness of power and cruelty. Pitiless as you have been towards me, I now see compassion in your eyes; let me seize the favourable moment, and persuade you to promise what I so ardently desire.'

'You propose,' replied I, 'to fly from the habitations of man, to dwell in those wilds where the beasts of the field will be your only companions. How can you, who long for the love and sympathy of man, persevere in this exile ? You will return, and again seek their kindness, and you will meet with their detestation ; your evil passions will be renewed, and you will then have a companion to aid you in the task of destruction. This may not be ; cease to argue the point, for I cannot consent.'

'How inconstant are your feelings ! but a moment ago you were moved by my representations, and why do you again harden yourself to my complaints ? I swear to you, by the earth which I inhabit, and by you that made me, that, with the companion you bestow, I will quit the neighbourhood of man, and dwell, as it may chance, in the most savage of places. My evil passions will have fled, for I shall meet with sympathy ; my life will flow quietly away, and, in my dying moments, I shall not curse my maker.'

His words had a strange effect upon me. I compassionated him, and sometimes felt a wish to console him ; but when I looked upon him, when I saw the filthy mass that moved and talked, my heart sickened, and my feelings were altered to those of horror and hatred. I tried to stifle these sensations ; I thought, that as I could not sympathize with him, I had no right to withhold from him the small portion of happiness which was yet in my power to bestow.

'You swear,' I said, 'to be harmless ; but have you not already shewn a degree of malice that should reasonably make me distrust you ? May not even this be a feint that will increase your triumph by affording a wider scope for your revenge ?'

'How is this ? I thought I had moved your compassion, and yet you still refuse to bestow on me the only benefit that can soften my heart, and render me harmless. If I have no ties and no affections, hatred and vice must be my portion ; the love of another will destroy the cause of my crimes, and I shall become a thing of whose existence every one will be ignorant. My vices are the children of a forced solitude that I abhor ; and my virtues will necessarily arise when I live in communion with an equal. I shall feel the affections of a sensitive being, and become linked to the chain of existence and events, from which I am now excluded.'

I paused some time to reflect on all he had related, and the various arguments which he had employed. I thought of the promise of virtues which he had displayed on the opening of his existence, and the subsequent blight of all kindly feeling by the loathing and scorn which his protectors had manifested towards him. His power and threats were not omitted in my calculations: a creature who could exist in the ice caves of the glaciers, and hide himself from pursuit among the ridges of inaccessible precipices, was a being possessing faculties it would be vain to cope with. After a long pause of reflection, I concluded, that the justice due both to him and my fellow-creatures demanded of me that I should comply with his request. Turning to him, therefore, I said —

'I consent to your demand, on your solemn oath to quit Europe for ever, and every other place in the neighbourhood of man, as soon as I shall deliver into your hands a female who will accompany you in your exile.'

'I swear,' he cried, 'by the sun, and by the blue sky of heaven, that if you grant my prayer, while they exist you shall never behold me again. Depart to your home, and commence your labours: I shall watch their progress with unutterable anxiety; and fear not but that when you are ready I shall appear.'

Saying this, he suddenly quitted me, fearful, perhaps, of any change in my sentiments. I saw him descend the mountain with greater speed than the flight of an eagle, and quickly lost him among the undulations of the sea of ice.

His tale had occupied the whole day; and the sun was upon the verge of the horizon when he departed. I knew that I ought to hasten my descent towards the valley, as I should soon be encompassed in darkness; but my heart was heavy, and my steps slow. The labour of winding among the little paths of the mountains, and fixing my feet firmly as I advanced, perplexed me, occupied as I was by the emotions which the occurrences of the day had produced. Night was far advanced, when I came to the half-way resting-place, and seated myself beside the fountain. The stars shone at intervals, as the clouds passed from over them; the dark pines rose before me, and every here and there a broken tree lay on the ground: it was a scene of wonderful solemnity, and stirred strange thoughts within me. I wept bitterly; and, clasping my hands in agony, I exclaimed, 'Oh! stars, and clouds, and winds, ye are all about to mock me: if ye really pity me, crush sensation and memory; let me become as nought; but if not, depart, depart and leave me in darkness.'

These were wild and miserable thoughts; but I cannot describe to you how the eternal twinkling of the stars weighed upon me, and how I listened to every blast of wind, as if it were a dull ugly siroc* on its way to consume me.

Morning dawned before I arrived at the village of Chamounix; but my presence, so haggard and strange, hardly calmed the fears of my family, who had waited the whole night in anxious expectation of my return.

The following day we returned to Geneva. The intention of my father in coming had been to divert my mind, and to restore me to my lost tranquillity; but the medicine had been fatal. And, unable to account for the excess of misery I appeared to suffer, he hastened to return home, hoping the quiet and monotony of a domestic life would by degrees alleviate my sufferings from whatsoever cause they might spring.

For myself, I was passive in all their arrangements; and the gentle affection of my beloved Elizabeth was inadequate to draw me from the depth of my despair. The promise I had made to the dæmon weighed upon my mind, like Dante's iron cowl* on the heads of the hellish hypocrites. All pleasures of earth and sky passed before me like a dream, and that thought only had to me the reality of life. Can you wonder, that sometimes a kind of insanity possessed me, or that I saw continually about me a multitude of filthy animals inflicting on me incessant torture, that often extorted screams and bitter groans?

By degrees, however, these feelings became calmed. I entered again into the every-day scene of life, if not with interest, at least with some degree of tranquillity.

END OF VOL. II

FRANKENSTEIN
Volume III

CHAPTER I

Day after day, week after week, passed away on my return to Geneva; and I could not collect the courage to recommence my work. I feared the vengeance of the disappointed fiend, yet I was unable to overcome my repugnance to the task which was enjoined me. I found that I could not compose a female without again devoting several months to profound study and laborious disquisition. I had heard of some discoveries having been made by an English philosopher, the knowledge of which was material to my success, and I sometimes thought of obtaining my father's consent to visit England for this purpose; but I clung to every pretence of delay, and could not resolve to interrupt my returning tranquillity. My health, which had hitherto declined, was now much restored; and my spiritis, when unchecked by the memory of my unhappy promise, rose proportionably. My father saw this change with pleasure, and he turned his thoughts towards the best method of eradicating the remains of my melancholy, which every now and then would return by fits, and with a devouring blackness overcast the approaching sunshine. At these moments I took refuge in the most perfect solitude. I passed whole days on the lake alone in a little boat, watching the clouds, and listening to the rippling of the waves, silent and listless. But the fresh air and bright sun seldom failed to restore me to some degree of composure; and, on my return, I met the salutations of my friends with a readier smile and a more cheerful heart.

It was after my return from one of these rambles that my father, calling me aside, thus addressed me :-

'I am happy to remark, my dear son, that you have resumed your former pleasures, and seem to be returning to yourself. And yet you are still unhappy, and still avoid our society. For some time I was lost in conjecture as to the cause of this; but yesterday an idea struck me, and if it is well founded, I conjure you to avow it. Reserve on such a point would be not only useless, but draw down treble misery on us all.'

I trembled violently at this exordium and my father continued –

'I confess, my son, that I have always looked forward to your marriage with your cousin as the tie of our domestic comfort, and the stay of my declining years. You were attached to each other from your earliest infancy, you studied together, and appeared, in dispositions and tastes, entirely suited to one another. But so blind is the experience of man, that what I conceived to be the best assistants to my plan may have entirely destroyed it. You, perhaps, regard her as your sister without any wish that she might become your wife. Nay, you may have met with another whom you may love and, considering yourself as bound in honour to your cousin, this struggle may occasion the poignant misery which you appear to feel.'

'My dear father, re-assure yourself. I love my cousin tenderly and sincerely. I never saw any woman who excited, as Elizabeth does, my warmest admiration and affection. My future hopes and prospects are entirely bound up in the expectation of our union.'

'The expression of your sentiments on this subject, my dear Victor, gives me more pleasure than I have for sometime experienced. If you feel thus, we shall assuredly be happy, however present events may cast a gloom over us. But it is this gloom, which appears to have taken so strong a hold of your mind, that I wish to dissipate. Tell me, therefore, whether you object to an immediate solemnization of the marriage. We have been unfortunate, and recent events have drawn us from that every-day tranquillity befitting my years and infirmities. You are younger; yet I do not suppose, possessed as you are of a competent future, that an early marriage would at all interfere with any future plans of honour and utility that you may have formed. Do not suppose, however, that I wish to dictate happiness to you, or that a delay on your part would cause me any serious uneasiness. Interpret my words with candour, and answer me, I conjure you, with confidence and sincerity.'

I listened to my father in silence, and remained for some time incapable of offering any reply. I revolved rapidly in my mind a multitude of thoughts, and endeavoured to arrive at some conclusion. Alas! to me the idea of an immediate union with my cousin was one of horror and dismay. I was bound by a solemn promise, which I had not yet fulfilled, and dared not break; or, if I did, what manifold miseries might not impend over me and my devoted family! Could I enter into a festival with this deadly weight yet hanging round my neck, and bowing me to the ground. I must perform my engagement, and let the monster depart with his mate, before I allowed myself to enjoy the delight of an union from which I expected peace.

I remembered also the necessity imposed upon me of either journeying to England, or entering into a long correspondence with those philosophers of that country, whose knowledge and discoveries were of indispensable use to me in my present undertaking. The latter method of obtaining the desired intelligence was dilatory and unsatisfactory: besides, any variation was agreeable to me, and I was delighted with the idea of spending a year or two in change of scene and variety of occupation, in absence of my family; during which period some event might happen which would restore me to them in peace and happiness: my promise might be fulfilled, and the monster have departed; or some accident might occur to destroy him, and put an end to my slavery for ever.

These feelings dictated my answer to my father. I expressed a wish to visit England; but, concealing the true reasons of this request, I clothed my desires under the guise of wishing to travel and see the world before I sat down for life within the walls of my native town.

I urged my entreaty with earnestness, and my father was easily induced to comply; for a more indulgent and less dictatorial parent did not exist upon earth. Our plan was soon arranged. I should travel to Strasbourg, where Clerval would join me. Some short time would be spent in the towns of Holland, and our principal stay would be in England. We should return by France; and it was agreed that the tour should occupy the space of two years.

My father pleased himself with the reflection, that my union with Elizabeth should take place immediately on my return to Geneva. 'These two years,' said he, 'will pass swiftly, and it will be the last delay that will oppose itself to your happiness. And, indeed, I earnestly desire that period to arrive, when we shall all be united, and neither hopes or fears arise to disturb our domestic calm.'

'I am content,' I replied, 'with your arrangement. By that time we shall both have become wiser, and I hope happier, than we at present are.' I sighed; but my father kindly forbore to question me further concerning the cause of my dejection. He hoped that new scenes, and the amusement of travelling, would restore my tranquillity.

I now made arrangements for my journey; but one feeling haunted me, which filled me with fear and agitation. During my absence I should leave my friends unconscious of the existence of their enemy, and unprotected from his attacks, exasperated as he might be by my departure. But he had promised to follow me wherever I might go; and would he not accompany me to England? This imagination was dreadful in itself, but soothing, inasmuch as it supposed the safety of my friends. I was agonized with the idea of the possibility that the reverse of this might happen. But through the whole period during which I was the slave of my creature, I allowed myself to be governed by the impulses of the moment; and my present sensations strongly intimated that the fiend would follow me, and exempt my family from the danger of his machinations.

It was in the latter end of Angust that I departed, to pass two years of exile. Elizabeth approved of the reasons of my departure, and only regretted that she had not the same opportunities of enlarging her experience, and cultivating her understanding. She wept, however, as she bade me farewell, and entreated me to return happy and tranquil. 'We all,' said she, 'depend upon you; and if you are miserable, what must be our feelings?'

I threw myself into the carriage that was to convey me away, hardly knowing whither I was going, and careless of what was passing around. I remembered only, and it was with a bitter anguish that I reflected on it, to order that my chemical instruments should be packed to go with me: for I resolved to fulfil my promise while abroad, and return, if possible, a free man. Filled with dreary imaginations, I passed through many beautiful and majestic scenes; but my eyes were fixed and unobserving. I could only think of the bourne* of my travels, and the work which was to occupy me whilst they endured.

After some days spent in listless indolence, during which I traversed many leagues, I arrived at Strasbourg, where I waited two days for Clerval. He came. Alas, how great was the contrast between us! He was alive to every new scene; joyful when he saw the beauties of the setting sun, and more happy when he beheld it rise, and recommence a new day. He pointed out to me the shifting colours of the landscape, and the appearances of the sky. 'This is what it is to live;' he cried, 'now I enjoy existence! But you, my dear Frankenstein, wherefore are you desponding and sorrowful?' In truth, I was occupied by gloomy thoughts, and neither saw the descent of the evening star, nor the golden sun-rise reflected in the Rhine. – And you, my friend, would be far more amused with the journal of Clerval, who observed the scenery with an eye of feeling and delight, than to listen to my reflections. I, a miserable wretch, haunted by a curse that shut up every avenue to enjoyment.

We had agreed to descend the Rhine in a boat from Strasbourg to Rotterdam, whence we might take shipping for London. During this voyage, we passed by many willowy islands, and saw several beautiful towns. We staid a day at Manheim, and, on the fifth from our departure from Strasbourg, arrived at Mayence. The course of the Rhine below Mayence becomes much more picturesque. The river descends rapidly, and winds between hills, not high, but steep, and of beautiful forms. We saw many ruined castles standing on the edges of precipices, surrounded by black woods, high and inaccessible. This part of the Rhine, indeed, presents a singularly variegated landscape. In one spot you view rugged hills, ruined castles overlooking tremendous precipices, with the dark Rhine rushing beneath; and, on the sudden turn of a promontory, flourishing vineyards, with green sloping banks, and a meandering river, and populous towns, occupy the scene.

We travelled at the time of the vintage, and heard the song of the labourers, as we glided down the stream. Even I, depressed in mind, and my spirits continually agitated by gloomy feelings, even I was pleased. I lay at the bottom of the boat, and, as I gazed on the cloudless blue sky, I seemed to drink in a tranquillity to which I had long been a stranger. And if these were my sensations, who can describe those of Henry? He felt as if he had been transported to Fairy-land, and enjoyed a happiness seldom tasted by man. 'I have seen,' he said, 'the most beautiful scenes of my own country; I have visited the lakes of Lucerne and Uri, where the snowy mountains descend almost perpendicularly to the water, casting black and impenetrable shades, which would cause a gloomy and mournful appearance, were it not for the most verdant islands that relieve the eye by their gay appearance; I have seen this lake agitated by a tempest, when the wind tore up whirlwinds of water, and gave you an idea of what the water-spout must be on the great ocean, and the waves dash with fury the base of the mountain, where the priest and his mistress were overwhelmed by an avalanche, and where their dying voices are still said to be heard amid the pauses of the nightly wind; I have seen the mountains of La Valais, and the Pays de Vaud : but this country, Victor, pleases me more than all those wonders. The mountains of Switzerland are more majestic and strange; but there is a charm in the banks of this divine river, that I never before saw equalled. Look at that castle which overhangs yon precipice; and that also on the island, almost concealed amongst the foliage of those lovely trees; and now that group of labourers coming from among their vines; and that village half-hid in the recess of the mountain. Oh, surely, the spirit that inhabits and guards this place has a soul more in harmony with man, than those who pile the glacier, or retire to the inaccessible peaks of the mountains of our own country.'

Clerval ! beloved friend ! even now it delights me to record your words, and to dwell on the praise of which you are so eminently deserving. He was a being formed in the 'very poetry of nature.*' His wild and enthusiastic imagination was chastened by the sensibility of his heart. His soul over-flowed with ardent affections, and his friendship was of that devoted and wondrous nature that the worldly-minded teach us to look for only in the imagination. But even human sympathies were not sufficient to satisfy his eager mind. The scenery of external nature, which others regard only with admiration, he loved with ardour :

> 'The sounding cataract
> Haunted *him* like a passion; the tall rock,
> The mountain, and the deep and gloomy wood,
> Their colours and their forms, were then to him
> An appetite; a feeling, and a love,
> That had no need of a remoter charm,
> By thought supplied, or any interest
> Unborrowed from the eye.'†

And where does he now exist ? Is this gentle and lovely being lost for ever ? Has this mind so replete with ideas, imaginations

* Leigh Hunt's 'Rimini.'
† Wordsworth's 'Tintern Abbey.'

fanciful and magnificent, which formed a world, whose existence depended on the life of its creator ; has this mind perished ? Does it now only exist in my memory ? No, it is not thus ; your form so divinely wrought, and beaming with beauty, has decayed, but your spirit still visits and consoles your unhappy friend.

Pardon this gush of sorrow ; these ineffectual words are but a slight tribute to the unexampled worth of Henry, but they soothe my heart, overflowing with the anguish which his remembrance creates. I will proceed with my tale.

Beyond Cologne we descended to the plains of Holland ; and we resolved to post* the remainder of our way ; for the wind was contrary, and the stream of the river was too gentle to aid us.

Our journey here lost the interest arising from beautiful scenery ; but we arrived in a few days at Rotterdam, whence we proceeded by sea to England. It was on a clear morning, in the latter days of December, that I first saw the white cliffs of Britain. The banks of the Thames presented a new scene ; they were flat, but fertile, and almost every town was marked by the remembrance of some story. We saw Tilbury Fort, and remembered the Spanish armada ; Gravesend, Woolwich, and Greenwich, places which I had heard of even in my country.

At length we saw the numerous steeples of London, St Paul's towering above all, and the Tower famed in English history.

CHAPTER II

London was our present point of rest; we determined to remain several months in this wonderful and celebrated city. Clerval desired the intercourse of the men of genius and talent who flourished at this time; but this was with me a secondary object; I was principally occupied with the means of obtaining the information necessary for the completion of my promise, and quickly availed myself of the letters of introduction, that I had brought with me, addressed to the most distinguished natural philosophers.

If this journey had taken place during my days of study and happiness, it would have afforded me inexpressible pleasure. But a blight had come over my existence, and I only visited these people for the sake of the information they might give me on the subject in which my interest was so terribly profound. Company was irksome to me; when alone, I could fill my mind with the sights of heaven and earth; the voice of Henry soothed me, and I could thus cheat myself into a transitory peace. But busy uninteresting joyous faces brought back despair to my heart. I saw an insurmountable barrier placed between me and my fellow-men; this barrier was sealed with the blood of William and Justine; and to reflect on the events connected with those names filled my soul with anguish.

But in Clerval I saw the image of my former self; he was inquisitive, and anxious to gain experience and instruction. The difference of manners which he observed was to him an inexhaustible source of instruction and amusement. He was for ever busy; and the only check to his enjoyments was my sorrowful and dejected mien. I tried to conceal this as much as possible, that I might not debar him from the pleasures natural to one who was entering on a new scene of life, undisturbed by any care or bitter recollection. I often refused to accompany him, alleging another engagement, that I might remain alone. I now also began to collect the materials necessary for my new creation, and this was to me like the torture of single drops of water continually falling on the head. Every thought that was devoted to it was an extreme anguish, and every word that I spoke in allusion to it caused my lips to quiver, and my heart to palpitate.

After passing some months in London, we received a letter from a person in Scotland, who had formerly been our visitor at Geneva. He mentioned the beauties of his native country, and asked us if those were not sufficient allurements to induce us to prolong our journey as far north as Perth, where he resided. Clerval eagerly desired to accept this invitation; and I, although I abhorred society, wished to view again mountains and streams, and all the wondrous works with which Nature adorns her chosen dwelling-places.

We had arrived in England at the beginning of October, and it was now February. We accordingly determined to commence our journey towards the north at the expiration of another month. In this expedition we did not intend to follow the great road to Edinburgh, but to visit Windsor, Oxford, Matlock, and the Cumberland lakes, resolving to arrive at the completion of this tour about the end of July. I packed my chemical instruments, and the materials I had collected, resolving to finish my labours in some obscure nook in the northern highlands of Scotland.

We quitted London on the 27th of March, and remained a few days at Windsor, rambling in its beautiful forest. This was a new scene to us mountaineers; the majestic oaks, the quantity of game, and the herds of stately deer, were all novelties to us.

From thence we proceeded to Oxford. As we entered this city, our minds were filled with the remembrance of the events that had been transacted there more than a century and a half before. It was here that Charles I, had collected his forces.* This city had remained faithful to him, after the whole nation had forsaken his cause to join the standard of parliament and liberty. The memory of that unfortunate king, and his companions, the amiable Falkland, the insolent Goring, his queen, and son, gave a peculiar interest to every part of the city, which they might be supposed to have inhabited. The spirit of elder days found a dwelling here, and we delighted to trace its footsteps. If these feelings had not found an imaginary gratification, the appearance of the city had yet in itself sufficient beauty to obtain our admiration. The colleges are ancient and picturesque; the streets are almost magnificent; and the lovely Isis, which flows besides it through meadows of exquisite verdure, is spread forth into a placid expanse of waters, which reflects its majestic assemblage of towers, and spires, and domes, embosomed among aged trees.

I enjoyed this scene; and yet my enjoyment was embittered both by the memory of the past, and the anticipation of the future. I was formed for peaceful happiness. During my youthful days discontent never visited my mind; and if I was ever overcome by *ennui*,* the sight of what is beautiful in nature, or the study of what is excellent and sublime in the productions of man, could always interest my heart, and communicate elasticity to my spirits. But I am a blasted tree; the bolt has entered my soul; and I felt then that I should survive to exhibit, what I shall soon cease to be – a miserable spectacle of wrecked humanity, pitiable to others, and abhorrent to myself.

We passed a considerable period at Oxford, rambling among its environs, and endeavouring to identify every spot which might relate to the most animating epoch of English history. Our little voyages of discovery were often prolonged by the successive objects that presented themselves. We visited the tomb of the illustrious Hampden,* and the field on which that patriot fell. For a moment my soul was elevated from its debasing and miserable fears to contemplate the divine ideas of liberty and self-sacrifice, of which these sights were the monuments and the remembrancers. For an instant I dared to shake off my chains, and look around me with a free and lofty spirit; but the iron had eaten into my flesh, and I sank again, trembling and hopeless, into my miserable self.

We left Oxford with regret, and proceeded to Matlock, which was our next place of rest. The country in the neighbourhood of this village resembled, to a greater degree, the scenery of Switzerland; but every thing is on a lower scale, and the green hills want the crown of distant white Alps, which always attend on the piny mountains of my native country. We visited the wondrous cave, and the little cabinets of natural history, where the curiosities are disposed in the same manner as in the collections at Servox and Chamounix. The latter name made me tremble, when prounounced by Henry; and I hastened to quit Matlock, with which that terrible scene was thus associated.

From Derby still journeying northward, we passed two months in Cumberland and Westmoreland. I could now almost fancy myself among the Swiss mountains. The little patches of snow which yet lingered on the northern sides of the mountains, the lakes, and the dashing of the rocky streams, were all familiar and dear sights to me. Here also we made some acquaintances, who almost contrived to cheat me into happiness. The delight of Clerval was proportionably greater than mine; his mind expanded in the company of men of talent, and he found in his own nature greater capacities and resources than he could have imagined himself to have possessed while he associated with his inferiors. 'I could pass my life here,' said he to me; 'and among these mountains I should scarcely regret Switzerland and the Rhine.'

But he found that a traveller's life is one that includes much pain amidst its enjoyments. His feelings are for ever on the stretch; and when he begins to sink into repose, he finds himself obliged to quit that on which he rests in pleasure for something new, which again engages his attention, and which also he forsakes for other novelties.

We had scarcely visited the various lakes of Cumberland and Westmoreland, and conceived an affection for some of the inhabitants, when the period of our appointment with our Scotch friend approached, and we left them to travel on. For my own part I was not sorry. I had now neglected my promise for some time, and I feared the effects of the demon's disappointment. He might remain in Switzerland, and wreak his vengeance on my relatives. This idea pursued me, and tormented me at every moment from which I might otherwise have snatched repose and peace. I waited for my letters with feverish impatience: if they were delayed, I was miserable, and overcome by a thousand fears; and when they arrived, and I saw the superscription of Elizabeth or my father, I hardly dared to read and ascertain my fate. Sometimes I thought that the fiend followed me, and might expedite my remissness by murdering my companion. When these thoughts possessed me, I would not quit Henry for a moment, but followed him as his shadow, to protect him from the fancied rage of his destroyer. I felt as if I had committed some great crime, the consciousness of which haunted me. I was guiltless, but I had indeed drawn down a horrible curse upon my head, as mortal as that of crime.

I visited Edinburgh with languid eyes and mind; and yet that city might have interested the most unfortunate being. Clerval did not like it so well as Oxford; for the antiquity of the latter city was more pleasing to him. But the beauty and regularity of the new town of Edinburgh, its romantic castle, and its environs, the most delightful in the world, Arthur's Seat, St Bernard's Well, and the Pentland Hills, compensated him for the change, and filled him with cheerfulness and admiration. But I was impatient to arrive at the termination of my journey.

We left Edinburgh in a week, passing through Coupar, St Andrews, and along the banks of the Tay, to Perth, where our friend expected us. But I was in no mood to laugh and talk with strangers, or enter into their feelings or plans with the good humour expected from a guest; and accordingly I told Clerval that I wished to make the tour of Scotland alone. 'Do you,' said I, 'enjoy yourself, and let this be our rendezvous. I may be absent a month or two; but do not interfere with my motions, I entreat you: leave me to peace and solitude for a short time; and when I return, I hope it will be with a lighter heart, more congenial to your own temper.'

Henry wished to dissuade me; but, seeing me bent on this plan, ceased to remonstrate. He entreated me to write often. 'I had rather be with you,' he said, 'in your solitary rambles, than with these Scotch people, whom I do not know: hasten then, my dear friend, to return, that I may again feel myself somewhat at home, which I cannot do in your absence.'

Having parted from my friend, I determined to visit some remote spot of Scotland, and finish my work in solitude. I did not doubt but that the monster followed me, and would discover himself to me when I should have finished, that he might receive his companion.

With this resolution I traversed the northern highlands, and fixed on one of the remotest of the Orkneys as the scene labours. It was a place fitted for such a work, being hardly more than a rock, whose high sides were continually beaten upon by the waves. The soil was barren, scarcely affording pasture for a few miserable cows, and oatmeal for its inhabitants, which consisted of five persons, whose gaunt and scraggy limbs gave tokens of their miserable fare. Vegetables and bread, when they indulged in such luxuries, and even fresh water, was to be procured from the main land, which was about five miles distant.

On the whole island there were but three miserable huts, and one of these was vacant when I arrived. This I hired. It contained but two rooms, and these exhibited all the squalidness of the most miserable penury. The thatch had fallen in, the walls were unplastered, and the door was off its hinges. I ordered it to be repaired, bought some furniture, and took possession; an incident which would, doubtless, have occasioned some surprise, had not all the senses of the cottagers been benumbed by want and squalid poverty. As it was, I lived ungazed at and unmolested, hardly thanked for the pittance of food and clothes which I gave; so much does suffering blunt even the coarsest sensations of men.

In this retreat I devoted the morning to labour; but in the evening, when the weather permitted, I walked on the stony beach of the sea, to listen to the waves as they roared, and dashed at my feet. It was a monotonous, yet ever-changing scene. I thought of Switzerland; it was far different from this desolate and appalling landscape. Its hills are covered with vines, and its cottages are scattered thickly in the plains. Its fair lakes reflect a blue and gentle sky; and, when troubled by the winds, their tumult is but as the play of a lively infant, when compared to the roarings of the giant ocean.

In this manner I distributed my occupations when I first arrived; but, as I proceeded in my labour, it became every day more horrible and irksome to me. Sometimes I could not prevail on myself to enter my laboratory for several days; and at other times I toiled day and night in order to complete my work. It was indeed a filthy process in which I was engaged. During my first experiment, a kind of enthusiastic frenzy had blinded me to the horror of my employment; my mind was intently fixed on the sequel of my labour, and my eyes were shut to the horror of my proceedings. But now I went to it in cold blood, and my heart often sickened at the work of my hands.

Thus situated, employed in the most detestable occupation, immersed in a solitude where nothing could for an instant call my attention from the actual scene in which I was engaged, my spirits became unequal; I grew restless and nervous. Every moment I feared to meet my persecutor. Sometimes I sat with my eyes fixed on the ground, fearing to raise them lest they should encounter the object which I so much dreaded to behold. I feared to wander from the sight of my fellow-creatures, lest when alone he should come to claim his companion.

In the mean time I worked on, and my labour was already considerably advanced. I looked towards its completion with a tremulous and eager hope, which I dared not trust myself to question, but which was intermixed with obscure forebodings of evil, that made my heart sicken in my bosom.

I sat one evening in my laboratory; the sun had set, and the moon was just rising from the sea; I had not sufficient light for my employment, and I remained idle, in a pause of consideration of whether I should leave my labour for the night, or hasten its conclusion by an unremitting attention to it. As I sat, a train of reflection occurred to me, which led me to consider the effects of what I was now doing. Three years before I was engaged in the same manner, and had created a fiend whose unparalleled barbarity had desolated my heart, and filled it for ever with the bitterest remorse. I was now about to form another being, of whose dispositions I was alike ignorant; she might become ten thousand times more malignant than her mate, and delight, for its own sake, in murder and wretchedness. He had sworn to quit the neighbourhood of man, and hide himself in deserts; but she had not; and she, who in all probability was to become a thinking and reasoning animal, might refuse to comply with a compact made before her creation. They might even hate each other; the creature who already lived loathed his own deformity, and might he not conceive a greater abhorence for it when it came before his eyes in the female form? She also might turn with disgust from him to the superior beauty of man; she might quit him, and he be again alone, exasperated by the fresh provocation of being deserted by one of his own species.

Even if they were to leave Europe, and inhabit the deserts of the new world, yet one of the first results of those sympathies for which the dæmon thirsted would be children, and a race of devils would be propagated upon the earth, who might make the very existence of the species of man a condition precarious and full of terror. Had I a right, for my own benefit, to inflict this curse upon everlasting, generations? I had before been moved by the sophisms* of the being I had created; I had been struck senseless by his fiendish threats : but now, for the first time, the wickedness of my promise burst upon me ; I shuddered to think that future ages might curse me as their pest, whose selfishness had not hesitated to buy its own peace at the price perhaps of the existence of the whole human race.

I trembled, and my heart failed within me : when, on looking up, I saw, by the light of the moon, the dæmon at the casement. A ghastly grin wrinkled his lips as he gazed on me, where I sat fulfilling the task which he had allotted to me. Yes, he had followed me in my travels ; he had loitered in forests, hid himself in caves, or taken refuge in wide and desert heaths ; and he now came to mark my progress, and claim the fulfilment of my promise.

As I looked on him, his countenance expressed the utmost extent of malice and treachery. I thought with a sensation of madness on my promise of creating another like to him, and, trembling with passion, tore to pieces the thing on which I was engaged. The wretch saw me destroy the creature on whose future existence he depended for happiness, and, with a howl of devilish despair and revenge, withdrew.

I left the room, and, locking the door, made a solemn vow in my own heart never to resume my labours ; and then, with trembling steps, I sought my own apartment. I was alone ; none were near me to dissipate the gloom, and relieve me from the sickening oppression of the most terrible reveries.

Several hours past, and I remained near my window gazing on the sea ; it was almost motionless, for the winds were hushed, and all nature reposed under the eye of the quiet moon. A few fishing vessels alone specked the water, and now and then the gentle breeze wafted the sound of voices, as the fishermen called to one another. I felt the silence, although I was hardly conscious of its extreme profundity until my ear was suddenly arrested by the paddling of oars near the shore, and a person landed close to my house.

In a few minutes after, I heard the creaking of my door, as if some one endeavoured to open it softly. I trembled from head to foot ; I felt a presentiment of who it was, and wished to rouse one of the peasants who dwelt in a cottage not far from mine ; but I was overcome by the sensation of helplessness, so often felt in frightful dreams, when you in vain endeavour to fly from an impending danger, and was rooted to the spot.

Presently I heard the sound of footsteps along the passage ;

the door opened, and the wretch whom I dreaded appeared.
Shutting the door, he approached me, and said, in a smothered
voice —

'You have destroyed the work which you began; what is it
that you intend? Do you dare to break your promise? I have
endured toil and misery: I left Switzerland with you; I crept
along the shores of the Rhine, among its willow islands, and
over the summits of its hills. I have dwelt many months in the
heaths of England, and among the deserts of Scotland. I have
endured incalculable fatigue, and cold, and hunger; do you dare
destroy my hopes?'

'Begone! I do break my promise; never will I create another
like yourself, equal in deformity and wickedness.'

'Slave, I before reasoned with you, but you have proved
yourself unworthy of my condescension. Remember that I have
power; you believe yourself miserable, but I can make you so
wretched that the light of day will be hateful to you. You are
my creator, but I am your master; — obey!'

'The hour of my weakness is past, and the period of your
power is arrived. Your threats cannot move me to do an act of
wickedness; but they confirm me in a resolution of not creating
you a companion in vice. Shall I, in cool blood, set loose upon
the earth a dæmon, whose delight is in death and wretchedness.
Begone! I am firm, and your words will only exasperate my
rage.'

The monster saw my determination in my face, and gnashed
his teeth in the impotence of anger. 'Shall each man,' cried he,
'find a wife for his bosom, and each beast have his mate, and I
be alone? I had feelings of affection, and they were requited by
detestation and scorn. Man, you may hate; but beware! Your
hours will pass in dread and misery, and soon the bolt will fall
which must ravish from you your happiness for ever. Are you to
be happy, while I grovel in the intensity of my wretchedness?
You can blast my other passions; but revenge remains — revenge,
henceforth dearer then light or food! I may die; but first you,
my tyrant and tormentor, shall curse the sun that gazes on your
misery. Beware; for I am fearless, and therefore powerful. I will
watch with the wiliness of a snake, that I may sting with its
venom. Man, you shall repent of the injuries you inflict.'

'Devil, cease; and do not poison the air with these sounds of
malice. I have declared my resolution to you, and I am no
coward to bend beneath words. Leave me; I am inexorable.'

'It is well. I go; but remember, I shall be with you on your wedding-night.'

I started forward, and exclaimed, 'Villain! before you sign my death-warrant, be sure that you are yourself safe.'

I would have seized him; but he eluded me, and quitted the house with precipitation: in a few moments I saw him in his boat, which shot across the waters with an arrowy swiftness, and was soon lost amidst the waves.

All was again silent; but his words rung in my ears. I burned with rage to pursue the murderer of my peace, and precipitate him into the ocean. I walked up and down my room hastily and perturbed, while my imagination conjured up a thousand images to torment and sting me. Why had I not followed him, and closed with him in mortal strife? But I had suffered him to depart, and he had directed his course towards the main land. I shuddered to think who might be the next victim sacrificed to his insatiate revenge. And then I thought again of his words – '*I will be with you on your wedding-night.*' That then was the period fixed for the fulfilment of my destiny. In that hour I should die, and at once satisfy and extinguish his malice. The prospect did not move me to fear; yet when I thought of my beloved Elizabeth, – of her tears and endless sorrow, when she should find her lover so barbarously snatched from her, – tears, the first I had shed for many months, streamed from my eyes, and I resolved not to fall before my enemy without a bitter struggle.

The night passed away, and the sun rose from the ocean; my feelings became calmer, if it may be called calmness, when the violence of rage sinks into the depths of despair. I left the house, the horrid scene of the last night's contention, and walked on the beach of the sea, which I almost regarded as an insuperable barrier between me and my fellow-creatures; nay, a wish that such should prove the fact stole across me. I desired that I might pass my life on that barren rock, wearily it is true, but uninterrupted by any sudden shock of misery. If I returned, it was to be sacrificed, or to see those whom I most loved die under the grasp of a dæmon whom I had myself created.

I walked about the isle like a restless spectre, separated from all it loved, and miserable in the separation. When it became noon, and the sun rose higher, I lay down on the grass, and was overpowered by a deep sleep. I had been awake the whole of the preceding night, my nerves were agitated, and my eyes inflamed by watching and misery. The sleep into which I now sunk refreshed me; and when I awoke, I again felt as if I belonged to a race of human beings like myself, and I began to reflect upon what had passed with greater composure; yet still the words of the fiend rung in my ears like a death-knell, they appeared like a dream, yet distinct and oppressive as a reality.

The sun had far descended, and I still sat on the shore, satisfying my appetite, which had become ravenous, with an oaten cake, when I saw a fishing-boat land close to me, and one of the men brought me a packet; it contained letters from Geneva, and one from Clerval, entreating me to join him. He said that nearly a year had elapsed since we had quitted Switzerland, and France was yet unvisited. He entreated me, therefore, to leave my solitary isle, and meet him at Perth, in a week from that time, when we might arrange the plan of our future proceedings. This letter in a degree recalled me to life, and I determined to quit my island at the expiration of two days.

Yet, before I departed, there was a task to perform, on which I shuddered to reflect: I must pack my chemical instruments; and for that purpose I must enter the room which had been the scene of my odious work, and I must handle those utensils, the sight of which was sickening to me. The next morning, at day-break, I summoned sufficient courage, and unlocked the door of my laboratory. The remains of the half-finished creature, whom I had destroyed, lay scattered on the floor, and I almost felt as if I had mangled the living flesh of a human being. I paused to collect myself, and then entered the chamber. With trembling hand I conveyed the instruments out of the room; but I reflected that I ought not to leave the relics of my work to excite the horror and suspicion of the peasants, and I accordingly put them into a basket, with a great quantity of stones, and laying them up, determined to throw them into the sea that very night; and in the mean time I sat upon the beach, employed in cleaning and arranging my chemical apparatus.

Nothing could be more complete than the alteration that had taken place in my feelings since the night of the appearance of the dæmon. I had before regarded my promise with a gloomy despair, as a thing that, with whatever consequences must be fulfilled; but I now felt as if a film had been taken from before my eyes, and that I, for the first time, saw clearly. The idea of renewing my labours did not for one instant occur to me; the threat I had heard weighed on my thoughts, but I did not reflect that a voluntary act of mine could avert it. I had resolved in my own mind, that to create another like the fiend I had first made would be an act of the basest and most atrocious selfishness; and I banished from my mind every thought that could lead to a different conclusion.

Between two and three in the morning the moon rose; and then, putting my basket aboard a little skiff, sailed out about four miles from the shore. The scene was perfectly solitary: a few boats were returning towards land, but I sailed away from them. I felt as if I was about the commission of a dreadful crime, and avoided with shuddering anxiety any encounter with my fellow-creatures. At one time the moon, which had before been clear, was suddenly overspread by a thick cloud, and I took advantage of the moment of darkness, and cast my basket into the sea; I listened to the gurgling sound as it sunk, and then sailed away from the spot. The sky became clouded; but the air was pure, although chilled by the north-east breeze that was then rising. But it refreshed me, and filled me with such agreeable sensations, that I resolved to prolong my stay on the water, and fixing the rudder in a direct position, stretched myself at the bottom of the boat. Clouds hid the moon, every thing was obscure, and I heard only the sound of the boat, as its keel cut through the waves; the murmur lulled me, and in a short time I slept soundly.

I do not know how long I remained in this situation, but when I awoke I found that the sun had already mounted considerably. The wind was high, and the waves continually threatened the safety of my little skiff. I found that the wind was north-east, and must have driven me far from the coast from which I had embarked. I endeavoured to change my course, but quickly found that if I again made the attempt the boat would be instantly filled with water. Thus situation, my only resource was to drive before the wind. I confess that I felt a few sensations of terror. I had no compass with me, and was so little acquainted with the geography of this part of the world that the sun was of little benefit to me. I might be driven into the wide Atlantic, and feel all the tortures of starvation, or be swallowed up in the immeasurable waters that roared and buffeted around me. I had already been out many hours, and felt the torment of a burning thirst, a prelude to my other sufferings. I looked on the heavens, which were covered by clouds that flew before the wind only to be replaced by others: I looked upon the sea, it was to be my grave. 'Fiend,' I exclaimed, 'your task is already fulfilled!' I thought of Elizabeth, of my father, and of Clerval; and sunk into a reverie, so despairing and frightful, that even now, when the scene is on the point of closing before me for ever, I shudder to reflect on it.

Some hours passed thus; but by degrees, as the sun declined towards the horizon, the wind died away into a gentle breeze, and the sea became free from breakers. But these gave place to a heavy swell; I felt sick, and hardly able to hold the rudder, when suddenly I saw a line of high land towards the south.

Almost spent, as I was, by fatigue, and the dreadful suspense I endured for several hours, this sudden certainty of life rushed like a flood of warm joy to my heart, and tears gushed from my eyes.

How mutable are our feelings, and how strange is that clinging love we have of life even in the excess of misery! I constructed another sail with a part of my dress, and eagerly steered my course towards the land. It had a wild and rocky appearance; but as I approached nearer, I easily perceived the traces of cultivation. I saw vessels near the shore, and found myself suddenly transported back to the neighbourhood of civilized man. I eagerly traced the windings of the land, and hailed a steeple which I at length saw issuing from behind a small promontory. As I was in a state of extreme debility, I resolved to sail directly towards the town as a place where I could most easily procure nourishment. Fortunately I had money with me. As I turned the promontory, I perceived a small neat town and a good harbour; which I entered, my heart bounding with joy at my unexpected escape.

As I was occupied in fixing the boat and arranging the sails, several people crowded towards the spot. They seemed very much surprised at my appearance; but, instead of offering me any assistance, whispered together with gestures that at any other time might have produced in me a slight sensation of alarm. As it was, I merely remarked that they spoke English; and I therefore addressed them in that language: 'My good friends,' said I, 'will you be so kind as to tell me the name of this town, and inform me where I am?'

'You will know that soon enough,' replied a man with a gruff voice. 'Maybe you are come to a place that will not prove much to your taste; but you will not be consulted as to your quarters, I promise you.'

I was exceedingly surprised on receiving so rude an answer from a stranger; and I was also disconcerted on perceiving the frowning and angry countenances of his companions. 'Why do you answer me so roughly?' I replied: 'surely it is not the custom of Englishmen to receive strangers so inhospitably.'

'I do not know,' said the man, 'what the custom of the English may be; but it is the custom of the Irish to hate villains.'

While this strange dialogue continued, I perceived the crowd rapidly increase. Their faces expressed a mixture of curiosity and anger, which annoyed, and in some degree alarmed me. I inquired the way to the inn; but no one replied. I then moved forward, and a murmuring sound arose from the crowd as they followed and surrounded me; when an ill-looking man approaching, tapped me on the shoulder, and said, 'Come, Sir, you must follow me to Mr Kirwin's, to give an account of yourself.'

'Who is Mr Kirwin? Why am I to give an account of myself? Is not this a free country?'

'Aye, Sir, free enough for honest folks. Mr Kirwin is a magistrate; and you are to give an account of the death of a gentleman who was found murdered here last night.'

This answer startled me; but I presently recovered myself. I was innocent; that could easily be proved: accordingly I followed my conductor in silence, and was led to one of the best houses in the town. I was ready to sink from fatigue and hunger; but, being surrounded by a crowd, I thought it politic to rouse all my strength, that no physical debility might be construed into apprehension or conscious guilt. Little did I then expect the calamity that was in a few moments to overwhelm me, and extinguish in horror and despair all fear of ignominy or death.

I must pause here; for it requires all my fortitude to recall the memory of the frightful events which I am about to relate, in proper detail, to my recollection.

CHAPTER IV

I was soon introduced into the presence of the magistrate, an old benevolent man, with calm and mild manners. He looked upon me, however, with some degree of severity; and then, turning towards my conductors, he asked who appeared as witnesses on this occasion.

About half a dozen men came forward; and one being selected by the magistrate, he deposed, that he had been out fishing the night before with his son and brother-in-law, Daniel Nugent, when, about ten o'clock, they observed a strong northerly blast rising, and they accordingly put in for port. It was a very dark night, as the moon had not yet risen; they did not land at the harbour, but, as they had been accustomed, at a creek about two miles below. He walked on first, carrying a part of the fishing tackle, and his companions followed him at some distance. As he was proceeding along the sands, he struck his foot against something, and fell all his length on the ground. His companions came up to assist him; and, by the light of their lantern, they found that he had fallen on the body of a man, who was to all appearance dead. Their first supposition was, that it was the corpse of some person who had been drowned, and was thrown on shore by the waves; but, upon examination, they found that the clothes were not wet, and even that the body was not then cold. They instantly carried it to the cottage of an old woman near the spot, and endeavoured, but in vain, to restore it to life. He appeared to be a handsome young man, about five and twenty years of age. He had apparently been strangled; for there was no sign of any violence, except the black mark of fingers on his neck.

The first part of this deposition did not in the least interest me; but when the mark of the fingers was mentioned, I remembered the murder of my brother, and felt myself extremely agitated; my limbs trembled, and a mist came over my eyes, which obliged me to lean on a chair for support. The magistrate observed me with a keen eye, and of course drew an unfavourable augury from my manner.

The son confirmed his father's account: but when Daniel Nugent was called, he swore positively that, just before the fall of his companion, he saw a boat, with a single man in it, at a short distance from the shore; and, as far as he could judge by the light of a few stars, it was the same boat in which I had just landed.

A woman deposed that she lived near the beach, and was standing at the door of her cottage, waiting for the return of the fishermen, about an hour before she heard of the discovery of the body, when she saw a boat, with only one man in it, push off from that part of the shore where the corpse was afterwards found.

Another woman confirmed the account of the fishermen having brought the body into her house; it was not cold. They put it into a bed, and rubbed it; and Daniel went to the town for an apothecary,* but life was quite gone.

Several other men were examined concerning my landing; and they agreed that with the strong north wind that had arisen during the night, it was very probable that I had beaten about for many hours, and had been obliged to return nearly to the same spot from which I had departed. Besides, they observed that it appeared that I had brought the body from another place, and it was likely, that as I did not appear to know the shore, I might have put into the harbour ignorant of the distance of the town of—from the place where I had deposited the corpse.

Mr Kirwin, on hearing this evidence, desired that I should be taken into the room where the body lay for interment, that it might be observed what effect the sight of it would produce upon me. This idea was probably suggested by the extreme agitation I had exhibited when the mode of the murder had been described. I was accordingly conducted, by the magistrate and several other persons, to the inn. I could not help being struck by the strange coincidences that had taken place during this eventful night; but, knowing that I had been conversing with several persons in the island I had inhabited about the time that the body had been found, I was perfectly tranquil as to the consequences of the affair.

I entered the room where the corpse lay, and was led up to

the coffin. How can I describe my sensations on beholding it ? I feel yet parched with horror, nor can I reflect on that terrible moment without shuddering and agony, that faintly reminds of the anguish of the recognition. The trial, the presence of the magistrate and witnesses, passed like a dream from my memory, when I saw the lifeless form of Henry Clerval stretched before me. I gasped for breath ; and, throwing myself on the body, I exclaimed, 'Have my murderous machinations deprived you also, my dearest Henry, of life ? Two I have already destroyed ; other victims await their destiny : but you, Clerval, my friend, my benefactor' –

The human frame could no longer support the agonizing suffering that I endured, and I was carried out of the room in strong convulsions.

A fever succeeded to this. I lay for two months on the point of death : my ravings, as I afterwards heard, were frightful ; I called myself the murderer of William, of Justine, and of Clerval. Sometimes I entreated my attendants to assist me in the destruction of the fiend by whom I was tormented ; and, at others, I felt the fingers of the monster already grasping my neck, and screamed aloud with agony and terror. Fortunately, as I spoke my native language, Mr Kirwin alone understood me ; but my gestures and bitter cries were sufficient to affright the other witnesses.

Why did I not die ? More miserable than man ever was before, why did I not sink into forgetfulness and rest ? Death snatches away many blooming children, the only hopes of their doating parents : how many brides and youthful lovers have been one day in the bloom of health and hope, and the next a prey for worms and the decay of the tomb ! Of what materials was I made, that I could thus resist so many shocks, which, like the turning of the wheel, continually renewed the torture.

But I was doomed to live ; and, in two months, found myself as awaking from a dream, in a prison, stretched on a wretched bed, surrounded by gaolers, turnkeys, bolts, and all the miserable apparatus of a dungeon. It was morning, I remember, when I thus awoke to understanding : I had forgotten the particulars of what had happened, and only felt as if some great misfortune had suddenly overwhelmed me ; but when I looked around, and saw the barred windows, and the squalidness of the room in which I was, all flashed across my memory, and I groaned bitterly.

This sound disturbed an old woman who was sleeping in a chair beside me. She was a hired nurse, the wife of one of the turnkeys, and her countenance expressed all those bad qualities which often characterize that class. The lines of her face were hard and rude, like that of persons accustomed to see without sympathizing in sights of misery. Her tone expressed her entire indifference; she addressed me in English, and the voice struck me as one that I had heard during my sufferings:

'Are you better now, Sir?' said she.

I replied in the same language, with a feeble voice, 'I believe I am; but if it be all true, if indeed I did not dream, I am sorry that I am still alive to feel this misery and horror.'

'For that matter,' replied the old woman, 'if you mean about the gentleman you murdered, I believe that it were better for you if you were dead, for I fancy it will go hard with you; but you will be hung when the next sessions come on. However, that's none of my business, I am sent to nurse you, and get you well; I do my duty with a safe conscience, it were well if everybody did the same.'

I turned with loathing from the woman who could utter so unfeeling a speech to a person just saved, on the very edge of death; but I felt languid, and unable to reflect on all that had passed. The whole series of my life appeared to me as a dream; I sometimes doubted if indeed it were all true, for it never presented itself to my mind with the force of reality.

As the images that floated before me became more distinct, I grew feverish; a darkness pressed around me; no one was near me who soothed me with the gentle voice of love; no dear hand supported me. The physician came and prescribed medicines, and the old woman prepared them for me; but utter carelessness was visible in the first, and the expression of brutality was strongly marked in the visage of the second. Who could be interested in the fate of a murderer, but the hangman who would gain his fee?

These were my first reflections; but I soon learned that Mr Kirwin had shown me extreme kindness. He had caused the best room in the prison to be prepared for me (wretched indeed was the best); and it was he who had provided a physician and a nurse. It is true, he seldom came to see me; for, although he ardently desired to relieve the sufferings of every human creature, he did not wish to be present at the agonies and miserable ravings of a murderer. He came, therefore, sometimes to see that I was not neglected; but his visits were short, and at long intervals.

One day, when I was gradually recovering, I was seated in a chair, my eyes half open, and my cheeks livid like those in death, I was overcome by gloom and misery, and often reflected I had better seek death than remain miserably pent up only to be let loose in a world replete with wretchedness. At one time I considered whether I should not declare myself guilty, and suffer the penalty of the law, less innocent than the poor Justine had been. Such were my thoughts, when the door of my apartment was opened, and Mr Kirwin entered. His countenance expressed sympathy and compassion; he drew a chair close to mine, and addressed me in French —

'I fear that this place is very shocking to you; can I do any thing to make you more comfortable?'

'I thank you; but all that you mention is nothing to me: on the whole earth there is no comfort which I am capable of receiving.'

'I know that the sympathy of a stranger can be but of little relief to one borne down as you are by so strange a misfortune. But you will, I hope, soon quit this melancholy abode; for, doubtless, evidence can easily be brought to free you from the criminal charge.'

'That is my least concern: I am, by a course of strange events, become the most miserable of mortals. Persecuted and tortured as I am and have been, can death be any evil to me?'

'Nothing indeed could be more unfortunate and agonizing than the strange chances that have lately occurred. You were thrown, by some surprising accident, on this shore, renowned for its hospitality; seized immediately, and charged with murder. The first sight that was presented to your eyes was the body of your friend, murdered in so unaccountable a manner, and placed, as it were, by some fiend across your path.'

As Mr Kirwin said this, notwithstanding the agitation I endured on this retrospect of my sufferings, I also felt considerable surprise at the knowledge he seemed to possess concerning me. I suppose some astonishment was exhibited in my countenance; for Mr Kirwin hastened to say — 'It was not until a day or two after your illness that I thought of examining your dress, that I might discover some trace by which I could send to your relations an account of your misfortune and illness. I found several letters, and, among others, one which I discovered from its commencement to be from your father. I instantly wrote to Geneva : nearly two months have elapsed since the departure of my letter. – But you are ill; even now you tremble : you are unfit for agitation of any kind.'

'This suspense is a thousand times worse than the most horrible event : tell me what new scene of death has been acted, and whose murder I am now to lament.'

'Your family is perfectly well,' said Mr Kirwin, with gentleness ; 'and someone, a friend, is come to visit you.'

I know not by what chain of thought the idea presented itself, but it instantly darted into my mind that the murderer had come to mock at my misery, and taunt me with the death of Clerval, as a new incitement for me to comply with his hellish desires. I put my hand before my eyes, and cried out in agony –

'Oh ! take him away ! I cannot see him; for God's sake, do not let him enter !'

Mr Kirwin regarded me with a troubled countenance. He could not help regarding my exclamation as a presumption of my guilt, and said, in rather a severe tone –

'I should have thought, young man, that the presence of your father would have been welcome, instead of inspiring such violent repugnance.'

'My father !' cried I, while every feature and every muscle was relaxed from anguish to pleasure. 'Is my father, indeed, come ? How kind, how very kind. But where is he, why does he not hasten to me ?'

My change of manner surprised and pleased the magistrate ; perhaps he thought that my former exclamation was a momentary return of delirium, and now he instantly resumed his former benevolence. He rose, and quitted the room with my nurse, and in a moment my father entered it.

Nothing, at this moment, could have given me greater pleasure than the arrival of my father. I stretched out my hand to him, and cried –

'Are you then safe – and Elizabeth – and Ernest ?'

My father calmed me with assurances of their welfare, and endeavoured by dwelling on these subjects so interesting to my heart, to raise my desponding spirits ; but he soon felt that a prison cannot be the abode of cheerfulness. 'What a place is this that you inhabit, my son !' said he, looking mournfully at the barred windows, and wretched appearance of the room. 'You travelled to seek happiness, but a fatality seems to pursue you. And poor Clerval – '

The name of my unfortunate and murdered friend was an agitation too great to be endured in my weak state; I shed tears.

'Alas! yes, my father,' replied I; 'some destiny of the most horrible kind hangs over me, and I must live to fulfil it, or surely I should have died on the coffin of Henry.'

We were not allowed to converse for any length of time, for the precarious state of my health rendered every precaution necessary that could insure tranquillity. Mr Kirwin came in, and insisted that my strength should not be exhausted by too much exertion. But the appearance of my father was to me like that of my good angel, and I gradually recovered my health.

As my sickness quitted me, I was absorbed by a gloomy and black melancholy, that nothing could dissipate. The image of Clerval was for ever before me, ghastly and murdered. More than once the agitation into which these reflections threw me made my friends dread a dangerous relapse. Alas! why did they preserve so miserable and detested a life? It was surely that I might fulfil my destiny, which is now drawing to a close. Soon, oh, very soon, will death extinguish these throbbings, and relieve me from the mighty weight of anguish that bears me to the dust; and, in executing the award of justice, I shall also sink to rest. Then the appearance of death was distant, although the wish was ever present to my thoughts; and I often sat for hours motionless and speechless, wishing for some mighty revolution that might bury me and my destroyer in its ruins.

The season for the assizes approached. I had already been three months in prison; and although I was still weak, and in continual danger of a relapse, I was obliged to travel nearly a hundred miles to the country-town, where the court was held. Mr Kirwin charged himself with every care of collecting witnesses, and arranging my defence. I was spared the disgrace of appearing publicly as a criminal, as the case was not brought before the court that decides on life and death. The grand jury rejected the bill, on its being proved that I was on the Orkney Islands at the hour the body of my friend was found, and a fortnight after my removal I was liberated from prison.

My father was enraptured on finding me freed from the vexations of a criminal charge, that I was again allowed to breathe the fresh atmosphere, and allowed to return to my native country. I did not participate in these feelings; for to me the walls of a dungeon or a palace were alike hateful. The cup of life was poisoned for ever; and although the sun shone upon me, as upon the happy and gay of heart, I saw around me nothing but a dense and frightful darkness, penetrated by no light but the glimmer of two eyes that glared upon me. Sometimes they were the expressive eyes of Henry, languishing in death, the dark orbs nearly covered by the lids, and the long black lashes that fringed them; sometimes it was the watery clouded eyes of the monster, as I first saw them in my chamber at Ingolstadt.

My father tried to awaken in me the feelings of affection. he talked of Geneva, which I should soon visit – of Elizabeth, and Ernest; but these words only drew deep groans from me. Sometimes, indeed, I felt a wish for happiness; and thought, with melancholy delight, of my beloved cousin; or longed; with a devouring *maladie du pays*,* to see once more the blue lake and rapid Rhone, that had been so dear to me in early childhood: but my general state of feeling was a torpor, in which a prison was as welcome a residence as the divinest scene in nature; and these fits were seldom interrupted, but by paroxysms of anguish and despair. At these moments I often endeavoured to put an end to the existence I loathed; and it required unceasing attendance and vigilance to restrain me from committing some dreadful act of violence.

I remember, as I quitted the prison, I heard one of the men say, 'He may be innocent of the murder, but he has certainly a bad conscience.' These words struck me. A bad conscience! yes, surely I had one. William, Justine, and Clerval, had died through my infernal machinations; 'And whose death,' cried I, 'is to finish the tragedy? Ah! my father, do not remain in this wretched country; take me where I may forget myself, my existence, and all the world.'

My father easily acceded to my desire; and, after having taken leave of Mr Kirwin, we hastened to Dublin. I felt as if I was relieved from a heavy weight, when the packet sailed with a fair wind from Ireland, and I had quitted for ever the country which had been to me the scene of so much misery.

It was midnight. My father slept in the cabin; and I lay on the deck, looking at the stars, and listening to the dashing of the waves. I hailed the darkness that shut Ireland from my sight, and my pulse beat with a feverish joy, when I reflected that I should soon see Geneva. The past appeared to me in the light of a frightful dream; yet the vessel in which I was, the wind that blew me from the detested shore of Ireland, and the sea which surrounded me, told me too forcibly that I was deceived by no vision, and that Clerval, my friend and dearest companion, had fallen a victim to me and the monster of my creation. I repassed, in my memory, my whole life; my quiet happiness while residing with my family in Geneva, the death of my mother, and my departure for Ingolstadt. I remembered shuddering at the mad enthusiasm that hurried me on to the creation of my hideous enemy, and I called to mind the night during which he first lived. I was unable to pursue the train of thought; a thousand feelings pressed upon me, and I wept bitterly.

Ever since my recovery from the fever I had been in the custom of taking every night a small quanity of laudanum;* for it was by means of this drug only that I was enabled to gain the rest necessary for the preservation of life. Oppressed by the recollection of my various misfortunes, I now took a double dose, and soon slept profoundly. But sleep did not afford me respite from thought and misery; my dreams presented a thousand objects that scared me. Towards morning I was possessed by a kind of night-mare; I felt the fiend's grasp in my neck, and could not free myself from it; groans and cries rung in my ears. My father, who was watching over me, perceiving my restlessness, awoke me, and pointed to the port of Holyhead, which we were now entering.

CHAPTER V

We had resolved not to go to London, but to cross the country to Portsmouth, and thence to embark for Havre. I preferred this plan principally because I dreaded to see again those places in which I had enjoyed a few moments of tranquillity with my beloved Clerval. I thought with horror of seeing again those persons whom we had been accustomed to visit together, and who might make inquiries concerning an event, the very remembrance of which made me again feel the pang I endured when I gazed on his lifeless form in the inn at—.

As for my father, his desires and exertions were bounded to the again seeing me restored to health and peace of mind. His tenderness and attentions were unremitting; my grief and gloom was obstinate, but he would not despair. Sometimes he thought that I felt deeply the degradation of being obliged to answer a charge of murder, and he endeavoured to prove to me the futility of pride.

'Alas! my father,' said I, 'how little do you know me. Human beings, their feelings and passions, would indeed be degraded, if such a wretch as I felt pride. Justine, poor unhappy Justine, was as innocent as I, and she suffered the same charge; she died for it; and I am the cause of this – I murdered her. William, Justine, and Henry – they all died by my hands.'

My father had often, during my imprisonment, heard me make the same assertion; when I thus accused myself, he sometimes seemed to desire an explanation, and at others he appeared to consider it as caused by delirium, and that, during my illness, some idea of this kind had presented itself to my imagination, the remembrance of which I preserved in my convalescence. I avoided explanation, and maintained a continual silence concerning the wretch I had created. I had a feeling that I should be supposed mad, and this for ever chained my tongue, when I would have given the whole world to have confided the fatal secret.

Upon this occasion my father said, with an expression of unbounded wonder, 'What do you mean, Victor? are you mad? My dear son, I entreat you never to make such an assertion again.'

'I am not mad,' I cried energetically; 'the sun and the heavens, who have viewed my operations, can bear witness of my truth. I am the assassin of those most innocent victims; they died by my machinations. A thousand times would I have shed my own blood, drop by drop, to have saved their lives; but I could not, my father, indeed I could not sacrifice the whole human race.'

The conclusion of this speech convinced my father that my ideas were deranged, and he instantly changed the subject of our conversation, and endeavoured to alter the course of my thoughts. He wished as much as possible to obliterate the memory of the scenes that had taken place in Ireland, and never alluded to them, or suffered me to speak of my misfortunes.

As time passed away I became more calm: misery had her dwelling in my heart, but I no longer talked in the same incoherent manner of my own crimes; sufficient for me was the consciousness of them. By the utmost self-violence, I curbed the imperious voice of wretchedness, which sometimes desired to declare itself to the whole world; and my manners were calmer and more composed than they had ever been since my journey to the sea of ice.

We arrived at Havre on the 8th of May, and instantly proceeded to Paris, where my father had some business which detained us a few weeks. In this city, I received the following letter from Elizabeth :-

'To Victor Frankenstein

MY DEAREST FRIEND

'It gave me the greatest pleasure to receive a letter from my uncle dated at Paris; you are no longer at a formidable distance, and I may hope to see you in less than a fortnight. My poor cousin, how much you must have suffered! I expect to see you looking even more ill than when you quitted Geneva. This winter has been passed most miserably, tortured as I have been by anxious suspense; yet I hope to see peace in your countenance, and to find that your heart is not totally devoid of comfort and tranquillity.

'Yet I fear that the same feelings now exist that made you so miserable a year ago, even perhaps augmented by time. I would not disturb you at this period, when so many misfortunes weigh upon you; but a conversation that I had with my uncle previous to his departure renders some explanation necessary before we meet.

'Explanation! you may possibly say; what can Elizabeth have to explain? If you really say this, my questions are answered, and I have no more to do than to sign myself your affectionate cousin. But you are distant from me, and it is possible that you may dread, and yet be pleased with this explanation; and, in a probability of this being the case, I dare not any longer postpone writing what, during your absence, I have often wished to express to you, but have never had the courage to begin.

'You well know, Victor, that our union had been the favourite plan of your parents ever since our infancy. We were told this when young, and taught to look forward to it as an event that would certainly take place. We were affectionate playfellows during childhood, and, I believe, dear and valued friends to one another as we grew older. But as brother and sister often entertain a lively affection towards each other, without desiring a more intimate union, may not such also be our case? Tell me, dearest Victor. Answer me, I conjure you, by our mutual happiness, with simple truth – Do you not love another?

'You have travelled; you have spent several years of your life at Ingolstadt; and I confess to you, my friend, that when I saw you last autumn so unhappy, flying to solitude, from the society of every creature, I could not help supposing that you might regret our connexion, and believe yourself bound in honour to fulfil the wishes of your parents, although they opposed themselves to your inclinations. But this is false reasoning. I confess to you, my cousin, that I love you, and that in my airy dreams of futurity you have been my constant friend and companion. But it is your happiness I desire as well as my own, when I declare to you, that our marriage would render me eternally miserable, unless it were the dictate of your own free choice. Even now I weep to think, that, borne down as you are by the cruelest misfortunes, you may stifle, by the word *honour*, all hope of that love and happiness which would alone restore you to yourself. I, who have so interested an affection for you, may increase your miseries ten-fold, by being an obstacle to your wishes. Ah, Victor, be assured that your cousin and playmate has too sincere a love for you not to be made miserable by this supposition. Be happy, my friend; and if you obey me in this one request, remain satisfied that nothing on earth will have the power to interrupt my tranquillity.

'Do not let this letter disturb you; do not answer it to-morrow, or the next day, or even until you come, if it will give you pain. My uncle will send me news of your health; and if I see but one smile on your lips when we meet, occasioned by this or any other exertion of mine, I shall need no other happiness.

Elizabeth Lavenza.
Geneva, May 18th, 17—.'

This letter revived in my memory what I had before forgotten, the threat of the fiend – '*I will be with you on your wedding-night!*' Such was my sentence, and on that night would the dæmon employ every art to destroy me, and tear me from the glimpse of happiness which promised partly to console my sufferings. On that night he had determined to consummate his crimes by my death. Well, be it so; a deadly struggle would then assuredly take place, in which if he was victorious, I should be at peace, and his power over me be at an end. If he were vanquished, I should be a free man. Alas! what freedom! such as the peasant enjoys when his family have been massacred before his eyes, his cottage burned, his lands laid waste, and he is turned adrift, homeless, penniless, and alone, but free. Such would be my liberty, except that in my Elizabeth I possessed a treasure; alas! balanced by those horrors of remorse and guilt, which would pursue me until death.

Sweet and beloved Elizabeth! I read and re-read her letter, and some softened feelings stole into my heart, and dared to whisper paradisaical dreams of love and joy; but the apple was already eaten,* and the angel's arm bared to drive me from all hope. Yet I would die to make her happy. If the monster executed his threat, death was inevitable; yet, again, I con-sidered whether my marriage would hasten my fate. My destruc-tion might indeed arrive a few months sooner; but if my torturer should suspect that I postponed it, influenced by his menaces, he would surely find other, and perhaps more dreadful means of revenge. He had vowed *to be with me on my wedding-night*, yet he did not consider that threat as binding him to peace in the mean time; for, as if to show me that he was not yet satiated with blood, he had murdered Clerval immediately after the enunciation of this threats. I resolved, therefore, that if my immediate union with my cousin would conduce either to her's or my father's happiness, my adversary's designs against my life should not retard it a single hour.

In this state of mind I wrote to Elizabeth. My letter was calm and affectionate. 'I fear, my beloved girl,' I said, 'little happiness remains for us on earth; yet all that I may one day enjoy is concentered in you. Chase away your idle fears; to you alone do I consecrate my life, and my endeavours for contentment. I have one secret, Elizabeth, a dreadful one; when revealed to you, it will chill your frame with horror, and then, far from being surprised at my misery, you will only wonder that I survive what I have endured. I will confide this tale of misery and terror to you the day after our marriage shall take place; for, my sweet cousin, there must be perfect confidence between us. But until then, I conjure you, do not mention or allude to it. This I most earnestly entreat, and I know you will comply.'

In about a week after the arrival of Elizabeth's letter, we returned to Geneva. My cousin welcomed me with warm affection; yet tears were in her eyes, as she beheld my emaciated frame and feverish cheeks. I saw a change in her also. She was thinner, and had lost much of that heavenly vivacity that had before charmed me; but her gentleness, and soft looks of compassion, made her a more fit companion for one blasted and miserable as I was.

The tranquillity which I now enjoyed did not endure. Memory brought madness with it; and when I thought on what had passed, a real insanity possessed me; sometimes I was furious, and burnt with rage, sometimes low and despondent. I neither spoke or looked, but sat motionless, bewildered by the multitude of miseries that overcame me.

Elizabeth alone had the power to draw me from these fits; her gentle voice would soothe me when transported by passion, and inspire me with human feelings when sunk in torpor. She wept with me, and for me. When reason returned, she would remonstrate, and endeavour to inspire me with resignation. Ah! it is well for the unfortunate to be resigned, but for the guilty there is no peace. The agonies of remorse poison the luxury there is otherwise sometimes found in indulging the excess of grief.

Soon after my arrival my father spoke of my immediate marriage with my cousin. I remained silent.

'Have you, then, some other attachment?'

'None on earth. I love Elizabeth, and look forward to our union with delight. Let the day therefore be fixed; and on it I will consecrate myself, in life or death, to the happiness of my cousin.'

'My dear Victor, do not speak thus. Heavy misfortunes have befallen us; but let us only cling closer to what remains, and transfer our love for those whom we have lost to those who yet live. Our circle will be small, but bound close by the ties of affection and mutual misfortune. And when time shall have softened your despair, new and dear objects of care will be born to replace those of whom we have been so cruelly deprived.'

Such were the lessons of my father. But to me the remembrance of the threat returned: nor can you wonder, that, omnipotent as the fiend had been in his deeds of blood, I should almost regard him as invincible; and that when he had pronounced the words, '*I shall be with you on your wedding-night*,' I should regard the threatened fate as unavoidable. But death was no evil to me, if the loss of Elizabeth were balanced with it; and I therefore, with a contented and even cheerful countenance, agreed with my father, that if my cousin, would consent, the ceremony should take place in ten days, and thus put, as I imagined, the seal to my fate.

Great God! if for one instant I had thought what might be the hellish intention of my fiendish adversary, I would rather have banished myself for ever from my native country, and wandered a friendless outcast over the earth, than have consented to this miserable marriage. But, as if possessed of magic powers, the monster had blinded me to his real intentions; and when I thought that I prepared only my own death, I hastened that of a far dearer victim.

As the period fixed for our marriage drew nearer, whether from cowardice or a prophetic feeling, I felt my heart sink within me. But I concealed my feelings by an appearance of hilarity, that brought smiles and joy to the countenance of my father, but hardly deceived the ever-watchful and nicer* eye of Elizabeth. She looked forward to our union with placid contentment, not unmingled with a little fear, which past misfortunes had impressed, that what now appeared certain and tangible happiness, might soon dissipate into an airy dream, and leave no trace but deep and everlasting regret.

Preparations were made for the event; congratulatory visits were received; and all wore a smiling appearance. I shut up, as well as I could, in my own heart the anxiety that preyed there, and entered with seeming earnestness into the plans of my father, although they might only serve as the decorations of my tragedy. A house was purchased for us near Cologny, by which we should enjoy the pleasures of the country, and yet be so near Geneva as to see my father every day; who would still reside within the walls, for the benefit of Ernest, that he might follow his studies at the schools.

In the meantime I took every precaution to defend my person, in case the fiend should openly attack me. I carried pistols and a dagger constantly about me, and was ever on the watch to prevent artifice; and by these means gained a greater degree of tranquillity. Indeed, as the period approached, the threat appeared more as a delusion, not to be regarded as worthy to disturb my peace, while the happiness I hoped for in my marriage wore a greater appearance of certainty, as the day fixed for its solemnization drew nearer, and I heard it continually spoken of as an occurrence which no accident could possibly prevent.

Elizabeth seemed happy; my tranquil demeanour contributed greatly to calm her mind. But on the day that was to fulfil my wishes and my destiny, she was melancholy, and a presentiment of evil pervaded her; and perhaps also she thought of the dreadful secret, which I had promised to reveal to her the following day. My father was in the meantime overjoyed, and, in the bustle of preparation, only observed in the melancholy of his niece the diffidence of a bride.

After the ceremony was performed, a large party assembled at my father's; but it was agreed that Elizabeth and I should pass the afternoon and night at Evian, and return to Cologny the next morning. As the day was fair, and the wind favourable, we resolved to go by water.

Those were the last moments of my life during which I enjoyed the feeling of happiness. We passed rapidly along: the sun was hot, but we were sheltered from its rays by a kind of canopy, while we enjoyed the beauty of the scene, sometimes on one side of the lake, where we saw Mont Salêve, the pleasant banks of Montalêgre, and at a distance, surmounting all, the beautiful Mont Blânc, and the assemblage of snowy mountains that in vain endeavour to emulate her; sometimes coasting the opposite banks, we saw the mighty Jura opposing its dark side to the ambition that would quit its native country, and an almost insurmountable barrier to the invader who should wish to enslave it.

I took the hand of Elizabeth: 'You are sorrowful, my love. Ah! if you knew what I have suffered, and what I may yet endure, you would endeavour to let me taste the quiet, and freedom from despair, that this one day at least permits me to enjoy.'

'Be happy, my dear Victor,' replied Elizabeth; 'there is I hope, nothing to distress you; and be assured that if a lively joy is not painted in my face, my heart is contented. Something whispers to me not to depend too much on the prospect that is opened before us; but I will not listen to such a sinister voice. Observe how fast we move along, and how the clouds which sometimes obscure, and sometimes rise above the dome of Mont Blânc, render this scene of beauty still more interesting. Look also at the innumnerable fish that are swimming in the clear waters, where we can distinguish every pebble that lies at the bottom. What a divine day! how happy and serene all nature appears!'

Thus Elizabeth endeavoured to divert her thoughts and mine from all reflection upon melancholy subjects. But her temper was fluctuating; joy for a few instants shone in her eyes, but it continually gave place to distraction and reverie.

The sun sunk lower in the heavens; we passed the river Drance, and observed its path through the chasms of the higher, and the glens of the lower hills. The Alps here come closer to the lake, and we approached the amphitheatre of mountains which forms its eastern boundary. The spire of Evian shone under the woods that surrounded it, and the range of mountain above mountain by which it was overhung.

The wind, which had hitherto carried us along with amazing rapidity, sunk at sunset to a light breeze; the soft air just ruffled the water, and caused a pleasant motion among the trees as we approached the shore, from which it wafted the most delightful scent of flowers and hay. The sun sunk beneath the horizon as we landed; and as I touched the shore, I felt those cares and fears revive, which soon were to clasp me, and cling to me for ever.

CHAPTER VI

It was eight o'clock when we landed; we walked for a short time on the shore, enjoying the transitory light, and then retired to the inn, and contemplated the lovely scene of waters, woods, and mountains, obscured in darkness, yet still displaying their black outlines.

The wind, which had fallen in the south, now rose with great violence in the west. The moon had reached her summit in the heavens, and was beginning to descend; the clouds swept across it swifter than the flight of the vulture, and dimmed her rays, while the lake reflected the scene of the busy heavens, rendered still busier by the restless waves that were beginning to rise. Suddenly a heavy storm of rain descended.

I had been calm during the day; but so soon as night obscured the shapes of objects, a thousand fears arose in my mind. I was anxious and watchful, while my right hand grasped a pistol which was hidden in my bosom; every sound terrified me; but I resolved that I would sell my life dearly, and not relax the impending conflict until my own life, or that of my adversary, were extinguished.

Elizabeth observed my agitation for some time in timid and fearful silence; at length she said, 'What it is that agitates you, my dear Victor? What is it you fear?'

'Oh! peace, peace, my love,' replied I, 'this night, and all will be safe: but this night is dreadful, very dreadful.'

I passed an hour in this state of mind, when suddenly I reflected how dreadful the combat which I momentarily expected would be to my wife, and I earnestly entreated her to retire, resolving not to join her until I had obtained some knowledge as to the situation of my enemy.

She left me, and I continued some time walking up and down the passages of the house, and inspecting every corner that might afford a retreat to my adversary. But I discovered no trace of him, and was beginning to conjecture that some fortunate chance had intervened to prevent the execution of his menaces; when suddenly I heard a shrill and dreadful scream. It came from the room into which Elizabeth had retired. As I heard it, the whole truth rushed into my mind, my arms dropped, the motion of every muscle and fibre was suspended; I could feel the blood trickling in my veins, and tingling in the extremities of my limbs. This state lasted but for an instant; the scream was repeated, and I rushed into the room.

Great God! why did I not then expire! Why am I here to relate the destruction of the best hope, and the purest creature of earth. She was there, lifeless and inanimate, thrown across the bed, her head hanging down, and her pale and distorted features half covered by her hair. Every where I turn I see the same figure – her bloodless arm and relaxed form flung by the murderer on its bridal bier. Could I behold this, and live? Alas! life is obstinate, and clings closest where it is most hated. For a moment only did I lose recollection; I fainted.

When I recovered, I found myself surrounded by the people of the inn; their countenances expressed a breathless terror: but the horror of others appeared only as a mockery, a shadow of the feelings that oppressed me. I escaped from them to the room where lay the body of Elizabeth, my love, my wife, so lately living, so dear, so worthy. She had been moved from the posture in which I had first beheld her; and now, as she lay, her head upon her arm, and a handkerchief thrown across her face and neck, I might have supposed her asleep. I rushed towards her, and embraced her with ardour; but the deathly languor and coldness of the limbs told me, that what I now held in my arms had ceased to be the Elizabeth whom I had loved and cherished. The murderous mark of the fiend's grasp was on her neck, and the breath had ceased to issue from her lips.

While I still hung over her in the agony of despair, I happened to look up. The windows of the room had before been darkened; and I felt a kind of panic on seeing the pale yellow light of the moon illuminate the chamber. The shutters had been thrown back; and, with a sensation of horror not to be described, I saw at the open window a figure the most hideous and abhorred. A grin was on the face of the monster; he seemed to jeer, as with his fiendish finger he pointed towards the corpse of my wife. I rushed towards the window, and drawing a pistol from my bosom, shot; but he eluded me, leaped from his station, and, running with the swiftness of lightning, plunged into the lake.

The report of the pistol brought a crowd into the room. I pointed to the spot where he had disappeared, and we followed the track with boats; nets were cast, but in vain. After passing several hours, we returned hopeless, most of my companions believing it to have been a form conjured by my fancy. After having landed, they proceeded to search the country, parties going in different directions among the woods and vines.

I did not accompany them; I was exhausted: a film covered my eyes, and my skin was parched with the heat of fever. In this state I lay on a bed, hardly conscious of what had happened; my eyes wandered round the room, as if to seek something that I had lost.

At length I remembered that my father would anxiously expect the return of Elizabeth and myself, and that I must return alone. This reflection brought tears into my eyes, and I wept for a long time; but my thoughts rambled to various subjects, reflecting on my misfortunes, and their cause. I was bewildered in a cloud of wonder and horror. The death of William, the execution of Justine, the murder of Clerval, and lastly of my wife; even at that moment I knew not that my only remaining friends were safe from the malignity of the fiend; my father even now might be writhing under his grasp, and Ernest might be dead at his feet. This idea made me shudder, and recalled me to action. I started up, and resolved to return to Geneva with all possible speed.

There were no horses to be procured, and I must return by the lake; but the wind was unfavourable, and the rain fell in torrents. However, it was hardly morning, and I might reasonably hope to arrive by night. I hired men to row, and took an oar myself, for I had always experienced relief from mental torment in bodily exercise. But the overflowing misery I now felt, and the excess of agitation that I endured, rendered me incapable of any exertion. I threw down the oar; and, leaning my head upon my hands, gave way to every gloomy idea that arose. If I looked up, I saw the scenes which were familiar to me in my happier time, and which I had contemplated but the day before in the company of her who was now but a shadow and a recollection. Tears streamed from my eyes. The rain had ceased for a moment, and I saw the fish play in the waters as they had done a few hours before; they had then been observed by Elizabeth. Nothing is so painful to the human mind as a great and sudden change. The sun might shine, or the clouds might lour; but nothing could appear to me as it had done the day before. A fiend had snatched from me every hope of future happiness : no creature had ever been so miserable as I was; so frightful an event is single in the history of man.

But why should I dwell upon the incidents that followed this last overwhelming event. Mine has been a tale of horrors; I have reached their *acme*,* and what I must now relate can but be tedious to you. Know that, one by one, my friends were snatched away; I was left desolate. My own strength is exhausted; and I must tell, in a few words, what remains of my hideous narration.

I arrived at Geneva. My father and Ernest yet lived; but the former sunk under the tidings that I bore. I see him now, excellent and venerable old man ! his eyes wandered in vacancy, for they had lost their charm and their delight – his niece, his more than daughter, whom he doated on with all that affection which a man feels, who, in the decline of life, having few affections, clings more earnestly to those that remain. Cursed, cursed be the fiend that brought misery on his grey hairs, and doomed him to waste in wretchedness ! He could not live under the horrors that were accumulated around him; an apoplectic fit was brought on, and in a few days he died in my arms.

What then became of me ? I know not; I lost sensation, and chains and darkness were the only objects that pressed upon me. Sometimes, indeed, I dreamt that I wandered in flowery meadows and pleasant vales with the friends of my youth; but awoke, and found myself in a dungeon. Melancholy followed, but by degrees I gained a clear conception of my miseries and situation, and was then released from my prison. For they had called me mad; and during many months, as I understood, a solitary cell had been my habitation.

But liberty had been a useless gift to me had I not, as I awakened to reason, at the same time awakened to revenge. As the memory of past misfortunes pressed upon me, I began to reflect on their cause – the monster whom I had created, the miserable dæmon whom I had sent abroad into the world for my destruction. I was possessed by a maddening rage when I thought of him, and desired and ardently prayed that I might have him within my grasp to wreak a great and signal revenge on his cursed head.

Nor did my hate long confine itself to useless wishes; I began to reflect on the best means of securing him; and for this purpose, about a month after my release, I repaired to a criminal judge in the town, and told him that I had an accusation to make; that I knew the destroyer of my family; and that I required him to exert his whole authority for the apprehension of the murderer.

The magistrate listened to me with attention and kindness: 'Be assured, sir,' said he, 'no pains or exertions on my part shall be spared to discover the villain.'

'I thank you,' replied I, 'listen, therefore, to the deposition that I have to make. It is indeed a tale so strange, that I should fear you would not credit it, were there not something in truth which, however wonderful, forces conviction. The story is too connected to be mistaken for a dream, and I have no motive for falsehood.' My manner, as I thus addressed him, was impressive, but calm; I had formed in my own heart a resolution to pursue my destroyer to death; and this purpose quieted my agony, and provisionally reconciled me to life. I now related my history briefly, but with the firmness and precision, marking the dates with accuracy, and never deviating into invective or exclamation.

The magistrate appeared at first perfectly incredulous, but as I continued he become more attentive and interested; I saw him sometimes shudder with horror, at others a lively surprise, unmingled with disbelief, was painted on his countenance.

When I had concluded my narration I said. 'This is the being whom I accuse, and for whose detection and punishment I call upon you to exert your whole power. It is your duty as a magistrate, and I believe and hope that your feelings as a man will not revolt from the execution of those functions on this occasion.'

This address caused a considerable change in the physiognomy of my auditor. He had heard my story with that half kind of belief that is given to a tale of spirits and supernatural events; but when he was called upon to act officially in consequence, the whole tide of his incredulity returned. He, however, answered mildly, 'I would willingly afford you every aid in your pursuit; but the creature of whom you speak appears to have powers which would put all my exertions to defiance. Who can follow an animal which can traverse the sea of ice, and inhabit caves and dens, where no man would venture to intrude?

Besides, some months have elapsed since the commission of his crimes, and no one can conjecture to what place he had wandered, or what region he may now inhabit.'

'I do not doubt that he hovers near the spot which I inhabit; and if he had indeed taken refuge in the Alps, he may he hunted like the chamois, and destroyed as a beast of prey. But I perceive your thoughts: you do not credit my narrative, and do not intend to pursue my enemy with the punishment which is his desert.'

As I spoke, rage, sparkled in my eyes; the magistrate was intimidated; 'You are mistaken,' said he, 'I will exert myself; and if it is in my power to seize the monster, be assured that he shall suffer punishment proportionate to his crimes. But I fear, from what you have yourself described to be his properties, that this will prove impracticable, and that, while every proper measure is pursued, you should endeavour to make up your mind to disappointment.'

'That cannot be; but all that I can say will be of little avail. My revenge is of no moment to you; yet, while I allow it to be a vice, I confess that it is the devouring and only passion of my soul. My rage is unspeakable, when I reflect that the murderer, whom I have turned loose upon society, still exists. You refuse my just demand. I have but one resource; and I devote myself, either in my life or death, to his destruction.'

I trembled with excess of agitation as I said this; there was a phrenzy in my manner, and something, I doubt not, of that haughty fierceness, which the martyrs of old are said to have possessed. But to a Genevan magistrate, whose mind was occupied by far other ideas than those of devotion and heroism, this elevation of mind had much the appearance of madness. He endeavoured to soothe me as a nurse does a child, and reverted, to my tale as the effects of delirium.

'Man,' I cried, 'how ignorant art thou in thy pride of wisdom! Cease; you know not what it is you say.'

I broke from the house angry and disturbed, and retired to meditate on some other mode of action.

CHAPTER VII

My present situation was one in which all voluntary thought was swallowed up and lost. I was hurried away by fury; revenge alone endowed me with strength and composure; it modelled my feelings, and allowed me to be calculating and calm, at periods when otherwise delirium or death would have been my portion.

My first resolution was to quit Geneva forever; my country, which, when I was happy and beloved, was dear to me, now, in my adversity, became hateful. I provided myself with a sum of money, together with a few jewels which had belonged to my mother, and departed.

And now my wanderings began, which are to cease but with life. I have traversed a vast portion of the earth, and have endured all the hardships which travellers, in deserts and barbarous countries, are wont to meet. How I have lived I hardly know; many times have I stretched my failing limbs upon the sandy plain, and prayed for death. But revenge kept me alive; I dared not die, and leave my adversary in being.

When I quitted Geneva, my first labour was to gain some clue by which I might trace the steps of my fiendish enemy. But my plan was unsettled; and I wandered many hours around the confines of the town, uncertain what path I should pursue. As night approached, I found myself at the entrance of the cemetery where William, Elizabeth, and my father, reposed. I entered it, and approached the tomb which marked their graves. Every thing was silent, except the leaves of the trees, which were gently agitated by the wind; the night was nearly dark; and the scene would have been solemn and affecting even to an uninterested observer. The spirits of the departed seemed to flit around, and to cast a shadow, which was felt but seen not, around the head of the mourner.

The deep grief which this scene had at first excited quickly gave way to rage and despair. They were dead, and I lived; their murderer also lived, and to destroy him I must drag out my weary existence. I knelt on the grass, and kissed the earth, and with quivering lips exclaimed, 'By the sacred earth on which I kneel, by the shades that wander near me, by the deep and eternal grief that I feel, I swear; and by thee, O Night, and by the spirits that preside over thee, I swear to pursue the dæmon, who caused this misery, until he or I shall perish in mortal conflict. For this purpose I will preserve my life: to execute this dear revenge, will I again behold the sun, and tread the green herbage of earth, which otherwise should vanish from my eyes for ever. And I call on you, spirits of the dead; and on you, wandering ministers of vengeance, to aid and conduct me in my work. Let the cursed and hellish monster drink deep of agony; let him feel the despair that now torments me.'

I had begun my adjuration with solemnity, and an awe which almost assured me that the shades of my murdered friends heard and approved my devotion; but the furies possessed me as I concluded, and rage choaked my utterance.

I was answered through the stillness of night by a loud and fiendish laugh. It rung on my ears long and heavily; the mountains re-echoed it, and I felt as if all hell surrounded me with mockery and laughter. Surely in that moment I should have been possessed by Frenzy, and have destroyed my miserable existence, but that my vow was heard, and that I was reserved for vengeance. The laughter died away; when a well-known and abhorred voice, apparently close to my ear, addressed me in a audible whisper — 'I am satisfied: miserable wretch! you have determined to live, and I am satisfied.'

I darted towards the spot from which the sound proceeded; but the devil eluded my grasp. Suddenly the broad disk of the moon arose, and shone full upon his ghastly and distorted shape, as he fled with more than mortal speed.

I pursued him; and for many months this has been my task. Guided by a slight clue, I followed the windings of the Rhone, but vainly. The blue Mediterranean appeared; and, by a strange change, I saw the fiend enter by night, and hide himself in a vessel bound for the Black Sea. I took my passage in the same ship; but he escaped, I know not how.

Amidst the wilds of Tartary and Russia, although he still evaded me, I have ever followed in his track. Sometimes the peasants, scared by this horrid apparition, informed me of his path; sometimes he himself, who feared that if I lost all trace I should despair and die, often left some mark to guide me. The snows descended on my head, and I saw the print of his huge step on the white plain. To you first entering on life, to whom care is new, and agony unknown, how can you understand what I have felt, and still feel? Cold, want, and fatigue, were the least pains which I was destined to endure; I was cursed by some devil, and carried about with me my eternal hell; yet still a spirit of good followed and directed my steps, and, when I most murmured, would suddenly extricate me from seemingly insurmountable difficulties. Sometimes, when nature, overcome by hunger, sunk under the exhaustion, a repast was prepared for me in the desert, that restored and inspirited me. The fare was indeed coarse, such as the peasants of the country ate; but I may not doubt that it was set there by the spirits that I had invoked to aid me. Often, when all was dry, the heavens cloudless, and I was parched by thirst, a slight cloud would bedim the sky, shed the few drops that revived me, and vanish.

I followed, when I could, the courses of the rivers; but the dæmon generally avoided these, as it was here that the population of the country chiefly collected. In other places human beings were seldom seen; and I generally subsisted on the wild animals that crossed my path. I had money with me, and gained the friendship of the villagers by distributing it, or bringing with me some food that I had killed, which, after taking a small part, I always presented to those who had provided me with fire and utensils for cooking.

My life, as it passed thus, was indeed hateful to me, and it was during sleep alone that I could taste joy. O blessed sleep! often, when most miserable, I sank to repose, and my dreams lulled me even to rapture. The spirits that guarded me had provided these moments, or rather hours, of happiness, that I might retain strength to fulfil my pilgrimage. Deprived of this respite, I should have sunk under my hardships. During the days I was sustained and inspirited by the hope of night: for in sleep I saw my friends, my wife, and my beloved country; again I saw the benevolent countenance of my father, heard the silver tones of my Elizabeth's voice, and beheld Clerval enjoying health and youth. Often, when wearied by a toilsome march, I persuaded myself that I was dreaming until night should come, and that I should then enjoy reality in the arms of my dearest friends.

What agonizing fondness did I feel for them! how did I cling to their dear forms, as sometimes they haunted even my waking hours, and persuade myself that they still lived! At such moments vengeance, that burned within me, died in my heart, and I pursued my path towards the destruction of the dæmon, more as a task enjoined by heaven, as the mechanical impulse of some power of which I was unconscious, than as the ardent desire of my soul.

What his feelings were whom I pursued, I cannot know. Sometimes, indeed, he left marks in writing on the barks of the trees, or cut in stone, that guided me, and instigated my fury. 'My reign is not yet over,' (these words were legible in one of these inscriptions); 'you live, and my power is complete. Follow me; I seek the everlasting ices of the north, where you will feel the misery of cold and frost, to which I am impassive. You will find near this place, if you follow not too tardily, a dead hare; eat, and be refreshed. Come on, my enemy; we have yet to wrestle for our lives; but many hard and miserable hours must you endure, until that period shall arrive.'

Scoffing devil! Again do I vow vengeance; again to do I devote thee, miserable fiend, to torture and death. Never will I omit my search, until he or I perish; and then with what ecstacy shall I join my Elizabeth, and those who even now prepare for me the reward of my tedious toil and horrible pilgrimage.

As I still pursued my journey to the northward, the snows thickened, and the cold increased in a degree almost too severe to support. The peasants were shut up in their hovels, and only a few of the most hardy ventured forth to seize the animals whom starvation had forced from their hiding-places to seek for prey. The rivers were covered with ice, and no fish could be procured; and thus I was cut off from my chief article of maintenance.

The triumph of my enemy increased with the difficulty of my labours. One inscription that he left was in these words: 'Prepare! your toils only begin: wrap yourself in furs, and provide food, for we shall soon enter upon a journey where your sufferings will satisfy my everlasting hatred.'

My courage and perseverance were invigorated by these scoffing words; I resolved not to fail in my purpose; and calling in heaven to support me, I continued with unabated fervour to traverse immense deserts, until the ocean appeared at a distance, and formed the utmost boundary of the horizon. Oh! how unlike it was to the blue seas of the south! Covered with ice it was only to be distinguished from land by its superior wildness and ruggedness. The Greeks wept for joy when they beheld the Mediterranean from the hills of Asia, and hailed with rapture the boundary of their toils. I did not weep; but I knelt down, and, with a full heart, thanked my guiding spirit for conducting me in safety to the place where I hoped, notwithstanding my adversary's gibe, to meet and grapple with him.

Some weeks before this period I had procured a sledge and dogs, and thus traversed the snows with inconceivable speed. I know not whether the fiend possessed the same advantages; but I found that, as before I had daily lost ground in the pursuit, I now gained on him; so much so, that when I first saw the ocean, he was but two day's journey in advance and I hoped to interrupt him before he should reach the beach. With new courage, therefore, I pressed on, and in two days arrived at a wretched hamlet on the seashore. I inquired of the inhabitants concerning the fiend, and gained accurate information. A gigantic monster they said, had arrived the night before, armed with a gun and many pistols; putting to flight the inhabitants of a solitary cottage, through fear of his terrific appearance. He had carried off their store of winter food, and, placing it in a sledge, to draw which he had seized on a numerous drove of trained dogs, he had harnessed them, and the same night, to the joy of the horror-struck villagers, had pursued his journey across the sea in a direction that led to no land; and they conjectured that he must speedily be destroyed by the breaking of the ice, or frozen by the eternal frosts.

On hearing this information, I suffered a temporary access of despair. He had escaped me; and I must commence a destructive and almost endless journey across the mountainous ices of the ocean, — amidst cold that few of the inhabitants could long endure, and which I, the native of a genial and sunny climate, could not hope to survive. Yet at the idea that the fiend should live and be triumphant, my rage and vengeance returned, and, like a mighty tide, overwhelmed every other feeling. After a slight repose, during which the spirits of the dead hovered round, and instigated me to toil and revenge, I prepared for my journey.

I exchanged my land sledge for one fashioned for the inequalities of the frozen ocean; and, purchasing a plentiful stock of provisions, I departed from land.

I cannot guess how many days have passed since then; but I have endured misery, which nothing but the eternal sentiment of a just retribution burning within my heart could have enabled me to support. Immense and rugged mountains of ice often barred up my passage, and I often heard the thunder of the ground sea, which threatened my destruction. But again the frost came, and made the paths of the sea secure.

By the quantity of the provision which I had consumed I should guess that I had passed three weeks in this journey; and the continual protraction of hope, returning back upon the heart, often wrung bitter drops of despondency and grief from my eyes. Despair had indeed almost secured her prey, and I should soon have sunk beneath this misery; when once, after the poor animals that carried me had with incredible toil gained the summit of a sloping ice mountain, and one sinking under his fatigue died, I viewed the expanse before me with anguish, when suddenly my eye caught a dark speck upon the dusky plain. I strained my sight to discover what it could be, and uttered a wild cry of ecstasy, when I distinguished a sledge, and the distorted proportions of a well-known form within. Oh! with what a burning gush did hope revisit my heart! warm tears filled my eyes, which I hastily wiped away, that they might not intercept the view I had of the demon; but still my sight was dimmed by the burning drops, until, giving way to the emotions that oppressed me, I wept aloud.

But this was not the time for delay; I disencumbered the dogs of their dead companion, gave them a plentiful portion of food; and, after an hour's rest, which was absolutely necessary, and yet which was bitterly irksome to me, I continued my route. The sledge was still visible; nor did I again lose sight of it, except at the moments when for a short time some ice rock concealed it with its intervening crags. I indeed perceptibly gained on it; and when, after nearly two days' journey, I beheld my enemy at no more than a mile distant, my heart bounded within me.

But now, when I appeared almost within grasp of my enemy, my hopes were suddenly extinguished, and I lost all trace of him more utterly than I had ever done before. A ground sea was heard; the thunder of its progress, as the waters rolled and swelled beneath me, became every moment more ominous and terrific. I pressed on, but in vain. The wind arose; the sea roared; and, as with the mighty shock of an earthquake, it split, and cracked with a tremendous and overwhelming sound. The work was soon finished: in a few minutes a tumultuous sea rolled between me and my enemy, and I was left drifting on a scattered piece of ice, that was continually lessening, and thus preparing for me a hideous death.

In this manner many appalling hours passed; several of my dogs died; and I myself was about to sink under the accumulation of distress, when I saw your vessel riding at anchor, and holding forth to me hopes of succour and life. I had no conception that vessels ever came so far north, and was astounded at the sight. I quickly destroyed part of my sledge to construct oars; and by these means was enabled with infinite fatigue, to move my ice-raft in the direction of your ship. I had determined, if you were going southward, still to trust myself to the mercy of the seas, rather than abandon my purpose. I hoped to induce you to grant me a boat with which I could still pursue my enemy. But your direction was northward. You took me on board when my vigour was exhausted, and I should soon have sunk under my multiplied hardships into a death, which I still dread, – for my task is unfulfilled.

Oh! when will my guiding spirit, in conducting me to the dæmon, allow me the rest I so much desire; or must I die, and he yet live? If I do, swear to me, Walton, that he shall not escape; that you will seek him, and satisfy my vengeance in his death. Yet, do I dare ask you to undertake my pilgrimage, to endure the hardships that I have undergone? No; I am not so selfish. Yet, when I am dead, if he should appear; if the ministers of vengeance should conduct him to you, swear that he shall not live – swear that he shall not triumph over my accumulated woes, and live to make another such a wretch as I am. He is eloquent and persuasive; and once his words had even power over my heart: but trust him not. His soul is as hellish as his form, full of treachery and fiend-like malice. Hear him not; call on the names of William, Justine, Clerval, Elizabeth, my father, and of the wretched Victor, and thrust your sword into his heart. I will hover near, and direct the steel aright.

Walton, *in continuation.*
August, 26th, 17—.

You have read this strange and terrific story, Margaret; and do you not feel your blood congealed with horror, like that which even now curdles mine? Sometimes, seized with sudden agony, he could not continue his tale; at others, his voice broken, yet piercing, uttered with difficulty the words so replete with agony. His fine and lovely eyes were now lighted up with indignation, now subdued to downcast sorrow, and quenched in infinite wretchedness. Sometimes he commanded his countenance and tones, and related the most horrible incidents with a tranquil voice, suppressing every mark of agitation; then, like a volcano bursting forth, his face would suddenly change to an expression of the wildest rage, as he shrieked out imprecations on his persecutor.

His tale is connected, and told with an appearance of the simplest truth; yet I own to you that the letters of Felix and Safie, which he showed me, and the apparition of the monster, seen from our ship, brought to me a greater conviction of the truth of his narrative than his asseverations, however earnest and connected. Such a monster has then really existence; I cannot doubt; yet I am lost in surprise and admiration.* Sometimes I endeavoured to gain from Frankenstein the particulars of his creature's formation; but on this point he was impenetrable.

'Are you mad, my friend?' said he 'or whither does your senseless curiosity lead you? Would you also create for yourself and the world a demoniacal enemy? Or to what do your quesions tend? Peace, peace! learn my miseries, and do not seek to increase your own.'

Frankenstein discovered that I made notes concerning his history: he asked to see them, and then himself corrected and augmented them in many places; but principally in giving the life and spirit to the conversations he held with his enemy. 'Since you have preserved my narration,' said he, 'I would not that a mutilated one should go down to posterity.'

Thus has a week passed away, while I have listened to the strangest tale that ever imagination formed. My thoughts, and every feeling of my soul, have been drunk up by the interest for my guest, which this tale, and his own elevated and gentle manners have created. I wish to soothe him; yet can I counsel one so infinitely miserable, so destitute of every hope of consolation, to live? Oh, no! the only joy that he can now know will be when he composes his shattered feelings to peace and death. Yet he enjoys one comfort, the offspring of solitude and delirium: he believes, that, when in dreams he holds converse with his friends, and derives from that communion consolation for his miseries, or excitements to his vengeance, that they are not the creations of his fancy, but the real beings who visit him from the regions of a remote world. This faith gives a solemnity to his reveries that render them to me almost as imposing and interesting as truth.

Our conversations are not always confined to his own history and misfortunes. On every point of general literature he displays unbounded knowledge, and a quick and piercing apprehension. His eloquence is forcible and touching; nor can I hear him, when he relates a pathetic incident, or endeavours to move the passions of pity or love, without tears. What a glorious creature must he have been in the days of his prosperity, when he is thus noble and godlike in ruin. He seems to feel his own worth, and the greatness of his fall.

'When younger,' said he, 'I felt as if I were destined for some great enterprise. My feelings are profound; but I possessed a coolness of judgment that fitted me for illustrious achievements. This sentiment of the worth of my nature supported me, when others would have been oppressed; for I deemed it criminal to throw away in useless grief those talents that might be useful to my fellow-creatures. When I reflected on the work I had completed, no less a one than the creation of a sensitive an rational animal, I could not rank myself with the herd of common projectors.* But this feeling, which supported me in the commencement of my career, now serves only to plunge me lower in the dust. All my speculations and hopes are as nothing; and, like the archangel who aspired to omnipotence,* I am chained in an eternal hell. My imagination was vivid, yet my powers of analysis and application were intense; by the union of these qualities I conceived the idea, and executed the creation of a man. Even now I cannot recollect, without passion, my reveries while the work was incomplete. I trod heaven in my thoughts, now exulting in my powers, now burning with the idea of their effects. From the infancy I was imbued with high hopes and a lofty ambition; but how am I sunk! Oh! my friend, if you had known me as I once was, you would not recognize me in this state of degradation. Despondency rarely visited my heart; a high destiny seemed to bear me on, until I fell, never, never again to rise.'

Must I then lose this admirable being? I have longed for a friend; I have sought one who would sympathize with and love me. Behold, on these desert seas I have found such a one; but, I fear, I have gained him only to know his value, and lose him. I would reconcile him to life, but he repulses the idea.

'I thank you, Walton,' he said, 'for your kind intentions towards so miserable a wretch; but when you speak of new ties, and fresh affections, think you that any can replace those who are gone? Can any man be to me as Clerval was; or any woman another Elizabeth? Even where the affections are not strongly moved by any superior excellence, the companions of our childhood always possess a certain power over our minds, which hardly any later friend can obtain. They know our infantine dispositions, which, however, they may be afterwards modified, are never eradicated; and they can judge of our actions with more certain conclusions as to the integrity of our motives. A sister or a brother can never, unless indeed such symptoms have been shewn early, suspect the other of fraud or false dealing, when another friend, however strongly he may be attached, may, in spite of himself, be invaded with suspicion. But I enjoyed friends, dear not only through habit and association, but from their own merits; and, wherever I am, the soothing voice of my Elizabeth, and the conversation of Clerval, will be ever whispered in my ear. They are dead; and but one feeling in such a solitude can persuade me to preserve my life. If I were engaged in any high undertaking or design, fraught with extensive utility to my fellow-creatures, then could I live to fulfil it. But such is not my destiny; I must pursue and destroy the being to whom I gave existence; then my lot on earth will be fulfilled, and I may die.'

September 2nd

MY BELOVED SISTER,

I write to you, encompassed by peril, and ignorant whether I am ever doomed to see again dear England, and the dearer friends that inhabit it. I am surrounded by mountains of ice which admit no escape, and threaten every moment to crush my vessel. The brave fellows, whom I have persuaded to be my companions, look towards me for aid; but I have none to bestow. There is something terribly appalling in our situation, yet my courage and hopes do not desert me. We may survive;

and if we do not, I will repeat the lessons of my Seneca,* and die with a good heart.

Yet what, Margaret, will be the state of your mind? You will not hear of my destruction, and you will anxiously await my return. Years will pass, and you will have visitings of despair, and yet be tortured by hope. Oh! my beloved sister, the sickening failings of your heart-felt expectations are, in prospect, more terrible to me than my own death. But you have a husband, and lovely children; you may be happy: heaven bless you, and make you so!

My unfortunate guest regards me with the tenderest compassion. He endeavours to fill me with hope; and talks as if life were a possession which he valued. He reminds me how often the same accidents have happened to other navigators, who have attempted this sea, and, in spite of myself, he fills me with cheerful auguries. Even the sailors feel the power of his eloquence: when he speaks, they no longer despair; he rouses their energies, and, while they hear his voice, they believe these vast mountains of ice are mole-hills, which will vanish before the resolutions of man. These feelings are transitory; each day's expectation delayed fills them with fear, and I almost dread a mutiny caused by this despair.

September 5th

A scene has just passed of such uncommon interest, that although it is highly probable that these papers may never reach you, yet I cannot forbear recording it.

We are still surrounded by mountains of ice, still in imminent danger of being crushed in their conflict. The cold is excessive, and many of my unfortunate comrades have already found a grave amidst this scene of desolation. Frankenstein has daily declined in health: a feverish fire still glimmers in his eyes; but he is exhausted, and, when suddenly roused to any exertion, he speedily sinks again into apparent lifelessness.

I mentioned in my last letter the fears I entertained of a mutiny. This morning, as I sat watching the wan countenance of my friend – his eyes half closed, and his limbs hanging listlessly, – I was roused by half a dozen of the sailors, who desired admission into the cabin. They entered; and their leader addressed me. He told me that he and his companions had been chosen by the other sailors to come in deputation to me, to make me a demand, which, in justice, I could not refuse. We were immured in ice, and should probably never escape; but they feared that if, as was possible, the ice should dissipate, and a free passage be opened, I should be rash enough to continue my voyage, and lead them into fresh dangers, after they might happily have surmounted this. They desired, therefore, that I should engage with a solemn promise, that if the vessel should be freed, I would instantly direct my course southward.

This speech troubled me. I had not despaired; nor had I yet conceived the idea of returning, if set free. Yet could I, in justice, or even in possibility, refuse this demand? I hesitated before I answered; when Frankenstein, who had at first been silent, and, indeed, appeared hardly to have force enough to attend, now roused himself; his eyes sparkled, and his cheeks flushed with momentary vigour. Turning towards the men, he said —

'What do you mean? What do you demand of your captain? Are you then so easily turned from your design? Did you not call this a glorious expedition? and wherefore was it glorious? Not because the way was smooth and placid as a southern sea, but because it was full of dangers and terror; because, at every new incident, your fortitude was to be called forth, and your courage exhibited; because danger and death surrounded, and these dangers you were to brave and overcome. For this was it a glorious, for this was it an honourable undertaking. You were hereafter to be hailed as the benefactors of your species; your name adored, as belonging to brave men who encountered death for honour and the benefit of mankind. And now, behold, with the first imagination of danger, or, if you will, the first mighty and terrific trial of your courage, you shrink away, and are content to be handed down as men who had not strength enough to endure cold and peril; and so, poor souls, they were chilly, and returned to their warm fire-sides. Why, that requires not this preparation; ye need not have come thus far, and dragged your captain to the shame of defeat, merely to prove yourselves cowards. Oh! be men, or be more than men. Be steady to your purposes, and firm as a rock. This ice is not made of such stuff as your hearts might be; it is mutable, cannot withstand you, if you say that it shall not. Do not return to your families with the stigma of disgrace marked on your brows.

Return as heroes who have fought and conquered, and who know not what it is to turn their backs on the foe.'

He spoke this with a voice so modulated to the different feelings expressed in his speech, with an eye so full of lofty design and heroism, that can you wonder that these men were moved. They looked at one another, and were unable to reply. I spoke; I told them to retire, and consider of what had been said: that I would not lead them further north, if they strenuously desired the contrary; but that I hoped that, with reflection, their courage would return.

They retired, and I turned towards my friend; but he was sunk in languor, and almost deprived of life.

How all this will terminate, I know not; but I had rather die, than return shamefully, — my purpose unfulfilled. Yet I fear such will be my fate; the men, unsupported by ideas of glory and honour, can never willingly continue to endure their present hardships.

September 7th.

The die is cast; I have consented to return, if we are not destroyed. Thus are my hopes blasted by cowardice and indecision; I come back ignorant and disappointed. It requires more philosophy than I possess, to bear this injustice with patience.

September 12th.

It is past; I am returning to England. I have lost my hopes of utility and glory; — I have lost my friend. But I will endeavour to detail these bitter circumstances to you, my dear sister; and, while I am wafted towards England, and towards you, I will not despond.

September the ninth, the ice began to move, and roarings like thunder were heard at a distance, as the islands split and cracked in every direction. We were in the most imminent peril; but, as we could only remain passive, my chief attention was occupied by my unfortunate guest, whose illness increased in such a degree, that he was entirely confined to his bed. The ice cracked behind us, and was driven with force towards the north; a breeze sprung from the west, and on the 11th the passage towards the south became perfectly free. When the sailors saw this, and that their return to their native country was apparently assured, a shout of tumultuous joy broke from them, loud and long-continued. Frankenstein, who was dozing, awoke, and asked the cause of the tumult. 'They shout,' I said, 'because they will soon return to England.'

'Do you then really return ?'

'Alas ! yes ; I cannot withstand their demands. I cannot lead them unwillingly to danger, and I must return.'

'Do so, if you will ; but I will not. You may give up your purpose ; but mine is assigned to me by heaven, and I dare not. I am weak ; but surely the spirits who assist my vengeance will endow me with sufficient strength.' Saying this, he endeavoured to spring from the bed, but the exertion was too great for him ; he fell back, and fainted.

It was long before he was restored ; and I often thought that life was entirely extinct. At length he opened his eyes, but he breathed with difficulty, and was unable to speak. The surgeon gave him a composing draught, and ordered us to leave him undisturbed. In the mean time he told me, that my friend had certainly not many hours to live.

His sentence was pronounced ; and I could only grieve, and be patient. I sat by his bed watching him ; his eyes were closed, and I thought he slept ; but presently he called to me in a feeble voice, and, bidding me come near, said – 'Alas ! the strength I relied on is gone ; I feel that I shall soon die, and he, my enemy and persecutor, may still be in being. Think not, Walton, that in the last moments of my existence I feel that burning hatred, and ardent desire of revenge, I once expressed, but I feel myself justified in desiring the death of my adversary. During these last days I have been occupied in examining my past conduct ; nor do I find it blameable. In a fit of enthusiastic madness I created a rational creature, and was bound towards him, to assure, as far as was in my power, his happiness and wellbeing. This was my duty ; but there was another still paramount to that. My duties towards my fellow-creatures had greater claims to my attention, because they included a greater proportion of happiness or misery. Urged by this view, I refused, and did right in refusing, to create a companion for the first creature. He showed unparalleled malignity and selfishness, in evil : he destroyed my friends ; he devoted to destruction beings who possessed exquisite sensations, happiness, and wisdom ; nor do I know where this thirst for vengeance may end. Miserable himself, that he may render no other wretched, he ought to die. The task of his destruction was mine, but I have failed. When actuated by selfish and vicious motives, I asked you to undertake my unfinished work; and I renew this request now, when I am only induced by reason and virtue.

'Yet I cannot ask you to renounce your country and friends, to fulfil this task; and now, that you are returning to England, you will have little chance of meeting with him. But the consideration of these points, and the well-balancing of what you may esteem your duties, I leave to you; my judgment and ideas are already disturbed by the near approach of death. I dare not ask you to do what I think right, for I may still be misled by passion.

'That he should live to be an instrument of mischief disturbs me; in other respects this hour, when I momentarily expect my release is the only happy one which I have enjoyed for several years. The forms of the beloved dead flit before me, and I hasten to their arms. Farewell, Walton! Seek happiness, in tranquillity, and avoid ambition, even if it be only the apparently innocent one of distinguishing yourself in science and discoveries. Yet why do I say this? I have myself been blasted in these hopes, yet another may succeed.'

His voice became fainter as he spoke; and at length, exhausted by his effort, he sunk into silence. About half an hour afterwards he attempted again to speak, but was unable; he pressed my hand feebly, and his eyes closed for ever, while the irradiation of a gentle smile passed away from his lips.

Margaret, what comment can I make on the untimely extinction of this glorious spirit? What can I say, that will enable you to understand the depth of my sorrow? All that I should express would be inadequate and feeble. My tears flow; my mind is overshadowed by a cloud of disappointment. But I journey towards England, and I may there find consolation.

I am interrupted. What do these sounds portend? It is midnight; the breeze blows fairly, and the watch on deck scarcely stir. Again; there is a sound as of a human voice, but hoarser; it comes from the cabin where the remains of Frankenstein still lie. I must arise, and examine. Good night, my sister.

Great God! what a scene has just taken place! I am yet dizzy with the remembrance of it. I hardly know whether I shall have the power to detail it; yet the tale which I have recorded would be incomplete without this final and wonderful catastrophe.*

I entered the cabin, where lay the remains of my ill-fated and admirable friend. Over him hung a form which I cannot find words to describe; gigantic in stature, yet uncouth and distorted in its proportions. As he hung over the coffin, his face was concealed by long locks of ragged hair; but one vast hand was extended, in colour and apparent texture like that of a mummy. When he heard the sound of my approach, he ceased to utter exclamations of grief and horror, and sprung towards the window. Never did I behold a vision so horrible as his face, of such loathsome, yet appalling hideousness. I shut my eyes involuntarily, and endeavoured to recollect what were my duties with regard to this destroyer. I called on him to stay.

He paused, looking on me with wonder; and, again turning towards the lifeless form of his creator, he seemed to forget my presence, and every feature and gesture seemed instigated by the wildest rage of some uncontrollable passion.

'That is also my victim!' he exclaimed; in his murder my crimes are consummated; the miserable series of my being is wound to its close! Oh, Frankenstein! generous and self-devoted being! what does it avail that I now ask thee to pardon me? I, who irretrievably destroyed thee by destroying all thou lovedst. Alas! he is cold; he may not answer me.'

His voice seemed suffocated; and my first impulses, which had suggested to me the duty of obeying the dying request of my friend, in destroying his enemy, were now suspended by a mixture of curiosity and compassion. I approached this tremendous being; I dared not again raise my looks upon his face, there was something so scaring and unearthly in his ugliness. I attempted to speak, but the words died away on my lips. The monster continued to utter wild and incoherent self-reproaches. At length I gathered resolution to address him, in a pause of the tempest of his passion: 'Your repentance,' I said, 'is now superfluous. If you had listened to the voice of conscience, and heeded the stings of remorse, before you had urged your diabolical vengeance to this extremity, Frankenstein would yet have lived.'

'And do you dream?' said the demon; 'do you think that I was then dead to agony and remorse? – He,' he continued, pointing to the corpse, 'he suffered not more in the consummation of the deed; – oh! not the ten-thousandth portion of the anguish that was mine during the lingering detail of its execution. A frightful selfishness hurried me on, while my heart was poisoned with remorse. Think ye that the groans of Clerval

were music to my ears ? My heart was fashioned to be suscep-
tible of love and sympathy ; and, when wrenched by misery to
vice and hatred, it did not endure the violence of the change
without torture, such as you cannot even imagine.

'After the murder of Clerval, I returned to Switzerland, heart-
broken and overcome. I pitied Frankenstein ; my pity amounted
to horror : I abhorred myself. But when I discovered that he, the
author at once of my existence of its unspeakable torments,
dared to hope for happiness ; that while he accumulated
wretchedness and despair upon me, he sought his own enjoyment in feelings and passions from the indulgence of which I
was for ever barred, then impotent envy and bitter indignation
filled me with an insatiable thirst for vengeance. I recollected my
threat, and resolved that it should be accomplished. I knew that
I was preparing for myself a deadly torture ; but I was the slave,
not the master of an impulse, which I detested, yet could not
disobey. Yet when she died ! – nay, then I was not miserable. I
had cast off all feeling, subdued all anguish to riot in the excess
of my despair. Evil thenceforth became my good. Urged thus
far, I had no choice but to adapt my nature to an element which
I had willingly chosen. The completion of my demoniacal design
became an insatiable passion. And now it is ended ; there is my
last victim !'

I was at first touched by the expressions of his misery ; yet
when I called to mind what Frankenstein had said of his powers
of eloquence and persuasion, and when I again cast my eyes on
the lifeless form of my friend, indignation was re-kindled within
me. 'Wretch !' I said, 'it is well that you come here to whine over
the desolation that you have made. You throw a torch into a
pile of buildings, and when they are consumed you sit among
the ruins, and lament the fall. Hypocritical fiend ! if he whom
you mourn still lived, still would he be the object, again would
he become the prey of your accursed vengeance. It is not pity
that you feel ; you lament only because the victim of your
malignity is withdrawn from your power.'

'Oh, it is not thus – not thus,' interrupted the being ; 'yet such
must be the impression conveyed to you by what appears to be
the purport of my actions. Yet I seek not a fellow-feeling in my
misery. No sympathy may I ever find. When I first sought it, it
was the love of virtue, the feelings of happiness and affection
with which my whole being overflowed, that I wished to be
participated. But now, that virtue has become to me a shadow,

and that happiness and affection are turned into bitter and loathing despair, in what should I seek for sympathy? I am content to suffer alone, while my sufferings shall endure : when I die, I am well satisfied that abhorrence and opprobrium should load my memory. Once my fancy was soothed with dreams of virtue, of fame, and of enjoyment. Once I falsely hoped to meet with beings, who, pardoning my outward form, would love me for the excellent qualities which I was capable of bringing forth. I was nourished with high thoughts of honour and devotion. But now vice has degraded me beneath the meanest animal. No crime, no mischief, no malignity, no misery, can be found comparable to mine. When I call over the frightful catalogue of my deeds, I cannot believe that I am he whose thoughts were once filled with sublime and transcendant visions of the beauty and the majesty of goodness. But it is even so ; the fallen angel becomes a malignant devil. Yet even that enemy of God and man had friends and associates in his desolation ; I am quite alone.

'You, who call Frankenstein your friend, seem to have a knowledge of my crimes and his misfortunes. But, in the detail which he gave you of them, he could not sum up the hours and months of misery which I endured, wasting in impotent passions. For whilst I destroyed his hopes, I did not satisfy my own desires. They were for ever ardent and craving ; still I desired love and fellowship, and I was still spurned. Was there no injustice in this? Am I to be thought the only criminal, when all human kind sinned against me? Why do you not hate Felix, who drove his friend from his door with contumely? Why do you not execrate the rustic who sought to destroy the saviour of his child? Nay, these are virtuous and immaculate beings ! I, the miserable and the abandoned, am an abortion, to be spurned at, and kicked, and trampled on. Even now my blood boils at the recollection of this unjustice.

'But it is true that I am a wretch. I have murdered the lovely and the helpless ; I have strangled the innocent as they slept, and grasped to death his throat who never injured me or any other living thing. I have devoted my creator, the select specimen of all that is worthy of love and admiration among men, to misery ; I have pursued him even to that irremediable ruin. There he lies, white and cold in death. You hate me ; but your abhorrence cannot equal that with which I regard myself. I look on the hands which executed the deed ; I think on the heart in which the imagination of it was conceived, and long for the moment when they will meet my eyes, when it will haunt my thoughts, no more.

'Fear not that I shall be the instrument of future mischief. My work is nearly complete. Neither yours nor any man's death is needed to consummate the series of my being, and accomplish that which must be done; but it requires my own. Do not think that I shall be slow to perform this sacrifice. I shall quit your vessel on the ice-raft which brought me hither, and shall seek the most northern extremity of the globe; I shall collect my funeral pile, and consume to ashes this miserable frame, that its remains may afford no light to any curious and unhallowed wretch, who would create such another as I have been. I shall die. I shall no longer feel the agonies which now consume me, or be the prey of feelings unsatisfied, yet unquenched. He is dead who called me into being; and when I shall be no more, the very remembrance of us both will speedily vanish. I shall no longer seen the sun or stars, or feel the winds play on my cheeks. Light, feeling, sense, will pass away; and in this condition must I find my happiness. Some years ago, when the images which this world affords first opened upon me, when I felt the cheering warmth of summer, and heard the rustling of the leaves and the chirping of the birds, and these were all to me, I should have wept to die; now it is my only consolation. Polluted by crimes, and torn by the bitterest remorse, where can I find rest but in death?

'Farewell! I leave you, and in you the last of human kind whom these eyes will ever behold. Farewell, Frankenstein! If thou wert yet alive, and yet cherished a desire of revenge against me, it would be better satiated in my life than in my destruction. But it was not so; thou didst seek my extinction, that I might not cause greater wretchedness; and if yet, in some mode unknown to me, thou has not yet ceased to think and feel, thou desirest not my life for my own misery. Blasted as thou wert, my agony was still superior to thine; for the bitter sting of remorse may not cease to rankle in my wounds until death shall close them for ever.

'But soon,' he cried, with sad and solemn enthusiasm, 'I shall die, and what I now feel be no longer felt. Soon these burning miseries will be extinct. I shall ascend my funeral pile triumphantly, and exult in the agony of the torturing flames. The light of that conflagration will fade away; my ashes will be swept into the sea by the winds. My spirit will sleep in peace; or if it thinks, it will not surely think thus. Farewell.'

He sprung from the cabin-window, as he said this, upon the ice-raft which lay close to the vessel. He was soon borne away by the waves, and lost in darkness and distance.

THE END

APPENDIX A

Preface to *Frankenstein*
by Mary Shelley (1831)

AUTHOR'S INTRODUCTION
to the Standard Novels Edition
(1831)

The publishers of the Standard Novels, in selecting *Frankenstein* for one of their series, expressed a wish that I should furnish them with some account of the origin of the story. I am the more willing to comply, because I shall thus give a general answer to the question, so very frequently asked me, 'How I, then a young girl, came to think of, and to dilate upon, so very hideous an idea?' It is true that I am very averse to bringing myself forward in print; but as my account will only appear as an appendage to a former production, and as it will be confined to such topics as have connection with my authorship alone, I can scarcely accuse myself of a personal intrusion.

It is not singular that, as the daughter of two persons of distinguished literary celebrity,* I should very early in life have thought of writing. As a child I scribbled; and my favourite pastime, during the hours given me for recreation, was to 'write stories'. Still I had a dearer pleasure than this, which was the formation of castles in the air – the indulging in waking dreams – the following up of trains of thought, which had for their subject the formation of a succession of imaginary incidents. My dreams were at once more fantastic and agreeable than my writings. In the latter I was a close imitator – rather doing as others had done, than putting down the suggestions of my own mind. What I wrote was intended at least for one other eye – my childhood's companion and friend; but my dreams were all my own; I accounted for them to nobody; they were my refuge when annoyed – my dearest pleasure when free.

I lived principally in the country as a girl, and passed a considerable time in Scotland. I made occasional visits to the more picturesque parts; but my habitual residence was on the blank and dreary northern shores of the Tay, near Dundee.

Blank and dreary on retrospection I call them; they were not so to me then. They were the eyry of freedom, and the pleasant region where unheeded I could commune with the creatures of my fancy. I wrote then – but in a most commonplace style. It was beneath the trees of the grounds belonging to our house, or on the bleak sides of the woodless mountains near, that my true compositions, the airy flights of my imagination, were born and fostered. I did not make myself the heroine of my tales. Life appeared to me too commonplace an affair as regarded myself. I could not figure to myself that romantic woes or wonderful events would ever be my lot; but I was not confined to my own identity, and I could people the hours with creations far more interesting to me at that age, than my own sensations.

After this my life became busier, and reality stood in place of fiction. My husband, however, was, from the first, very anxious that I should prove myself worthy of my parentage, and enrol myself on the page of fame. He was forever inciting me to obtain literary reputation, which even on my own part I cared for then, though since I have become infinitely indifferent to it. At this time he desired that I should write, not so much with the idea that I could produce anything worthy of notice, but that he might himself judge how far I possessed the promise of better things hereafter. Still I did nothing. Travelling, and the cares of a family, occupied my time; and study, in the way of reading, or improving my ideas in communication with his far more cultivated mind, was all of literary employment that engaged my attention.

In the summer of 1816, we visited Switzerland, and became the neighbours of Lord Byron.* At first we spent our pleasant hours on the lake, or wandering on its shores; and Lord Byron, who was writing the third canto of *Childe Harold*, was the only one among us who put his thoughts upon paper. These, as he brought them successively to us, clothed in all the light and harmony of poetry, seemed to stamp as divine the glories of heaven and earth, whose influences we partook with him.

But it proved a wet, ungenial summer, and incessant rain often confined us for days to the house. Some volumes of ghost stories, translated from the German into French, fell into our hands. There was the *History of the Inconstant Lover*, who, when he thought to clasp the bride to whom he had pledged his vows, found himself in the pale arms of her whom he had deserted. There was the tale of the sinful founder of his race,

whose miserable doom it was to bestow the kiss of death on all
the younger sons of his fated house, just when they reached the
age of promise. His gigantic, shadowy form, clothed like the
ghost in *Hamlet*, in complete armour, but with the beaver up,
was seen at midnight, by the moon's fitful beams, to advance
slowly along the gloomy avenue. The shape was lost beneath
the shadow of the castle walls; but soon a gate swung back, a
step was heard, the door of the chamber opened, and he
advanced to the couch of the blooming youths, cradled in
healthy sleep. Eternal sorrow sat upon his face as he bent down
and kissed the forehead of the boys, who from that hour
withered like flowers snapped upon the stalk. I have not seen
these stories since then; but their incidents are as fresh in my
mind as if I had read them yesterday.

'We will each write a ghost story,' said Lord Byron; and his
proposition was acceded to. There were four of us. The noble
author began a tale, a fragment of which he printed at the end
of his poem of *Mazeppa*. Shelley, more apt to embody ideas and
sentiments in the radiance of brilliant imagery, and in the music
of the most melodious verse that adorns our language, than to
invent the machinery of a story, commenced one founded on the
experiences of his early life. Poor Polidori* had some terrible
idea about a skull-headed lady, who was so punished for peeping
through a keyhole — what to see I forget — something very
shocking and wrong of course; but when she was reduced to a
worse condition than the renowned Tom of Coventry,* he did
not know what to do with her, and was obliged to dispatch her
to the tomb of the Capulets,* the only place for which she was
fitted. The illustrious poets also, annoyed by the platitude of
prose, speedily relinquished their uncongenial task.

I busied myself *to think of a story* – a story to rival those
which had excited me to this task. One which would speak to
the mysterious fears of our nature, and awaken thrilling horror
– one to make the reader dread to look round, to curdle the
blood, and quicken the beatings of the heart. If I did not
accomplish these things, my ghost story would be unworthy of
its name. I thought and pondered – vainly. I felt that blank
incapacity of invention which is the greatest misery of authorship, when dull Nothing replies to our anxious invocations.
Have you thought of a story? I was asked each morning, and
each morning I was forced to reply with a mortifying negative.

Everything must have a beginning, to speak in Sanchean

phrase ;* and that beginning must be linked to something that
went before. The Hindus give the world an elephant to support
it, but, they make that elephant stand upon a tortoise. Invention,
it must be humbly admitted, does not consist in creating out of
void, but out of chaos ; the materials must, in the first place, be
afforded : it can give form to dark, shapeless substances, but
cannot bring into being the substance itself. In all matters of
discovery and invention, even of those that appertain to the
imagination, we are continually reminded of the story of Colum-
bus and his egg. Invention consists in the capacity of seizing on
the capabilities of a subject, and in the power of moulding and
fashioning ideas suggested to it.

Many and long were the conversations between Lord Byron
and Shelley, to which I was a devout but nearly silent listener.
During one of these, various philosophical doctrines were discussed, and among others the nature of the principle of life, and
whether there was any probability of its ever being discovered
and communicated. They talked of the experiments of Dr
Darwin (I speak not of what the Doctor really did, or said that
he did, but, as more to my purpose, of what was then spoken of
as having being done by him), who preserved a piece of
vermicelli in a glass case, till by some extraordinary means it
began to move with voluntary motion. Not thus, after all, would
life be given. Perhaps a corpse would be reanimated ; galvanism*
had given token of such things : perhaps the component parts of
a creature might be manufactured, brought together, and endued
with vital warmth.

Night waned upon this talk, and even the witching hour had
gone by, before we retired to rest. When I placed my head on
my pillow, I did not sleep, nor could I be said to think. My
imagination, unbidden, possessed and guided me, gifting the
successive images that arose in my mind with a vividness far
beyond the usual bounds of reverie. I saw – with shut eyes, but
acute mental vision – I saw the pale student of unhallowed arts
kneeling beside the thing he had put together. I saw the hideous
phantasm of a man stretched out, and then, on the working of
some powerful engine, show signs of life, and stir with an
uneasy, half-vital motion. Frightful it must be ; for supremely
frightful would be the effect of any human endeavour to mock
the stupendous mechanism of the Creator of the World. His
success would terrify the artist ; he would rush away from his
odious handiwork, horror-stricken. He would hope that, left to

itself, the slight spark of life which he had communicated would fade; that this thing, which had received such imperfect animation, would subside into dead matter; and he might sleep in the belief that the silence of the grave would quench forever the transient existence of the hideous corpse which he had looked upon as the cradle of life. He sleeps; but he is awakened; he opens his eyes; behold the horrid thing stands at his bedside, opening his curtains, and looking on him with yellow, watery, but speculative eyes.

I opened mine in terror. The idea so possessed my mind, that a thrill of fear ran through me, and I wished to exchange the ghastly image of my fancy for the realities around. I see them still; the very room, the dark parquet, the closed shutters, with the moonlight struggling through and the sense I had that the glassy lake and white high Alps were beyond. I could not so easily get rid of my hideous phantom; still it haunted me. I must try to think of something else. I recurred to my ghost story, my tiresome, unlucky ghost story! Oh! If I could only contrive one which would frighten my reader as I myself had been frightened that night!

Swift as light and as cheering was the idea that broke in upon me. 'I have found it! What terrified me will terrify others; and I need only describe the spectre which had haunted my midnight pillow.' On the morrow I announced that I had *thought of a story*. I began that day with the words, *It was on a dreary night of November*, making only a transcript of the grim terrors of my waking dream.

At first I thought of but a few pages – of a short tale; but Shelley urged me to develop the idea at greater length. I certainly did not owe the suggestion of one incident, nor scarcely of one train of feeling, to my husband, and yet but for his incitement, it would never have taken the form in which it was presented to the world. From this declaration I must except the preface. As far as I can recollect, it was entirely written by him.

And now, once again, I bid my hideous progeny go forth and prosper. I have an affection for it, for it was the offspring of happy days, when death and grief were but words, which found no true echo in my heart. Its several pages speak of many a walk, many a drive, and many a conversation, when I was not alone: and my companion was one who, in this world, I shall never see more. But this is for myself; my readers have nothing to do with these associations.

I will add but one word as to the alterations I have made. They are principally those of style. I have changed no portion of the story, nor introduced any new ideas or circumstance.* I have mended the language where it was so bald as to interfere with the interest of the narrative; and these changes occur almost exclusively in the beginning of the first volume. Throughout they are entirely confined to such parts as are mere adjuncts to the story, leaving the core and substance of it untouched.

M.W.S.
London, October 15, 1831

---

* Modern scholarship disputes these claims. See introduction, pp. vii–viii.

APPENDIX B

Presumption
or
The Fate of Frankenstein
(1823)

by
Richard Brinsley Peake

Richard Brinsley Peake (1792–1847),
treasurer of the Lyceum Theatre,
London and successful writer of
farces and comic opera libretti. *He*
was known as 'quaintly humorous
speaker'. He compiled the memoirs
of the eighteenth-century theatrical
family, the Colmans.

PRESUMPTION
or
The Fate of Frankenstein
(1823)

by
Richard Brinsley Peake

DRAMATIS PERSONAE

* * *	Mr T P Cooke
FRANKENSTEIN	Mr Wallack
CLERVAL (*his friend, in love with* ELIZABETH)	Mr Bland
ELIZABETH (*sister of* FRANKENSTEIN)	Mrs Austin
WILLIAM (*brother of* FRANKENSTEIN)	Master Boden
FRITZ (*servant of* FRANKENSTEIN)	Mr Keeley
MADAME NINON (*wife of* FRITZ)	Mrs T Weippert
DE LACEY (*a banished gentleman – blind*)	Mr Rowbotham
FELIX DE LACEY (*his son*)	Mr Pearman
AGATHA (*daughter of* DE LACEY)	Miss L Dance
SAFIE (*an Arabian girl, bethrothed to* FELIX)	Miss Povey
TANSKIN (*a gipsy*)	Mr Shield
HAMMERPAN (*a tinker*)	Mr Salter
A GUIDE (*an old man*)	Mr R Phillips

Gipsies, peasants, choristers, and dancers (male and female).

SCENE – *Geneva and its vicinity.*

COSTUME

THE MONSTER'S APPEARANCE AND DRESS: Dark black flowing hair – *à la Octavian* – his face, hands, arms and legs all bare, being one colour, the same as his body, which is light blue or French grey cotton dress, fitting quite close, as if it were his flesh, with a slate colour scarf round his middle, passing over one shoulder.

FRANKENSTEIN: Black velvet vest and trunk breeches – grey tunic, open, the sleeves open in front, slashed with black – black silk pantaloons and black velvet shoes – black velvet hat.

CLERVAL: Blue-coloured tunic, trimmed with velvet, and silk puffs at arms – braided pantaloons – boots – drab hat and white feather.

ELIZABETH: Grey silk dress – trimmed with white fur – hat to correspond.

WILLIAM: Fawn-coloured tunic, trimmed with light blue – white silk pantaloons – scarlet bottoms – white satin Italian cap.

FRITZ: Buff jacket and trunks, trimmed with orange – blue stockings – russet shoes – small three-cornered drab hat.

NINON – A showy Italian peasant's dress, with apron – head-dress hair confined by long gold pins.

DE LACEY – Dark green doublet – vest trunk breeches to match – brown stockings – russet shoes – and cloth hat.

FELIX – Green hunting tunic, trimmed with black braid – russet boots – black hat and feather.

AGATHA – Short pelisse of a dark brown, over a slate-coloured petticoat – dark brown Italian cap.

SAFIE – Short frock of crimson cloth, trimmed with silk – turban head-dress – red shoes – and full silk trousers – large silk shawl or scarf to give an Oriental appearance.

TANSKIN – A tight goatskin jacket, leaving the throat and arms bare – a coarse canvas shirt seen through it, with ragged sleeves, extending nearly down to the elbow, and hanging loose there – goatskin breeches, extending half way down the thighs, with ragged underdress or trousers of canvas, reaching within an inch of the knees – legs bare, sandalled with leather thongs, the hair confined in a long Italian net – the dress confined at the waist by a belt, in which a knife is stuck – slouched hat.

HAMMERPAN – Same as Tanskin, with the addition of a leather apron – wallet – bald wig – and one eye blind.

GUIDE – Peasant's tunic – red pantaloons – russet boots.

ACT ONE SCENE I

A Gothic Chamber in the House of Frankenstein

[FRITZ *discovered in a Gothic arm-chair, nodding asleep. During the symphony of the song, he starts, rubs his eyes, and comes forward.*]

Air

FRITZ :   Oh, dear me ! What's the matter ?
How I shake at each clatter.
   My marrow
   They harrow.
Oh, dear me ! What's the matter ?
If mouse squeaks, or cat sneezes,
Cricket chirps, or cock wheezes,
   Then I fret,
   In cold sweat.
Ev'ry noise my nerves teases ;
Bless my heart — heaven preserve us !
I declare I'm so nervous.
   Ev'ry knock
   Is a shock.
I declare I'm so nervous !
I'm so nervous.

FRITZ :   Oh, Fritz, Fritz ! What is it come to ! You are frightened out of your wits. Why did you ever leave your native village ! Why couldn't you be happy in the country with an innocent cow for your companion (bless its sweet breath !) instead of coming here to the city of Geneva to be hired as a servant ! [*starts*] What's that ? — Nothing. And then how complimentary ! Master only hired me because he thought I looked so stupid ! Ha, ha, ha ! But am I stupid though ? To be sure Mr Frankenstein is a kind man, and I should respect him, but that I thinks as how he holds converse with somebody below with a long tail, horns, and hoofs, who shall be nameless. [*starts again*] What's that ! Oh, a gnat on my nose ! Oh, anything frightens me now — I'm so very nervous ! I spill all my bread and milk when I feed myself at breakfast ! Lauk, Lauk ! In the country, if a dog brayed or a donkey barked ever so loud, it had no effect upon me. [*Two distinct loud knocks – Fritz jumps*] Oh, mercy! I jump like a maggot out of a cheese! How my heart beats!

CLERVAL: [*offstage*] Fritz. Fritz! Open the door, Fritz!

FRITZ: Yes, it's only Mr Clerval, master's friend, who is going to marry Miss Elizabeth, master's sister. [*opens door*]
        Enter CLERVAL

FRITZ: How d'ye do, sir!

CLERVAL: Good morning, Fritz! Is Mr Frankenstein to be seen?

FRITZ: I fear not, sir, he has as usual been fumi – fumi – fumi-

CLERVAL: Fumigating.

FRITZ: Yes, sir – fumigating; thank'ee, sir – fumigating all night at his chemistry. I have not dared disturb him.

CLERVAL: Mr Frankenstein pursues his study with too much ardour.

FRITZ: And what can be the use of it, Mr Clerval? Work, work, work – always at it. Now, putting a case to you. Now, when I was in the country, with my late cow (she's no more, poor thing!) if I had set to and milked her for a fortnight together, day and night, without stopping, do you think I should have been any the better for it? I ask you as a gentleman and a scholar.

CLERVAL: Ha, ha, ha! Certainly not!

FRITZ: Nor my own neither, poor creature. [*wipes his eyes*] Excuse my crying – she's defunct, and I always whimper a little when I think on her; and my wife lives away from me, but I don't care so much for that. Oh! Mr Clerval, between ourselves – hush! didn't you hear a noise! – between ourselves, I want to unbosom my confidence.

CLERVAL: Well!

FRITZ: Between ourselves – there's nobody at the door, is there? – [*goes to door*] – No! Well, between ourselves, Mr Clerval, I have been so very nervous since I came to this place.

CLERVAL: Pshaw!

FRITZ: Nay, don't 'Pshaw!' till you've heard me out. Oh, Mr Clerval! I'll tell you. One night Mr Frankenstein did indulge himself by going to bed. He was worn with fatigue and study. I had occasion to go into his chamber. He was asleep, but frightfully troubled; he groaned and ground his teeth setting mine on edge. 'It is accomplished!' said he. *Accomplished!* I knew that had nothing to do with me, but I listened. He started up in his sleep, though his eyes were opened and dead as oysters, he cried, 'It is animated – it rises – walks !' Now my shrewd guess, sir, is that, like Dr Faustus,* my master is raising the Devil.

CLERVAL :   Fritz, you are simple : drive such impressions from your mind. You must not misconstrue your master's words in a dream. Do you never dream ?

FRITZ :   [*mournfully*] I dream about my cow sometimes.

CLERVAL :   Your master is a studious chemist – nay, as I sometimes suspect, an alchemist.

FRITZ :   Eh ! Ah, I think he is. What is an alchemist, Mr Clerval ?

CLERVAL :   Does he not sometimes speak of the art of making gold ?

FRITZ :   Lauk, sir ! Do you take Mr Frankenstein for a coiner ?

CLERVAL :   Did you never hear him make mention of the grand elixir which can prolong life to immortality ?

FRITZ :   Never in all my life.

CLERVAL :   Well, go – find out if it is possible I can see him. I will not detain him.

FRITZ :   Yes, sir. Oh, that laboratory ! I've got two loose teeth, and I am afraid I shall lose them, for whenever I go up towards that infernal place my head shakes like a dice-box ! [*goes to door*] Oh, mercy ! what's that ? Two shining eyes – how they glisten ! Dear, dear, why I declare it's only the cat on the stairs. Puss, puss, pussy ! How you frightened me, you young *dog*, when you know I am so very nervous !

[*Exit* FRITZ]

CLERVAL :   Frankenstein, friend of my youth, how extraordinary and secret are thy pursuits ! – How art thou altered by study ! Strange, what a hold has philosophy taken of thy mind – but thou wert always enthusiastic and of boundless ambition. But Elizabeth – the fair Elizabeth, his sister – what a difference in disposition ! Everyone adores her. Happy Clerval, to be now the possessor of Elizabeth, who, unconscious of her beauty, stole thy heart away !

Song
CLERVAL : Ere witching love my heart possessed,
           And bade my sighs the nymph pursue,
           Calm as the infant's smiling rest,

No anxious hope nor fear it knew.
But doom'd – ah ! doom'd at last to mourn,
What tumults in that heart arose !
An ocean tumbling, wild, and torn
By tempests from its deep repose.
Yet lem me not the virgin blame.
As tho' she wish'd my heart despair,
How could the maid suspect a flame,
Who never knew that she was fair.
– But Frankenstein approaches.

Enter FRANKENSTEIN, *thoughtful, shown in by* FRITZ, *who then exits.*

CLERVAL : My dear friend !

FRANKENSTEIN :   Clerval !

CLERVAL :   Frankenstein, how ill you appear – so pale ! You look as if your night-watchings had been long and uninterrupted.

FRANKENSTEIN :   I have lately been so deeply engaged in one occupation that I have not allowed myself sufficient rest. But how left you my sister, Elizabeth ?

CLERVAL :   Well, and very happy, only a little uneasy that she sees you so seldom.

FRANKENSTEIN : Aye ; I am engaged heart and soul in the pursuit of a discovery – a grand, unheard-of wonder ! None but those who have experienced them can conceive the enticements of science ; he who looks into the book of nature, finds an inexhaustible source of novelty, of wonder, and delight. What hidden treasures are contained in her mighty volume – what strange, un-dreamed-of mysteries !

CLERVAL :   But some little respite – your health should be considered.

FRANKENSTEIN :   [*abstracted*] After so much time spent in painful labour, to arrive at last at the summit of my desires, would be indeed a glorious consummation of my toils !

CLERVAL :   How wild and mysterious his abstractions – he heeds me not !

FRANKENSTEIN :   This discovery will be so vast, so overwhelming, that all the steps by which I have been progressively led will be obliterated, and I shall behold only the astounding result.

CLERVAL :   Frankenstein !

FRANKENSTEIN :   Ha ! [*to Clerval*] I see by your eagerness that you expect to be informed of the secret with which I am acquainted. That cannot be.

CLERVAL: I do not wish to pry into your secrets, Frankenstein. I am no natural philosopher; my imagination is too vivid for the details of science. If I contemplate, let it be the charms of your fair sister, Elizabeth. My message hither now – I wish to fix the day for our nuptials. But we must be certain, on so important and happy an event, that we shall enjoy the society of our Frankenstein.

FRANKENSTEIN: Pardon me, Clerval! My first thoughts should recur to those dear friends whom I most love, and who are so deserving of my love – name the day !

CLERVAL: On the morn after tomorrow, may I lead the charming Elizabeth to the alter ?

FRANKENSTEIN: E'en as you will – e'en as you will ! [*aside*] The morn after tomorrow – ere that – my wonderful task will be completed. It will be animated ! It will live – will think !

[*Crosses in deep reflection – afterwards turns up the stage.*]

CLERVAL: [*apart*] Again in reverie ! this becomes alarming – surely his head is affected. I am bound in duty to counteract this madness, and discover the secret of his deep reflections.

[FRANKENSTEIN *sits down – musing.*]

CLERVAL: Farewell, Frankenstein ! He heeds me not – 'tis in vain to claim his notice – but I will seek the cause, and, if possible, effect his cure. No time must be lost. Fritz must assist me, and this way he went.   [*Exit* CLERVAL]

FRANKENSTEIN: Every moment lost fevers me. What time have I devoted ? [*rises*] Had I not been heated by an almost supernatural enthusiasm, my application to this study would have been irksome, disgusting, and almost intolerable. To examine the causes of life – I have had recourse to death – I have seen how the fine form of man has been wasted and degraded – have beheld the corruption of death succeed to the blooming cheek of life ! I have seen how the worm inherited the wonders of the eye and brain – I paused – analysing all the minutiae of causation as exemplified in the change of life from death – until from the midst of this darkness, the sudden light broke in upon me ! A light so brilliant and dazzling, some miracle must have produced the flash ! The vital principle ! The cause of life ! – Like Prometheus of old, have I daringly attempted the formation – the animation of a Being ! To my task – away with reflection, to my task – to my task !

[*Exit* FRANKENSTEIN]

Enter FRITZ *and* CLERVAL.

FRITZ :   Yes, there he goes again, amongst otamies, and phials, and crucibles, and retorts, and charcoal, and fire, and the Devil – for I'm sure he's at the bottom of it, and that makes me so nervous.

CLERVAL :   Fritz, you love your master, and are, I know, a discreet servant – but his friends and relations are all unhappy on his account. His health is rapidly sinking under the fatigue of his present labours – will you not assist to call him back to life and to his family ?

FRITZ :   La ! I'd call out all day long, if that would do any good.

CLERVAL :   I know his mind has been devoted to abtruse and occult sciences – that his brain has been bewildered with the wild fancies of Cornelius Agrippa, Paracelsus, Albertus Magnus, and –

FRITZ :   Oh ! Mr Clerval ! How can you mention such crazy tooth-braking names ? There sounds something wicked in them.

CLERVAL :   Wicked ! Pshaw, man ! they are the renowned names of the earliest experimental philosophers. The sages who promised to the hopes of the laborious alchemist the transmutation of metals and the elixir of life.

FRITZ :   Oh ! Ah ! Indeed ! Lack-a-daisy me !

CLERVAL :   [*aside*] I suspect this fellow is more knave than fool – he wants a bribe. Now, sirrah ! answer me with candour. What is it you like best in the world ?

FRITZ :   Milk !

CLERVAL :   Simpleton ! I mean what station of life would you covet ?

FRITZ :   Station ?

CLERVAL :   Yes. Would you like to be master of a cottage ?

FRITZ :   What, and keep a cow ? – The very thing. Why, Mr Clerval, you're a conjuror, and know my thoughts by heart.

CLERVAL :   Fritz, I want to discover – but you must be prudent. [*Takes out purse and gives a florin to* FRITZ.] Here's an earnest of my future intentions touching the cows and cottage.

FRITZ :   Bodikins ! A florin ! [*examining money*]

CLERVAL : Friend Fritz, you must some time, when Mr Frankenstein is absent from home, admit me into his study.

FRITZ : Oh, dear, I can't ! — Don't take your florin back again — [*puts up money*] — for he always locks the door. To be sure, there's a little window a-top of the staircase, where I can see when he puffs up his fire.

CLERVAL : Well, they say the end justifies the means ; and in this case I admit the maxim. You can peep through that window, and inform me minutely of what you see.

FRITZ : But what is to become of my nerves ?

CLERVAL : Remember your cottage —

FRITZ : And the cow !

CLERVAL : Put me in possession of the secret, and both shall be secured to you. Some one approaches.

FRITZ : Mr Clerval, I'm your man. I'm so nervous, and the devil sticks in my gizzard ; but the cow will drive it out again. [*starts*] What's that ? Oh, nothing — oh, dear, I'm so nervous.

[*Exeunt* FRITZ *and* CLERVAL]

ACT ONE SCENE II

*Part of the villa residence of Elizabeth, at Belrive, Garden terrace.
Entrance into the house.*

[WILLIAM *discovered sleeping on a garden bench.
During symphony, enter* ELIZABETH *from house.*]

Song

ELIZABETH : The summer sun shining on tree and on tower,
And gilding the landscape with radiance divine,
May give to the heart o'er which pleasure has
power,
But even's beauties are dearer to mine.
Through trees gently sighing, the cool breeze of
even
Seems sympathy's voice to the ear of despair ;
And the dew-drops (like tears shed by angels of
heaven)
Revive the frail hopes in the bosom of care.

[*During this scene the stage becomes progressively dark.*]

NINON :   [*offstage*] William ! Little William !

ELIZABETH :   Where can our little favourite have secreted himself ?

Enter MADAME NINON *from the house.*

NINON :   Heaven bless Mont Blane and all the neighbouring hills ! Why, where is the boy ? How angry shall I be with him for staying out so late.

ELIZABETH :   Why, Ninon, assuage your friendly wrath — yonder is William.

NINON :   [*goes to the child*] Fast asleep, I declare, the pretty boy — how like his poor mother, who is gone. La, la, I daresay my Fritz was just such another, only his hair was red. Pretty William — he was the pin basket. Bless the thirteen cantons, I nursed him. William — [*kisses him*] — a pair of gloves, sir ! [WILLIAM *waking*] Fie, you little urchin, sleeping so early this beautiful evening.

[WILLIAM *rises. All come forward.*]

WILLIAM :   Indeed, dear Ninon, I know not how I fell asleep ; but I rose with the sun, and thinking I would lie down with it. I closed my eyes, and —

NINON :   Slumbered like a young dormouse ?

ELIZABETH :   But, William, you have not neglected your books ?

WILLIAM :   Oh, no ; for then I should not be such a scholar as my elder brother, Victor Frankenstein.

[*Runs to the end of terrace.*]

ELIZABETH :   Alas, poor Frankenstein ! he studies indeed too deeply ; but love — blighted love, drove him to solitude and abstruse research.

NINON :   Ah, madame, may love make you happy ! Mr Clerval was here this morning, and looked as handsome —

ELIZABETH :   Peace, Ninon ! And yet, why should I check your cheerfulness ? Ninon, I have given orders to my milliner to make you a handsome new cap. When your husband, Fritz, comes from Geneva, he may call and bring it.

NINON :   Thank you, dear madam ; but see —

Re-enter WILLIAM *from terrace and runs, crossing behind.*

WILLIAM :   Oh, sister — oh, Madame Ninon ! Two travellers are coming up the hill — such a beautiful lady — but her guide, I think, has fallen from his horse. See — here's the lady, helping the poor man.

[*Melo-music*] *Enter* SAFIE, *supporting the* GUIDE, *from terrace.*

ELIZABETH : Madame, allow me to offer you assistance.

SAFIE :   Thanks — thanks, fair lady; it is not for myself I require rest or help, for I am young. But this aged man, my faithful follower, is completely worn with fatigue.

ELIZABETH :   Ninon, see him conveyed into the house. Give him your support, and assist to welcome our guests.

NINON :   [*crossing to* GUIDE] Lean on me, old sir — aye, as heavy as you like; bless you my arm is strong. Come, gently — gently — there — there —

[NINON *leads the* GUIDE *into house,* WILLIAM *following them. By this time the wing lights are turned off.*]

SAFIE :   I can only weep my thanks. Of late I have been unused to kindness.

ELIZABETH :   Your garb and manner denote you a stranger here — yet you are acquainted with our language, and you appear to have travelled a great distance.

SAFIE :   From Leghorn, a wearisome journey. How far am I distant from the Valley of the Lake?

ELIZABETH :   But a few leagues.

SAFIE :   [*animated*] Then tonight I probably could reach it?

ELIZABETH :   I would not advise the attempt till the morning — the sun is down now; you are distant from any inn; your horses are fatigued; permit me to offer in my house refreshment and repose.

SAFIE :   No, no; no repose until my purpose is accomplished. Yet my poor follower needs rest; generous stranger, I gratefully accept your hospitality.

ELIZABETH :   And be assured such comfort as Eliza Frankenstein can offer shall be freely yours.

SAFIE :   You — you mention the name of Frankenstein!

ELIZABETH :   I bear that appellation.

SAFIE :   How fortunate! Happy chance that brought me to your hospitable door. Know you the family of De Lacey?

ELIZABETH :   I knew it well, but years have elapsed since I have heard of them.

SAFIE :   I seek their retreat. Exiled from France, they now exist in the Valley of the Lake.

ELIZABETH :   So near, and I not acquainted with their residence! Does the gentle Agatha de Lacey yet live?

SAFIE :   Tomorrow's noon I trust I shall discover her.

ELIZABETH :   What rapturous news for my dear brother,
Frankenstein. Let us in and converse further on this subject,
which is of deep interest to me. Night approaches.

SAFIE :   On such a night was I torn from Agatha's brother.
Felix, Felix ! Sad was the moment when you last enfolded
poor Safie in your affectionate embrace.

Song

SAFIE :   Each mountain was tinged with the sun's latest beam,
Sinking red in the fathomless deep ;
The pale watch lights of heaven shed their rays o'er
the stream ;
And nature seem'd lulled into sleep.
All was silent and hush'd over lake, lawn, and fell,
Save the whisper that breathed in the lover's
farewell ;
When at Fate's stern command two fond hearts
doom'd to sever,
And poor Felix and Safie were parted for ever.

[*Exeunt into house*]

ACT ONE SCENE III

The Sleeping Apartment of Frankenstein. Dark.

[*The bed is within a recess, enclosed by dark green curtains.
A sword hanging on wall. A large French window; a
staircase leading to a gallery across the stage, on which is
the door of the laboratory above. A small high lattice in
centre of scene, next the laboratory door. A Gothic table
on stage. A Gothic chair in centre, and footstool.
Music expressive of the rising of a storm. Enter* FRANKEN-
STEIN *with a lighted lamp, which he places on the table.
Distant thunder heard.*]

FRANKENSTEIN :   This evening – this lowering evening, will,
in all probability, complete my task. Years have I laboured,
and at length discovered that to which so many men of genius
have in vain directed their inquiries. After days and nights of
incredible labour and fatigue, I have become master of the
secret of bestowing animation upon lifeless matter. With so

astonishing a power in my hands, long, long long did I hesitate how to employ it. The object of my experiment lies there [*pointing up to the laboratory*] – a huge automaton in human form. Should I succeed in animating it, Life and Death would appear to me as ideal bounds, which I shall break through and pour a torrent of light into our dark world. I have lost all soul or sensation but for this one pursuit. I have clothed the inanimate mass, lest the chilly air should quench the spark of life newly infused. [*thunder and heavy rain heard*] 'Tis a dreary night, the rain patters dismally against the panes; 'tis a night for such a task. I'll in and complete the wondrous effort.

[*Music.* FRANKENSTEIN *takes up lamp, cautiously looks around him, ascends the stairs, crosses the gallery above, and exits into door of laboratory.*]

Enter FRITZ *with a candle.*

FRITZ : Master isn't here – dare I peep. Only think of the reward Mr Clerval promised me, a cow and a cottage, milk and a mansion. Master is certainly not come up yet. My candle burns all manner of colours, and spits like a roasted apple. [*Runs against the chair and drops his light, which goes out.*] There, now, I'm in the dark. Oh my nerves. [*A blue flame appears at the small lattice window above, as from the laboratory.*] What's that? Oh, lauk; there he is, kicking up the devil's own flame! Oh my cow! I'll venture up – oh my cottage! I'll climb to the window – it will be only one peep to make my fortune.

[*Music.* FRITZ *takes up footstool, he ascends the stairs; when on the gallery landing place, he stands on the footstool tiptoe to look through the small high lattice window of the laboratory, a sudden combustion is heard within. The blue flame changes to one of a reddish blue.*]

FRANKENSTEIN : [*offstage*] It lives! it lives!

FRITZ : [*speaks through music*] Oh, dear! Oh, dear! Oh, dear!

[FRITZ *greatly alarmed, jumps down hastily, totters tremblingly down the stairs in vast hurry; when in front on stage, having fallen flat in fright, with difficulty speaks.*]

FRITZ : There's a hob-, – hob-goblin, seven-and-twenty feet high! Oh, my nerves; I feel as if I had just come out of strong fits, and nobody to throw cold water in my face – if my legs

won't lap under me, I'll just make my escape. [*crosses towards exit*] Oh, my poor nerves !   *Exit* FRITZ, *crawling off*
[*Music.* FRANKENSTEIN *rushes from the laboratory, without lamp, fastens the door in apparent dread, and hastens down the stairs, watching the entrance of the laboratory.*]

FRANKENSTEIN :   It lives ! I saw the dull yellow eye of the creature open, it breathed hard, and a convulsive motion agitated its limbs. What wretch have I formed, his legs are in proportion and I had selected his features as beautiful ! Ah, horror ! his cadaverous skin scarcely covers the work of muscles and arteries beneath, his hair lustrous, black, and flowing – his teethy of pearly whiteness – but these luxuriances only form more horrible contrasts with the deformities of the monster. [*He listens at the foot of the staircase.*] What have I accomplished ? The beauty of my dream has vanished ! And breathless horror and disgust now fill my heart. For this I have deprived myself of rest and health, have worked my brain to madness ; and when I looked to reap my great reward, a flash breaks in upon my darkened soul, and tells me my attempt was impious, and that the fruition will be fatal to my peace for ever. [*He again listens*] All is still ! The dreadful spectre of a human form – no mortal could withstand the horror of that countenance – a mummy embued with animation could not be so hideous as the wretch I have endowed with life ! – Miserable and impious being that I am ! Elizabeth ! Brother ! Agatha ! – Fairest Agatha ! Never more dare I look upon your virtuous faces. Lost ! Lost ! Lost !
[*Music.* FRANKENSTEIN *sinks on a chair ; sudden combustion heard, and smoke issues the door of laboratory breaks to prices with a loud crash – red fire within. The* MONSTER *discovered at door entrance in smoke, which evaporates – the red flame continues visible. The* MONSTER *advances forward, breaks through the balustrade or railing of gallery immediately facing the door of laboratory, jumps on the table beneath, and from thence leaps on the stage, stands in attitude before* FRANKENSTEIN, *who had started up in terror ; they gaze for a moment at each other.*]

FRANKENSTEIN :   The horrid corpse to which I have given life !
[*Music.* The MONSTER *looks at* FRANKENSTEIN *most intently, approaches him with gestures of conciliation.* FRANKENSTEIN *retreats, the* MONSTER *pursuing him.*]

FRANKENSTEIN: Fiend! dare not approach me — avaunt, or dread the fierce vengeance of my arm.

[*Music.* FRANKENSTEIN *takes the sword from off nail, points with it at* MONSTER, *who snatches the sword, snaps it in two and throws it on stage. The* MONSTER *then seizes* FRANKENSTEIN — *loud thunder heard* — *throws him violently on the floor, ascends the staircase, opens the large window, and disappears through the casement.* FRANKENSTEIN *remains motionless on the ground.* — *Thunder and lightning until the drop falls.*]

·ACT TWO SCENE I

An apartment in the house of Elizabeth, at Belrive. — *Table and chairs.*

[*The hurried music from the close of the First Act to play in continuance until this scene is discovered, and* FRANKEN-STEIN *enters, hastily, to centre of stage. Music ceases.*]

FRANKENSTEIN: At length in my sister's house! — And safe! I have paced with quick step, but at every turn feared to meet the wretch — my heart palpitates with the sickness of fear! What have I cast on the world? A creature powerful in form, of supernatural and gigantic strength, but with the mind of an infant. Oh, that I could recall my impious labour, or suddenly extinguish the spark which I have so presumptuously bestowed. — Yet that were murder — murder in its worst and most horrid form — for he is mine — my own formation. Ha! Who approaches?
  Enter ELIZABETH; *they embrace.*
ELIZABETH: My dear Victor! My dear brother!
FRANKENSTEIN: Elizabeth!
ELIZABETH: You come to stay, I hope, till our wedding is over. Clerval will be here presently. Alas! Frankenstein! your cheek is pallid — your eye has lost its wonted lustre. Oh, Victor, what are the secrets that prey upon your mind and form? — The pernicious air of your laboratory will be fatal to you.

FRANKENSTEIN :   [*apart*] Fatal indeed !

ELIZABETH :   I pray you, for my sake, cease – I understand upon one subject you have laboured incessantly.

FRANKENSTEIN :   One subject ! [*aside*] Am I discovered ?

ELIZABETH :   You change colour, my dear brother. I will not mention it – I – there is a wildness in your eyes for which I cannot account.

FRANKENSTEIN :   [*starts*] See – see – he is there !

ELIZABETH :   Dearest Frankenstein – what is the cause of this ?

FRANKENSTEIN :   Do not ask me. I – I thought I saw the dreaded spectre glide into the room.

ELIZABETH :   Calm your mind, Victor.

FRANKENSTEIN :   Pardon me, Elizabeth. I know not what you will think of me.

ELIZABETH :   I have intelligence of one dear to you, and for whom, prior to your close attention to study, you had the tenderest regard. – Say, Victor, will you not be glad to hear that I have a clue to lead you to your lost love, Agatha de Lacey !

FRANKENSTEIN :   Agatha ! Dearest Agatha ! Her name recalls my sinking spirits – where – where is she to be found ? Oh, would that I ne'er had been robbed of her ! 'Twas her loss that drove me to deep and fatal experiments !

ELIZABETH :   A traveller, a beautiful Arabian girl, was here but last night ; she was seeking Felix de Lacey, the brother of Agatha, to whom she had been betrothed – she gave me the information that the family are but a short distance from hence – the Valley of the Lake.

FRANKENSTEIN :   And Agatha there ? – Agatha ! there is yet life and hope for me – Ah, no. [*aside*] The dreadful monster I have formed ! – Away with thought ! Elizabeth, I will instantly seek her. Agatha's smiles shall move this heavy pressure – to the Valley of the Lake. – Farewell, sister, farewell !

                    [*They embrace, and exeunt separately.*]

ACT TWO SCENE II

A wood in the neighbourhood of Geneva.

[*On one side a bush, on the other a gipsy's fire, flaming, over which hangs a cauldron. A group of* GIPSIES *discovered surrounding the fire in various positions. All laugh as the scene discovers them.* TANSKIN, HAMMPERPAN, *with others (male and female) advance to sing the following :*]

Chorus

GIPSIES :   Urge the slow rising smoke,
              Give the faggot a poke,
              For unroofed rovers are we ;
              Whilst our rags flutt'ring fly,
              We the brown skin espy,
              Our vellum of pedigree.
              Behold each tawny face
              Of our hard-faring race,
              Which the cold blast ne'er can feel ;
              See our glossy hair wave,
              Hear us, loud, as we crave
              But dumb only when we steal !

TANSKIN :   I tell you it was even so, friend Hammerpan – a giant creature, with something of a human shape; but ugly and terrible to behold as you would paint the Devil.

HAMMPERPAN :   And does this monster any mischief, or is he a pacific monster ?

TANSKIN :   I never heard of any being harmed by him.

HAMMERPAN :   Then why are you so frightened, Master Tanskin ? For my part, should he come across my path, let who will fly, I'll stand my ground like an anvil !

TANSKIN :   And get well beat for once for your pains. [*flute heard*] What sounds are those ?

HAMMERPAN :   [*returning to the fire*] Why, 'tis Felix, the son of old De Lacey. The young fellow is much famed for his excellence upon the flute, as the father for his piety, charities, and twanging on the harp, which, together with the beauty of his daughter, seems to have turned the heads and won the hearts of all the surrounding country. But come, my merry wanderers, our meal is smoking. I'faith, I'm in a rare relishing humour for it, so, prithee, dame, ladle us out our porridge.

Fegs, it scents rarely! [*sniffs*] Leeks, mutton, porridge, with a whole dead sheep in it.

[*The* GIPSIES *crowd round the fire with their bowls.*]

TANSKIN: [*pointing offstage*] See there! that's he! that's the tall bully. He looks like the steeple of Ingoldstadt taking a walk. See yonder, comrades!

HAMMERSPAN: See what?

TANSKIN: (*trembling*) As I'm a living rogue, 'tis he!

HAMMERSPAN: One of the Devil's grenadiers, mayhap! Pooh! Pooh! Old Tanskin, we all know you are a living rogue, but you won't frighten us with your ten feet. Come, give me my drink, I say. [*One of the Gipsies gives him a wooden bowl.*] Gentlemen Gipsies, here's all your good – Ha! Ha! Ha! –

[*Music. The* MONSTER *appears on an eminence of the bush, or a projecting rock.*]

HAMMERPAN: Help! Murder! Wouns! 'Tis the Devil himself? Away with the porridge!

[*Music.* HAMMERPAN *and all the* GIPSIES *shriek and run off.*]
[*The* MONSTER *descends, portrays by action his sensitiveness to light and air, perceives the Gipsies' fire, which excites his admiration – thrusts his hand into the flame, withdraws it hastily in pain. Takes out a lighted piece of stick, compares it with another faggot which has not been ignited. Tastes the food expressive of surprise and pleasure. Footsteps heard, and the* MONSTER *retreats behind the bush.*]
Enter AGATHA, *followed by* FELIX, *his flute slung at his back.*

AGATHA: Yes, my dear Felix, our father is anxious for your return. He bade me seek you, and conducted by the mellifluous sounds of your flute, the task was not one of great difficulty. Oh, Felix! How delightful is the reflection that both you and my father possess the skill of banishing for a few moments the horrors of our present misery. In the midst of poverty, how consoling it is to possess such a brother as you are. Dear, thoughtful Felix, the first little white flower that peeped out from beneath the snowy ground you brought, because you thought it would give pleasure to your poor Agatha.

FELIX: We are the children of misfortune – poverty's chilling grasp nearly annihilates us. Our poor blind father, now the inmate of our cottage – he who has been blessed with prosperity to be thus reduced – the noble-minded old De Lacey. Wretched man that I am, to have been the cause of ruin to both father and sister.

AGATHA : Nay Felix, we suffered in a virtuous cause ! Poor Safie, thy beloved –

FELIX : Is, I fear, lost to me for ever. The treacherous Mahometan, her father, whose escape I aided from a dungeon in Paris (where he was confined as a State prisoner), that false father has doubtless arrived at Constantinople, and is triumphing at the fate of his wretched dupes.

AGATHA : Nay, Felix –

FELIX : Alas, Agatha ! For aiding that escape, my family – my beloved family – are suffering exile and total confiscation of fortune.

AGATHA : But Safie still loves you ?

FELIX : That thought is the more maddening ! Safie ! Fairest Safie ! And she was my promised reward for liberating her faithless father – dragged away with him and forced to comply with his obdurate wishes. Oh, she is lost – lost to me for ever ! The early passion of each of us has been blighted, our rigorous imprisonment and sudden banishment have driven all trace of thee from thy admirer, young Frankenstein.

AGATHA : Dear Felix, press not more wretched recollections on my mind. I consider Frankenstein lost to me for ever. In abject poverty, dare I hope that the brilliant and animated student could e'er think of the unfortunate Agatha. [*weeps*] Let me dry these unworthy tears and exert a woman's firmest fortitude. My soul is henceforth devoted exclusively to the service of my poor dark father. Felix, you shall behold me no longer unhappy.

Duet

FELIX *and*   Of all the knots which Nature ties,
AGATHA :   The secret, sacred sympathies,
That, as with viewless chains of gold,
The heart a happy prisoner hold,
None is more chaste – more bright – more pure,
Stronger, stern trials to endure ;
None is more pure of earthly leaven,
More like the love of highest heaven,
Than that which binds in bonds how blest
A daughter to a father's breast.

[*Exeunt* AGATHA *and* FELIX.]

[*Music. The* MONSTER *cautiously ventures out — his mantle having been caught by the bush, he disrobes himself, leaving the mantle attached to the rock; he watches* FELIX *and* AGATHA *with wonder and rapture, appears irresolute whether he dares to follow them; he hears the flute of Felix, stands amazed and pleased, looks around him, snatches at the empty air, and with clenched hands puts them to each ear — appears vexed at his disappointment in not possessing the sound; rushes forward afterwards, again listens, and delighted with the sound, steals off, catching at it with his hands.*]

ACT TWO SCENE III

Exterior of the Cottage of Old De Lacey.

[*On one side a hovel, with a low door, near which are two or three large logs of wood and a hatchet; a small basket with violets on a stool at the side of the cottage door, and a stool also by the side of the cottage, whereon* DE LACEY *is discovered seated, leaning on his cane, a common harp at his side. — Music.*]

DE LACEY :   Another day is added to the life of banished De Lacey. [*rises and comes forward*] But how will it be passed — like the preceding days — in wretched poverty, hopeless grief, and miserable darkness ! [*calls*] Agatha ! Felix ! Alas ! I am alone. Hark ! 'Tis the flute of Felix ! — My children come. They must not suppose me cheerless — my harp is here — 'tis a fair deceit on them — my harp which has so oft been damped with the tears from my sightless eyes — the sound of it is the only indication I can give that I am contented with my lot !
[*Music.* DE LACEY *returns to his seat beside the cottage, and plays the harp. The* MONSTER *enters, attracted by the harp, suddenly perceives* DE LACEY *and approaches towards him — expresses surprise by action that* DE LACEY *does not avoid him — discovers his loss of sight, which the* MONSTER *appears to understand by placing his hand over his own eyes, and feeling his way. At the conclusion of the music on the harp — occasioned, as it were, by the* MONSTER *having*

placed his hand on the instrument – a short pause, and during which the MONSTER, *having lost the sound, appears to be looking for it, when the harp music is again resumed. In the midst of the music [without ceasing] a voice is heard.*]

FELIX: [*offstage*] This way, Agatha.

[*The* MONSTER, *alarmed, observes the little door of hovel, which he pushes open signifies that he wishes for shelter, and retreats into this hovel or wood-house by the ending of the harp music by* DE LACEY, *when enter* FELIX *and* AGATHA.]

FELIX: [*apart to* AGATHA] Observe his countenance, beaming with benevolence and love – behold those silver hairs – and, Agatha, I – I have reduced him to this pitiable state of poverty!

AGATHA: Cease, Felix, this self-reproach. [*goes to her father*] We have returned, dear father. Have you wanted us?

[AGATHA *leads her father forward.*]

DE LACEY: No, no, Agatha! You anticipate all my wants, and perform every little office of affection with gentleness.

AGATHA: Is it not my duty, and am I not rewarded by your kind smiles?

DE LACEY: Amiable girl, let thy poor father kiss thee. [*they embrace*] Felix, my son, where are you? [FELIX *comes forward, and takes his hand.*] Now I am cheerful – I am happy! – Indeed I am, my children! Let me encourage you to cast off your gloom. What – a tear, Agatha!

AGATHA: Nay, dear sir!

DE LACEY: 'Tis on my hand.

[*Pressing her hand to his lips, which he had held in his while speaking to* FELIX.]

FELIX: [*assuming gaiety*] Now must I to labour again. Our fuel is nearly exhausted. My time has been so lately occupied I have omitted my task in the forest.

[*Music.* FELIX *takes up a hatchet and chops a log of wood.*]

SAFIE: [*at a distance, offstage*] Felix!

AGATHA: What voice was that?

FELIX: It cannot be – no – it was but fancy!

[*Music resumed.* FELIX *chops the log in continuance – at a similar break in the tune the same voice heard again nearer.*]

SAFIE: [*offstage*] Felix!

[*No music.*]

FELIX: That magic sound! Alas! No – there is no such happainess in store for me!

SAFIE: [*offstage, louder*] Felix! Felix!

[*Music.* FELIX *drops the hatchet, rushes forward. At the same instant* SAFIE *enters, and falls into the arms of* FELIX]

FELIX: 'Tis she ! – Safie ! Beloved of my soul ! – Ah ! Revive !

DE LACEY: Safie, the traitor's daughter ? Impossible !

AGATHA: 'Tis, indeed, our sweet Safie !

FELIX: We never will part more ! Father ! Father ! Would that you could behold her ! It is my dear, lost Safie.

[*Music.* SAFIE *revives, crosses to old* DE LACEY, *kneels, and kisses his hand, during which the* MONSTER *appears at the little hovel, watching them, and then retires within again.*]

DE LACEY: Bless you, my child ! Where is your father – where the treacherous friend who devoted us to ignominy ?

[SAFIE *rises.*]

SAFIE: I have fled from him: he would have sacrificed his daughter, loathing the idea that I should be united to one of Christian faith. I – I have sought the love and protection of my Felix !

FELIX: Faithful girl ! Your constancy shall be crowned by my eternal love and gratitude.

AGATHA: But, Safie, you are fatigued. Come, dear girl, and on my lowly couch seek repose.

[*Music.* SAFIE *affectionately kisses and presses* DE LACEY's *hand, embraces* FELIX, *crosses back to* AGATHA, *and is led into the cottage by* AGATHA *and* FELIX.]

FELIX: [*who returns with a gun from cottage-door*] Father, I am wild with joy ! – No longer the sad, pining Felix. The sun of prosperity again gleams on us – Safie has returned ! I am rich ! – Happy ! But hold ! I must procure refreshment for our guest. Our lander* is not too much encumbered with provision. I'll to the village – I'll cross the forest – I'll hunt, shoot – and all in ecstasy ! Farewell, father ! I'll soon be back. Farewell !   [*Exit* FELIX]

[*Music.* DE LACEY *turns up the stage, and again seats himself on his cottage stool, at the side of door. – Re-enter* MONSTER, *examines log of wood, takes up hatchet, intimating he understands the use of it, and rushes off with the hatchet. Music ceases.*]

DE LACEY: [*calls*] Agatha !

Enter AGATHA *from cottage*

AGATHA: Did you call, father ?

DE LACEY   Sleeps your sweet guest?

AGATHA: Fatigue will soon lull her to repose. I should not have left her had not I thought I heard you call me.

[*Exit* AGATHA *into cottage again.* DE LACEY *rises and takes up the basket of flowers from stool by the side of the cottage door.*]

DE LACEY: [*smelling the violets*] How delightful is the perfume! — More exquisite because I am debarred the pleasure of beholding these sweet emblems of spring! The touch and scent elevate my spirits! How ungrateful am I to complain! In the contemplation of thee, oh, Nature, the past will be blotted from my memory! — The present is tranquil, and the future gilded by the past will be blotted from my memory! — The present is tranquil, and the future gilded by bright rays of hope and anticipations of joy!

[*Music.* DE LACEY *replaces the basket of flowers, and returns to his seat, leaning pensively on his cane. — The* MONSTER *enters with a pile of green faggots with foliage on his shoulders. — Crosses and throws them loosely on the stage. — Smiles with gratulation at that which he has accomplished. — Approaches* DE LACEY, *falls flat at his feet then kneels to him, and is about to press his hand. —* DE LACEY *feels around him with his cane and hand, without the knowledge of anyone being near him, and seated all the time — then calls.*]

DE LACEY: Agatha! Agatha!

[*Music. The* MONSTER *instantly retreats into hovel, and* AGATHA *enters from cottage door.*]

DE LACEY: Agatha, child, I pray you lead me in.

[*Rises from his seat, and comes forward.*]

AGATHA: Yes, father. Good heavens! Why, Felix could not have returned from the forest so quickly? What a quantity of wood!

DE LACEY: How!

AGATHA: Here is fuel to last us for a long time. How could we have been so bountifully supplied? Come, father, to the cottage — come!

[*Music. —* AGATHA *leads* DE LACEY *into cottage, afterwards comes forward.*]

AGATHA: Frankenstein! Vain is the endeavour to drive you from my recollection. Each bird that sings, each note of music that I hear, reminds me of the sweet moments of my former love !

Song [*flute accompaniment, behind the scenes*]

AGATHA :   In vain I view the landscapes round,
      Or climb the highest hill ;
   In vain, in vain, I listen to the sound
      Of ev'ry murmuring rill.
   For vain is all I hear or see,
   When Victor dear is far from me. [*thrice*]
   But hark, hark, hark,
   My love, my love is near.
   His well-known dulcet notes I hear. [*thrice*]
   Oh, yes, my love is near,
      I hear him in the grove ;
   Soon will be here,
      And breathe soft vows of love.
   Oh, fly not yet, ye blissful hours,
      Oh, fly not yet away ;
   While love its soft enchanting pours.
      Prolong, prolong your stay ! [*thrice*]
   Oh, yes, my love is near,
      I hear him in the grove,
   Soon will be here,
      and breathe soft vows of love !

[*Exit* AGATHA *into cottage*]

ACT TWO SCENE IV

A Wild Forest

Enter FELIX *with his gun.*

FELIX :   Not a shot yet — and, egad, joy has made my hand so unsteady, that were a fine pheasant to get up, I could not bring it down again. Thy return, sweet Safie, has restored me to existence. When I thought I had lost thee for ever, I was occupied by gloomy thoughts, and neither heeded the descent of the evening star nor the golden sunrise reflected on the lake; but now my love fills my imagination, and all is enjoyment !

Song

FELIX :   Thy youthful charms, bright maid, inspire,
              And grace my fav'rite theme,
            Whose person kindles soft desire,
              Whose mind secures esteem.
            Oh, hear me then my flame avow,
              And fill my breast with joy —
            A flame which taught by time to grow,
              No time can e'er destroy.
            My tender suit with smiles approve,
              And share the sweets of mutual love.
            When autumn yields her ripen'd corn,
              Or winter, darkening, lowers,
            With tenderest care I'll soothe thy morn,
              And cheer thy evening hours.
            Again, when smiling spring returns,
              We'll breathe the vernal air ;
            And still when summer sultry burns,
              To woodland walks repair —
            There seek retirement's sheltered grove,
              and share the sweets of mutual love.

[FELIX retires up stage]

Enter FRANKENSTEIN.

FRANKENSTEIN :   In vain do I seek a respite from these
dreadful thoughts — where'er I turn my eyes I expect to behold
the supernatural Being ! — To see him spring from each woody
recess — but on, on to Agatha, and repose.

FELIX :   A traveller ! And surely I know his air and manner.
[*comes forward*]

FRANKENSTEIN :   Good stranger, can you direct me to the
habitation of old De Lacey ?

FELIX :   Better than most persons, I trust.

FRANKENSTEIN :   How ! Felix De Lacey !

FELIX :   The same ! Frankenstein Your hand, my friend — 'tis
long since we have met.

FRANKENSTEIN :   Your strange and sudden disappearance
from Paris —

FELIX :   Makes as strange a story, with which I shall not now
detain you. Come to our humble cottage. Egad ! I'm overjoyed
to see you !

FRANKENSTEIN :   And Agatha ?

FELIX :   Has still a warm corner of her heart for you. Come, we have only to cross the wood.

HAMMERPAN :   [*offstage*] Any good Christians in the neighbourhood ?

FELIX :   What have we here !

Enter HAMMPERPAN, *with a long pole, tinker's utensils, fire kettle, etc.*

HAMMERPAN :   Real Christians ! Human beings ! Oh, good gentlemen, have you seen it ?

FELIX :   It ! What ? [*goes to him*]

HAMMERPAN :   Ah ! that's it ! As I live, an hour ago, I saw it in the forest !

FELIX :   What do you mean by *it* ?

HAMMERPAN :   My hair stood on end like mustard and cress, and so will yours when you see it !

FELIX :   Get you gone ! You are tipsy !

HAMMERPAN :   I wish I was. As I take it, you are Master Felix, of the Valley of the Lake ; we've done business together before now.

FELIX :   I know you not !

HAMMERPAN :   I mended your kettle t'other day. You did me a good turn – one good turn deserves another – I'll put you on your guard – the very devil is abroad.

FRANKENSTEIN :   [*aside*] How !

FELIX :   [*laughs*] Ha ! ha ! ha ! You romancing tinker !

HAMMERPAN :   You may laugh, but the other gentleman don't laugh. You may perceive *he* believes it. [*to* FRANKEN-STEIN] I saw it with *this one eye.*

FELIX :   One eye !

HAMMERPAN :   Yes, I've lost the other – a little boy threw a pebble at it, and I've been *stone* blind ever since, gentlemen. He was ten feet six long, [*holds his pole high up*] with a head of black lanky locks down to his very elbows.

FRANKENSTEIN :   'Tis the demon ! [*apart to himself*] What did this strange object !   [*to* HAMMERPAN]

HAMMERPAN :   It didn't speak to me, nor I to *it.* I saw it at first in the forest picking acorns and berries – and then, after it had dispersed our tribe like a ferret among the rats – it took a drink of our broth, and burnt its fingers in our fire.

FRANKENSTEIN :   And what became of this creature ?

HAMMERPAN :   I wasn't curious enough to inquire. My wife

was in fits at the sight of the devil – so I was obliged to keep my one eye upon her.

FELIX: Your one eye has been pretty well employed. Come, come, gipsy, we'll cross the wood, and see if this man mountain is to be met.

HAMMERPAN: The good genius of wandering tinkers forbid !

FELIX: [*to* FRANKENSTEIN] And now, my friend, we'll on to the cottage.

FRANKENSTEIN: So, so ! [*apart*] I will follow ye !

[*Exeunt* HAMMERPAN *and* FELIX]

FRANKENSTEIN: So ! The peasants have already been terrified by the ungainly form ! Ambitious experimentalist ! The consciousness of the crime I have committed eternally haunts me ! I have indeed drawn a horrible curse on my head ! He may be malignant, and delight in murder and wretchedness ! A whole country may execrate me as its pest ! Every thought that bears towards my baneful project causes my lips to quiver and heart to palpitate. I must now to the cottage of Felix. Agatha, fairest Agatha, instead of smiles, your lover will meet you with dark and hopeless despondency. [*Exit* FRANKENSTEIN]

ACT TWO SCENE V

Evening. Interior of the cottage of DE LACEY.

[*The thatched roof in sight. To one side, a wood fire. Through an open rustic porch, are visible a rivulet, and small wooden bridge. A wooden couch,* DE LACEY *discovered seated thereon, with* AGATHA *next to him in attendance. Music. The* MONSTER *appears through the portico, watching them, and regards* AGATHA *with rapture.* AGATHA *kisses her father's hand, crosses stage and takes a small pail or hand bucket, and trips through the portico on to the bridge to procure water. The* MONSTER *having retreated on* AGATHA's *approach, pursues her on the bridge.* AGATHA, *turning suddenly, perceives the* MONSTER, *screams loudly, and swoons, falling into the rivulet. The* MONSTER *leaps from the bridge, and rescues her.*]

DE LACEY: [*speaks during the melo music*] Gracious
Heaven! [*starting forward from the couch*] That cry of
horror! Agatha! – Despair! – My sweet child where art
thou? Agatha! Agatha!
     [*The* MONSTER *appears at the portico entrance, with* AGATHA
     insensible in his arms. The MONSTER *comes forward, gently
     places* AGATHA *in her father's arms, tenderly guiding the
     hand of old* DE LACEY *to support his daughter.* AGATHA
     recovers, and perceiving the MONSTER, *with a shriek, again
     faints – the* MONSTER *hovering over them with fondness.*
     FELIX *with his gun* [*loaded*] *suddenly enters through the
     open portico, and speaks whilst entering.*]
FELIX: Agatha! Victor Frankenstein is here! What horrid
monster is this! Agatha! – My father in danger!
     [*Music. The* MONSTER *retreats,* FELIX *following him – dis-
     charges his gun – wounds the* MONSTER *in the shoulder –
     who writhes under the agony of the wound from which the
     blood flows – would rush on* FELIX, *who keeps the gun
     presented – he is deterred by fear of a repetition of the
     wound.* FELIX *remaining on the defensive.* – SAFIE *alarmed
     at the firing of the gun by* FELIX, *rushes on to* AGATHA *and*
     DE LACEY.]
     Enter FRANKENSTEIN *through the portico.* [*The* MONSTER
     rushes up to FRANKENSTEIN, *and casts himself at his feet,
     imploring protection.*]
FRANKENSTEIN: Misery! The Fiend! [*crosses stage*] Hence,
avoid me! Do not approach me – thy horrid contact would
spread a pestilence throughout my veins! – Hence – no, no!
You shall not quit this spot – but thus – I destroy the wretch
I have created!
     [*Music.* FRANKENSTEIN *endeavours to stab him with his
     dagger, which the* MONSTER *strikes from his hand – and
     expresses that his kindly feeling towards the human race
     have been met by abhorrence and violence; that they are
     all now converted into hate and vengeance. In desperation,
     the* MONSTER *pulls a flaming brand from the fire, and in
     agony of feeling dashes through the portico, setting fire to
     the whole portico and entire back of the cottage – the
     thatched roof and rafters.*]
[FELIX: Ha! Frankenstein 'tis no time to parley – the cottage
is on fire! That fierce gigantic figure of terrific aspect waves
aloft his torch, as if in triumph of the deed.

[*The large doors in the centre are suddenly closed from without, as if to prevent escape. A coarse yelling laugh is heard.*]

FRANKENSTEIN: Ha! 'Tis that hideous voice! Quick, quick, let us fly! His hellish malice pursues me, and but with his death or with mine, will this persecution cease. Could I but place you beyond his power.

[FELIX *and* FRANKENSTEIN [*as soon as the* MONSTER *disappears, having climbed outside of the portico] force open the doors, when flaming faggots are thrown down at the portico, and falling trees on fire block up the entrance.* FELIX *and* FRANKENSTEIN *place the couch longways over the fallen trees, and Felix forces his way through the flames with old* DE LACEY *and then* SAFIE – *and, lastly,* FRANKENSTEIN *rushes out, bearing* AGATHA *in his arms over the couch, in the midst of which parts of the building fall. The* MONSTER *brandishing the burning brand on the bridge, laughs exultingly, on which the drop falls. Continue the 'Presto music' until end of act.*]

ACT THREE SCENE I

The Garden of Elizabeth, at Belrive – morning (same as Act One, Scene II)

Enter CLERVAL, *from entrance.*

CLERVAL: What a delightful morning! It is an auspicious commencement of the day which is to make me happy in the possession of my love! Elizabeth yet sleeps, peaceful be her slumbers, soft, she approaches.

Enter ELIZABETH *from the house.*

CLERVAL: Elizabeth, my love, why that look of anxiety?

ELIZABETH: Oh, Clerval! We have had strange occurrences since you quitted me yesterday; our house is full of guests, my brother has brought here the family of De Lacey of whom you have heard me so often speak –

CLERVAL: The family of De Lacey, the relatives of Agatha.

ELIZABETH: By some extraordinary mystery, which is yet unexplained to me, the cottage in which Frankenstein discovered his mistress and her family was destroyed by fire;

they arrived late last night, and all appear overcome with fatigue and terror; some dreadful calamity hangs about my dear brother.

CLERVAL: How astonishing in his conduct. Alas! My sweet Elizabeth, in the midst of all this misery I am selfish – I trust these singular occurrences will not postpone our marriage. Consider, our friends are invited, the church is prepared.

ELIZABETH: A few hours may explain these mysterious transactions. See now [*looks towards house*] Frankenstein approaches – observe his agitated countenance and restless step; he has not slept since his return – he has armed himself with pistols and appears continually watching.

CLERVAL: We will retire and avoid him for the present. This way, love.

[*Exeunt* ELIZABETH *and* CLERVAL, *and enter* FRANKENSTEIN *from house.*]

FRANKENSTEIN: Oh! how to avoid the powerful vengeance of the monster formed by my cursed ambition. I gave him energy and strength, to crush my own guilty head! My hours pass in dread, and soon the bolt may fall which will deprive me of existence! Yet *he* preserved the life of Agatha – he had some feeling of affection – how were those feelings requited! – By detestation, scorn, and wounds! – His look of everlasting malice! He will watch with the wiliness of a serpent, that he may sting with its venom! There is no hope but in his destruction. [*takes out pistol*] I dare not cease to guard and protect my friends. [*going to the door*] Agatha has arisen. [*conceals pistol*]

Enter AGATHA, *a locket round her neck, from the house.*

AGATHA: Frankenstein, I behold you unhappy – flying to solitude – and I cannot help supposing that you might regret the renewal of our intercourse. Dear Frankenstein, I still love you, and confess that in my airy dreams of futurity you have been my constant friend and companion.

FRANKENSTEIN: Agatha, you shall be mine! I will then divulge to you the secret which disturbs – nay, distracts me. [*Music: the Harmonica. Distant bells.*] Those cheerful chimes announce the wedding day of Elizabeth and Clerval. My care-worn looks will but damp their merriment.

[*Music.*]   [*Exeunt* FRANKENSTEIN *and* AGATHA]
Enter FELIX *and* SAFIE *from house.*

FELIX :   Listen, Safie, to those merry village bells; they ring a
rare contrast to our last night's misery. Soon, my Eastern
rose, will they chime for us; and then away with care. This
kiss – [*embracing her*]

SAFIE :   Fie, Felix! in open daylight. You will deepen the
blush of your Eastern rose.

Duet

SAFIE *and*   Come with me, dear, to my mountain home,
FELIX :   And Hymen shall hallow the peaceful dome.
                 Leave all the world for love and for me,
                 And I will be all the world to thee.
                 Our life shall be all holiday –
                     Shall be all holiday.
                 Come o'er the dew-bespangled vale,
                 Where the violet blue and primrose pale
                 Peep from the verdant shade.
                 Come o'er the dew-bespangled vale,
                 Where the violet blue and primrose pale,
                 Where the violet blue and primrose pale
                 Peep from the verdant shade.
                 Come o'er the dew, &c, &c.
                 We'll fly to the shady grove,
                 And sigh and whisper, love
                 Till day begins to fade,
                 Till day begins, &c., &c.
                 We'll roam, and I woo thee, love,
                 Where birds sing sweetly through the grove –
                 Where birds sing sweetly thro' the grove
                 Till day begins to fade.
                 We'll roam, and I will woo thee, love,
                 Where birds sing sweetly thro' the grove –
                 While birds sing, &c., &c., &c.

[*Music, with the Bells. Enter* MADAME NINON, *leading a
group of Dancing Villagers, from the terrace entrance, and*
ELIZABETH, *with* CLERVAL, *re-enter, the dancers having all
ranged themselves on one side.*]

NINON :   Now, Madame Elizabeth – now, Mr Clerval – we
are all ready, and the priest is in waiting.

[*Music resumes.* ELIZABETH *and* CLERVAL, *as also* SAFIE *and*
FELIX, *join the procession, and all the villagers dance off to
music along the terrace, except* MADAME NINON.]

NINON :   There they go to be coupled, pretty dears ! [*calls offstage*] Fritz ! Fritz ! where is my stupid husband ? I've stretched my neck out of joint looking for him. I expect him from the market at Geneva with a cargo of eatables and my new-fashioned beehive cap — all for our wedding festival of Mr Frankenstein, who has brought his bride and her family here in consequence, as I am told, of their cottage being accidentally destroyed by fire last night. Oh ! Here the fellow comes, with his basket at his back, creeping like a snail.

> *Enter* FRITZ, *from terrace, with hamper at his back containing various articles, a lady's cap, and a live duck.*

FRITZ :   Here I am, spousy. I've brought your list of articles. [NINON *assists him in putting down the basket*] Here's the trout, and the sugar-loaf, and the melons, and the nutmegs.

NINON :   But dear Fritz, where's my new beehive you were to bring from the milliner's at Geneva ?

FRITZ :   Somewhere, I know. [*Looking and examining the contents of the hamper, cautiously opening the top.*] The three live ducks are lying a top of the macaroni, squeezed up under the large Gruyere cheese.

NINON :   I hope to goodness my cap is not squeezed up !

FRITZ :   It's quite safe, I tell you. I put it at the very bottom of the basket.

NINON :   It will be in a nice state for my head, then !

FRITZ :   Lord, here's a rummaging fuss for the cap. I'm so nervous about it — you cautioned me so, you know. [*still kneeling and searching the hamper*] Oh, dear, where is it now ? Oh, la, to be sure, spousy — here it is at last ; la, I knew it was safe.

> [*He pulls the cap out, with a live duck in it.*]

NINON :   [*takes her cap from him*] Oh, Fritz, it's spoiled ! That duck has been laying in it !

FRITZ :   Not an egg, I hope, Ninon !

NINON :   Alas ! See how it is rumpled.

> [*She takes from the cap two or three of the duck's small feathers, which fall on the stage.*]

FRITZ :   [*aside*] Ha ! He ! He ! Cap and feathers !

NINON :   You careless, good-for-nothing fellow ! Take the basket in, you sinner ! [*having first replaced her cap in the hamper*]

FRITZ :   Oh ! [*to the duck*] You look very jolly, my fine fellow, considering you are going to be killed for dinner. Wait till the peas are ready ! I never saw such a piece of *quackery* as that cap in all my life !

[*Draws the basket after him into the house, and comes forward during the duet.*]

NINON :   My finery destroyed by that varlet ! But even *that* shall not disconcert me. My sweet mistress is united to-day to the man of her heart, and in spite of my loss I will be merry, and dance till I can dance no longer.

Duet [Welsh air.]

NINON :   Oh, I'll hail the wedding day,
And be the gayest of the gay,
Till age has tripp'd my steps away.

FRITZ :   [*re-entering from house*] Away !

NINON :   Your manners were not taught in France.

FRITZ :   La, wife ! you never learnt to dance,
A horse at fifty – [*aside*] – cannot prance –
Ah, nay !

NINON :   While pipes and tabors playing sweetly,
With all my soul I'll toot it featly,

FRITZ :   Yes I guess you'll hobble neatly.
Wife !

NINON :   Don't wife me, you saucy fellow !
Don't wife me, you saucy fellow !
Sure you're tipsy –

FRITZ :   Only mellow.
We'll all be so, for that is fun and life !

NINON :   Don't wife me, you saucy fellow.
FRITZ :   I won't wife you, I'm only mellow.   } together
NINON :   I ne'er was tipsy.
FRITZ :   You ne'er were tipsy, only mellow.
Wife !

[FRITZ *dances her up to the house,* NINON *turns, boxes his ear, and they exeunt into house. Music. The* MONSTER *appears from terrace entrance, watching about, and retreats as* FRITZ *re-enters from house.*]

FRITZ :   Oh ! [*rubbing his cheek*] What's the use of a fine cap to her ? She's so short, unless she stood on a chair, in a crowd – no one would see her, or her new-fashioned bee-hive either.

[*During the above speech* WILLIAM *comes from the house, behind* FRITZ *on tiptoe, and gives* FRITZ *a smack on the back, who being fearfully alarmed, cries out lustily.*]

FRITZ : Oh, dear ! Who's that ? There now, that's the way just to make me nervous again. What do you want, Master William ?

WILLIAM : I can't get a soul to speak to me in the house – some are busy – some are gone to be married – will you play with me, Fritz ?

FRITZ : I like a game of play – it's so relaxing. When work was over I used to play with my cow's calf.

WILLIAM : Do play with me, Fritz.

[*Music. Dances backwards towards the balustrade of terrace, where the* MONSTER, *during the foregoing speeches has been watching the child, then disappearing by falling flat on his face between the balustrades of the terrace, waits the opportunity as* WILLIAM *is tripping backwards, and suddenly seizes the child, throws him across his shoulder* [à la Rolla], *and rushes off, terrace entrance, to hurried music.* FRITZ, *turning round, sees them, utters a cry of horror, and speaks through the music.*]

FRITZ : Help, help, murder ! Wife ! The devil ! Oh, my nerves ! [*Exit* FRITZ, *frightened, into house*]

ACT THREE SCENE II

A Country View

Rustic Church in the distance. A large Yew Tree, spread plentifully with boughs, with pathway behind it.

[*Music. The procession, as before, returning from the marriage ceremony. The corps de ballet, Villagers, preceding, dancing, followed by* FELIX, SAFIE, CLERVAL *and* ELIZABETH.]

NINON : [*heard from offstage*] Oh, mistress ! Oh !

FRITZ : [*offstage*] I couldn't help it – murder !

Enter NINON *and* FRITZ.

NINON : But where did you leave him ?

FRITZ : I didn't leave him, he left me. Oh dear. [*cries*] Murder ! My nerves !

NINON : Oh, wicked Fritz !

ELIZABETH :   What is the matter, good Ninon ?

FRITZ :   She says her husband's wicked.

NINON :   [*to* ELIZABETH] William, your brother William is the matter; the boy is lost, no one can find him. I sent him to that Fritz, that he might be out of the way.

FRITZ :   Yes; and now he's out of everybody's way.

ELIZABETH :   This is most extraordinary – a frolic of the little rogue.

FRITZ :   No, no, it isn't; I saw – my nerves ! Oh, dear ! I saw – a great something snatch him up. [*cries*] I – oh ! – Oh – dear ! Oh, oh, oh ! Murder !

CLERVAL :   There's Frankenstein.

Enter FRANKENSTEIN, *with a pistol.*

ELIZABETH :   My dear Victor, know you aught of William ? The child has been missed in a most unaccountable manner.

FRANKENSTEIN :   My brother missing !

NINON :   Fritz was with him.

FRITZ :   Oh, master ! A great creature – oh ! Oh ! Oh !

FRANKENSTEIN :   Oh, horror ! The demon !

CLERVAL :   Hasten, my friends, one and all – all search. Our pastime is marr'd till the boy is found.

[*Music. All exeunt in consternation at different entrances, excepting* FRANKENSTEIN, *who appears lost in desponding reverie. He turns: the boughs of the yew tree, are pulled apart, and the* MONSTER *is discovered behind it, with* WILLIAM *in his grasp. –* FRANKENSTEIN *draws a pistol, and points it – the* MONSTER *holds forth the child, when* FRANKENSTEIN *lowers his pistol, and kneels. – The* MON-STER *again shoulders the child, and rushes off within the path,* FRANKENSTEIN *rises, and pursues them in despair.*]

ACT THREE SCENE III

An Apartment in the Villa at Belrive

A wide folding window opening to the Garden, closed. A side door, a table centre of stage, with red baize covering.

AGATHA *and* NINON *enter.*

NINON: The most unaccountable disappearance of my dear little boy, at such a moment – on such a day – when we should have been so merry !

AGATHA: It is indeed strange and fearful; let us hope that William will soon be discovered, and brought home. [*aside*] The wild phantom that fired our cottage, surely, is not concerned.

NINON: I can do nothing but think of William – that is your room, ma'm – [*points to door*] – you will find it well furnished – with such sweet blue eyes – everything is comfortable – unhappy little boy ! There's a fine grate in the room – with two little dimples on each cheek ! There's a cabinet in the corner – curly locks ! Forgive me, ma'am ; I fostered the pretty child, and I cannot get him out of my head.

AGATHA: Pray leave me, Ninon, and give me the earliest intelligence of Mr Frankenstein's return.

NINON: All the festivities of the wedding-day destroyed, till the dear unlucky urchin is found. [*sobbing*] The sweet little, naughty, rosy-cheek'd rogue ! How I will whip him when he comes home.   [*Exit* NINON]

[*During the above the* MONSTER *is seen at the window watching, and disappears.*]

AGATHA: Frankenstein ! what a singular fatality is attached to you – with wealth and friends, doomed to be miserable ! – This mystery ! – I feel a heavy foreboding of mischance ! A presentiment of evil pervades my mind. I may regret the day that I have given my affection to Frankenstein – I may rue the hour that I left our homely hut.   [*Exit* AGATHA]

[*Afterwards, enter* FRANKENSTEIN, *reflecting – two pistols in his belt.*]

FRANKENSTEIN: One sudden and desolating change has taken place – the fangs of remorse tear my bosom and will not forego their hold ! – Pursue the wretch ! One might as well attempt to overtake the winds, or confine a mountain torrent. My poor brother – I – I am thy murderer – the author of unalterable evils. There is scope for fear, so long as anything I love remains. [*goes to door*] Agatha ! She reclines sleeping on yon sofa.

[*The* MONSTER *during the above soliloquy reappears on the balcony of the window – and while* FRANKENSTEIN *is looking in at the door, the* MONSTER *creeps in at the window, crouching beneath the table, unseen.*]

FRANKENSTEIN: Sleep on, sweet innocence! I dare not leave you; I will stay and guard your slumber, or the remorseless fiend will snatch your breath away.

[*Music.* FRANKENSTEIN *takes out a pistol and primes it – holding it in his hand.*]

FRANKENSTEIN: The wretch e'en now may be haunting the room – let me search around.

[*Music.* FRANKENSTEIN *fearfully examines each avenue, advancing to the front. The* MONSTER, *unperceived by him, follows his footsteps, making an ineffectual attempt occasionally to gain his loaded pistol.* FRANKENSTEIN *leads on, looking in at door, passes behind table, when the* MONSTER *falls flat before table, still unseen by* FRANKENSTEIN, *who then places the loaded pistol on table, and turns to close the folding large window. While* FRANKENSTEIN *has his back turned, the* MONSTER *snatches up the pistol, hugs it, and escapes through door.* FRANKENSTEIN, *having closed the window, comes forward.*]

FRANKENSTEIN: Oh, Agatha! would that I had banished myself for ever from my native country, and wandered a friendless outcast over the earth, rather than I had again met you – perhaps to bring you in the grasp of my fiendish adversary – perhaps to –

[*Pistol shot heard, and a piercing shriek*]

– My blood curdles! [*goes to door*] Ah! what do I behold? My last, last hope!

[*Music. He rushes off.*]

ACT THREE SCENE IV

An Ante-chamber in Belrive

Enter ELIZABETH, *hastily, meeting* NINON. – *Music ceases.*

ELIZABETH: Whence is this fresh alarm?

NINON: I know not, madam. Oh, wretched day for poor Ninon! I know not, madam, Oh, wretched day for poor Ninon! Mr Frankenstein is stark mad; he ran out but this instant, jumped into his boat, and rowed off rapidly.

Enter FRITZ, *alarmed.*

FRITZ :   Oh, oh, oh ! – I've seen it again ! The great creature, it got out of one of our windows and scudded off in a boat, and is going after the great creature like lightning.

ELIZABETH :   Where – where are our friends ?

FRITZ :   Oh, I don't know ; there's Mr Frankenstein gone after the great creature, Mr Clerval and Mr Felix have gone after Mr Frankenstein, and I'm going after them all.   [*Runs off.*]

SAFIE :   [*offstage*] Help ! Ah, help !

   Enter SAFIE, *who goes to* ELIZABETH, *and throws herself into her arms.*

SAFIE :   Ah, Madame ! Agatha, my sister – the gentle Agatha – I fear, is no more.

OMNES :   Agatha !

ELIZABETH :   Gracious Heaven ! what horrible destiny hangs over us ?

SAFIE :   Stretched on the ground she lies. Ah ! Elizabeth, the spark of life may yet not be extinct.

ELIZABETH : Hasten – hasten to the apartment.

   [*Hurried music. Exeunt hastily,* ELIZABETH, SAFIE, *and Madame* NINON.]

ACT THREE SCENE V

Wild Border of the Lake

At the extremity of the stage [*into flies*], *a lofty overhanging mountain of snow.*

[*Music. All the* GIPSIES *discovered in various groups. A pistol shot is heard. The* GIPSIES *start up alarmed. A second pistol is fired nearer. The* MONSTER *rushes on with the locket worn by* AGATHA *during the piece. The* GIPSIES *scream out and fly in all directions.* HAMMERPAN *is on the point of escaping when the* MONSTER *seizes him, and* HAMMERPAN *falls down on being dragged back. The* MONSTER *points off to intimate that* FRANKENSTEIN *is approaching, throws down the locket, commands the gipsy.* HAMMERPAN, *to show it to* FRANKENSTEIN – *the* MONSTER *threatens him, and rushing up the mountain, climbs and disappears.*]

Enter FRANKENSTEIN *with two loaded pistols and a musket unloaded. At the same time* HAMMERPAN *rises and gets near.*

FRANKENSTEIN: In vain do I pursue the wretch, in vain have I fired on him. [*throws his gun from him*] He eludes the bullet. Say fellow, have you seen aught pass here?

HAMMPERPAN: The giant creature, who aroused us in the forest, and pointing to the path by which you came, intimated that I should give you this. [*presents locket to* FRANKENSTEIN]

FRANKENSTEIN: 'Tis Agathaa's – the murdered Agatha! Malicious fiend! It will joy you to know that my lacerated heart bleeds afresh. Revenge shall henceforth be the devouring and only passion of my soul. I have but one resource – I devote myself either in my life or death to the destruction of the Demon! Agatha! William! You shall be avenged.

HAMMERPAN: See yonder [*points offstage*], the monster climbs the snow.

FRANKENSTEIN: Then this recontre shall terminate his detested life or mine!

[*Music.* FRANKENSTEIN *draws his pistol – rushes off at back of stage. The Gipsies return at various entrances. At the same time, enter* FELIX *and* CLERVAL *with pistols, and* SAFIE, ELIZABETH *and* NINON *following. The* MONSTER *appears at the base of the mountain,* FRANKENSTEIN *pursuing.*]

CLERVAL: Behold our friend and his mysterious enemy.

FELIX: See – [FRANKENSTEIN *overtakes him*] – let us follow and assist him. [*is going up stage with* CLERVAL *towards them*]

HAMMERPAN: Hold, master! If the gun is fired, it will bring down a mountain of snow. Many an avalanche has fallen there.

[*Music.* FRANKENSTEIN *discharges his pistol. The* MONSTER *and* FRANKENSTEIN *meet at the very extremity of the stage.* FRANKENSTEIN *fires his second pistol – the avalanche falls and annihilates the* MONSTER *and* FRANKENSTEIN. *A heavy fall of snow succeeds. Loud thunder heard, and all the characters form a picture as the curtain falls.*]

END

NOTES

p. 1 **The Modern Prometheus:** in classical legend Prometheus stole fire from heaven for the benefit of mankind. For this he was punished by the gods. In Mary Shelley's version Victor Frankenstein steals the secret of life from God or Nature.

p. 2 **William Godwin:** the dedicatee was Mary Shelley's father (1756–1836).

p. 3 **Dr Darwin:** Erasmus Darwin (1731–1802), scientist who produced theories of evolution. Charles Darwin was his grandson.

p. 7 **the region of beauty and delight:** there was a popular belief that explorers, once inside the polar zone, would discover a warm land whose inhabitants led peaceful lives.

p. 8 **a passage near the pole:** the North-West passage, around the north coast of Canada, was for centuries the goal of explorers in their search for a shorter route from the Atlantic to the Pacific.

p. 11 **keeping:** harmonious proportions.

p. 11 **prize-money:** money gained from captured enemy ships.

p. 12 **'the land of mist and snow;' but I shall kill no albatross:** the quotation is from Coleridge's *The Ancient Mariner* (1798), a poem partly set, like *Frankenstein*, in the polar regions. The mariner shoots an albatross, and the crew and voyage are cursed as a result.

p. 15 **ground sea:** a heavy sea.

p. 15 **capitulated:** laid down terms.

p. 16 **dæmon:** evil being.

p. 19 **series:** logical sequence.

p. 20 **syndics:** the principal magistrates of Geneva.

p. 21 **plain work:** needlework.

p. 23 **Orlando, Robin Hood, Amadis, and St George:** heroes of chivalrous stories from literature or myth.

p. 24 Natural philosophy: physics particularly, but the term can extend to other sciences.

p. 24 Cornelius Agrippa: renaissance expert on magic and the occult (1486–1535).

p. 24 chimerical: imaginary.

p. 24 Paracelsus and Albertus Magnus: Paracelsus (1493–1541) was a doctor and alchemist; St Albertus Magnus (1200–1280), a scientist and churchman.

p. 25 the philosopher's stone and the elixir of life: the supreme quest of the alchemists was to discover the substances that would convert ordinary metals into gold (the philosopher's stone) or provide eternal life (the elixir). Both of these were presumed to exist.

p. 26 Pliny and Buffon: Pliny the Elder (AD23–79) was the Roman author of 'Historia Naturalis'; Buffon (1707–88) was a French naturalist and among the first to raise the question of evolution.

p. 28 the university of Ingolstadt: in Bavaria.

p. 31 reprobated: condemned.

p. 35 charnel houses: places where bones are stored.

p. 36 like the Arabian: in *The Arabian Nights* Sinbad the sailor is buried alive with his dead wife during one of his many adventures.

p. 40 accidents: events, generally unforeseen.

p. 41 Dante: Italian poet (1265–1321) who created a vision of Hell in the *Divine Comedy*.

p. 42 diligences: stage-coaches.

p. 43 the Vicar of Wakefield: novel published in 1766 by Oliver Goldsmith.

p. 47 Ariosto . . . Angelica: Angelica is a character in *Orlando Furioso* (1532) by the Italian poet Ariosto.

p. 55 Stoics: a philosophical sect, originally Greek, which held that true happiness was to be found in cultivating indifference to both pleasure and suffering.

p. 55 cabriole: small carriage.

p. 56 'the palaces of nature': from a description of the Alps in Byron's poem *Childe Harold's Pilgrimage*.

p. 57 discovered: revealed.

p. 77 *aiguilles:* peaks.

p. 77 *dome:* mountain top.

p. 79 **more necessary beings:** living things more at the mercy of external circumstances. Mary Shelley's point is that human beings are governed not only by appetites, like animals, but also by the smallest changes of mood induced by our surroundings.

p. 79 **We rest . . . but mutability!:** The last two verses of 'Mutability' (1816) by Mary Shelley's husband, Percy Bysshe Shelley (1792–1822).

p. 81 **the fallen angel:** Satan.

p. 87 **Pandaemonium:** in Book I of Milton's *Paradise Lost* (1667) the fallen angels, driven out of heaven for attempting to overthrow God, build a vast and lavish meeting-place in Hell. Milton invented the term 'Pandemonium' for this place.

p. 91 **viands:** food.

p. 95 **It was as the ass and the lap-dog:** in La Fontaine's fable the ass resents the attention the lap-dog gets from its master. Imitating the dog and trying to paw the man, all it receives is a beating.

p. 98 **Volney's *Ruins of Empires:*** the Comte de Volney (1757–1820) was a French historian who made a particular study of the causes of revolution.

p. 101 **Mahometan:** Muslim.

p. 106 ***Paradise Lost:*** Milton's *Paradise Lost* (1667) tells the story of the fall of man and the expulsion of Adam and Eve from the Garden of Eden. The monster identifies himself with both Adam and Satan.

p. 106 ***Plutarch's Lives:*** Plutarch was a Greek historian writing in the first century AD. He produced a series of lives of famous people such as Julius Caesar and Mark Antony.

p. 106 ***Sorrows of Werter:*** the German writer Goethe produced this very popular and influential novel in 1774.

p. 107 **'The path of my departure was free':** from 'Mutability' (see note to p. 79).

p. 107 **Numa, Solon, and Lycurgus:** a group of rulers and law-givers. Numa was a legendary figure from the early days of Rome, while Solon and Lycurgus were Athenian and Spartan respectively.

p. 107 **Romulus and Theseus:** early and legendary rulers in Rome and Greece. (These five biographies begin *Plutarch's Lives*.)

p. 110 **revolved:** considered.

p. 114 toils: net used for catching wild animals.

p. 114 I, like the arch fiend, bore a hell within me: one of several references to Milton's Satan, with whom the monster identifies himself. Milton writes of 'the hot hell that always in him burns' (*Paradise Lost*, Book X).

p. 120 sanguinary: bloodthirsty.

p. 122 contemns: despises.

p. 126 siroc: the sirocco, a hot wind that blows from the North African desert.

p. 126 Dante's iron cowl: in Dante's *Divine Comedy* the hypocrites consigned to Hell wear leaden cloaks and hoods in punishment for their sins.

p. 132 bourne: limit.

p. 135 post: travel rapidly by horse.

p. 137 It was here that Charles I had collected his forces: shortly after the beginning of the English Civil War, King Charles I moved his court and his military headquarters to Oxford.

p. 138 *ennui:* apathy.

p. 138 Hampden: John Hampden (1594–1643) was one of the leaders of the anti-Royalist Parliamentarians.

p. 142 sophisms: false arguments.

p. 151 apothecary: combination of chemist and doctor.

p. 157 *maladie de pays:* homesickness.

p. 158 laudanum: preparation of opium widely available in the nineteenth century and used for medicinal purposes, to assist sleep, etc.

p. 162 the apple was already eaten: a reference to Genesis (Chapter 3) the story of the fall of man (and a further echo of *Paradise Lost*). Frankenstein means that the chain of events which will lead to disaster has already been initiated.

p. 164 nicer: more pentrating.

p. 170 acme: topmost point.

p. 180 admiration: amazement.

p. 181 projectors: planners, designers, entrepreneurs.

p. 181 the archangel who aspired to omnipotence: Satan, who attempted to rebel against God.

p. 183 Seneca: Roman playwright and Stoic (*c.* 4 BC–*c.* AD 65).

p. 187 catastrophe: last event, climax.

p. 195 **the daughter of two persons of distinguished literary celebrity:** Mary Shelley's parents were Mary Wollstonecraft and William Godwin, both famous authors and radical thinkers.

p. 196 **Lord Byron:** Lord Byron (1788–1824) was the most famous and influential of the poets in the Romantic movement at the beginning of the nineteenth century.

p. 197 **Polidori:** Dr John Polidori (1795–1821) was a companion of Byron and one of the group challenged by the poet to produce a ghost story. His contribution was a short story, 'The Vampyre'.

p. 197 **Tom of Coventry:** the Peeping Tom of the Lady Godiva legend. He was struck blind for gazing at her as she rode naked through Coventry.

p. 197 **tomb of the Capulets:** reference to Shakespeare's *Romeo and Juliet*. Juliet is from the Capulet family.

p. 198 **in Sanchean phrase:** like Sancho Panza in Cervantes's novel *Don Quixote*.

p. 198 **galvanism:** the process of stimulating movement by passing an electric current through an object. A follower of Luigi Galvani, from whom the term comes, had 'animated' animal remains and even the body of a recently hanged criminal in the early part of the nineteenth century.

p. 203 ***: Mary Shelley commented when she saw the way in which the monster had been billed in the programme: 'This nameless mode of naming the unnameable is rather good'.

p. 209 **Dr Faustus:** the legendary figure who sold his soul to the devil. In the sixteenth-century play of the same name by Christopher Marlowe, Faustus was, like Frankenstein, a dabbler in forbidden sciences.

p. 226 **lander:** province.

Frankenstein has never been out of the public eye since its publication in 1818. What Mary Shelley herself described as her 'hideous progeny' retains its power to shock and baffle, though in ways that might not have occurred to Shelley's contemporaries. Even during periods when the novel has not been valued for its own sake it has taken on other incarnations in film and television or on stage. Our standard idea of Frankenstein's creation, derived less from Mary Shelley than from the cycle of films initiated by Boris Karloff's monster in 1931, is a twentieth-century icon, domesticated and familiar enough (sometimes to the point of comedy) but always threatening to break loose.

In *In Frankenstein's Shadow* (1987), Chris Baldick maintains that 'as a published work, it escapes Mary Shelley's textual frame and acquires its independent life outside it, as a myth.'

The early reception of *Frankenstein* was mixed. For some, the fact that it was dedicated to William Godwin was sufficient to damn it. The reviewer in the conservative *Quarterly Review* assumed that he was confronting a male author, possibly Mary's husband Percy Bysshe Shelley. After a laboriously ironic treatment of the way the events of the novel stretch the reader's belief, he continues:

'Our readers will guess from this summary, what a tissue of horrible and disgusting absurdity this works presents. It is piously dedicated to Mr. Godwin, and is written in the spirit of his school. The dreams of insanity are embodied in the strong and striking language of the insane, and the author, notwithstanding the rationality of his preface, often leaves us in doubt whether he is not as mad as his hero.'

In conclusion the reviewer had to concede that there were 'passages which appal the mind and make the flesh creep'. A similar note was struck by Sir Walter Scott, reviewing in *Blackwood's*, with the difference that he willingly acknowledged the author's 'uncommon powers of poetic imagination', but described how the 'feeling with which we perused the unexpected and fearful, yet, allowing the possibility of the event, very natural conclusion of Frankenstein's experiment, shook a little even our firm nerves . . . '

Shock and horror, tempered by a grudging admiration, characterised the reaction of Mary Shelley's contemporaries. Although *Frankenstein* has much more to offer than a pleasant frisson of terror, it has until recently been lumped together with the Gothic novels of the Romantic period which specialised in providing exactly that for their largely female readership. As late as 1968 *Frankenstein* appeared as one of *Three Gothic Novels* (Penguin). Curiously, the introductory essay by Mario Praz comments on the implausibility of certain events in the novel, such as the monster's self-education from a cache of books, in terms that recall the original objections in the *Quarterly Review* of 1818. Although, for Praz, *Frankenstein* 'ranks as the greatest achievement of the Gothic school', in that edition Mary Shelley's unique work is safely corralled with two lesser pieces: Walpole's *The Castle of Otranto* and Beckford's *Vathek*. Mary Shelley began *Frankenstein* in response to Byron's famous challenge – 'We will each write a ghost story' – and the genesis of the story came to her in a dream (as *Otranto* did to Walpole), but the urges driving the narrative far transcend the desire to produce a titillating Gothic diversion.

In the last two decades *Frankenstein* criticism has enjoyed an extraordinary expansion as the novel has burst its Gothic bounds. The psychological reading was an early example of the willingness to see the novel in a new light. Christopher Small in *Ariel Like a Harpy* (1972) links the character of Frankenstein to Percy Bysshe Shelley and treats the work as, in part, a drama of guilt and innocence:

[Frankenstein] is accused of one murder (of Clerval) and even imprisoned, but soon cleared and released with apologies and expressions of sympathy. From time to time he accuses himself, asserting that all the victims 'died by my hands', but it is taken, and meant to be taken, as the extravagant self-reproach of an over-sensitive soul. He is unable to explain what he means by these self-reproaches because, of course, the very existence of the Monster is a secret, a truly guilty secret, which he cannot share. From the very start, before any crime has been committed, the close secrecy in which Frankenstein sets about his work and, having accomplished it, his extreme anxiety lest its result should become known point to the strongest feelings of guilt. His immediate repulsion and rejection of the Monster have already been noted, but even these are not so strong as his desire for concealment; when, the day after the Monster has been brought to life Frankenstein's friend Clerval turns up, there is no question of unburdening himself; on the contrary, Frankenstein is terrified lest Clerval should find out what has happened. When the two return to his room, where the newly living creature may yet be, 'I dreaded', he says, 'to behold this monster; but I feared still more that Henry should see him.'

That, of course, is before the Monster has revealed – or has developed – his 'malignity'. After the first murder, with Franken-stein's immediate certainty that the Monster is the murderer, his absolute inability to reveal his knowledge is even more striking. The servant-girl, Justine, is accused of the crime and her life is at stake; Frankenstein, knowing the truth and even promising before-hand that he will be able to save her, is quite unable to declare it. He even reaches the absurd position of contemplating a bogus confession: 'A thousand times rather would I have confessed myself guilty of the crime ascribed to Justine; but I was absent when it was committed . . .'; he cannot, however, tell the truth. We are reminded, throughout the story of Justine's wrongful conviction and execution, of the murder in *Caleb Williams* to which Falkland *cannot* confess, although two innocent men are hanged for it; but the effect is hugely enhanced here, is indeed removed to another level of expression, by changing Falkland's overriding regard for his 'reputation', which makes it impossible for him to acknowledge his crime, to the actual innocence, in literal terms, of Frankenstein. In this he never alters, though continuing to express it ambiguously: after the murder of Clerval has been added to the list, he may say that he has been the cause of all these deaths and exclaim that 'they all died by my hands', but he says it, of course, in such a way that no one believes him, and even in the same breath (speaking here of Justine) describes her as being '*as innocent as I*'.

* * *

Frankenstein's innocence, the unsullied and conscious uprightness of his motives, is no less than Shelley's: who was, of course, in his own eyes and the eyes of all but his enemies, the most blameless of men, actually incapable of doing wrong.

Critics have frequently linked Mary Shelley's text with her life. The way in which Frankenstein's family is slowly slaughtered around him is a playing-out, it has been suggested, of Mary's suppressed anger against her father or against Shelley himself. For Chris Baldick, examining a diversity of approaches in *In Frankenstein's Shadow*, there is much to be said for interpreting the relationship between the monster and his creator 'as a drama of repression'. He focuses on the wedding-night scene in Volume III:

> As with Adam in *Paradise Lost*, it is just this moment of separation from his wife which allows the fatal attack on her to be made. The fact that Victor leaves Elizabeth in the mistaken hope of obtaining knowledge makes the passage an unusually condensed résumé of the action of the novel as a whole.
>
> Perhaps more disturbingly, as Robert Kiely has pointed out, the ambiguity of this passage, in which the identity of the 'adversary' is left unspecified, allows us to read Victor's agitation as a sign that he fears the 'dreadful . . . combat' of sexual initiation itself, the more traditional 'impending conflict' of the wedding night. The coincidence of terms seems to imply that Victor's fear of sexuality and Elizabeth's murder are parts of a single 'complex'; and if we remember that the creation of the monster is an attempt to create life without encountering female sexuality, we begin to see how this connection might work. Nuptial forebodings are of course an established preoccupation of the Gothic from Bluebeard to Hammer Films, but few fictional wedding nights can have been as loaded with guilt as Frankenstein's. Just as Victor has called himself the true murderer of William, Justine, and Henry, so he knows that he is his wife's assassin too, having condemned her indirectly but certainly to death by tearing up the unfinished female monster. In the relentless logic of this 'return of the repressed', what returns is not so much the monster as the content of Victor's earlier dream: the transformation of Elizabeth into a corpse, which in dream-logic is itself an 'exchange' for the transformation of a corpse into a living being.
>
> Observing Victor's anxious demeanour after his return home from Ingolstadt, his father and Elizabeth herself both guess that he wishes to break off his engagement to his childhood sweetheart, having formed another attachment while at university. Although in the plainest sense he proves them wrong by marrying Elizabeth, they are still right in a deeper sense. The monster is indeed a sort of matrimonial rival to Elizabeth, a dependent whose ties to Victor are, he claims, indissoluble until death. [. . .] Frankenstein delays his marriage because he remembers his solemn promise, his 'engagement' to the monster. In so far as the monster is Victor's own persecuting *Doppelgänger*, he is in Freudian terms a symptom of a profound narcissism, displayed in his solitary and guilty

attempt to achieve reproduction without a sexual partner. Viewed from a further stage of Freudian interpretation, Frankenstein's enterprise is a model of sublimation.

One of the things that gives *Frankenstein* its mythic status, quite apart from the entry of the monster into modern consciousness independent of his literary source, is the way in which the novel opens itself to a range of fruitful interpretation. It refuses to be stabilised, but shifts according to the reader's perspective. Anne K. Mellor in *Mary Shelley: Her Life, Her Fiction, Her Monsters* (1988) refers to the Marxist point of view:

> Frankenstein's scientific project is clearly an attempt to gain power. Inspired by Waldman's description of scientists who 'acquired new and almost unlimited powers', Frankenstein has sought both the power of a father over his children, and, more omnipotently, of God over his creation. More subtly, yet more pervasively, Frankenstein has sought power over the female. He has 'pursued nature to her hiding places' in an attempt not only to penetrate nature and show how her hidden womb works but actually to steal or appropriate that womb. To usurp the power of reproduction is to usurp the power of production as such. Marx identified childbirth as the primary example of pure, or unalienated, labor. Victor Frankenstein's enterprise can be viewed from a Marxist perspective as an attempt to exploit nature or labor in the service of a ruling class. Frankenstein wishes to harness the modes of reproduction in order to become the acknowledged, revered, and gratefully obeyed father of a new species. His project is thus identical with that of bourgeois capitalism: to exploit nature's resources for both commercial profit and political control.

A less specifically political view turns the novel into an attack on social injustice. This has the monster's own endorsement: 'I was benevolent and good; misery made me a fiend. Make me happy, and I shall again be virtuous' (p. 81). It is a view that was congenial to Godwin, Mary's father, as well as to Shelley himself, as an essayist pointed out in *Tait's Edinburgh Magazine* (1847): 'her protest against society is his, copied out in a fine female hand'.

But perhaps the most radical reworking of *Frankenstein* comes from the feminist critics who have rescued Mary Shelley from the shadow of her genius-husband and given her a status unrelated to his. Commentary ranges from the provokingly stark

— 'From a feminist viewpoint, *Frankenstein* is a book about what happens when a man tries to have a baby without a woman' (from Anne K. Mellor's *Mary Shelley*) — to the complex argument that the novel is to be seen as Mary Shelley's revision of Milton's *Paradise Lost*. Milton's epic is the most significant of the three books discovered by the monster (p. 106), and he identifies himself with both Adam and Satan. For Sandra M. Gilbert and Susan Gubar in *The Madwoman in the Attic* (1979), Frankenstein the creator 'enacts the roles of Adam and Satan like a child trying on costumes'; principally, though, Frankenstein becomes Eve (a male becoming a mother). Gilbert and Gubar's most suggestive piece of casting, however, is to link the monster himself with Eve:

> Nevertheless, one of the most notable facts about the monster's ceaselessly anxious study of *Paradise Lost* is his failure even to mention Eve. As an insistently male monster, on the surface of his palimpsestic narrative he appears to be absorbed in Milton's epic only because, as Percy Shelley wrote in the preface to *Frankenstein* that he drafted for his wife, *Paradise Lost* 'most especially' conveys 'the truths of the elementary principles of human nature,' and conveys that truth in the dynamic tensions developed among its male characters, Adam, Satan, and God. Yet not only the monster's uniquely ahistorical birth, his literary anxieties, and the sense his readings (like Mary's) foster that he must have been parented, if at all, by *books*; not only all these facts and traits but also his shuddering sense of deformity, his nauseating size, his namelessness, and his orphaned, motherless isolation link him with Eve and with Eve's double, Sin. Indeed, at several points in his impassioned analysis of Milton's story he seems almost on the verge of saying so, as he examines the disjunctions among Adam, Satan, and himself:

> > Like Adam, I was apparently united by no link to any other being in existence; but his state was far different from mine in every other respect. He had come forth from the hands of God a perfect creature, happy and prosperous, guided by the especial care of his Creator; he was allowed to converse with and acquire knowledge from beings of a superior nature, but I was wretched, helpless, and alone. Many times I considered Satan as the fitter emblem of my condition, for often, like him, when I viewed the bliss of my protectors, the bitter gall of envy rose within me [. . .] Accursed creator! Why did you form a monster so hideous that even *you* turned from me in disgust? God, in pity, made man beautiful and alluring, after his own image; but

my form is a filthy type of yours, more horrid even from the very resemblance. Satan had his companions, fellow devils, to admire and encourage him, but I am solitary and abhorred.

It is Eve, after all, who languishes helpless and alone, while Adam converses with superior beings, and it is Eve in whom the Satanically bitter gall of envy rises, causing her to eat the apple in the hope of adding 'what wants/In Female Sex.' It is Eve, moreover, to whom deathly isolation is threatened should Adam reject her, an isolation more terrible even than Satan's alienation from heaven. And finally it is Eve whose body, like her mind, is said by Milton to resemble 'less/His Image who made both, and less [to express]/The character of that Dominion giv'n/O'er other Creatures . . .' (PL 8. 543–46). In fact, to a sexually anxious reader, Eve's body might, like Sin's, seem 'horrid even from [its] very resemblance' to her husband's, a 'filthy' or obscene version of the human form divine.

In her overview of *Frankenstein* Anne K. Mellor ties together various strands, whether biographical, social/political or scientific/creative, to show how the novel functions as an extensive critique of male power. It has long been conventional to see Mary Shelley's story in cautionary terms, as a warning against *hubris*, human arrogance usurping what should be left to nature or, in the Promethean scheme, the gods. For Mellor, however, Frankenstein's enterprise is not merely anti-human but fundamentally misogynistic:

> One of the deepest horrors of this novel is Frankenstein's implicit goal of creating a society for men only: his creature is male; he refuses to create a female; there is no reason that the race of immortal beings he hoped to propagate should not be exclusively male.

From this perspective the skewed society that would result, that is in a sense already in place, denies female sexuality, promotes power and competition at the expense of co-operation, and is ultimately nihilistic. *Frankenstein* is not crudely anti-science:

> Mary Shelley's critique of objective, rationalistic thought goes beyond Wordworth's organicist notion that 'we murder to dissect.' Perhaps because she was a woman, she perceived that inherent in most scientific thought was a potent gender identification. Professor Waldman taught Frankenstein that scientists 'penetrate into the recesses of nature, and shew how *she* works in *her* hiding

places' [my emphasis]. In Waldman's trope, nature is a passive female who can be penetrated in order to satisfy male desire.

The enduring relevance of *Frankenstein*, its freshness for us here and now, are also persuasively indicated by Mellor:

> Although we have not yet discovered Frankenstein's procedure for reanimating corpses, recent research in biochemistry – the discovery of DNA, the technique of gene-splicing, and the development of extra-uterine fertilization – has brought us to the point where human beings are able to manipulate life-forms in ways previously reserved only to nature and chance. The replacement of natural childbirth by the mechanical eugenic control systems and baby-breeders envisioned in Aldous Huxley's *Brave New World* or Marge Piercy's *Woman on the Edge of Time* is now only a matter of time and social will. Worse by far, of course, is the contemporary proliferation of nuclear weapons systems resulting from the Los Alamos Project and the political decision to drop atomic bombs on Hiroshima and Nagasaki in 1945. As Jonathan Schell has so powerfully reminded us in *The Fate of the Earth*, as such docudramas as 'The Day After' (1983) and 'Threads' (1984) have starkly portrayed, a morally irresponsible scientific development has released a monster that can destroy human civilisation. As Frankenstein's monster proclaims, 'Remember that I have power; ... I can make you so wretched that the light of day will be hateful to you'. Mary Shelley's tale of horror is no fantastical ghost story, but rather a profound insight into the probable consequences of 'objective' – gendered – or morally insensitive scientific and technological research.

At the end of *Frankenstein* the monster leaps on an ice-raft and Walton the narrator soon loses sight of him 'in darkness and distance'. The novel is open-ended: the monster has promised to destroy himself on a funeral pyre at the North Pole but there is no certainty that he has done, or will ever do so. This extraordinary creation of a nineteen year-old girl is with us still. Whatever revisions and adjustments are made in our understanding of *Frankenstein* – and there is no sign that we have exhausted the capacity of the novel for creative surprise – Mary Shelley's work will always discomfit.

SUGGESTIONS FOR FURTHER READING

WRITINGS BY MARY WOLLSTONECRAFT SHELLEY

Frankenstein, or The Modern Prometheus (The 1818 Text), ed. James Rieger (New York: Bobbs-Merrill, 1974; Chicago: University of Chicago Press, 1982).

The Journals of Mary Shelley 1814–1844, ed. Paula R. Feldman and Diana Scott-Kilvert (Oxford: Clarendon Press, 1987), 2 vols.

The Last Man, ed. Hugh J. Lake, Jnr (Lincoln: University of Nebraska Press, 1965).

The Letters of Mary W. Shelley, ed. Betty T. Bennett (Baltimore: Johns Hopkins University Press, 1980, 1983, 1988), 3 vols.

Mathilda, ed. Elizabeth Nitchie (Chapel Hill: University of North Carolina Press, 1959).

BIOGRAPHY AND CRITICAL REPUTATION

Baldick, Chris. *In Frankenstein's Shadow: Myth, Monstrosity and Nineteenth-Century Writing* (Oxford: Clarendon Press, 1987).

Dunn, Jane. *Moon in Eclipse: A Life of Mary Shelley* (London: Weidenfeld & Nicolson, 1978).

Mellor, Anne K. *Mary Shelley: Her Life, Her Fiction, Her Monsters* (New York: Methuen Inc., 1988; London: Routledge, 1989).

Nitchie, Elizabeth. *Mary Shelley – Author of 'Frankenstein'* (New Brunswick: Rutgers University Press, 1953).

St Claire, William, *The Godwins and the Shelleys* (London: Faber, 1989).

Small, Christopher, *Ariel Like a Harpy* (London: Gollancz, 1972).

Spark, Muriel. *Child of Light: A Reassessment of Mary Wollstonecraft Shelley* (Hadleigh, Essex: Tower Bridge Publications, 1951); revised and republished as *Mary Shelley: A Biography* (New York: E. P. Dutton, 1987; London: Constable, 1988).

Sunstein, Emily W., *Mary Shelley: Romance and Reality* (Baltimore: John Hopkins University Press, 1989).

260   *Suggestions for Further Reading*

CRITICAL STUDIES

Alexander, Meena. *Women in Romanticism: Mary Wollstonecraft, Dorothy Wordsworth and Mary Shelley* (Basingstoke: Macmillan, 1989).

Botting, Fred. *Making Monstrous: Frankenstein, Criticism, Theory* (Manchester: University of Manchester Press, 1991).

Clifford Gay. '*Caleb Williams* and *Frankenstein*: First Person Narration and Things as They Are', *Genre* (1977): pp. 601–17.

Forry, Stephen Earl. *Hideous Progenies: Dramatizations of Frankenstein from the Nineteenth Century to the Present* (Pennsylvania: University of Pennsylvania Press, 1990).

Gilbert, Sandra M., and Gubar, Susan. *The Madwoman in the Attic – The Woman Writer and the Nineteenth Century Literary Imagination* (New Haven: Yale University Press, 1979).

Homans, Margaret. *Bearing the Word: Language and Female Experience in Nineteenth Century Women's Writing* (Chicago: Chicago University Press, 1986).

Howells, Coral Ann. *Love, Mystery and Misery – Feeling in Gothic Fiction* (London: Athlone Press, 1978).

Jacobus, Mary. 'Is there a Woman in This Text?' *New Literary History* (1982): pp. 117–41.

Jackson, Rosemary. *Fantasy: the Literature of Subversion* (London: Methuen, 1982).

Johnson, Barbara. 'My Monster / My Self', *Diacritics* (1982): pp. 2–10.

Kahane, Claire. 'The Gothic Mirror' in *The (M)other Tongue: Essays in Feminist Psychoanalytic Interpretation*, eds. Shirley Nelson Garner, Claire Kahane, and Madelon Sprengnether (Ithaca: Cornell University Press, 1985): pp. 243–61.

Levine, George, and U. C. Knoepflmacher, eds. *The Endurance of Frankenstein* (Los Angeles: University of California Press, 1979).

Moers, Ellen. *Literary Women* (New Jersey: Doubleday, 1976).

Moretti, Franco. *Signs Taken for Wonders – Essays in the Sociology of Literary Form* (London: Verso, 1983).

Musselwhite, David E. *Partings Welded Together: Politics and Desire in the Nineteenth Century Novel* (London and New York: Methuen, 1987).

O'Flinn, Paul. 'Production and reproduction: *Frankenstein*' in *Popular Fictions: Essays in Literature and History*, eds Peter Humm, Paul Stigant and Peter Widdowson (London: Routledge, 1986): pp. 196–211.

Poovey, Mary. *The Proper Lady and the Woman Writer – Ideology as Style in the works of Mary Wollstonecraft, Mary Shelley and Jane Austen* (Chicago: University of Chicago Press, 1984).

Punter, David. *The Literature of Terror: A History of Gothic Fictions from 1765 to the Present Day* (Harlow: Longman, 1980).

Rubenstein, Marc A. ' "My Accursed Origin": The Search for the Mother in *Frankenstein*', *Studies in Romanticism* (1976): pp. 165–94.

Sage, Victor. *Horror Fiction in the Protestant Tradition* (London: Macmillan, 1988).

Sedgwick, Eve Kosofsky. *The Coherence of Gothic Conventions* (New York and London: Methuen, 1986).

Spivak, Gayatri Chakravorty. 'Three Women's Texts and a Critique of Imperialism', *Critical Inquiry* (1985): pp. 243–61.

Veeder, William. *Mary Shelley and Frankenstein: The Fate of Androgyny* (Chicago: University of Chicago Press, 1986).

TEXT SUMMARY

VOLUME I

Letter I
From St Petersburgh Robert Walton writes to his sister, Mrs Margaret Saville – explains why he intends to explore the polar regions and his plan to charter a boat in the northern Russian port of Archangel.

Letter II
Writing from the port, Walton regrets that he has no true companion on board – he outlines the characters of the lieutenant and captain.

Letter III
Walton reports on a so-far uneventful voyage to the North Pole.

Letter IV
Walton's ship is ice-bound – the crew sees in the distance a giant figure passing on a sledge – as the ice breaks up an exhausted man is floated to the ship on a large fragment of ice – on board, he reveals that he is in pursuit of the giant – Walton admires the man, Victor Frankenstein, and willingly listens to his life-story.

Chapter I
Frankenstein tells of his childhood in Geneva in a loving family – his friendship with his cousin Elizabeth, who everyone considers will be his future wife – his early interest in pre-scientific occult theories and thinkers.

Chapter II
Frankenstein's parents intend to send him to the university at Ingolstadt – before he leaves his mother dies – at university one lecturer criticises him for studying outmoded systems but

another stimulates his interest in modern science, particularly chemistry.

Chapter III

During his studies Frankenstein becomes obsessed with the question of the source of life – his discovery of 'the principle of life' enables him to animate lifeless matter – disgusted with himself yet driven by the urge to create, he constructs a being out of human remains.

Chapter IV

Frankenstein gives life to his creature – horrified at the result – the man-made being appears pitifully at his creator's bedside but Frankenstein runs away from him – next morning Frankenstein's childhood friend Henry Clerval arrives on a vist – to Frankenstein's delight the monster has vanished but the strain brings about a nervous collapse – Clerval nurses him through it.

Chapter V

A letter from his cousin Elizabeth gives Frankenstein news of others in the family home, notably Justine, a girl adopted by Frankenstein's mother, and his young brother William – Frankenstein and Clerval go on a walking tour of the area round Ingolstadt.

Chapter VI

Frankenstein's father tells him in a letter of the murder of William – as Frankenstein is returning home he glimpses the monster during a thunderstorm – he is immediately certain that the man-made being is William's murderer – he says nothing because he does not think he will be believed – once home Frankenstein discovers that Justine has been accused of the murder.

Chapter VII

Justine's trial – she pleads innocence but circumstantial evidence is against her – she is condemned to death – Frankenstein and Elizabeth visit her in prison.

VOLUME II

Chapter I
Frankenstein's family is grief-stricken at William's death and Justine's apparent treachery – Frankenstein knows himself to be in effect 'the true murderer' – the family goes on a tour of the Alpine area near Chamonix.

Chapter II
Walking alone in mountains Frankenstein meets the monster – his first impulse is to try to destroy what he has himself created – the monster begs him to listen to his story.

Chapter III
The monster remembers his early days after leaving Frankenstein's laboratory – his struggles to survive in the wild, his responsiveness to nature – any human he encounters reacts with revulsion and fear – the monster takes refuge in a shed attached to a cottage and spies on the people inside.

Chapter IV
The monster is fascinated by the people in the cottage, a brother and sister and their father – he admires their grace and wishes to learn their language – he dreams of winning their favour and love.

Chapter V
An Arabian woman arrives at the cottage – the young man, Felix, instructs her in the language and teaches her something of history – the monster eavesdrops and also learns – he contrasts his own state, without family, love or friends, with that of the cottagers.

Chapter VI
The monster learns the background to the cottagers' lives – they are French, of good family – attempting to help the imprisoned father of Safie, the Arabian girl, they have been cheated by him after his escape – they have ended up in poverty and exile from their own country – Safie has disobeyed her father to return to Felix.

Chapter VII

The monster discovers some books – compares his own situation
with that of the characters he reads about – he enters the cottage
in an attempt to befriend its inhabitants – only the old (blind)
man is there – as the monster is about to confide in him the
three young people appear and drive the monster off in horror.

Chapter VIII

The monster explains to Frankenstein how he burned the now-
abandoned cottage to the ground – how he was shot at after
rescuing a child from drowning – how by chance he encountered
young William Frankenstein – in fury at his creator he strangled
the boy – he planted a cameo picture carried by William on a
sleeping woman (Justine) – now the monster demands that his
creator should provide him with a mate because he will never
find companionship in the human world.

Chapter IX

The monster promises that, if Frankenstein constructs a mate
for him, they will live far away from human society.

VOLUME III

Chapter I

Frankenstein plans to go to England where recent scientific
discoveries will help him in his work of constructing a mate for
the monster – he agrees to marry Elizabeth on his return in two
years' time – he and Clerval travel down the Rhine before sailing
to England.

Chapter II

With Clerval, Frankenstein tours England – leaves his companion to travel to one of the remotest of the Orkney Islands –
rents broken-down accommodation and begins, in a spirit of
disgust and fear, to fulfil his obligation to the monster and create
a mate.

Chapter III

At the last moment Frankenstein has second thought – visualises
the monster and his mate producing 'a race of devils' – he tears
to pieces the nearly finished female – the monster is watching
and promises revenge – in despair Frankenstein sets sail for the

mainland – is blown off course and lands on Irish coast – he is arrested on suspicion of the murder of a gentleman.

Chapter IV
Frankenstein is charged with murdering Clerval, whose body has been found near where he landed – Frankenstein is certain that the monster strangled his friend – a kindly magistrate summons his father from Switzerland – the case never goes to court because Frankenstein was on the Orkneys when body was found – he and his father return home.

Chapter V
On the way back, Frankenstein receives letter from Elizabeth – she offers to release him from the marriage obligation if he loves someone else – he assures her he is happy for marriage to proceed – Frankenstein always aware of monster's threat of vengeance.

Chapter VI
The monster murders Elizabeth on the night of her wedding to Frankenstein – Frankenstein's father dies of grief – Frankenstein goes to a magistrate to lay a charge against the monster – magistrate doubts that the monster could be captured, and Frankenstein suspects that he does not believe his tale.

Chapter VIII
Frankenstein describes how he has dedicated his life to pursuit of the monster – followed him into Russia and the polar regions – and so come to Walton's ship – Walton resumes story in letters to his sister – Frankenstein is dying – he rebukes mutinous sailors for their wish to turn back from the polar expedition – nevertheless Walton decides to return as passage opens in ice – Frankenstein dies – Walton confronts the monster over the body of his creator – monster justifies himself, arguing that he was driven to persecute Frankenstein and his family – he assures Walton that now his work is complete, he will destroy himself on a funeral pyre at the North Pole – he leaps from the ship and is quickly lost in darkness.

ACKNOWLEDGEMENTS

The editor and publishers wish to thank the following for permission to use copyright material.

Victor Gollancz Ltd for material from Christopher Small, *Ariel Like a Harpy*, 1972;

Oxford University Press for material from Chris Baldick, *In Frankenstein's Shadow*, 1987;

Routledge for material from Anne K. Mellor, *Mary Shelley: Her Life, Her Fiction, Her Monsters*, Methuen, 1988;

Every effort has been made to trace all the copyright holders, but if any have been inadvertently overlooked the publishers will be pleased to make the necessary arrangement at the first opportunity.

WOMEN'S WRITING
IN EVERYMAN

Poems and Prose
CHRISTINA ROSSETTI
A collection of her writings, poetry and prose, published to mark the centenary of her death
£5.99

Women Philosophers
edited by Mary Warnock
The great subjects of philosophy handled by women spanning four centuries, including Simone de Beauvoir and Iris Murdoch
£6.99

Glenarvon
LADY CAROLINE LAMB
A novel which throws light on the greatest scandal of the early nineteenth century – the infatuation of Caroline Lamb with Lord Byron
£6.99

Women Romantic Poets
1780 – 1830: **An Anthology**
edited by Jennifer Breen
Hidden talent from the Romantic era rediscovered
£5.99

Memoirs of the Life of Colonel Hutchinson
LUCY HUTCHINSON
One of the earliest pieces of women's biographical writing, of great historic and feminist interest
£6.99

The Secret Self 1: Short Stories by Women
edited by Hermione Lee
'A superb collection' The Guardian
£4.99

The Age of Innocence
EDITH WHARTON
A tale of the conflict between love and tradition by one of America's finest women novelists
£4.99

Frankenstein
MARY SHELLEY
A masterpiece of Gothic terror in its original 1818 version
£3.99

The Life of Charlotte Brontë
ELIZABETH GASKELL
A moving and perceptive tribute by one writer to another
£4.99

Victorian Women Poets
1830 – 1900
edited by Jennifer Breen
A superb anthology of the era's finest female poets
£5.99

Female Playwrights of the Restoration: Five Comedies
edited by Paddy Lyons
Rediscovered literary treasure in a unique selection
£5.99

All books are available from your local bookshop or direct from:
Littlehampton Book Services Cash Sales, 14 Eldon Way, Lineside Estate,
Littlehampton, West Sussex BN17 7HE (*prices are subject to change*)

To order any of the books, please enclose a cheque (in sterling) made payable to
Littlehampton Book Services, or phone your order through with credit card details (Access,
Visa or Mastercard) on 01903 721596 (24 hour answering service) stating card number
and expiry date. (*Please add £1.25 for package and postage to the total of your order.*)

In the USA, for further information and a complete catalogue call 1-800-526-2778

CLASSIC FICTION
IN EVERYMAN

The Impressions of Theophrastus Such
GEORGE ELIOT
An amusing collection of character sketches, and the only paperback edition available
£5.99

Frankenstein
MARY SHELLEY
A masterpiece of Gothic terror in its original 1818 version
£3.99

East Lynne
MRS HENRY WOOD
A classic tale of melodrama, murder and mystery
£7.99

Holiday Romance and Other Writings for Children
CHARLES DICKENS
Dickens's works for children, including 'The Life of Our Lord' and 'A Child's History of England', with original illustrations
£5.99

The Ebb-Tide
R. L. STEVENSON
A compelling study of ordinary people in extreme circumstances
£4.99

The Three Impostors
ARTHUR MACHEN
The only edition available of this cult thriller
£4.99

Mister Johnson
JOYCE CARY
The only edition available of this amusing but disturbing twentieth-century tale
£5.99

The Jungle Book
RUDYARD KIPLING
The classic adventures of Mowgli and his friends
£3.99

Glenarvon
LADY CAROLINE LAMB
The only edition available of the novel which throws light on the greatest scandal of the early nine-teenth century – the infatuation of Caroline Lamb with Lord Byron
£6.99

Twenty Thousand Leagues Under the Sea
JULES VERNE
Scientific fact combines with fantasy in this prophetic tale of underwater adventure
£4.99

All books are available from your local bookshop or direct from:
Littlehampton Book Services Cash Sales, 14 Eldon Way, Lineside Estate,
Littlehampton, West Sussex BN17 7HE (*prices are subject to change*)

To order any of the books, please enclose a cheque (in sterling) made payable to
Littlehampton Book Services, or phone your order through with credit card details (Access,
Visa or Mastercard) on 01903 721596 (24 hour answering service) stating card number
and expiry date. (*Please add £1.25 for package and postage to the total of your order.*)

In the USA, for further information and a complete catalogue call 1-800-526-2778

CLASSIC NOVELS
IN EVERYMAN

The Time Machine
H. G. WELLS
*One of the books which defined
'science fiction' – a compelling
and tragic story of a brilliant
and driven scientist*
£3.99

Oliver Twist
CHARLES DICKENS
*Arguably the best-loved of
Dickens's novels. With all the
original illustrations*
£4.99

Barchester Towers
ANTHONY TROLLOPE
*The second of Trollope's
Chronicles of Barsetshire,
and one of the funniest of all
Victorian novels*
£4.99

The Heart of Darkness
JOSEPH CONRAD
*Conrad's most intense, subtle,
compressed, profound and
proleptic work*
£3.99

Tess of the d'Urbervilles
THOMAS HARDY
*The powerful, poetic classic
of wronged innocence*
£3.99

Wuthering Heights and Poems
EMILY BRONTË
*A powerful work of genius – one of
the great masterpieces of literature*
£3.99

Pride and Prejudice
JANE AUSTEN
*Proposals, rejections, infidelities,
elopements, happy marriages –
Jane Austen's most popular novel*
£2.99

North and South
ELIZABETH GASKELL
*A novel of hardship, passion
and hard-won wisdom amidst the
conflicts of the industrial revolution*
£4.99

The Newcomes
W. M. THACKERAY
*An exposé of Victorian polite
society by one of the nineteenth-
century's finest novelists*
£6.99

Adam Bede
GEORGE ELIOT
*A passionate rural drama enacted
at the turn of the eighteenth
century*
£5.99

All books are available from your local bookshop or direct from:
Littlehampton Book Services Cash Sales, 14 Eldon Way, Lineside Estate,
Littlehampton, West Sussex BN17 7HE (*prices are subject to change*)

To order any of the books, please enclose a cheque (in sterling) made payable to
Littlehampton Book Services, or phone your order through with credit card details (Access,
Visa or Mastercard) on 01903 721596 (24 hour answering service) stating card number
and expiry date. (*Please add £1.25 for package and postage to the total of your order.*)

In the USA, for further information and a complete catalogue call 1-800-526-2778

DRAMA
IN EVERYMAN

The Oresteia
AESCHYLUS
New translation of one of the greatest Greek dramatic trilogies which analyses the plays in performance
£5.99

Everyman and Medieval Miracle Plays
edited by A. C. Cawley
A selection of the most popular medieval plays
£4.99

Complete Plays and Poems
CHRISTOPHER MARLOWE
The complete works of this great Elizabethan in one volume
£5.99

Restoration Plays
edited by Robert Lawrence
Five comedies and two tragedies representing the best of the Restoration stage
£7.99

Female Playwrights of the Restoration: Five Comedies
edited by Paddy Lyons
Rediscovered literary treasures in a unique selection
£5.99

Plays, Prose Writings and Poems
OSCAR WILDE
The full force of Wilde's wit in one volume
£4.99

A Dolls House/The Lady from the Sea/The Wild Duck
HENRIK IBSEN
introduced by Fay Weldon
A popular selection of Ibsen's major plays
£4.99

The Beggar's Opera and Other Eighteenth-Century Plays
JOHN GAY et. al.
Including Goldsmith's She Stoops To Conquer *and Sheridan's* The School for Scandal, *this is a volume which reflects the full scope of the period's theatre*
£6.99

Female Playwrights of the Nineteenth Century
edited by Adrienne Scullion
The full range of female nineteenth-century dramatic development
£6.99

All books are available from your local bookshop or direct from:
Littlehampton Book Services Cash Sales, 14 Eldon Way, Lineside Estate,
Littlehampton, West Sussex BN17 7HE *(prices are subject to change)*

To order any of the books, please enclose a cheque (in sterling) made payable to
Littlehampton Book Services, or phone your order through with credit card details (Access,
Visa or Mastercard) on 01903 721596 (24 hour answering service) stating card number
and expiry date. *(Please add £1.25 for package and postage to the total of your order.)*

In the USA, for further information and a complete catalogue call 1-800-526-2778

POETRY
IN EVERYMAN

**Amorous Rites: Elizabethan
Erotic Verse**
edited by Sandra Clark
*Erotic and often comic poems deal-
ing with myths of transformation
and erotic interaction between
humans and gods*
£4.99

Selected Poems
JOHN KEATS
*An excellent selection of the poetry
of one of the principal figures of
the Romantic movement*
£6.99

Poems and Prose
CHRISTINA ROSSETTI
*A new collection of her writings,
poetry and prose, marking the centenary of her death*
£5.99

Poems and Prose
P. B. SHELLEY
The essential Shelley in one volume
£5.99

**Silver Poets of the
Sixteenth Century**
edited by Douglas Brooks-Davies
*An exciting and comprehensive
collection*
£6.99

Complete English Poems
JOHN DONNE
*The father of metaphysical verse
in this highly-acclaimed collection*
£6.99

**Complete English Poems,
Of Education, Areopagitica**
JOHN MILTON
*An excellent introduction to
Milton's poetry and prose*
£6.99

Women Romantic Poets
1780–1830: **An Anthology**
edited by Jennifer Breen
*Hidden talent from the Romantic
era rediscovered*
£5.99

Selected Poems
D. H. LAWRENCE
*An authoritative selection
spanning the whole of Lawrence's
literary career*
£4.99

The Poems
W. B. YEATS
*Ireland's greatest lyric poet
surveyed in this ground-breaking
edition*
£7.99

All books are available from your local bookshop or direct from:
Littlehampton Book Services Cash Sales, 14 Eldon Way, Lineside Estate,
Littlehampton, West Sussex BN17 7HE (*prices are subject to change*)

To order any of the books, please enclose a cheque (in sterling) made payable to
Littlehampton Book Services, or phone your order through with credit card details (Access,
Visa or Mastercard) on 01903 721596 (24 hour answering service) stating card number
and expiry date. (*Please add £1.25 for package and postage to the total of your order.*)

In the USA, for further information and a complete catalogue call 1-800-526-2778